ARENA

By Simon Scarrow

The *Roman* Series

Under the Eagle
The Eagle's Conquest
When the Eagle Hunts
The Eagle and the Wolves
The Eagle's Prey
The Eagle's Prophecy
The Eagle in the Sand
Centurion
The Gladiator
The Legion
Praetorian

The *Wellington and Napoleon* Quartet

Young Bloods
The Generals
Fire and Sword
The Fields of Death

Sword and Scimitar
Arena

SIMON SCARROW
AND T. J. ANDREWS

ARENA

headline

First published in Great Britain in 2013
by HEADLINE PUBLISHING GROUP

1

Cataloguing in Publication Data is available from the British Library

ISBN 978 0 7553 9822 5 (Hardback)
ISBN 978 1 4722 0739 5 (Trade paperback)

Typeset in Bembo by Palimpsest Book Production Ltd, Falkirk, Stirlingshire

Printed and bound in Great Britain by Clays Ltd, St Ives plc

Headline's policy is to use papers that are natural, renewable and
recyclable products and made from wood grown in sustainable
forests. The logging and manufacturing processes are expected to conform
to the environmental regulations of the country of origin.

HEADLINE PUBLISHING GROUP
An Hachette UK Company
338 Euston Road
London NW1 3BH

www.headline.co.uk
www.hachette.co.uk

For John Bracey,
fearless warrior and middle-school teacher

CHAPTER ONE

Rome, late AD *41*

The imperial gladiator blinked sweat from his eyes and watched the stadium officials drag away the dead bodies carpeting the arena floor.

From his position in the shadows of the passageway, Gaius Naevius Capito had a panoramic view of the aftermath of the mock battle. A crude reconstruction of a Celtic settlement stood in the middle of the Statilius Taurus amphitheatre, which was littered with the dead. Capito lifted his eyes to the galleries. He could see the new Emperor at the podium, flanked by a cabal of freedmen jostling for attention, with the senators and imperial high priests seated at the periphery in their distinctive togas. Above the podium the crowd was squeezed shoulder to shoulder on the stone seats lining the upper galleries. Capito felt a shiver in his bones as the crowd roared. He looked on as a pair of officials prodded a slumped barbarian with a heated iron. The man jolted. The crowd jeered at his attempt to play dead and one of the officials signalled to a servant wielding a massive double-sided hammer. A second official finished sprinkling fresh white sand over the blood-flecked arena floor. Then they retreated to the passageway, resting in the shadows a few paces away from Capito.

'Look at this shit,' one of the officials moaned as he held up his blood-smeared hands. 'It'll take me bloody ages to clean this mess off.'

'Gladiators,' the other official grumbled. 'Selfish buggers.'

Capito frowned at them as the servant with the hammer strode over to the Gaul and towered over the fallen man, smiling glee-fully as he smashed the hammer into the barbarian's skull. Capito

1

heard the crack of shattering bone and grimaced. As the highest-ranked gladiator of the imperial ludus in Capua, he took great pride in his handiwork. But this spectacle had left a bitter taste in his mouth. He'd looked on from the passageway as gladiators dressed as legionaries had massacred their opponents – a mixture of condemned men and slaves armed with blunted instruments. There had been little skill involved. He considered it an affront to his profession.

An arena servant dragged away the last of the dead with a metal hook.

'A bloodbath,' Capito muttered to himself. 'Just a bloodbath.'

'What did you say?' one of the officials demanded.

'Nothing,' Capito replied.

The official was about to speak again when the editor called out Capito's name in a sonorous tone that soared up to the highest galleries. The crowd roared. The official jerked a thumb towards the blood-splattered sand.

'You're on,' he growled. 'Now remember. This is the showpiece event. Twenty thousand people have come here to see this. The Emperor is up there and he's counting on you to give Britomaris a bloody good hiding. Don't let him down.'

Capito nodded cautiously. His fight represented the main event of the first major spectacle given to the people by Emperor Claudius. The afternoon had seen a re-creation of a pitched battle involving hundreds of men, with the gladiators predictably triumphing over the ill-equipped barbaric horde. Now the pride of the imperial gladiators would fight a barbarian playing the chief of a Celtic tribe. But this was not any old barbarian. Britomaris had already notched up five victories in the arena, to the surprise of seasoned observers. Barbarians without any proper schooling in the way of the sword usually met a grisly demise on their debut, and Britomaris's run of wins had unsettled the veterans at the imperial school. Capito dismissed such concerns and reassured himself that the men Britomaris had faced in previous bouts were lesser warriors than he. Capito was a legend of the arena. A bringer of death and winner of glory. He flexed his neck muscles as he swore to teach Britomaris a lesson. His confidence was further boosted by the fact that he wore the full complement of equipment, including leg greaves, arm manicas and a plate cuirass, as well as a long red cloak draped over his back. The armour was to guarantee victory. With the Emperor in attendance, the idea of a Roman – even a gladiator dressed as a Roman – losing to a barbarian was too much to stomach. But the armour had its drawbacks. With the heavily decorated helmet over his head, the complete panoply caused Capito to break out in a suffocating sweat.

The official handed him a short sword and a rectangular legionary shield. Capito gripped the sword in his right hand and took the shield with his left. He focused on the dark mouth of the passageway facing him from the opposite side of the arena floor and saw a figure slowly emerge from the shadows, head glancing left and right, as if bemused by his surroundings.

A barbarian who'd notched up a few fortuitous wins, Capito told himself. Armed with a blunted weapon. The gladiator vowed to put Britomaris in his place.

Capito stepped out into the arena and marched towards the centre, where the umpire stood tapping his wooden stick against the side of his right leg. The sun glared down and rendered the sand blisteringly hot under his bare feet. He glanced up at the crowd lining the galleries. Some were slaking their thirst from small wine jars, while others fanned themselves. A large group of legionaries packed into one corner of the gallery were in bois-terous mood. There were women too, Capito thought with a lustful smile. He felt a pang of pride that so many people had come to see him, the great Capito.

The metallic stench of blood choked the air as Capito felt the full force of the heat rising from the ground. Right at the top of the arena, above the highest gallery, dozens of sailors manipulated vast awnings in an attempt to provide shade to the crowd. But the sun had shifted position and foiled their efforts. The freedmen in the upper galleries were in shade, while the dignitaries below had to suffer the heat.

Trumpets blasted. Capito tightened his grip on the sword. The crowd simultaneously craned their necks at the passageway opposite him. The gladiator shut out the noise of the arena and focused solely on the barbarian pacing heavily towards him.

Capito suppressed a smile. Britomaris looked almost too big for his own good. His legs were wide as tree trunks at the thigh and his arm and shoulder muscles were buried under a layer of fat. He tramped ponderously into the centre of the arena, as if every step required great exertion. Capito couldn't quite bring himself to believe that Britomaris had won five fights. His opponents must have been even worse than he had first imagined. The barbarian wore a pair of brightly coloured trousers and a sleeveless woollen tunic fastened at the waist with a belt. He had no armour. No leg greaves or manicas or helmet. His weapons consisted of a leather-covered wooden shield with a metal boss, and a spear with a blunted tip. The umpire motioned with his stick for the gladiators to stop, face to face. The men stood two sword-lengths apart.

'All right, lads,' the umpire said. 'I want a fair and clean fight. Now remember, this is a fight to the death. There will be no mercy, so don't waste your time begging the Emperor. Accept your fate with honour. Understood?'

Capito nodded. Britomaris showed no reaction. He probably didn't even speak Latin, thought the imperial gladiator with a sneer. The umpire looked to the editor in the podium, seated not far from the Emperor himself. The editor gave the sign.

'Engage!' the umpire bellowed, and with a swoosh of his stick the fight began.

The barbarian immediately lumbered towards Capito. His swift attack caught the imperial gladiator by surprise. But Capito read the jerk of his opponent's elbow as he made to thrust his spear and quickly sidestepped, dropping his right shoulder and leaving the barbarian stabbing at thin air. The barbarian lurched forward as momentum carried his cumbersome frame beyond Capito, and now the imperial gladiator angled his torso at his rival and slashed at his right calf. Britomaris let out an animal howl of agony as the blade cut into his flesh. The crowd appreciated the move, cheering at the sight of blood flowing freely from the calf wound and spattering the white sand.

Capito revelled in the roar of the mob.

The barbarian staggered and launched his spear at the gladiator. Capito anticipated the move and ducked. The spear hurtled over him and thwacked uselessly into the sand to his rear. Fuming, Britomaris charged towards Capito, bellowing with pain, rage and fear. Capito calmly jerked his shield up sharply – a carefully rehearsed move practised many times before on the ludus training ground. There was a sudden thud as the iron edge of the shield crashed into the underside of Britomaris's jawbone. The barbarian grunted. The cheers in the crowd grew feverish, and amid the din the gladiator could hear individual voices. Men and women shrieking his name. Down in the blood-soaked arena, the barbarian hobbled backwards. Blood oozed from his nose and mouth. Sweat flowed freely down his neck. He could hardly stand.

A voice in the lower galleries shouted at Capito, 'Finish him!'

'Don't show the bastard any mercy!'

'Go for the throat!' a woman screamed.

Capito didn't care if the spectacle was a little short. The crowd wanted blood, and he would provide it. He moved in for the kill, stepping towards the barbarian, his shield hoisted and his sword elbow tucked tightly to his side. The barbarian raised his fists, making one last stand as the gladiator closed in. Advancing swiftly, Capito thrust his sword at his opponent and stabbed at an upward angle, aiming just above the ribcage.

But the barbarian stunned Capito by kicking the bottom of his shield. As he did so, the top tilted forward and in a flash the barbarian wrenched it down at the gladiator's feet. Capito grunted as the metal rim crushed the toes of his left foot. The barbarian ripped the shield away from Capito and kicked him in the groin. Capito staggered backwards, dazed by what had happened, rattled by the same thought as the five gladiators who had faced Britomaris previously. *How could such a large man move so quickly?*

The barbarian followed up with a weighted punch that struck Capito on the shoulder and shuddered through his bones. He collapsed on to the sand, and in a flash Britomaris threw himself forward. The two men rolled on the ground, exchanging blows while the umpire stood a few paces away and ordered them both to their feet. But he was powerless to intervene. Capito tried to scrabble clear, but the barbarian smashed a fist into him and sent the gladiator crashing face down into the sand. The blow stunned Capito. He lay there for a moment in dumb shock and wondered what had happened to his sword. Then he felt a powerful blow on his back, like teeth sinking into his flesh. Something warm and wet was draining out of his back and down his legs. He rolled on to his side and saw Britomaris towering over him, grasping a sword. It was Capito's sword.

Capito became conscious of blood pooling around him, gushing out of his back. 'What?' he said disbelievingly. 'But . . . how . . .?'

The crowd went deadly quiet. Capito felt sick. His mouth was suddenly very dry. Blotches bubbled across his vision. The crowd implored him to get up and fight, but he couldn't. The blow had struck deep. He could feel blood filling his lungs.

'I call on you, gods,' he gasped. 'Save me.'

He glanced up at the podium in despair. The Emperor stared down with cold disapproval. Capito knew he could expect no mercy. None of the gladiators could be granted a reprieve – not even the highest-ranking imperial warrior. His reputation demanded that he accept death fearlessly.

Capito trembled as he struggled to his knees, clamped his hands around the solid legs of Britomaris and bowed deeply, presenting himself for execution. He stared hopelessly at the bloodied sand as he cursed himself for underestimating his opponent. He prayed that whoever faced Britomaris next would not make the same mistake.

His limbs spasmed as the sword plunged into his neck behind his collarbone, and tore deep into his heart.

CHAPTER TWO

The officer raised his head slowly from his cup of wine and focused on the two Praetorian Guards standing in front of him, dimly lit by the dull glow of a single oil lamp. Outside the inn, the street was pitch black.

'Lucius Cornelius Macro, optio of the Second Legion?' the guard on the left barked. The officer nodded with pride and raised his cup to the guards. They wore plain white togas over their tunics, he noticed, which was the distinctive garb of the Praetorian Guard.

'That's me,' he slurred. 'Come to hear the story behind my decoration too, I suppose. Well, take a seat, lads, and I'll give you every grisly detail. But it'll cost you a jug of wine. None of that Gallic swill, though, eh?'

The guard stared humourlessly at Macro. 'You're required to come with us.'

'What, right now?' Macro looked at the young guard on the right. 'Isn't it past your bedtime, lad?'

The young Praetorian glared with outrage at the officer. The guard on the left cleared his throat and said, 'We are here on orders from the imperial palace.'

Macro sobered up. A summons to the imperial household, well after dusk? He shook his head.

'You must be mistaken. I've already collected my award.' He proudly tapped the bronze medals strapped across his chest, which he'd been presented with by the Emperor before the festivities at the Statilius Taurus amphitheatre earlier that day. The defeat of Capito had cast a cloud over proceedings and Macro had left his seat as soon as the gladiator had fallen, sensing the mood of the crowd was about to turn ugly. He'd sunk a skinful of wine at the

7

Sword and Shield tavern not far from the amphitheatre. It was a stinking hovel with foul wine, redeemed by the fact that the owner was an old sweat from the Second Legion who insisted on plying Macro with free drinks in recognition of his decoration.

'The Praetorian Guard doesn't make mistakes,' the guard said bluntly. 'Now come with us.'

'No use arguing with you boys, is there?' Macro slid out of his bench and reluctantly followed the guards outside.

The crowds had taken their anger out on everything in the streets. Market stalls had been overthrown. Carved miniature statuettes of Capito with their heads smashed off littered the ground, and Macro had to watch his step as he ambled down the covered portico of the Flaminian Way towards the Fontinalian Gate. The Julian plaza stood at his right, its ornate marble facade commemorating Caesar. To his left stood rows of extravagant private residences.

'What's this all about, then?' Macro asked the guards.

'No idea, mate,' the one at his left shoulder replied, blunt as the spear Britomaris had been equipped with. 'We were just told to find you and bring you to the palace. What you're wanted for is none of our business.'

Gods, thought Macro as the guards escorted him through the gate towards the Capitoline Hill. A Praetorian who wasn't sticking his nose where it wasn't wanted? He couldn't quite believe it.

'You never get used to the smell here, I suppose,' Macro said, creasing his nose at the fetid stench coming from an open section of the great sewer that carried the city's filth out from the Forum.

The guard nodded. 'You think it's bad here,' he said, 'wait till you visit the Subura. Smells like a fucking Gaul's arse down there. We steer well clear of the place, thank the gods. Spend most of our time up at the imperial palace, being in the Guard and all. Clean air, fresh cunny and all the figs you can eat.' He grinned at the other guard to Macro's right. 'And that fifteen thousand sestertii bonus from the new Emperor came in very handy.'

A bewildering array of smells fanned over the officer. Although the markets had closed a few hours earlier, the potent aroma of cinnamon and pepper, cheap perfume and rotten fish lingered in the air, mixing with the smell of the sewers and conspiring to churn Macro's guts. He hated being in Rome. Too much noise, too much dirt, too many people. And too many bloody Praetorians, he thought. Acrid billows of dull grey smoke wafted up from forges and blanketed the sky, rendering the air muggy and leaden. It was like walking through a giant kiln. Fires glowered dimly in the dark. Apartment blocks tapered along the distant hills and valleys, their blackened upper storeys barely visible against the night sky.

'All the lads in the camp are talking about your award,' the guard said, his voice carrying a hint of jealousy. 'It's not every day that his imperial majesty personally decorates a lowly officer, you know. You're the toast of Rome.' He narrowed his eyes to slits. 'You must have some friends in high places, I suppose.'

'Afraid not,' Macro replied drily. 'My boys and I were part of a punitive expedition against a tribe from across the Rhine. We got caught in the thick of it. Killed three hundred of the wildest-looking Germans you could imagine. I led the men back after our centurion copped it. All in a day's work for the Second. Honestly, I don't know what all the fuss is about.'

The Praetorian swapped an impressed look with the second guard. Macro felt a sudden hankering to be back on the Rhine Frontier. Rome disagreed with him, even though he had lived there in his childhood. He'd left the city under a cloud some thirteen years ago, after avenging the death of his uncle Sextus by slaying a violent gang leader. He had journeyed north to Gaul and enlisted for twenty-five years at the fortress of the Second Legion. He'd not expected to ever return to the city, and being back felt strange.

'Yes,' he said, patting his stomach. 'It's tough being a hero. Everyone buying you drinks. Tarts fawning over you, of course. The ladies love a man with a shiny set of medals.' The guard glanced back enviously across his shoulder. 'Especially the posh ones. They can't resist a bit of rough.'

Macro struggled to match pace with the guards as they weaved their way through a wave of exotic faces – Syrians and Gauls,

Nubians and Jews. Synagogues and a variety of temples he hadn't seen before loomed between the tenements along the main thoroughfare.

'A word to the wise,' said the guard. 'From one soldier to another. Things aren't like they used to be around here. A lot's changed.'

'Oh?' Macro asked, his interest piqued. 'How do you mean?'

'Claudius may be emperor, but his accession hasn't exactly been smooth. That unfortunate business of Caligula getting the chop a few months back caused a bit of a mess.'

'As I recall,' said Macro frostily, 'it was one of your own who stuck his blade into Caligula.'

News of the assassination of the previous emperor in January had been greeted with a mixture of dismay and relief by the men of the Second. Dismay that there was a chance they might return to the days of the Republic, but relief that Caligula's reign had ended. The Emperor had been dogged by scandal. It was common knowledge that he'd committed incest with his sisters and turned the imperial palace into a brothel, and an attempt on his life from the offended aristocracy and Senate had been all too predictable. In the end, a trio of officers from the Praetorian Guard, led by Cassius Chaerea, had taken matters into their own hands. The conspirators had stabbed Caligula thirty times, slain his wife and smashed his young daughter's head against a wall to end the bloodline. For a short while, a new Roman republic had seemed on the cards. Until the Praetorians turned to Claudius.

The guard stopped in his tracks and, turning to face Macro, lowered his voice. 'Look, between you and me, old Chaerea was a decent bloke, but he never had much support among the Guard. He forgot the golden rule. Praetorians stick by the Emperor through thick and thin.' He paused, took a calming breath and continued. 'Anyway, after Caligula died, a few unsavoury types crawled out of the woodwork, announcing that they were opposed to Claudius becoming emperor. One or two of them had the idea that they deserved the job instead. Or worse, wanted to turn Rome into a republic again! To have us return to the dark days of civil war and bloodletting on the streets . . .' The guard shivered at the thought. 'Obviously the Emperor can't rule with dissent in the ranks.'

'Obviously,' Macro said.

'Right. So we've had to spend these last few months rooting out the ones who were opposed to Claudius and making them disappear.'

Macro made a face. 'Disappear?'

'Yes,' the guard said, his eyes darting left and right to check no one was snooping on their conversation. 'We quietly take them off the streets, bring 'em to the palace and deal with them.' He made a throat-slitting gesture. 'Senators, knights, magistrates. Even the odd legate. The sons get exiled, or worse, thrown into the ludus. The list seems to grow by the week. No one is safe, I'm telling you.'

'Not sure I like the sound of that,' Macro said tersely. 'Soldiers shouldn't get involved in politics.'

The guard raised a hand in mock surrender. 'Hey, don't look at me. You know how it is. Orders are orders. If you ask me, it's those freedmen the Emperor has been surrounding himself with we need to watch. You should see the way they talk to us. But they've got his ear.'

The guard straightened his back and approached a set of wrought-iron gates at the entrance to the imperial palace complex. A blast of cool evening air swept through the street as the guards ushered Macro up a wide staircase leading into a dimly lit hall with marbled walls and a bas-relief frieze depicting the famous battle of Zama, the decisive victory against Carthage masterminded by Publius Cornelius Scipio, the great reformer of the Roman military. They swept along a vast corridor and cut through a lavish garden adorned with fountains and statues and surrounded by marble arcades. Beyond, Macro could see the rooftops of the Forum and the columns of the Temple of Castor and Pollux. Arriving at the opposite side of the garden, they climbed a flight of stone stairs and entered a large hall with an apse at the far end. The guards escorted Macro across the hall to where a shadowed figure stood at the step of a raised dais used by the Emperor when he was holding court.

The man at the dais was not the Emperor. He had the dark curly hair and sloping nose of a Greek. His smooth skin and willowy physique suggested he had never done a day's hard labour. He wore the simple tunic of a freedman, although Macro noted that it appeared to be made of fine-spun wool. His eyes were black like the holes in a stage mask.

'Ah, the famous Macro!' the freedman said with an exaggerated tone of praise. 'A true Roman hero!'

He approached Macro, his thin lips twisted into a smile.

'Leave us,' he ordered the guards in a sharp, shrill voice. The Praetorians nodded and paced back down the centre of the hall. The freedman followed them with his dark eyes until they were out of earshot.

'You have to be careful who you speak around these days,' he said. 'Particularly the Praetorians. They have the misguided impression that his imperial majesty owes them an eternal debt. What is the world coming to when the guards think they hold sway over the most powerful man in the world?'

Macro bit his tongue. He'd heard that after Caligula had been assassinated, Claudius had been discovered hiding in the imperial palace by members of the Praetorian Guard. Desperate for stability, the Praetorians had promptly acclaimed as emperor a fifty-year-old man with practically no experience of government and who, if the rumours were to be believed, didn't even want the job. Without the backing of the Praetorians, there might have been another face stamped on every coin in the Empire. No wonder the freedman felt so threatened by their presence, thought Macro.

The freedman said, 'My name is Servius Ulpius Murena. I report to the imperial secretary, Marcus Antonius Pallas. I presume you're familiar with the name?'

'Sorry, but no,' Macro replied with a shrug. 'It's been a while since I've been around polite society. I've spent the last few years chopping down Germans.'

Murena grunted. 'I'm aware of your background, officer. As a matter of fact, that's why you're here. Pallas is a secretary to his imperial majesty. He helps the Emperor administer Rome and her provinces. As do I. Tell me, how many Germans do you think you've killed during your time at the Rhine?'

Macro shrugged. 'Depends.'

'On what?' Murena said, cocking his head at the officer.

'Your average German takes a number of cuts before he drops,' Macro said. 'Sometimes you'll give one a good few stabs and he'll still be charging at you and foaming at the mouth. You don't actually see them shuffle off to the Underworld. They drag themselves away to die somewhere nice and quiet. But they die all the same. We have a saying in the Second: swords can't tell the difference between Germans and Greeks.'

'I see.' The freedman shifted awkwardly on his feet, clearly unsettled by the violent turn the conversation had taken. 'And what precisely does that mean?'

'A stab's a stab,' said Macro. 'Give a man a good twist in the guts and he's done for, whether he's a whacking great barbarian or a skinny little toga-lifter.'

Murena wrung his hands as he turned away from Macro towards the gardens and the pair of Praetorian Guards hovering under the arched walkway. 'What a pity the great Capito did not heed such sagacious advice.'

'Sagacious?'

'Yes, almost synonymous with judicious.' Seeing the quizzical look on Macro's face, the freedman rolled his eyes. 'Never mind,' he went on. 'My point is, you have lots of experience of slaying the barbaric enemies of Rome.'

'More than most, I'd say,' Macro said, puffing out his chest.

'Good. Because I have a task for you.'

Macro frowned as anxiety spilled through his guts. 'Task?'

'Yes. A task. For me.'

Macro gritted his teeth. 'Find someone else to do your dirty work. I take orders from my centurion, my legate and the Emperor. No one else.'

The freedman laughed and inspected his fingernails. 'I hear you haven't set foot in this city for a while?'

'Thirteen years or so.'

'Then I will give you the benefit of the doubt just this once.

Rome is different now. I may be a simple freedman, but you would do well to treat me with respect. I have a certain influence within these walls. Enough to rescind your decoration . . . and your promotion to centurion.'

'Centurion?' Macro repeated with a start. 'What are you talking about?'

Murena produced a scroll, and Macro noticed the imperial seal on the wax. The freedman opened it and read aloud, '"Orders from his imperial majesty to the legate of the Second Legion, instructing the immediate promotion to centurion of Optio Lucius Cornelius Macro." A position that interests you, I believe?'

Macro frowned at Murena.

'Sadly, I cannot dispatch the letter until you carry out a certain task for the Emperor,' Murena explained.

'What kind of task?' Macro said uneasily.

Murena smiled wanly. 'Permit me to elaborate. You were there at the arena earlier today to receive your decoration. A proud moment, sadly marred by the defeat of our dear Capito.' The freedman tutted. 'Highly embarrassing for the Emperor. Capito was not only the finest fighter in the imperial school and therefore the personal property of Claudius himself, he was the sixth imperial gladiator to fall at the hands of Britomaris.'

Murena circled the officer. Macro eyed him warily. 'These are stressful days for the new Emperor,' the freedman continued. 'There are many doubters in Rome. Some of them are openly hostile to Claudius. Not just men of the Senate, but in the Forum and the taverns too. I speak frankly now. The Emperor was not a unanimous choice. The vagaries of bloodline and birthright mean that no man can wear the laurel crown without facing nefarious challenges to his supremacy. You heard the rumbles of discontent in the crowd after Capito died. A defeat like this threatens to undermine our regime in its infancy. We must demonstrate to the mob that Claudius is the strong, decisive leader we have craved since the golden age of Augustus.'

'So invade somewhere,' Macro said with a shrug. 'That usually does the trick.'

Murena laughed like a tutor humouring a brash student. 'Thank you for that truly enlightening insight, Optio. Your genius makes me wonder why you haven't elevated yourself higher up the ranks.'

Macro fought a powerful urge to punch Murena in the face.

'Rest assured, plans are afoot for the near future,' the freedman went on. 'But the more pressing problem is Britomaris. Six gladiators defeated! That is more than a stain on the Emperor's name; it is a veritable boil, one we must lance before it overwhelms us. We cannot afford any more defeats by this barbarian. Whoever faces him next must triumph, demonstrating to all that no one defies the Emperor, and that Claudius is the right man to occupy the throne.'

Macro said, 'What about getting Hermes to fight him? He's just about the toughest gladiator there's ever been. He'd chop up a thug like Britomaris as quick as boiling asparagus.'

'Out of the question,' Murena said flatly.

'Why?'

A pained expression wrinkled unpleasantly across the freedman's bony face. As if he were chewing on a mouthful of rotten fish guts, thought Macro.

'I must confess, I am not a fan of Hermes. Neither is Pallas. We find him somewhat brutish. However, the problem with Hermes is not one of style. Indeed, in the event of Capito dying, another of the Emperor's advisers – a wretched, snivelling fellow by the name of Narcissus – had arranged for Hermes to fight Britomaris next.'

'So what's the problem?' Macro asked.

'This morning, Hermes suffered a . . . a rather unfortunate accident.'

'Accident?' Macro repeated.

'He was robbed in the street, would you believe.' Murena shook his head. 'Thugs broke several of his bones. The man could be out for months. But we cannot wait for him to recover from his inconvenient beating. We need a substitute urgently.'

Murena finished circling Macro, stopping directly in front of him.

'You will train a substitute gladiator to fight Britomaris,' he said.

Macro looked quizzically at him. 'Why me?' he stuttered. 'I've never worked at a ludus. You've more than enough doctores at the imperial establishment for the job.'

'Ordinarily, yes. But this is no ordinary fight. We must send a powerful message to the mob, and what better way to do that than by having a hero of the Empire employ his military know-how to destroy a barbarian like Britomaris?' Murena teased out a twisted smile.

Macro shook his head firmly.

'It's too risky,' he said. 'Training someone up, I mean. You're better off just picking one of the gladiators from the imperial school. That lot are supposed to be the best swordsmen in Capua. You'd have far better odds on one of them defeating Britomaris than some wet-behind-the-ears recruit.'

Murena sucked his teeth. 'Unfortunately the imperial school is severely depleted. Caligula has used most of the best men up in the arena. He's left us with just a few stragglers, none of whom would be fit for this purpose.'

The imperial aide folded his hands behind his back and walked the width of the central aisle, his gait slow and methodical, as if pacing out the perimeter of a building. The sound of his sandals against the floor echoed throughout the hall.

'Happily, Fortuna smiles on us.'

Macro clicked his tongue. 'Hard to believe.'

A flicker of a smile crossed Murena's face before he continued. 'It appears we have a ready-made candidate. A young man with military experience who was instructed by a gladiator as a boy. A man who, I am reliably informed, demonstrates utter fearless-ness when facing raw steel. A rare quality, as I'm sure a man of violence such as yourself will appreciate. With the right guidance, he could be just the ticket.'

'A soldier, eh?' Macro said. 'What's the lad's name?'

Murena looked down. 'Marcus Valerius Pavo.' He pulled a face at his sandal, as if he had trodden in a puddle of sewage. 'Although you may well be more familiar with his father's name. Titus?'

'The legate of the Fifth Legion?'

'Formerly the legate,' Murena corrected icily. 'Latterly rotting

in an unmarked grave on the Appian Way. The predictable consequence of trying to return Rome to a republic. We're still debating
whether to decimate the Fifth, since his men appeared so eager
to support him in his treachery.'

A cold shiver crawled down Macro's spine. News of the execution of the Fifth's legate had not yet reached the Rhine, but the
more the officer heard about how the imperial palace now dealt
with its enemies, the less he liked the sound of it. Bashing up
barbarians in Germany and Gaul was all well and good, but the
thought of Romans stabbing each other in the back reminded
him of the civil wars that had dogged Rome during the darkest
days of the Republic.

'Dissent in the ranks cannot be tolerated,' Murena said, as if
reading Macro's mind. 'We had to set an example.'

'But you let the son live?'

'He wasn't in Rome at the time. Pavo was a military tribune
in the Sixth Legion. We had him placed under arrest and returned
to Rome. The Emperor had planned to execute the young man
in the arena, and to that end we slung him into a ludus in Paestum.
The lanista has promised to see to it that he dies in the arena
within the year.'

Macro curled up his lips in thought. 'And now you want him
to save the honour of Rome?'

'These are desperate times. With Hermes out of the picture,
we need Pavo. At least for the time being. Training him, however,
may not be so straightforward. The young man is rather upset
about the whole business of his father being killed.'

'How did he die?' Macro asked cautiously.

Murena chuckled to himself and shook his head. 'Condemned
to death in the arena. The Emperor paired him with Hermes, no
less. Titus put up rather a good show. I'm surprised he had a drop
of blood left him in when the time came for Hermes to finish
him off.'

'No bloody wonder the lad is angry,' Macro murmured, in a
voice low enough that his words evaded Murena's ear.

'I'm told that you have soldierly qualities in abundance, Macro.
I believe you're just the right man to whip him into shape. You're

to head to Paestum, train your charge and escort him to Rome for the fight. You have one month.'

'A month?' Macro cried. 'You must be joking!'

'On the contrary,' Murena replied. 'I'm deadly serious.'

'But . . . a month! That's nowhere near enough time to prepare for battle.'

'It's not a battle. Just a fight in the arena.'

'Just a fight?' Macro shook his head wearily. 'I have plenty of experience in training legionaries. Even the best take months to whip into any kind of shape, and the worst can take three or four times that.'

'Pavo is different. His natural talent with the sword is exceptional.'

'I've heard that before,' said Macro.

'Well this is no mere boast. The gladiator who first trained him happens to be the doctore at the imperial ludus. He claims he has never known a boy with such prodigious skill. And by all accounts the men of the Sixth haven't seen a tribune handle a sword so well.' Murena sighed as he lifted his gaze to the ceiling. 'It's his temperament that is the problem.'

'What about the Emperor? He's happy to have his skin saved by the son of a traitor?'

'In the current climate, we can't afford to be picky,' Murena replied sourly. 'Domestic squabbles have to be set to one side, for we cannot allow this barbarian to hang over us any longer.' Murena inspected the sleeve of his tunic. 'Besides, I have reassured the Emperor that it is he, and not Pavo, who will bask in the glory of Rome's honour being restored.'

As will you, no doubt, Macro thought. For once he managed to keep his opinion to himself. Macro's tongue was his worst enemy at times. His lack of diplomacy was part of the reason why it had taken him so long to be in contention for promotion to centurion. He didn't want to let the opportunity slip through his fingers now. Even if it meant working for a snake like Murena.

'You could push the fight back a month or two,' he offered. 'Give me some more time with the lad.'

'I'm afraid that's not possible,' Murena sniffed. 'Announcements have already been made and the wheels have been put in motion for the fight. We cannot backtrack and we cannot tolerate any challenge to the Emperor's authority. You must appreciate the precariousness of our situation.'

Macro cursed the gods under his breath. A short while ago he'd been licking his lips at the thought of indulging himself for a few days before returning to the Rhine and enjoying his new status as the toast of the Second. Now he was looking at a month in a backwater training a troubled gladiator in a ludus whilst surrounded by prisoners of war, errant slaves and wastrels. And the cost of losing to Britomaris and heaping further embarrassment on the Emperor didn't bear thinking about.

'I've dispatched a messenger by horse with instructions for the lanista at the ludus in Paestum. He'll be expecting you. We'll be hosting the match at the Julian plaza. The plaza is a somewhat more intimate venue than the arena, but it's the perfect setting: rich and full of history. Caesar built it and Augustus hosted gladiator fights in it. Now the Emperor will assert his credentials there.'

The freedman called over the two Praetorian Guards. 'You are to leave immediately,' he said without looking at Macro. 'A horse has been saddled for you, and I'll have my clerks draft an imperial warrant to give you the necessary authority to do as you need at the ludus. It is a five-day journey to Paestum, I believe. Five days there and the same back leaves you with twenty days of training with your charge. Use it wisely. Questions?'

'Just one,' Macro said. 'What if this Pavo doesn't want to fight? I mean, if he bears a grudge against the Emperor for what happened to his family, he's not exactly going to be enthusiastic about helping him out, is he? Especially since you've already condemned him to death.'

Murena smiled cruelly. 'I've got something that should provide him with a strong incentive . . .'

CHAPTER THREE

Paestum

The doctore cracked his short leather whip on the blistering
sand and glared at the new recruits. 'Straighten your backs!'
he growled. 'Raise your heads, you worthless buggers!'

The men shuffled into the training ground and arranged themselves in a rough line in front of Calamus. The doctore cast his
eye over the men the way a butcher inspects cattle at a market.
He'd have his work cut out getting this lot into shape, he thought
grimly. Calamus knew from experience how hard the training
regime was, and how few men made it through the selection
process. He'd once fought as a gladiator himself, yet all he had to
show for it was a noticeable limp and a face lacerated with scars.

'You're here because you're the lowest of the low,' he said.
'Common criminals look down on you. Whores wouldn't sleep
with you. Even bloody slaves laugh at you. Rome shits on each
and every one of you daily, and if I had my way, I'd pack the lot
of you off to the mines. But today is your lucky day, ladies. Our
master is in a generous mood for a change. He's given you a
once-in-a-lifetime chance to make something of your pathetic
little lives.'

A silence fell across the training ground. The doctore looked
for someone to make an example of and fixed his piercing eyes
on a young man at the end of the line. He had an angular and
awkward physique, and appeared somehow shorter than his actual
height. His eyes radiated a defiance of everything around him and
he wore an intricately decorated pallium cloak over his tunic. The
mere sight of the cloak caused Calamus to blaze with anger.

'You!' he shouted as he marched over to the young man. 'That's a rich-looking cloak. Very nice.' He narrowed his eyes to dagger slits. 'Who'd you steal it from?'

The young man shook his head. 'Nobody,' he said. 'It's mine.'

Calamus elbowed him in the solar plexus. The recruit grunted as he doubled over and dropped to his knees, coughing and sputtering on the ground. Calamus towered above him. 'That's "sir" to you, you little shit!' he snarled. 'What's your name?'

'Marcus Valerius Pavo,' the recruit said between desperate draws of breath. 'Sir.'

'Tell me, Pavo, do you think I was born yesterday?'

'No, sir.'

Calamus grabbed a fold of the cloak and shoved it in front of the recruit's face. 'And yet you expect me to believe that a desperate lowlife like you can afford a piece of finery like this?'

'I didn't steal it.'

'Bollocks! Are you calling me a liar?' Calamus said, lowering his voice.

'It was a gift, sir.'

'A gift?' Calamus spat. 'Scum like you don't get gifts.'

'I swear, sir. My father gave it to me.'

Calamus laughed and rubbed his hands with glee. 'Oh, that's a rich one! You don't have a father, son. You were born a bastard like every other man in this ludus. But entertain me some more. Who do you reckon your old man is?'

'Titus Valerius Pavo, sir. Legate of the Fifth Legion. Or at least he was.'

That caught Calamus off guard. He worked his features into a heavyset frown and paused, unsure for a moment how to proceed. In his twenty years' experience in the business, Calamus had never heard of the son of a legate enrolling at a ludus.

'Another rich-boy volunteer, eh?' he seethed. 'I know your kind. Pissed away your inheritance, did you? What was your poison, lad? Tarts? Booze? Gambling? Chariot races? Can't be bothered to get a proper job? If you've come here thinking it's an easy ride, you're in for a fucking shock.'

'I'm not a volunteer,' Pavo said, scraping himself off the ground. 'I'm here against my will. My father was killed by—'

'Shut up,' the doctore thundered. 'Frankly I couldn't give a toss why you're here. As far as I'm concerned, you're a fucking recruit and nothing else.'

Pavo kept his mouth shut. He had been beaten and spat on and shouted at by men below his station ever since a guard of Praetorians arrived at the camp of the Sixth Legion and placed him under arrest. The doctore didn't scare him. Not much did now. Not after what had happened to his family.

He watched Calamus wheel away in disgust and pace up and down in front of the men, his voice echoing around the porticoes and travertine columns surrounding the training ground. Pavo noticed that the tendons of the doctore's bare feet were bulbous and distorted from years of fighting on sand.

'This isn't the army,' Calamus said. 'Gladiators aren't legionaries.' He shot a scathing look at Pavo. 'If you want to spend the next twenty-five years digging holes and collecting seashells for the Emperor, you've come to the wrong place.'

One of the recruits to Pavo's right laughed uneasily. Pavo watched Calamus glower and turn to look at him. He was a short man with cropped dark hair and a nose with a break at the bridge. He had a layer of fat about his waist and wore a plain, tattered tunic.

'You! Name?'

'Manius Salvius Bucco, sir,' the man replied nervously.

'Bucco? I know a Bucco. He's a toga-lifter. Are you a toga-lifter, son?'

'No, sir.'

'Bollocks, of course you are! Are you a volunteer or a slave?'

'Volunteer, sir.'

'Want to be a gladiator, do you, Bucco?'

'Yes, sir.'

'Don't make me laugh. You don't look like gladiator material to me, Bucco. You look like something I'd scrape off my boot. Tell me, why are you disgracing my ludus? Murder someone and now on the run? Shag your master's missus when he was away on business at the forum? Is that it?'

'No, sir.' Bucco lowered his head in shame. Pavo squirmed.

Although he felt sorry for poor Bucco, he was also glad that Calamus had found someone else to bully. 'I gambled. Fell in with some bad people, sir. Figured I would enrol and pay off my debts.'

'A gambler! What'd you play?'

'Dice mainly, sir.'

Calamus smirked. 'I should've known! You look like a mug. Only idiots play dice, Bucco. How much did you lose?'

'Ten thousand sestertii.'

'Good gods, man!' Calamus exclaimed. 'And look at the shape of you! You'd have to win twenty fights to earn that much, and I've never seen a fat bastard win once. Or the son of a legate, for that matter.'

Pavo frowned. He didn't approve of the doctore's attitude to the military. His father Titus had been something of a hero to his men – a real soldier's soldier – in stark contrast to the halfwits and aristocrats who populated most of the senior posts in the legions. Titus had further endeared himself with his love of chariot races, and he could often be seen at the Circus Maximus cheering on his beloved Greens. But his enjoyment of the races was nothing compared to his devotion to gladiatorial combat. Pavo remembered with fondness his father explaining how Rome had been founded on blood and sacrifice, and that no man could be worthy of leading others without understanding those twin virtues. He had often regaled Pavo with the story of the beleaguered General Publius Decius Mus, who had sacrificed himself to the gods of the Underworld during the Samnite Wars in exchange for success in battle.

Twenty years of service, and Rome had repaid Titus by condemning him to death. The back of Pavo's throat burned with outrage at the memory of seeing his father's bowels slashed open by the tip of a sword and his entrails scooped out by his murderer, while the shrill voices of the crowd bayed for blood.

'Gladiators don't build forts or go on marches,' Calamus boomed as he wheeled away from Bucco and addressed the recruits as one. 'Make no mistake, when you're lying on your arse in the sand and some bastard has a blade to your throat, there will be no comrades charging to save you. Gladiator fighting is a precise skill, ladies. It is not an art, as some poseurs make out. Art is for women, or worse, Greeks. A gladiator goes into the arena alone and comes out alone, and the only difference is whether he walks out or has to be dragged. Gladiators dedicate themselves to one-on-one warfare. Bucco, why is your fucking hand raised?'

'When do we get to eat, sir?'

The question made Pavo wince. He suddenly remembered how hungry he was – it had been a long morning. They'd been escorted to the ludus at dawn for a thorough examination by the medic, a mealy-eyed old Greek called Achaeus. There had been a lot of waiting around since, the men fidgeting tensely as they waited to see what lay in store for them.

'You'll get to eat, Bucco, when I say so. You shit when I say so, you sleep when I say so. You don't even think without getting permission from me first. Got it?'

'Yes, sir!'

Calamus jerked his head at a huddle of men under the north-facing portico. Pavo noted their overly developed muscles and heavily scarred torsos. The doctore summoned one of them over. 'Amadocus!'

A veteran turned and trudged towards the doctore with a grunt. Pavo studied the man. He had skin the colour of chalk and a mane of light hair, with a darker beard shaved close at the cheeks. His muscles were clearly defined. His veins bulged like rope on his forearms and neck. He stopped beside Calamus as the doctore gestured to his scars.

'Tell the men how many matches you've fought.'

'Thirteen, sir,' answered the veteran in heavily accented Latin. Pavo noticed that he had a stubborn, hostile look in his deep-set eyes.

'And how many times have you lost, Amadocus?'

'Never, sir.'

'Never!' The doctore beamed with pride at the reply and swung his icy stare back to the recruits. 'You miserable buggers might look at this haggard face and see a man who's taken his fair share of knocks. Amadocus is a scrapper, plain and simple. But thanks to my instruction, he's still alive, while his many opponents are taking a nice long trip through the Underworld.'

Calamus nodded at the veteran. 'That will be all, Amadocus.'

'Yes, sir,' the Thracian replied, no discernible expression on his face.

Pavo watched Amadocus march back towards the huddle of veterans as Calamus glared at the new recruits. The doctore took a deep breath and turned his head in the direction of a balcony overlooking the courtyard. 'Now stand upright, the lot of you. Your lanista, Vibius Modius Gurges, wishes to introduce himself.'

Calamus stepped aside. Pavo craned his neck and saw a figure float into view on the balcony. He had thin lips, and eyes set deep into their sockets. His skin was stretched tightly across his small face. He rested his hands on the balcony plinth and stared curiously at Pavo for a moment before addressing the men.

'Calamus is your mentor, your doctore. He will turn some of you into legends of the arena, gods willing,' he said, flicking his eyes from Pavo over the rest of the group. 'But I am your master. I own you, body and soul. All of you have made a solemn promise to me to be burned, bound, beaten and killed by the sword. Some of you will fulfil that promise before the year is out. A lucky few will live a little longer. Most Romans consider you the dregs of humanity. But I don't.' Gurges raised his head to the heavens, then clasped his hands in front of his face. 'In fact, I envy you.'

He paused and sucked in a deep breath. 'I envy you because you get the chance to die a glorious death. In Rome, as some of you might know, there is no greater honour. Crowds will cheer your name. Women will want to be with you. Even some men will want to be you. Children will talk of your legend for years after your blood has run dry.'

A wicked smile tickled the corners of Gurges's mouth as a slave emerged carrying a silver tray with a single wine goblet balanced on top. The lanista scooped it up and toasted the recruits. 'To your success,' he said. 'Or not.'

He drained the wine in a single gulp, then nodded to Calamus. 'As you were.'

'Back to training!' Calamus barked at the gladiators. 'New recruits at the palus. Move it!'

Pavo paced with a heavy heart towards the wooden posts located in the middle of the training ground. The posts were a short step from a sundial used to time the length of each exercise. Training like a common legionary, he thought. His privileged life as a tribune in the Sixth Legion suddenly seemed a distant dream.

'Not you, rich boy,' the doctore ordered. Pavo stopped in his tracks and shot a puzzled look at Calamus.

'Is there a problem?'

'The lanista wants a word,' Calamus replied.

CHAPTER FOUR

A household slave ushered Pavo down a wide passageway with a vaulted ceiling painted in bright colours. At the end the slave turned left and stopped outside a bronze-panelled door with posts sheathed in carved marble. An intricate mosaic on the floor depicted a gladiator combat between a pair of lightly armoured fighters with whips.

At that moment the door swung open and Pavo lifted his eyes from the mosaic. The lanista stood in the doorway. Up close, he looked even shorter and thinner than he had on the balcony, Pavo thought, as if he had shrivelled up. His arrogant demeanour had disappeared. Now a serious, dark expression was cast over his features.

'Come in,' Gurges said.

Pavo followed the lanista into an office with contrasting marble tiles covering the floor, and richly decorated walls. The lanista eased himself on to a chair behind an oak desk and nodded to his slave.

'Fetch more wine. The Falernian. Not that piss I ply my guests with.'

The slave shuffled outside. Gurges leaned back in his chair. Pavo stood in front of the desk, his arms resting by his sides.

'I am the lanista of the oldest and grandest ludus in Paestum,' Gurges said. 'Well, the oldest, though perhaps no longer the grandest. Fucking hard to make an honest living these days.'

Pavo said nothing, unsettled by the lanista's loose tongue. He saw that Gurges's eyes were glazed and it occurred to Pavo that this probably wasn't the lanista's first drink of the day. Gurges folded his arms behind the back of his head and pushed out his bottom lip.

'The high priests might turn their noses up at my work, but when it comes to keeping the mob happy, they need people like me. Men who live and work among the lowest scum Rome has to offer, looking for a champion.'

The slave returned with a fresh goblet of wine. Like everything else in the lanista's home, it appeared expensive and crass. Gurges admired the goblet for a moment. Then he said to the slave, 'Fetch Calamus. I want an update on the injured gladiators.'

'Yes, master,' the slave replied and quickly departed from the study. Gurges took a gulp of wine, and set the cup down on the desk with a sharp rap. A few drops splashed over the oak. His eyes were wide and angry as they fixed on Pavo.

'You can handle a sword, from what I hear.'

Pavo shrugged. 'Well enough.'

'Good. I trust you're aware of the deal I cut with that slippery Greek?'

'Pallas,' Pavo muttered through clenched jaws. 'The snake.'

'You're to die within the year, for twenty thousand of the Emperor's sestertii. I'll honour the deal, because I'm a man of my word. But there's nothing from Pallas to dictate what I do with you in the interim. For one year you belong to me, body and soul. And for that year, you'll fight. A lot. I intend to pitch you into the arena at every opportunity. And I expect you to win. I know what you posh lads are like, I've had a few pass through my ludus in my time. One boy, he shoved his head through the wheels of the cart on the way to a fight. Chose to snap his bloody neck in half rather than face the arena, and left me out of pocket, the selfish prick.'

Pavo took a deep breath. 'There's only one man I want to face. The man who killed my father.'

Gurges stroked his chin thoughtfully. 'And who might that be?'

'Hermes of Rhodes,' said Pavo icily. 'The Emperor ordered my father to fight him to the death in the arena. Hermes showed him no mercy or respect. Disembowelled him, then cut off his head and paraded it around the arena like a trophy. He disgraced my father and my family name in front of thousands. I will fight him, and I will have my revenge.'

Gurges steepled his fingers on the desk and studied the son of the legate in silence. 'Hermes, eh?' he said after a long pause. 'That won't be easy to arrange. Hermes is officially retired now. He only comes out into the arena for a hefty fee. We're talking a hundred thousand sestertii.'

'I don't care,' Pavo said. 'I'll find a way.'

Gurges picked at a morsel of food lodged in his teeth. Pulling his finger out of his mouth, he rubbed the morsel between his thumb and forefinger. 'Arrogant lad, aren't you?'

'No,' Pavo said. 'Just wronged.'

A chill gripped Pavo as an image flashed across his mind of Hermes lying prostrate on the arena floor, blood spilling from his slit throat. He burned with rage. His father had been humiliated in the arena. His family's wealth had been seized by Claudius and pumped into the imperial coffers. Pavo's son, Appius, had vanished and he feared the worst. The child could have been sold into slavery or butchered in some dark alley, joining his mother Sabina – who had died during childbirth – in the afterlife. Pavo had been stripped of his position as tribune and condemned to a barbaric death. He had nothing left to live for, except the prospect of killing Hermes.

'Perhaps we can come to an arrangement,' Gurges said. Calamus arrived and waited patiently by the study door. 'If you earn me some good victories, I may be able to help you in your quest to fight Hermes.'

Pavo said nothing.

'Give it some thought,' Gurges continued. 'In the meantime, watch your back. Some of the gladiators in this ludus are prisoners of war. One or two might even have been captured by your old man. As for the rest, well . . .' He swept his arms across his desk as if clearing away imaginary clutter. 'Let's just say they don't like high-born brats like you intruding on their ludus.'

He reached for his wine cup and raised it to his lips, forgetting that he'd already emptied it. Frowning, he rose abruptly from his seat as Calamus brushed past Pavo. The doctore watched the recruit depart down the passageway. Once he was out of earshot, he turned to the lanista.

'He's trouble, that one,' Calamus grumbled. 'We should just be rid of him.'

'That's where you're wrong,' Gurges replied, flattening out a slight crease in his tunic. 'Times are hard. We haven't had a champion since the great Proculus, seven bloody long years ago.'

Calamus made to reply, but Gurges levelled his eyes with the doctore and cut in before he could speak. 'With his raw talent and the fame of his family name, crowds will flock to see Pavo. We'll fill the arena ten times over.' He looked back down the passageway at Pavo's shrinking figure. 'He could save us. And gods know, we need a new champion. Either that, or we go out of business. Now, tell me how the injured gladiators in the infirmary are faring. The useless bastards . . .'

Calamus stabbed at the sky, as if drawing blood from the bellies of the clouds.

'This is a sword,' the doctore said. 'Look at it. Admire the blade. Consider the craftsmanship that has gone into making such a fine weapon.' He smiled for a moment before making a thrusting motion at the recruits. 'Now imagine the point puncturing your ribcage,' he said. 'Cutting through your flesh.' He twisted the sword in his hand. 'Carving up your vitals.'

He held the weapon outstretched and pointed the tip at Pavo, who stood at the end of the line. Pavo felt the other recruits' eyes burning holes in him. In the shadows beneath the balcony he could see the veteran fighters occasionally throwing angry stares at him between training exercises. Word of his privileged upbringing had spread quickly, Pavo realised. Since arriving in the ludus, he had learned that most of the men in the gladiator school were prisoners of war, slaves or criminals. There was a sprinkling of freedmen volunteers, men of lowly status and desperate circumstances willing to accept the stain on their characters inflicted by becoming a gladiator in exchange for a chance of glory and money. But all the men were of a much lower social status than Pavo. He knew from long experience in the Sixth that nothing bred resentment like an upper-class accent. Still, he had been at the ludus for less than a day, and already the trainer and most of the recruits despised him. It must be some kind of record, he thought moodily, as he took a deep breath and pretended not to notice.

'A gladiator only gets to use a real sword when he fights in the arena, since no Roman worth his salt trusts a gladiator with a real sword in the ludus. You have that ungrateful wretch Spartacus to thank for that.'

The doctore squinted at the sun gleaming off the sword.

'Plenty of you may know about Spartacus. Some of you may even admire the bastard,' he said, staring down the barrel of his bulbous nose at the recruits. 'Don't. Spartacus fought as a gladiator, received three square meals a day and a warm bed, and instead of seeking glory in the arena, he chose to piss it all away. When he died, six thousand of his followers were crucified along the road to Capua, so you can see how well that worked out. Learn from me, and you might end up better off than old Spartacus. One or two of you may live long enough to taste freedom.'

Calamus plunged the sword into the sand and pointed at the dozen wooden posts to his right. They were arranged in two rows of six, spaced two sword-widths apart, one post for each new recruit, standing at roughly the same height as a tall Roman.

'Until you prove yourselves worthy of the brotherhood, you will practise at the palus using a wooden sword. You will practise day and night. You will practise in your sleep. You will practise until your arms drop off. From this day on, your life is nothing but this palus,' Calamus tapped the nearest post on the head, like a star student, 'and your sword. Bucco!'

'Yes, sir?'

The doctore puckered his brow. 'Extra rations for the men if you can tell me what this wooden post really is.'

Bucco wiped his forehead. Pavo watched the other recruits glaring at him with hungry eyes, willing him to get the right answer so they could fill their empty bellies.

'Come on then, fatso,' Calamus growled. 'I don't have all fucking day.'

'A wooden post?' Bucco ventured between snatches of breath.

Calamus looked ready to explode.

'A . . . *post*? Fuck me, Bucco, you're even thicker than you look. And believe me, from where I'm standing, that is no mean feat.'

Calamus took an angry step towards Bucco, and for a moment Pavo thought the trainer might thrash him with his whip. Instead he grabbed Bucco by the fleshy folds of his neck and hauled him in front of the nearest palus, venting his anger.

'This is no post. This is the palus! This is your sworn enemy! This is the merchant who stole your girlfriend and the father who kicked you senseless when he came home pissed every night. You will learn to hate the palus with every bone in your body. Despise it. Unleash your rage on it, and it will reward you by making you a decent swordsman.'

Calamus released Bucco and shoved him back towards the line of recruits as he turned to address the group.

'You will all be assigned your own palus. Each man will paint a face on his. Not the face of your girlfriend – or boyfriend for you, Bucco – but someone you truly hate. You will stab your sword at that face every day, until your rage has been channelled fully. Bucco!'

'Yes, sir?'

Pavo looked on as the doctore pointed at Bucco. 'Let's see if you've learned anything in your miserable little life.'

The recruit cautiously approached the nearest palus, which had a practice sword lying beside it. The silence was broken only by the clashing thud of wood against wood as the veteran gladiators battled each other in pairs at the other end of the courtyard. Bucco didn't strike Pavo as a natural gladiator. But he had bulk, and some of the better gladiators he had seen in the arena carried a reasonable amount of fat on them. More flesh to protect their vitals. One of two were even obese. Perhaps he will surprise me, Pavo thought.

'Come on,' Calamus barked with barely disguised contempt. 'Don't just stand there gawping at the sword like it's a bit of posh cunny. Pick it up.'

Bucco tentatively picked up the sword. His shoulder sagged as he struggled with the weight of it. Lifting it in a two-handed grip, he puffed out his cheeks as he aimed at a low point on the post, swiping the sword in a wide arc from his side rather than bringing it over his head with a reckless slashing motion. The point of the sword clattered meekly into the post four feet off the ground. It was an almost apologetic thrust. Pavo winced as the doctore looked on in disgust.

'Gods below,' Calamus fumed. 'You're trying to slay a man, not touch him up.' He snatched the sword back from Bucco. 'Maybe tomorrow you can show me how to dress like a Greek as well as fight like one.'

Pavo watched Bucco sink back into line. He looked crestfallen. Calamus cast his eyes over the rest of the recruits. 'Who wants to see if they can do better than the toga-lifter, then?'

No one spoke up. The doctore settled his cold grey gaze on Pavo. 'Rich boy! Get your arse over here.'

A tense atmosphere fell over the recruits as Pavo stepped forward and wrapped the fingers of his right hand around the grip. The training sword was surprisingly heavy. Much heavier than a real blade, he thought. He stood level with the palus, his feet planted shoulder-width apart. He took a deep breath. He felt a heft in his arm muscles as he lifted the sword. In the same breath he felt his heart burn with resentment at the humiliation that had been inflicted upon his family since Claudius had come to the throne. He grasped the sword so tightly his knuckles whitened. The palus disappeared. Instead Pavo saw the figure of Hermes standing in front of him. An uncontrollable frenzy washed over the recruit as he suddenly dropped his right shoulder and twisted his torso, thrusting the sword against the palus with such force that both post and weapon shuddered. In the same blur of motion Pavo retracted his arm, angling his wrist so that his thumb was perpendicular to the ground, and thrust near the top of the palus at the point of an imaginary neck. There was a crack as the post shuddered. Pavo quickly launched a third attack lower down, driving the point of the sword into the groin area. Calamus waved for him to stop. The son of the legate took a step back from the post, his muscles inflamed as he stared coldly at three coin-sized divots on the post.

A bout of silence swept like the shadow of a cloud across the training ground. His veins pulsing, Pavo retreated a couple more steps from the palus and let the sword clatter to the ground.

'Well, that wasn't completely shit.' The doctore pursed his lips. He made a point of not looking at Pavo. 'Right, I've seen enough for one day. It's fair to say none of you will be giving me nightmares about my own proud record in the arena. Remove yourselves to the barracks. We resume tomorrow at dawn. Anyone late to roll call will be flogged and given half-rations for the day. Dismissed!'

CHAPTER FIVE

'About bloody time!' Bucco announced to Pavo as half a dozen lightly armoured guards ushered the new recruits under the east-facing portico and down a gloomy corridor. From a room up ahead to the left, Pavo could hear the crackle of meat sizzling on a grill. Bucco patted his belly in anticipation and beamed at Pavo. 'I don't know about you, but I'm starving.'

Bucco licked his lips as he drew near to the cookhouse entrance. Pavo peered inside and looked on longingly as several slaves toiled over a side of pork hanging above a large grill. He feasted his eyes on bowls of sweet figs, grilled mushrooms layered with cheese, and a mouth-watering assortment of pickled fruit, all carefully arranged on silver trays, together with cakes dripping with honey and a large bunch of freshly picked grapes. His empty belly rumbled with hunger.

'Let's get stuck in,' Bucco said.

'Hold it.' A guard gripped Bucco by the shoulder. 'Where do you think you're going?'

'To eat.' Bucco gestured to the cookhouse. 'What does it look like?'

The guard sniggered. 'This isn't for scum like you,' he said. 'That's the lanista's dinner they're preparing.'

Before the men could protest, the guard brusquely shoved them beyond the cookhouse and further down the corridor. They passed a heavily guarded armoury sealed off with a wrought-iron gate. Armour and swords gleamed on wall racks. The guards stopped the recruits when they reached a dark, damp room at the end of the corridor, located next to the stairs that led up to the cells on the second storey of the ludus.

'This is where you lot eat,' the guard grinned as he waved a hand around the canteen.

A powerful stench of manure hit Pavo, and he realised the canteen was right next to the stables. Straw had been scattered across the floor, and from its damp, rotten texture, he guessed it had already been used for the horses. He spotted a cockroach scuttling across the floor. Blowflies buzzed in the air. The other recruits scuttled towards the far end of the canteen, where a cook with teeth like old tombs poured small rations of barley gruel into clay bowls.

Pavo felt his heart sink at the sight of the squalor. There were two trestle tables with a pair of benches either side taken up by the veterans. The recruits had to content themselves with squatting on the floor. Many seemed accustomed to their surroundings, ignoring the insects crawling over their legs, and the rancid smell. Pavo supposed these men had grown up as slaves and were familiar with such appalling living conditions. At the roll call that morning he'd been surprised to discover that Bucco was the only volunteer recruit. Eighteen of the other men were runaway slaves and four had been accused of murder. Laws introduced by Augustus and reinforced by subsequent emperors had attempted to rein in the number of volunteer gladiators, and the fact that most of the men around Pavo came from a much lower station only increased his sense of isolation.

A brief pang of nostalgia hit him as he remembered the feasts that had been laid on for his father at the imperial palace. Titus had been highly respected by Emperor Tiberius, Caligula's predecessor and a military man to the bone. Titus and Tiberius would often relive past glories on the battlefield over jars of honeyed wine late into the evening, whilst Pavo played at gladiators with the other children in the palace gardens.

'Here,' Bucco said, snapping Pavo out of his daydream and handing him a small bowl of gruel. 'Get stuck in before it's all gone.'

Pavo looked despondently at his meagre ration. A maggot wriggled in the mixture. Pavo felt his stomach churn. 'I'm not feeling hungry,' he said, passing the bowl to Bucco, who accepted it with a shrug.

'Fine by me. More for old Bucco.'

'How do they expect us to live like this?' Pavo said quietly.

'Oh, it's not all that bad,' Bucco replied between greedy mouthfuls of gruel. 'Three square meals a day, a bed to sleep in and the chance to earn a few sestertii. There's plenty in Rome who'd give anything for that.'

Pavo threw up his hands. 'You're right,' he announced drily. 'What am I thinking? I should be grateful for being thrown into a ludus and forced to work myself to the bone every day, feeding on scraps and living with a bunch of criminals and the very dregs of society.'

Bucco looked hurt. Pavo offered a weak smile.

'Present company excluded, of course,' he said.

'Well, you'd better get used to it.' Bucco finished licking his bowl clean and stifled a belch. 'Gurges has a reputation as a right vicious bastard. Step out of line and you'll find yourself being crucified in the arena instead of fighting in it.'

Pavo fell quiet as he mulled over his conversation with the lanista. Gurges had dropped a hint that he might have some leverage with enticing Hermes into the arena. But only if Pavo was victorious against lesser opponents, he presumed. As he made a silent prayer to the gods that he would survive long enough to face Hermes, a grim thought occurred to Pavo. His greatest fear wasn't dying in the arena. It was dying before he had a chance for revenge.

'Anyway,' Bucco said. 'At least you can use a sword. You heard the doctore. I was bloody useless out there. Got the skills of a leper.'

'Then why join a ludus? You must have had some other means of paying off your debts.'

Bucco harrumphed. 'Don't count on it. Ten thousand sestertii might not sound like so much to someone born into class, but that's a lot of money for a man like me. It'd take a soldier the best part of twelve years to pay off that kind of sum. And I'm no soldier. I don't have a brain for numbers, and I don't fancy collecting piss for a living,' he said, referring to the fullers who collected jugs filled with urine for cleaning togas. 'On top of that,

I've got a wife and two boys back in Ostia, so that's three mouths to feed. All in all, I didn't have a lot of options, all right?'

'I'm sorry. I didn't mean to judge.'

Bucco sighed. 'Forget it. Not your fault I'm here, is it?'

'Your sons – how old are they?'

'Papirius is seven, Salonius is four.' Bucco stared wistfully at his empty bowl, lost in thought. 'They're good boys. The little 'un wants to be a soldier when he grows up. Says he wants to conquer Britain all by himself.'

'I have a son of my own,' Pavo said. 'Or I did,' he added quietly. He moved on quickly, before Bucco could ask about Appius and open the still-sore wound. 'It must be hard for them to see their father in a ludus.'

'Well I don't imagine I'll be here for very long,' Bucco replied casually.

'Oh?' Pavo raised his eyebrows. 'I hate to point it out to you, Bucco, but it'll take you a long time before you've got enough money to settle your debts in full. Even with the signing-on fee, that still leaves you short by six thousand sestertii.'

Bucco lowered his voice and tapped the side of his nose furtively. 'Between you and me, I've got a plan for settling up sooner rather than later.'

Pavo puckered his brow. 'What are you talking about?'

The volunteer leaned in to Pavo, a slovenly grin stretched across his flabby jowls. 'There's a bookmaker who visits the ludus every so often. You can place bets with him on the fights. The way I see it, being here I'll be able to judge the form and ability of the gladiators: injuries, training, that sort of thing. I can't lose! I'm going to use the money I received when signing my contract to buy my way out of here before the year is out.'

'What if you get the bets wrong?' the recruit asked.

'I won't. Come on, don't give me that look! Can you honestly see me leaving the ludus in one piece? Look at the size of some of the veterans. Bloody beasts! What chance do I stand against any of that lot? This way I can make enough money to repay my debts and settle my contract with old Gurges. It's got to be a better bet than bleeding to death in some godforsaken arena.'

Pavo was about to reply, but he was interrupted by a call from the doctore, ordering the recruits to their cells. Bucco grudgingly stood up. The others began to file out of the canteen. Pavo remained for a moment on the floor. He wanted a moment of peace to himself as he made a solemn vow to see his quest through to the bitter end. He wouldn't stop before he had a chance to watch the life drain out of Hermes. Nothing would stand in his way. Opening his eyes, Pavo rose to his feet, suddenly alone. He turned towards the corridor and noticed someone blocking his path.

'Going somewhere?' Amadocus whispered.

Pavo froze as light from a nearby lamp illuminated the veteran's features. Up close, Pavo could see that he had the bulbous nose and cauliflower ears of a man who had been in his fair share of brawls. He towered over Pavo, his eyes glinting. The recruit was dimly aware of three more veterans behind Amadocus. The Thracian stood his ground while the other men slowly circled Pavo, breathing heavily through their nostrils.

'Let me through,' Pavo said.

Amadocus stood his ground. Pavo could hear the three other men at his back. 'Son of a legate, they say. Military tribune. Pah!' He flicked his eyes up at Pavo. 'I fucking hate Romans. And if there's one thing I hate more than Romans, it's Roman soldiers.'

Pavo looked around. The canteen was empty. The rest of the gladiators and the servants had left. There was no one to help him.

'I saw you at the palus today, Roman. And I tell you, there's only one thing worse than a Roman soldier. Any idea what that is?'

'No.' Pavo shrugged. He saw that Amadocus had balled his right hand into a fist. He took a step back from Pavo and grinned at the other three men.

'He doesn't know, lads,' Amadocus said as his accomplices steered back behind the enlarged shoulders of the veteran. They laughed meanly and glared at Pavo, and the recruit craned his neck past Amadocus as he tried to catch sight of the guards. They had disappeared, and Pavo had an awful feeling that they had abandoned their post on purpose.

'A Roman soldier who's a show-off, that's what,' Amadocus went on, staring viciously at Pavo. 'Just because you can hit a bit of wood, don't go around thinking you're a gladiator. You have to earn this in blood.' The veteran raised his left wrist to reveal a reddish 'G', representing the house of Gurges, branded on his flesh. Pavo had noticed that all of the veteran gladiators sported the same brand. He had overheard another recruit explain that to receive a branding was an honour bestowed only when a trainee gladiator triumphed in the arena and became a veteran.

The recruit said nothing. Amadocus chuckled as he cupped his hand to his ear and turned it towards Pavo.

'What's that, Roman? Something to say?'

Pavo still said nothing.

'That's what I thought.' Amadocus clucked as he stepped closer. Pavo could smell the foul breath coming off him. 'A fucking coward. Just like your old man.'

A hot rage burst inside Pavo. He spat into Amadocus's face, the thick globule catching him on the forehead, sliding down between his eyes and on to his nose. For a moment the veteran was stunned. He took a step back, his muscles palpitating with anger as he wiped the spit away from his face and studied it in the palm of his hand. His eyes were wide and his brow furrowed, as if he couldn't quite believe what had just happened.

Then he punched Pavo in the stomach. The recruit doubled up in pain and fell forward. Amadocus grabbed him by the nape of his tunic and smashed a knee into his face, the dome of the bone slamming into the bridge of his nose. Agony shot through Pavo's skull, and he lost his balance abruptly. He dropped to the ground, and a flurry of hard feet to his chest and abdomen winded him further. He rolled on to his front, curling up into a tight ball to shield himself from the repeated wave of blows. Each time he tried scrabbling to his feet, another hit thudded down on the small of his back and struck him like a hammer. His face was smeared with the foul hay that had been raked across the canteen floor. His nostrils were violated by the thick stench of sweat and piss.

'Spit on me, will you!' Amadocus fumed above the pounding between his temples. 'I'll teach you some manners, you little prick!'

Pavo tried crawling away from Amadocus and the other veterans, his face and hands tarnished with dirt, the salty taste of blood in his mouth. He clawed his way towards the far end of the canteen, towards the trestle tables and the cooking pots filled with gruel. Then a boot plummeted down on to his hand, and there was a sickening crunch as it crushed his fingers. Pavo winced in pain. The boot ground his fingers underfoot, as if crushing grapes in a wine vat. It rose suddenly, freeing his hand, but Pavo felt himself being lifted off the ground and thrown forward. There was a crashing din as he fell head-first into a stack of pans, pots and clay bowls. His skull jarred as he landed with a thud, and beyond the piercing sound in his ears he could faintly hear Amadocus stomping towards him. Pavo grabbed a bronze pot emptied of gruel and in the same blur of motion he rolled on to his right side and swung it at Amadocus just as the veteran reached down to grab him. Amadocus grunted as the pot clattered against the side of his skull with a hollow thud. He stumbled backwards, dazed and shocked. He shook his head clear and turned to his shocked accomplices.

'Fucking get him!'

The three other men closed in on Pavo. The middle one rushed at him, a couple of steps ahead of the other two. He had a dense beard and a thickset frame. He swung a roundhouse punch which Pavo jerked away from, and as momentum carried the blow on its trajectory above his head, Pavo lunged at the man and butted him in the middle of his chest. He grunted as the force of the blow sent him stumbling backwards. His comrades stepped out of the way as he tripped over a bench and fell to the ground amid a cacophony of shattering cups and bowls. The man to the right, a gaunt-looking figure with an angular frame and gaps in his front teeth, spun around and grabbed Pavo from behind, wrapping a bony arm around his neck and clamping his other hand to the recruit's forehead while the third man, a bear of a figure and a head taller than the others, made to unload a punch at his guts.

Pavo struck first, launching a high kick at the larger man, bending his leg at the knee and aiming at his chest. The man

41

shrieked as the sole of the recruit's foot thumped into his midriff, winding him and turning him purple in the face. Pavo jerked his shoulders to try and shake off the smaller man, who had him in a headlock, but his grip was surprisingly firm despite his bony physique. Pavo tried backtracking a few steps, building up momentum in his feet in a bid to slam his assailant into the canteen wall and wind him. He heard a crack at his back and the harsh exhalation of breath as his attacker crashed into the canteen wall. But still the man refused to relinquish his grip. Pavo felt himself going faint as the arm constricted his air passage. Ahead of him, the bear-like gang member had recovered from the brutal kick to the stomach and staggered towards him.

'Now I'm going to make you fucking sorry.'

Then Pavo saw a flicker of movement behind the man.

'That's enough!'

Amadocus and his men spun around to see Gurges standing in the corridor, flanked by an exasperated Calamus and a third man Pavo didn't recognise. This third man was stocky, a little shorter than the doctore, and wore a simple tunic with a pair of leather sandals and a red cloak. The clobber of an off-duty soldier, thought Pavo as he wiped blood from his mouth and eyed the lanista warily.

'What's going on here?' Calamus demanded, baring his teeth. He locked his sunken eyes on Amadocus. 'You. What are you doing out of your cell at this time of night? Explain yourself.'

Amadocus lowered his eyes deferentially. 'Sir. I am sorry.' He twisted his neck towards Pavo. 'This recruit was causing a disturbance.'

'Is this true, Pavo?' The doctore turned to face him.

'No!' the recruit protested. 'I didn't—'

'Forget it,' Gurges interrupted. He gestured to Amadocus and the three other veterans, and shot them a final withering look. 'Calamus. See these men to their cells. I'll deal with them later. Pavo and I have a pressing matter to discuss.'

'Yes, sir,' the doctore replied. He marched the veterans through the door one by one. Amadocus was the last to leave. He flashed a fierce scowl at the recruit as he stormed out of the canteen.

Pavo felt a cold tremor of fear shoot up his spine at the thought of having made an enemy of Amadocus and his thugs. He wondered how his day could get any worse.

Then the man in the military-issue clothing stepped out of the shadows. Pavo studied him. He had the grizzled look of a battle-hardened veteran and the scars to prove it, even though his eyes told Pavo that he couldn't be much older than thirty. As a military tribune, Pavo had encountered dozens of men like this in the Sixth – career soldiers, men who'd signed away their lives at the age of eighteen, or earlier perhaps, lying to enlist as soon as they could. Men who made it their business to shed blood for Rome in far-flung corners of the Empire. A cause that Pavo had once believed in himself. Until Rome had sunk its teeth into his neck.

'It appears your stay here is to be rather shorter than I had hoped,' Gurges said, choosing his words carefully, glancing at the stocky man out of the corner of his eye. Pavo thought he detected a trace of resentment in the lanista's voice.

'What are you talking about?' Pavo said, his voice barely a whisper. In the distance he could hear the roars and shouts of Amadocus and the other veterans being manhandled into their cells.

Gurges wrinkled his lips. He hesitated, gesturing to the scroll he held in his hands. He went on, 'This man is a soldier, Pavo. Sent from Rome, on imperial orders, no less. You are to fight the barbarian Britomaris. To the death.'

Pavo looked stony-faced at the soldier. He knew the name Britomaris. At training that morning the recruits had been talking of his defeat of Capito. Rumours had swirled through the ludus: that Britomaris ate babies for breakfast, that he was born in the Underworld, that his manhood could snap a vestal virgin in half.

'I understand the fight will be held at the Julian plaza in Rome. An impressive venue,' Gurges said, drawing Pavo out of his stupor. The lanista frowned again. 'A great pity that we won't get the chance to see you in action here in Paestum. For your sake as well as mine.'

The soldier grunted. 'If I may,' he began gruffly. Gurges nodded jadedly and the soldier turned to Pavo. 'My name is Lucius Cornelius Macro. I'm an optio in the Second Legion. I'm here to train you for the fight.'

'Who sent you?'

Macro pursed his lips. 'The order was signed by Marcus Antonius Pallas.'

Pavo laughed. 'So it's as good as from the Emperor himself, then.'

'That's about the size of it, lad.' He narrowed his eyes at Pavo. 'You're familiar with the name?'

'You could say that,' the young recruit replied, his mood improving rapidly. 'Pallas was the man who convinced the Emperor to condemn my father to death in the arena. I've heard that Claudius was set to spare his life until that arse-licking Greek swayed his decision. That aide of his does most of his bidding.'

'Murena,' Macro muttered.

'That's the one,' Pavo nodded. 'Thick as thieves, those two.'

'Tell me about it.' Macro cut himself short, aware of the political danger of criticising the imperial household in the presence of the lanista. Gurges struck Macro as an untrustworthy sort of fellow. 'Enough talk. Let's knuckle down to business. As you can see, I've already cleared this matter with your lanista. From what I've been told, you're a natural with a sword, so we're not totally fucked.'

Gurges cleared his throat. Macro shot a look at him.

'About my compensation,' the lanista said carefully. 'This is a fine young specimen of a man. I won't sell him off for less than the going rate.'

Macro produced a bag filled with coins from under his tunic and chucked it at the lanista, who caught it in his cupped hands and licked his lips as he peeked inside.

'I suppose this looks to be an adequate level of compensation,' he said greedily. 'And I presume you'll be staying with us, Optio?'

'You must be joking,' Macro said. 'I'll get myself a nice warm bed at a cosy inn in town.' He watched a cockroach scuttle across the floor. 'Although even a shit bed would be better than staying in this armpit of a house.'

Gurges grunted irritably and turned to leave. Macro watched him go, then frowned at the pots and cups scattered across the ground. He sized Pavo up, and the expression on his face suggested to the recruit that the soldier did not approve of what he saw.

'It's been a bloody long journey,' he said finally. 'We begin tomorrow at dawn. You'd better pray you're more effective with a sword than you are with your fists, lad. For both our sakes.'

CHAPTER SIX

Just as he had promised, Macro was waiting for Pavo on the ludus training ground the following morning. The optio fixed his steely gaze on the young recruit as he strode across from the east-facing portico. The men of the gladiator school had been given a piece of stale bread washed down with a cup of vinegary wine as breakfast in their cells. Bucco and the other recruits resumed their work at the paluses positioned near the sundial in the middle of the courtyard, while Amadocus and the veterans practised fighting in pairs at the far end. A single palus had been erected for Macro at the opposite end. A pair of pigskins and a set of full legionary armour comprising a helmet, cuirass and bronze belt, as well as a shield and a marching yoke, were laid out on the ground in the shadow of the optio. The lanista gazed down from the balcony and stared intently at Macro. He looked displeased at the prospect of a soldier training a recruit in his ludus. There was a risk that Macro might make Calamus look bad, Pavo supposed, and in a ludus the authority of the doctore was absolute. He tried to shut everything else out and approached the officer with a sinking feeling in his stomach at the thought of being paired against Britomaris.

'You're late,' Macro growled, gesturing up at the sun gleaming over the roof tiles.

'Sorry,' said Pavo.

'Sorry, *sir*,' Macro corrected him.

Pavo glared at the officer. 'You're forgetting who you're talking to, *Optio*. You're a mere drill instructor. I'm a military tribune, second in command of the Sixth Legion. Address me correctly in the future.'

'And you're forgetting that you're in a fucking ludus,' Macro thundered, his face darkening, his blood boiling between his temples. 'You're not a tribune any more. And frankly I don't care much for some privileged broad-striper talking down to Rome's newest hero.'

'Hero?'

Macro nodded curtly. 'Decorated by the Emperor himself.'

Pavo dug his fingernails into the palms of his hands, sealing his lips tightly shut. Much as he hated to admit it, Macro was right. He was the man in charge. He had imperial authority. Pavo had been stripped of his rights and condemned to the arena. According to the strict social mores of Rome, he was no better than a common slave.

'Question my authority again, and I'll have Calamus thrash you. Understood?'

'Yes . . . sir,' Pavo said through clenched jaws.

Macro was in a foul mood. The only inn that had any rooms available in the middle of the night had been the Drunken Goat, a stinking cesspit on the outskirts of Paestum. The wine had tasted like donkey piss and the bill had been eye-watering. He'd spent the night on an uncomfortable hay mattress and had been awoken by the innkeeper's wife kicking him out an hour before dawn. That morning Macro had made his way to the ludus bleary-eyed and ferociously hungry, and to his shock found himself regretting the day he'd been decorated. What should have been the proudest moment of his life had quickly descended into a nightmare. Not only did he have precious little time before the fight, but his charge was a belligerent brat.

Macro stepped closer to Pavo. He eyed him from head to toe, the way an officer instructor inspects his men on parade.

'Your face is covered in bruises,' he said. 'A bit of advice for you, Pavo. Next time you're trading punches with someone much bigger than you, learn how to block.' The officer caught sight of the recruit's right hand and gestured towards it. 'What in Hades' name happened there?'

Pavo glanced down. His fingers had swollen to twice their size and his palm was badly purpled. He hadn't noticed the injury last night. He'd gone to sleep with his mind reeling at the idea of saving the reputation of the very man who'd ordered his father to fight in the arena. But when he had woken up, he'd felt a dull ache spreading up his forearm, and at breakfast he could barely flex his fingers.

'That rat Amadocus did it,' he said with a snarl, 'when he cornered me last night in the canteen. Can't hold a sword, thanks to that bastard.'

Macro shook his head. 'Never mind. You're not going to be using a sword much.'

'I'm not sure I follow,' said Pavo.

Macro grinned. 'You're not going to fight like a gladiator, boy. Capito has tried that against Britomaris already and you know the result. Trading blows with that barbarian is suicide. You're bound to lose.'

Pavo huffed. 'You're implying that I've agreed to fight Britomaris.'

'You don't have a choice,' said Macro. 'You're a trainee gladiator now, not a citizen.'

'I could lose. Heap further shame on the Emperor. I'm sentenced to die anyway in this bloody ludus. I've nothing to lose by letting Britomaris kill me. My old life has been taken away.'

'That's where you're wrong.' The officer met the trainee's eye. 'You do have something to lose.'

Pavo cocked his head at Macro. 'What are you talking about?'

'You have a son, yes?'

'Appius.' Pavo nodded. 'He's almost two. His mother died during childbirth. My father Titus and mother Drusilla raised him.' He swallowed. 'Until they were murdered.'

'I have good news for you. Well, good and bad,' Macro said, weighing up the thoughts in his head. 'Appius is alive. He's being held at the imperial palace. If you win, the Emperor has promised to release him.'

A tingle of cold dread flared at the back of Pavo's scalp. His muscles went numb with rage and shock. His son. Alive. At the mercy of that snake Pallas and his lackey Murena. Pavo booted the foot of the palus and belted out an explosive roar of anger. Macro backed off a step.

'Is there no end to Pallas and his cruelty?' Pavo growled bitterly.

'First he takes my father away from me. Then he dangles my only son before me like a carrot in front of a donkey.'

Macro watched Pavo wrestle with his rage. Taming this lad would be tricky, he thought to himself. The trainee paced up and down the ground furiously, his muscles trembling, his fists clenched, a ball of uncontrollable rage. Then he stopped, took a deep breath and glanced at Macro.

'Fine,' he said. 'I'll fight Britomaris. But I don't need advice from a mere optio. I'm good with a sword. I can take that barbarian perfectly well on my own. Be on your way.'

Macro folded his arms across his barrel-like chest. 'Have you seen Britomaris fight?'

'No . . . sir,' Pavo said hesitantly.

'Well, it just so happens that I have. And I can tell you a couple of things about our barbarian friend. One: he's big. Much bigger than you. Two: he's bloody strong. Same as any barbarian. They grow up in a cruel world. There are none of life's little luxuries for these monsters. You could be Hercules himself with a sword, it wouldn't matter. He'd knock you down just by breathing on you.'

Pavo visibly deflated. He felt a cold knot of fear in the pit of his stomach as the scale of the task in front of him grew more ominous. He'd been cocky about his chances against Hermes in a fight. Perhaps too cocky, he reflected. Now, as he was forced to confront the reality of an actual fight to the death, he found his confidence rapidly draining.

'Cheer up,' Macro said, patting Pavo on the back. 'You're going to fight in front of the Emperor, for the glory of Rome, watched by thousands of people. Fights don't get much bigger. And this is only your first one, you lucky bugger. You should be kissing Fortuna's arse.'

Pavo shrugged him off. 'You have a perverse idea of luck.'

'Just trying to put some fire in your belly,' Macro said, furrowing his brow at his student's prickly nature. 'Look, there's no point moping about feeling sorry for yourself. If you go into the arena with that kind of attitude, you'll stand no chance.'

Pavo shrugged as the sun simmered and swelled on the horizon.

'I don't deserve this,' he said, turning away from Macro. 'Everything that's happened to me. To my family. First my father. Then me. Now they've made a prisoner out of my son. How much more suffering does that wretch Pallas wish to inflict? It's not fair.'

'Bollocks!' Macro barked with such venom that it sent a jolt quivering like an arrow up Pavo's spine. 'This is Rome, lad. There's no such thing as fair. Even a high-born boy like you must know that. And yes, I know all about your family squabble. I'm sorry about what happened with Titus. He had respect, even from us hard-to-please men in the Second. But that's all in the past now, lad. You have to focus on Britomaris.'

Pavo closed his eyes and sighed.

'Do you know how my father died?' he asked Macro, keeping his eyes closed, as if he was trying to seek peace in the dark. 'Did that rat Murena tell you about how Rome treated a man who sacrificed everything to the city?'

Macro cleared his throat. 'He told me that Hermes killed your old man in the arena.'

'Killing is putting it rather mildly,' Pavo muttered. 'Hermes gutted him like a pig. Cut off his head. When he was done, Claudius had his servants drag my father's body out of the arena on a hook and dump it in the street outside, as if he were some common thief.'

Macro cleared his throat again, but said nothing. An awkward silence lingered between the two men. At the far end of the training ground Pavo caught sight of Amadocus leaning against a palus, his hands choking the post as Calamus flogged him repeatedly on his back with his short whip. The other veterans looked on blankly, suggesting that such brutality was commonplace. Amadocus stole a sideways glance at Pavo. He winced as Calamus lashed his back again and drew blood. Then he grinned at the recruit. Pavo gulped and turned back to Macro.

'Everything has been taken away from me, Optio. My old life is gone for ever. But there is one thing I want before I die, and that's a chance to face Hermes in the arena.' He turned stiffly away from Macro. 'I have no quarrel with Britomaris. If he's giving

Murena and Pallas sleepless nights, so much the better. I don't see why I should help out that pair of devious Greeks.'

'Sod Pallas. Sod Murena. Sod them all. Do this for yourself and for your son.'

Pavo said nothing. But Macro thought he spotted some weakening in the lad's hostile stance. He drew closer to Pavo and gripped him by the shoulders.

'Whatever you think, we don't have time to sit around and talk.'

Pavo frowned and stepped back from Macro. 'What do you mean?'

'Patience is in short supply in the imperial household,' the optio replied. 'The Emperor wishes to see Britomaris lose before the month is out.' He raised a hand to stifle the trainee's protest. 'Now I know what you're thinking. Normally it takes at least six months to prepare a gladiator to fight in the arena, and that's just so you can face some Egyptian armpit-plucker with a blunted sword, not a vicious bastard like Britomaris. Nevertheless, that's the way the dice have fallen. Besides, you've got the talent, from what I've been told by the doctore. We can skip the basics and knuckle down to the strategy for beating Britomaris. It's no different to sorting out your tactics before going into battle. So let's just get on with it, eh?'

Pavo fell quiet. Macro weighed up his young charge. Pavo lacked the build of a gladiator. He looked more like a clerk – you'd think a gust of wind might break every bone in his body. But Macro detected some sliver of inner steel in the lad that reminded him a little of himself as a fresh-faced recruit. He thought briefly back to his own harsh treatment at the hands of Bestia, the legion's legendary drill instructor.

But Macro could never recall being as difficult as Pavo. Then again, he had never been cast into a ludus in the knowledge that he'd soon be dead.

Macro said, 'You may not like the Emperor—'

'That's a rather mild way of putting it,' Pavo interrupted.

'But you'd do well to remember that it's not only your neck on the line. Mine is too.'

Pavo blinked. 'How so?'

Macro scowled at the clear morning sky. 'Our good friend Murena made a not-so-subtle suggestion that if you lost, I'd be equally culpable.'

A sudden feeling of guilt swept over Pavo. 'Sir. I'm sorry you got dragged into this.'

'That makes two of us. But sorry gets us nowhere. The only thing for it is to teach this Britomaris a sharp, bloody lesson. One that ends with him on his knees, cradling his guts and begging for a quick death.'

The recruit flashed a pained expression at the ground. Three weeks. No time at all before he would be confronting Britomaris, the barbarian who had dispatched the best of the imperial school with consummate ease.

'If you win,' Macro went on, 'you'll be a hero, like me.' The officer thumped a fist against his chest with unconcealed pride. 'Rome doesn't kill its heroes. Not if it can help it, anyway. Get one over on old Britomaris and your name will be in graffiti on the walls of every inn across the Empire. You'll have prize money, tarts, fame.' Macro counted the rewards off on his fingers one by one. 'And you know what? That'll piss old Hermes off no end.'

Pavo glanced up at Macro. 'Do you think so?'

'Of course!' Macro snorted, warming to his theme. 'Hermes may be a legend, but at the end of the day he's a glory-seeking tosser just like every other gladiator. You win and he'll see you as a threat to his status. You'll be one step closer to having your showdown.'

Pavo paced a few steps away from Macro and stared up at the porticoes. Gurges had left the balcony and made his way down to the training ground, where the veterans had gathered around him in a semicircle. The lanista was waving a hand at Amadocus's grossly lacerated back as he boomed a warning at them. Pavo couldn't quite hear him but he got the gist of the message. Anyone stepping out of line would suffer similar treatment. At least I won't have to worry about being jumped in the canteen for a while, Pavo thought.

'Beating Britomaris is the best way to honour your old man's name,' Macro said.

Pavo laughed nervously. 'Easy for you to say. You're not the one who's got to fight him to the death. With a crocked hand.'

Macro grinned slyly as he replied, 'I have a secret plan.'

CHAPTER SEVEN

'Come on,' Pavo snapped impatiently. 'Let's hear it.' Macro looked rather too pleased with himself, the trainee thought.

'Britomaris has a weakness,' the optio announced.

'What is it?'

Casting glances from the corner of his eye, Macro leaned in to Pavo as if to whisper in his ear. 'His stamina,' the optio said in a low voice. 'It's shit.'

'Wonderful,' Pavo replied as he pulled away from Macro. 'What a pity I'm not challenging him to a marathon race instead of a fight to the death.'

The optio wagged a finger at him. 'You're not following me, lad. I saw it after Capito had a sword plunged into his heart at the amphitheatre. Everyone else was too shocked to notice, but the barbarian was sweating out of his arse. I'm telling you, he could barely stand on his feet by the end of the contest. And that was just a short fight. Think about what would happen if you really made the bastard work!'

Pavo raised a sceptical eyebrow at Macro.

'Hide and seek. That's how you're going to beat Britomaris.'

'Hide . . . and . . . seek?' Pavo repeated doubtfully. 'It sounds rather defensive, sir.'

Macro stared at him for a moment. 'Stubborn bastard, aren't you?'

Pavo shrugged. 'Runs in the family. And I may be the one calling you "sir", but that doesn't mean I can't question your tactics. It seems to me that the trick is to go in hard and fast against Britomaris and overwhelm him with speed.'

'Won't work,' Macro said with an abrupt shake of his head. 'Britomaris is big, but from what I've seen, he's deceptively light on his toes. Capito lost because he thought he was facing a big, slow lump. You won't make the same mistake. You'll fight on the back foot. Let Britomaris come forward and attack you. Every time he thrusts, you take a step back. Each missed thrust is wasted energy on his part. Eventually he'll tire. When he does, that's when you strike.'

'And what if Britomaris doesn't tire? What if I tire first?'

Macro shrugged. 'Then you're fucked.'

'Great.' The recruit clapped his hands sardonically. Macro ignored him, content to indulge Pavo in his tantrum. As far as the officer was concerned, anger was good, so long as it was directed towards the opponent. He knew that from experience. Throughout his career as a soldier Macro had frequently let his temper get the better of him, which had landed him in hot water more than once. He was sure it was one of the reasons he still hadn't made the step up from optio to centurion. That, and his woeful reading and writing ability. But in the ferocity of battle, that same inner rage kept him alive and helped him to fend off the enemy, even when his body screamed with agony and fear. The angrier Pavo was at Britomaris, the better his chance of winning. But as things stood, Pavo was angry with the whole world. And that was a problem.

Macro nodded towards a sand-filled pigskin. 'Let's start off with twenty circuits. Fast as you can.'

'Twenty? Is that it?' Pavo scoffed. 'I thought you're supposed to be training me for the fight of my life, sir, not ordering me to go on a light jog.'

'I wasn't finished,' Macro growled, his expression turning a darker shade of black. He kicked the legionary armour with a sandalled foot. 'Twenty circuits, in full kit, shield in one hand, marching yoke in the other. That little lot should weigh you down a bit, lad. Make you put a bit of effort into it, eh?'

Pavo watched speechlessly as Macro drew a line in the sand with the tip of a wooden sword, roughly in the middle of the training ground. Then the optio stuffed two of the sand-filled pigs' bladders on to a legionary marching yoke. Pavo reluctantly strapped on the cuirass and helmet and picked up the shield.

'You'll remember from your basic training,' Macro said as he hefted the yoke off the ground and laid it out on Pavo's shoulder, 'that the first thing a legionary is taught to do is march with a full complement of equipment.'

'But sir, this is too much,' Pavo said glumly, his legs nearly buckling under the weight.

'Britomaris is going to make you sweat like never before. He will come at you like a bull. You can't do anything about that. But you can prepare for when the going gets tough.' Macro pointed with his wooden sword to the porticoes at the north and south ends of the training ground. 'First circuit: run the length of the ground and back.'

Pavo grumbled as he broke into a lumbering trot towards the north portico.

'I said run, not bloody crawl!' Macro roared.

'I am running!'

'I am running, *sir*!'

'Sir . . .' Pavo grunted as he picked up the pace, his cheeks puffing and his face reddening with effort. He could feel his heart thumping inside his chest. Dry, hot air singed his throat. The yoke dug into his shoulder. In the army, the young trainee had completed his fair share of marches with full equipment, but that had been at a steady pace. Now he was sprinting, and the exertion quickly took its toll. He broke out in a hot, salty sweat.

'Now get back here!' Macro barked.

Pavo muttered curses under his breath as he lurched back to the line, sweat streaking down his back. As he made to release the yoke, Macro dropped his left shoulder and thrust his sword at the recruit's midriff. Pavo instinctively jerked his shield up to block the attack. The force of the blow took him by surprise. He stumbled backwards, his toes digging into the sand as he scrambled for purchase, feeling a shuddering up his left forearm that reverberated through his bicep and shoulder muscles.

'Again!' Macro shouted. 'And sprint both ways this time. I want to see you sweat.'

'But—'

'Don't answer me back, boy!'

Pavo shuttled off.

'Now!' Macro roared. Pavo hefted the pigskin and began jogging around the perimeter.

By the eighth lap he could feel blisters forming on the soles of his feet. As he completed the twelfth lap his steady run had become staggered and frantic and his legs pleaded with him to stop. Nausea tickled the back of his throat. Still he ran. His feet ached. On the sixteenth lap his blisters burst and hot sand rubbed into the exposed sores, causing him great discomfort every time he planted his foot on the ground. He gritted his teeth and practically stumbled the final lap. At last he hit the portico steps with a thirsty sigh of relief and a painful stitch spearing his right side. He lifted his head up and vomited on the sand with a weak groan.

'Get up!' Macro boomed. Pavo tried to say something between snatches of breath but the soldier cut him short. 'The first rule of fighting is you never fall over. If you're on your arse, you're as good as dead.'

Pavo struggled wearily to his feet.

'Ten more laps,' Macro said.

'Ten?' Pavo sputtered. 'But—'

'Faster this time! Put some bloody sweat into it.'

Pavo bent over, his hands on his knees and spittle dangling from his lips. His shield weighed heavily in his left hand, while his right was burdened by the pigskin. His wrist tendons burned with the stress of holding both objects upright, and the pain twisted his shoulder muscles into excruciating knots.

'We never trained like this in the legions, sir,' he rasped. 'Not with all this bloody kit.'

'I didn't learn this in the Second,' Macro replied. 'I learned it when I was a boy. Four or five years younger than you. I had the good fortune to be trained by a retired gladiator. He taught me a few tricks of the trade.'

Pavo snatched at the air. 'What was his name?'

'Draba of Ethiopia. Bloody good swordsman.'

'Never heard of him.'

'Pity. You could have learned a lot from that man. He's not

around any more. But I am, and I'm going to pass on to you what he told me. If you know what's good for you, you'll take every word to heart.'

Between gasped breaths, Pavo spat on the ground. 'In case it escaped your notice, Optio, I received plenty of sword training in my own youth, and from a gladiator far more famous than your Draba. Felix was one of the best fighters of his era. And he never had me running up and down, over and bloody over.'

Macro shook his head patiently. 'Whatever Felix taught you isn't going to help in the arena. Capito fought like a true gladiator against Britomaris and lost. What you need is to forget the basic principles of gladiator combat. As I said, we have to work on a new way of winning against the barbarian. You see, Draba's skill wasn't just with a sword. It was with his feet. His movement meant that he'd tire his opponent before he stabbed them.'

Pavo cocked his head inquisitively at Macro. 'Why did you receive instruction from a gladiator?'

'Let's just say I had a score to settle, and Draba helped me do it. Now get a move on!'

'Yes, sir.' The trainee winced as he hauled himself upright and staggered down the training ground, his muscles sagging under the load of the marching yoke, shield and armour. But the fact that he had addressed Macro as 'sir' told the optio he was getting somewhere with his young charge. Pavo was finally channelling his aggression into the training. Macro nodded to himself in satisfaction as Pavo set off on another lap, a grimly determined look stitched into his features.

The rest of the morning passed in a blur of sweat and aggression for Pavo. After twenty laps of the training ground the optio got him to perform a set of nausea-inducing strength exercises under the unseasonably hot sun. Pavo carried out a hundred abdominal crunches and a series of hanging leg raises from wooden posts mounted at head-height at the porticoes on the west side of the training ground. He then practised lumbering two pigs' bladders loaded with sand, one in each hand, from one end of the training ground to the other. By the end of the session he could hardly move. His muscles were sore and stiff, his veins stretched out like tense rope. Life as a military tribune had been relatively soft on his body compared to the hardships the enlisted soldiers had to endure, and it had been a long time since he had trained with such intensity. But with every drop of sweat and strain of sinew, he began to relish the challenge in front of him. News of Appius had refocused him. Now he vowed to redouble his efforts. If he could not set himself free, he could at least see to it that his son avoided the same fate he had endured.

For his part Macro was impressed and a little surprised by the determination and drive of his young charge. He'd never seen a man born into privilege throw himself so hungrily into his labours. The only concern picking away at the back of Macro's head was Pavo's damaged hand. The injury had deprived the officer of the chance to size up his charge's skills at the palus and his natural ability with a sword. With a sigh, he realised he'd have to take Murena's word for it.

'I swear to the gods I'll make a champion of him yet,' Macro mumbled to himself.

For the next nineteen days Macro worked tirelessly on Pavo's fitness. During agonising sprint sessions he instructed the trainee to practise dashing from one end of the training ground to the other, before counting to five and sprinting back in the opposite direction. Pavo ran until his legs could carry his body no further, and then ran some more. He ran with a constant feeling of sickness in his mouth and a stitch spearing his right side. Macro forced him to run until he could do a hundred laps without breaking into a sweat. He worked with Pavo on endless long jumps, high jumps and lunges to put some extra spring into his gangly legs. Gradually Pavo noticed that his muscle ache was wearing off as he crawled out of his cell each morning and dragged himself to the training ground. By the end of the circuit programme he could feel his thighs and abdominal muscles becoming firmer and more supple. He had found his stride and was standing upright instead of spilling his guts on the floor. He felt leaner, faster and more agile. He was ready to face Britomaris.

On the twentieth day, Macro made preparations for their return to Rome. Pavo's hand had healed sufficiently for him to grasp a sword without too much pain, although he grimly understood that the injury would not be gone entirely by the time of his bout. He'd be taking on Britomaris with a damaged hand.

Pavo awoke with a feeling of dread in his guts that morning. Macro had arranged to meet him at dawn with a pair of horses at the ludus gates. As he rose, he noticed Bucco watching him from the other side of the cell. On most mornings Bucco over-slept, his loud snoring echoing through the barracks and incurring the wrath of the doctore. This morning, though, the volunteer was wide awake.

'You'll be off to Rome, then?' he said, stretching his arms and legs. Bucco had already lost an alarming amount of weight since enlisting. The tortuously long hours spent at the palus, combined with the limited diet, had left him pale and lean. The palms of his hands were covered in calluses.

Pavo nodded as he rolled up his cloak and tucked it under his arm. 'It appears so.'

'Never been there myself. What's it like?'

'Rome?' Pavo chuckled. 'The weather is stifling, the food is rubbish, the streets are filthy, everything is overpriced and every-one's in a mad rush, but other than that, it's fine.'

'Oh,' Bucco said with a frown. He stared out of the small window that afforded the men a view of Paestum's dilapidated forum. 'I rather thought it might be . . .' He shrugged. 'You know, centre of the world and all that.'

'I'm being harsh. It's a wonderful city, really. Just one full of bad memories for me.'

Pavo ran a hand over his cloak. It was stained with the filth of the ludus and it reeked of sweat and urine. But he felt a strange attachment to it. It was, he reflected, his only worldly possession.

Bucco rose to his feet. 'Good luck,' he said.

Pavo nodded. 'Thanks, Bucco.'

A guard unlocked their cell and ushered Pavo towards the stone stairs that led to the ground floor. As they passed each of the other cells, veteran gladiators bellowed abuse at Pavo. The kinder ones wished him a quick death in the arena. The less kind ones he tried not to think about. He descended the stairs, the guard close behind with one hand resting on the pommel of his sword at all times in case Pavo tried to make a break for freedom. From the ground floor they passed down the corridor that led towards the training ground. The guard escorted Pavo around the perimeter towards the main building at the northern end, which housed the servants' quarters, medical facilities and the administrative offices. Daylight had not yet broken, and a gritty, speckled darkness accompanied by an eerie silence hung like a veil over the empty ground. Not a soul in sight, Pavo realised.

Then he saw a shadow skulking towards them from across the training ground. Pavo stopped in his tracks to focus on it. He smelled Amadocus before he recognised him. The trainee wrinkled his nose as the veteran drew nearer.

'Pavo!' Amadocus thundered. 'I want a word with you.'

Just my luck, thought Pavo as Amadocus pounded across the training ground, his club-like feet thudding on the crisp sand with every giant stride. He halted at the verge of the ground.

'Gurges has got me on latrine duty,' Amadocus said, raising his shit-flecked palms at Pavo. 'Four fucking weeks. This is your fault.'

Pavo smiled to himself. 'If I recall, you were the one who attacked me,' he said.

Amadocus snarled, then spat on the ground. 'You started it the moment you stepped into this ludus. Pissing about with your fancy handiwork at the palus.' He rubbed dirt out of his eye. 'I hear you're off to fight Britomaris.'

Pavo felt his neck muscles stiffen. 'Not that it's any of your business, but yes.'

Amadocus pulled an unpleasant face as he took a step closer to Pavo. 'It should be me fighting in the arena. The great Amadocus! Champion of the house of Gurges! Not some woman born with a silver spoon in his mouth.'

He went to take another step towards Pavo. But the guard began to unsheath his sword and barked, 'Back to work.'

Amadocus smiled as he retreated across the ground, pointing a filthy finger at Pavo. 'Better pray you die in Rome, rich boy,' he said. 'If I see you in this ludus again, I'll rip your guts out.'

CHAPTER EIGHT

The crowd rumbled expectantly as Macro made a final check on Pavo's equipment. The two men were in a small, dark room on the western side of the Julian plaza. A short corridor led towards the colonnades that lined the arcades surrounding the roofed forum, which had been converted into an arena for the purposes of the day's spectacle. Macro remembered his father taking him around the plaza as a boy. He recalled the rich smell of spices, cinnamon and incense that came from shops selling luxury goods on the walkways off the arcade, and the vast sculptures of the great Emperor Augustus and Julius Caesar mounted on plinths behind the travertine columns. The plaza looked very different now. Temporary wooden galleries had been erected in front of the colonnades, blocking out much of the sunlight. Through the corridor Macro could see the forum floor blanketed with bright white sand. He could hear the creak of the gallery walkways as the last members of the audience made their way to their allocated seating.

'Nervous?' the optio asked Pavo.

The trainee knitted his brow in the middle and stared defiantly at Macro. 'I'm not afraid of dying, sir. I'm afraid of losing.'

The optio suddenly felt a pang of pity for his charge. He sympathised with Pavo. As a soldier, Macro's greatest fear in battle wasn't dying, but letting down his comrades. But he had had the grain of comfort of knowing that he had seventy-nine men around him who were thinking the same thing. Pavo, however, was all on his own.

Pavo adjusted the metal guard on his right shoulder until it was secure. From the arena the master of ceremonies began his preamble, though his authoritative voice was lost in the din of the crowd. Pavo could barely make out his thanks to the Emperor on behalf of the audience for hosting the spectacle. His warning about throwing objects at the gladiators, jumping into the arena or otherwise interfering in the contest was also greeted roundly with boos and heckles. The mood among the mob was more rowdy than Pavo could ever remember hearing. Even the crowds at the chariot races seemed fairly hushed by comparison. The roar trembled in his bones as Macro threw an arm over his shoulder and patted him on the back.

'Cheer up, lad,' he said. 'Tell you what, if the worst happens out there, I'll organise a whip-round with some of the lads in the Second. Buy you a decent burial spot. Can't have the son of a legate being slung into a pit grave, can we?'

'Great,' Pavo replied.

Macro looked his charge in the eye. 'Britomaris is scum. Back home he shags sheep and whores out his daughters. He probably even drinks milk. You're not going to let an animal like that steal the glory of the arena, are you?'

'No, sir!' Pavo shouted, his voice trembling with adrenalin.

The master of ceremonies bellowed out the recruit's name. Macro prodded Pavo in the chest. 'Britomaris didn't kill your old man, but I want you to go out there feeling like he did. Imagine he's the one who stabbed Titus. The blood is on his hands, lad.'

A flicker of hatred glowed in Pavo's eyes. The officer could tell he'd hit a raw nerve with talk of his father.

Macro gave his charge a final slap on the back. 'You're fighting for yourself. For your boy, Appius. But most of all you're fighting for your father's name.' He thumbed at the galleries. 'This lot were probably cheering when your old man died. Why don't you show them what a Valerius is really made of! Wherever Titus is, make him proud.'

He watched Pavo depart down the corridor towards the servants at the arena entrance. Macro had a space reserved for himself at the podium, not far from the Emperor, and close to Pallas and Murena. As he made his way through the bowels of the plaza he passed a hastily erected surgeon's counter, where a set of instruments were laid out on a table: a sickening array of forceps, scalpels, catheters and bone saws that turned Macro's blood cold. There was a bowl of vinegar and a bucket of fresh water with a set of white cloths and a row of wine goblets set to one side. Macro knew from previous spectacles that the goblets were used by surgeons to save the blood from a newly dead gladiator to sell on the black market. Gladiator blood fetched a high price, especially for those seeking a cure for epilepsy. Macro hurried on, confounded by the layout of the plaza. There had to be an entrance to the stands somewhere near, he thought, glancing left and right and trying to get his bearings.

He slowed his stride as he heard two voices coming from within a second room. Thank the gods for that, he thought. I can ask them for directions. The voices were hushed and hurried, the soldier realised as he drew close to the door.

'Hurry!' one of the men implored angrily. Macro froze. He vaguely recognised the voice but couldn't remember where he'd heard it. 'It's about to begin!'

'Wait,' the second man replied in a panicked tone. 'I've got to get the mix right first. Too little poison and it won't kill him!'

Intrigued, Macro poked his head inside. He saw a guard huddled over a gaunt older man who was pouring liquids into a bowl. With a start he recognised the guard as one of the Praetorians who had escorted him to the imperial palace a month ago. In addition to the sword he carried in a scabbard by his hip, the guard cradled a long spear of the type used by Britomaris in the arena. He was carefully dipping the tip of the spear into the bowl.

'What the bloody Hades is going on here?' Macro barked.

The surgeon looked up in horror and jumped back from the table. The Praetorian Guard looked up at Macro too. He grinned, seemingly unflustered by the optio's sudden entrance.

'Hang on,' said Macro. 'Where's your mate?'

The Praetorian grinned still. Confusion clouded Macro. Then he heard footsteps behind him, too late for him to spin around. A dull thud crashed down on the optio's skull. His world went black.

Pavo made his way under the temporary wooden stands into the main arena, his heart thumping against his breastbone, a rasping dryness in his throat. Britomaris had already entered the arena to a chorus of jeers as members of the crowd rained down obscenities on him. Britomaris seemed to be enjoying playing the role of villain, slowly turning to each quarter of the crowd in turn and raising a balled fist high above his head in a posture of defiance. His striped tunic and trousers had been replaced with a simple loincloth, so that just a cone-like helmet with a horse-tail crest signified his Celtic origins. He carried a long, narrow leather-bound shield with a decorated ceremonial bronze boss and his hair had been dyed blue. Pavo could make out the wild streaks of it as he reached the end of the corridor. A pair of officials stood guard at the entrance to the arena. The younger of the two held a convex shield fashioned in the style of a legionary's, but without an emblem on the front.

The official handed Pavo the shield, then placed a legionary helmet over his head. The trainee hefted his shield to chest height as the crowd shouted impatiently for him to enter the arena.

'Best of luck, eh,' the older official said in a rough voice. He smirked at the trainee, revealing a set of rotten teeth with a gap at the front wide enough to push a thumb between. 'Do us all a favour and try not to make too much of a mess. I don't want to spend all bloody evening cleaning your guts off the sand.'

Pavo grunted. Then he burst out of the corridor and emerged to a wave of tumultuous cheers and applause. Adrenalin surged in his blood. He forgot about the nausea at the back of his throat and the fear in his bones. His muscles swelled and loosened. Riding a wave of euphoria, he glanced up at the central portico on the west side of the arena. Above the ornamented balustrade stood the makeshift imperial box. The two Greek freedmen were positioned to the left of the Emperor. Pavo recognised the good-looking one as Pallas. The other had curly dark hair and delicate features. Murena. Pallas looked anxious. Murena smiled thinly at Pavo, who felt the burning sensation in his throat boil up.

The next few moments passed in a blur. The master of ceremonies introduced the contenders to the crowd and reminded them that today would be a fight to the death. Trumpets blared. Drums beat an insistent rhythm. Another pair of servants entered the arena carrying the weapons. The servant on the left had a spear propped against his shoulder. The servant on the right carried a short sword sheathed in a scabbard which lay flat across his arms. The umpire – a stumpy man with a bald pate and a belly drooping over the belt of his tunic – ordered the servant to unsheathe the sword. He cursorily examined the tip of the blade to check its sharpness, then performed the same action with the spear. Pavo noted the spear's wide iron head, with secondary tangs to inflict greater damage. An iron spike was attached to the base of the weathered ash shaft.

The umpire looked to Emperor Claudius and gave an approving nod to confirm the killing power of both weapons. The servants handed the spear to Britomaris and the sword to Pavo and hurried aside. Pavo gripped the double-edged short sword. He was still familiarising himself with the feel of the weapon when the Emperor gave the signal and the umpire shouted, 'Engage!'

Pavo backtracked from Britomaris as soon as the words left the umpire's mouth, just as Macro had instructed during those gruelling hours of training. The barbarian promptly charged at him, again just as the optio had warned. Taking six swift steps back from the centre of the arena, Pavo raised his shield in a defensive posture as Britomaris stabbed angrily at thin air with his spear. Pavo caught sight of the tangs glinting six inches from his face. He retreated further. The plaza floor covered a sprawling rectangular area roughly twice the size of the amphitheatre at Paestum. Pavo quickly discovered that the enormous space was ideal for his evasive tactics, permitting him to keep dropping away from Britomaris without the risk of being fatally cornered against a wall. Britomaris stormed after the recruit, his thickset legs bounding forward in big strides, his gargantuan torso already gleaming with sweat from his toil.

Pavo relaxed a little. Britomaris was straining with effort and working himself into a frenzy, exactly as he and Macro had planned.

Then Britomaris surged forward with astonishing speed and slashed his spear in a downward arc at Pavo's legs, as if meaning to sever his feet. The low attack caught Pavo by surprise, his shield raised high to protect his chest. In a heartbeat he corrected his stance by ramming the shield down. The metal trim smacked into the sand an inch ahead of his feet and there was a dull clunk as the spear struck the lower half. Britomaris bared his teeth in anger and with a brief flick of the wrist jabbed his spear up at Pavo's upper torso. The recruit frantically jacked his shield up again and deflected the attack. The spear continued thrusting upwards above Pavo. Britomaris lurched forward as his spear arm rose high above his head, putting him off balance. With a rush of blood, Pavo saw an opportunity for a counterattack. He jerked his sword in a sharp upward thrust, aiming for the barbarian's neck. But Britomaris bewildered the recruit a second time with his reflexes, leaning back from the blow and withdrawing his spear arm, in the same giddy motion slamming his narrow shield into Pavo and catching him square in the face. Pavo's helmet clanged. The noise of the crowd dampened. A tinny, high-pitched note squealed between his temples. His world blurred for a moment. Then he saw the iron tangs of the spear rushing towards him. He yanked his head back and to the side just in time, the tip of the spear screeching across the metal plate of his helmet.

Pavo backed away from Britomaris in a daze. A groggy fog settled behind his eyelids as the enormity of the task in front of him finally began to set in. Macro had been correct in his tactical assessment, but Pavo knew from his days as a military tribune that there was a world of difference between giving orders and having the blood, sweat and toil to physically carry them out. Britomaris bided his time several paces away from Pavo, a thirsty grin visible under his beard. He was happy to let Pavo retreat, comfortable in the knowledge that he had the upper hand. The crowd implored Pavo to attack the barbarian again. A feeling of outrage welled up inside him as he observed the thousands of faces lining the galleries. They had come here to see blood. To them it didn't matter whose blood was spilled. He searched the crowd for Macro. He couldn't see the optio anywhere.

Where is he? Pavo thought. Then he looked ahead as the barbarian clumped towards him once more.

Shaking his groggy head clear, Pavo recalled Macro's instructions and quickly abandoned any thought of attacking Britomaris.

He staggered backwards, occasionally glancing over his shoulder to see how much space he had left between himself and the wall. Britomaris chased him down, thrusting his spear to gauge the state of his opponent and see how much fight he had left in him. As Pavo neared the wall, he switched his stance and began circling Britomaris, careful to remain two spears' lengths from the barbarian. He moved nimbly. His arms were aching from wielding the sword and shield, but his legs were strong and willing. Britomaris roared with anger at this new tactic. The crowd seemed to agree with the barbarian. Shouts of 'Coward!' and 'Shame!' rained down from the galleries and swelled to a deafening chorus of boos. As Pavo finished his first circuit of the arena, he noticed one or two spectators leaving their seats in disgust. But he ignored them. Macro's strategy was paying off. Pavo wasn't here to please the mob. He was here to win a fight. Spurred on by the heavy breathing coming from the barbarian and his blundering strides, Pavo backtracked as Britomaris laboured to keep up his relentless pursuit.

'Stand and fight!' a voice shouted from the lower galleries.

'Get stuck into him!' another boomed.

Pavo noticed Pallas and his fellow Greek freedman squirming in their seats, desperate for victory, barely able to watch. The Emperor seemed oblivious to both his freedmen and the intimidating mood among the crowd, as he shouted with childlike excitement at the fighters. Pavo quickly reset his gaze to Britomaris. The barbarian carted towards him, his gait heavier as he tucked his right elbow tight to his side and drew the tip of his spear level with the cusp of his shield. Then he lunged at Pavo, thrusting his spear at the recruit's jugular. Pavo hurried backwards as fast as he could, narrowly avoiding the spear but losing his footing and almost slipping to the arena floor.

Britomaris flew at him with a sudden urgency to his movements, breathing heavily as he sensed the tide of the battle turning in his favour. Pavo scrambled back in a frantic stoop. Despite his stamina training, the recruit was short of breath and sweating heavily. The stress of facing raw steel was taking its toll. Britomaris kept swiping, Pavo kept scrabbling clear. Several members of the crowd chucked their tickets into the arena in disgust, pelleting Pavo with the numbered clay chips. One spectator lobbed his wine jug at the youth. It shattered a foot away from the gladiators, dyeing the sand deep red. A couple of stadium officials dragged the man responsible kicking and screaming towards the nearest exit. Britomaris slashed at Pavo. The recruit jumped clear and felt a thud against his spine as he backed up against the wall.

He was cornered.

CHAPTER NINE

Britomaris towered over Pavo, jabbing his spear at the recruit's upper chest. With his muscles screaming and the blood pounding in his ears, Pavo hefted his shield upwards. There was a nerve-jangling clang as the spear tip clattered into the centre of the shield, iron hammering into bronze. The barbarian howled a Celtic war cry. Then he unleashed a torrent of thrusts and slashes, forcing Pavo to shelter behind his shield. The force the barbarian summoned for each attack stunned Pavo. He gripped the handle for dear life and muttered a prayer to Fortuna to save him as a second thrust of the spear split through the leathered surface of the shield above the boss, showering splinters of wood at his face. Tugging back on the spear, Britomaris kicked the bottom of Pavo's shield and wrenched his weapon free. The crowd roared in murderous expectation. Out of the corner of his eye Pavo could see the Emperor rising gawkily to his feet, his mouth agape. Pallas wrung his hands, shooting agitated glances across the Emperor to an older freedman sitting opposite.

Pavo was conscious of the spear tip plummeting towards his chest. A hot wave of anger flushed through him. His reflex was automatic, rolling his body to the right as the spear stabbed the sand. He looked up, saw Britomaris adjusting his aim and stabbing downwards again and desperately rolled to the left, his heart in his mouth as he felt the whoosh of the spear tip skating past his neck and the dull thwack of iron on the sand.

In the next instant Pavo arched his back up and to the left, driving his sword towards the barbarian in a whirl of motion. Britomaris was still lifting the spear out of the sand as Pavo's blade pierced his flesh at a spot just below his elbow. The tip glanced off his lower ribs as Pavo wrenched the sword out. The spectators gasped as the barbarian let out a howl like a wolf being skinned alive before whirling towards Pavo and clattering the recruit on the head with the side of his shield. A shard of white light flashed in front of Pavo's eyes as he dropped to his knees. Blood oozed out of his nostrils. He staggered away from Britomaris. The barbarian let out another animal roar. He cast aside his shield to staunch the blood pulsing from his own wound with his left hand. It landed with a heavy clunk. Britomaris was bleeding, but not heavily. His loincloth glistened as the crimson stain spread. Peeling his hand away from his side, he raised his blood-soaked palm to his face. The icy blue points of his eyes glowered at Pavo. He flashed his teeth at the young man and breathed heavily out of his nostrils. A tense silence hung over the spectators. Britomaris wiped his hand on his thigh and blind rage took over. Ignoring his discarded shield, holding his spear in a two-handed grip with his right hand wrapped under the throat of the oak shaft in front of his chest and his left hand gripping the base tucked close to his side, he charged at Pavo.

The recruit watched numbly as his opponent stampeded towards him in a lumbering gait, stunned by the way he had shaken off his injury. The horse tails at the back of Britomaris's helmet flapped wildly. His legs wobbled. He almost lost his footing and stopped. He looked around in a daze at the crowd, as if noticing them for the first time. Growling as he tried to shake his head clear, the barbarian made a renewed charge towards Pavo. He dominated Pavo's line of vision, blocking out the arena floor and the cries from the galleries baying for blood as the spear tip rushed at him. Drawing closer to Pavo now, the barbarian raised the spear over his head parallel to his right shoulder and prepared to make a final downward thrust with the iron spike attached to the base of the shaft. But his movements had become sluggish and unco-ordinated. Slow enough for Pavo to read. The menacing spike snapped Pavo out of his shock. With a drop of his left shoulder he feinted a half-step to the right and then thrust his sword upwards. A crude look of horror briefly flashed across the face of the barbarian as he realised too late that by attacking overhead he had left his torso fatally exposed. He plunged his spear uselessly into the sand and Pavo struck him in the groin.

Britomaris froze. Pavo ripped the sword across, the weapon making a tearing sound as if splitting open a sack of grain. The blade diced up the barbarian's bowels and severed his femoral artery. Blood fountained out of the wound as Pavo withdrew his sword and collapsed on the ground. Ten thousand people rose to their feet around the Julian plaza, watching Britomaris. The barbarian was rooted to the spot, looking down dumbly at the blood spraying his feet. He stood defiantly for a few moments longer, then ripped off his helmet, his eyes rolling into the backs of his sockets as he gasped for air. His face had turned pale, and he was shivering and foaming at the mouth. He looked feverish. His legs buckled. Then he collapsed on to the sand with a colossal thud.

Salty sweat dripped from Pavo's brow into his eyes, blurring his vision. He tasted blood in his mouth. His heartbeat pulsed violently, the veins on his neck throbbing and echoing inside his head. He could hear the ghoulish whimpers coming from Britomaris as he bled out on the sand, his helmet by his feet, vomit oozing from his slackened mouth.

There was a moment's silence. Then the crowd broke into rapturous cheers. Pavo picked himself off the ground. He was so weary it took every last ounce of strength to stand tall. He wiped the sweat from his eyes.

'Pavo! Pavo!' the crowd chanted, over and over. The same people who had been roundly booing him only a short while earlier, the recruit thought. Up in the podium a Praetorian Guard clumsily shuffled his way past the podgy imperial high priests and whispered something into Pallas's ear. The Greek freedman furrowed his brow, then turned to Murena and muttered something. Abruptly the two men rose from their seats and followed the Praetorian out of the arena as the master of ceremonies handed Claudius a victory palm and a box of coins to present to the victor. The Emperor accepted the coins with a cold and distant expression in his greying eyes. He looked displeased. He scowled in disgust and glanced in Pavo's direction with stony-faced contempt as the chanting of the victor's name swelled in the plaza.

Pavo stared defiantly back at the Emperor. He barely noticed the officials dragging Britomaris away with a meat hook, just as they had dragged away Titus months before. They left a streak of blood stretching like a tongue from the arena entrance to the place where the barbarian had fallen. His limbs were the same pale colour as his face. The feverish look in the barbarian's eyes, and the way he had foamed at the mouth, troubled Pavo.

Then the pair of officials who had been stationed at the arena entrance grabbed Pavo and hurried him away from the floor towards the corridor and a flight of stairs leading up to the podium, where the trainee would accept his prize from the Emperor in person. Pavo was still running his eyes over the galleries as the officials hauled him down the corridor, the hoarse cheers of the crowd echoing off the dank walls, the air stifled with hot dust and sweat, the crowd shrinking from view.

'Where the hell did he disappear to?' Pavo wondered aloud.

'You mean your friend? The soldier?' snarled the older official with the rotten teeth. 'Don't worry. You'll get to see him soon enough. In fact, we're taking you to him as soon as you've collected your prize . . .'

Macro awoke with the din of the crowd buzzing in his ears. The optio shook his groggy head and acquainted himself with his surroundings. He was back in the small room on the western side of the plaza that he and Pavo had occupied in the build-up to the fight. But the two Praetorian Guards now blocked the doorway, and Macro's young charge was nowhere to be seen. A dim image came back to the optio through the haze. He recalled stumbling across the surgeon's counter, and witnessing the Praetorian dipping Britomaris's spear tip into a bowl of poison.

The image forced Macro to shoot upright. He rushed towards the door but the Praetorians blocked his path. 'What in Hades' name is going on?' the optio rasped.

The Praetorians said nothing. Both their expressions were tight and blank.

'Did he win?' Macro demanded.

'Pavo? Oh, he won,' a voice quivered from the corridor behind the guards. Macro's joy was short-lived as the Praetorians stepped out of the way and four figures appeared from the shadows of the colonnades. Macro watched two stadium officials bundling an exhausted Pavo towards the room. Murena led the way, a stern expression plastered across his gaunt face. Pavo was too tired to try and wrench himself away. The freedman nodded at the guards as the officials slung Pavo into the room. The trainee dropped to his knees beside Macro, his exertion in the arena having drained his muscles and left him weary. In the background, Macro could hear the crowd roaring Pavo's name. He flicked his eyes to Murena lingering in the doorway; the Greek smiled pityingly back at the optio.

'You were going to poison Pavo,' Macro growled.

'Poison?' Pavo whispered, a disbelieving look on his face.

The optio nodded grimly. He was conscious of blood flowing out of a wound at the back of his scalp, from when the second Praetorian had clobbered him earlier, matting his hair and dripping down his neck. 'I caught these two fools in the act,' he said, jerking his head furiously at the guards.

'But I just saved the reputation of Rome,' Pavo hissed as he glowered with rage at Murena. 'The Emperor's too. Not to mention your own and that of Pallas! And this is how you repay me?'

Murena chuckled weakly as he placed his hands behind his back. He kept his distance from Pavo, as if avoiding a rabid dog. 'Our plan was simple,' he said. 'We needed to guarantee victory. Even with someone as skilled with a sword as you, however, nothing in life is guaranteed. We poisoned the tips of both your weapons. That way Britomaris would perish in the arena, thus restoring the glory of Rome.' Murena chuckled. 'Why on earth do you think our barbaric friend collapsed so easily at the end?'

'But you were going to kill me too!' Pavo roared, his face turning crimson with rage.

Murena knitted his wispy brow. 'Two birds, one stone. Both Pallas and I knew that your victory, whilst necessary for his imperial majesty, would also make you a hero in the eyes of the mob. Listen to them,' he grumbled scathingly as the crowd continued to roar in the background, ecstatic at the outcome of the fight. 'They think you're a legend, young man! We took a calculated risk in getting you to fight Britomaris. But we hoped to avoid the celebration of your name by arranging your death in the arena. There would have been some applause from the crowd for your efforts, of course. A few tawdry poems written to celebrate your feat. The odd inscription. But dead gladiators don't live long in memory. By the following month you would have been forgotten.' Murena sighed. 'If only that idiot Britomaris had done his job, and stabbed you.'

Despite his ragged condition, Pavo mustered his precious last reserves of energy and lunged at Murena. The freedman took a frightened step back out of the doorway, his eyes wide with fear.

'You tried to kill me, you bastard!' Pavo roared.

The Praetorians jerked into action. One kicked Pavo in the midriff and sent him flying backwards, landing on the ground with a thud, while the other guard glared at Macro, who had balled his hands into tight fists. The guard began to unsheathe his sword. Macro got the message and reluctantly loosened his fists.

'What about my son?' Pavo seethed. 'I was told he would be released after I won.'

'Appius?' Murena asked, wearing an expression of feigned ignorance. 'You must be mistaken, young man. The Emperor was to release him upon your glorious death in the arena. Since you failed to stick to your side of the bargain and die, I'm afraid the deal is off. Appius will remain the possession of the imperial palace. He'll grow up with the other slave children, and when he's old enough he'll fetch grapes and figs for those who control the Empire. Men like Pallas and me. In future generations the name of Valerius will be synonymous with slaves, not military heroes and victorious gladiators.'

Pavo fumed, his nostrils flaring with rage. 'You can't do this.'

'Oh, but I can,' Murena replied condescendingly. He began to turn away from the room. 'I can do whatever I please. Your victory means that the Emperor is in debt to Pallas, and don't forget that Pallas is my boss. It would've taken years for us to win the complete confidence of Claudius. You've helped us achieve it in a mere few months. Thank you, Pavo.'

Pavo simmered with rage. The freedman paused and rubbed his hands together, as if warming them on a cold winter's night. 'I suppose it's all worked out rather well in the end,' he went on. 'All that remains is for me to take care of loose ends.' He cast his eyes over Macro and Pavo in turn. 'As I promised Pallas.'

'What do you mean?' Pavo snapped, narrowing his eyes at Murena.

'The Emperor won't tolerate the mob chanting the name of the son of a traitor.' Murena barked at the Praetorians as he clicked his fingers: 'Take him away.'

Pavo hung his head low as the guards hauled him to his feet, grabbing a weary arm each. The fight had dimmed in him, Macro noticed. Despair had doused the flames of rage burning inside his belly.

'Appius . . . my boy . . .' the trainee muttered under his breath, his dry lips cracking as the guards manhandled him out of the room and dragged him down the corridor. Away from the arena. Away from the noise and buzz of the crowd chanting his name.

'Pavo was right,' Macro growled at the smug Greek when they were left alone. 'You are a bastard.'

Murena stroked his chin thoughtfully and smiled at Macro as if he had just given him a compliment.

'What's going to happen to him?' the optio asked.

'There's a wagon waiting outside. He's to return to the ludus in Paestum,' Murena replied as he gazed down the corridor. 'We'll find another opponent for him to fight locally, in the more modest surroundings of Paestum's amphitheatre. Someone with a poor reputation.'

Macro scoffed and folded his arms. 'What for? Pavo's a great fighter. Pair him with a low-ranking gladiator and he'll carve up his opponent in a heartbeat. If you ask me, I say the lad's been through enough.'

'Pavo's survival is an embarrassment to Claudius. He must die,' Murena said icily. 'He must die in disgrace, in a way that leaves his reputation in tatters. And you are going to help me achieve that.'

The optio shifted on the balls of his feet and felt his pulse quicken with fear. 'Why the bloody hell would I do that? I've already honoured my end of the deal. I trained Pavo. He won. Now I'm due my promotion, as promised.'

Murena looked back at Macro.

'It's not that simple, Optio. You know our dirty little secret. And if the mob discover that Claudius tried to poison the new hero of the arena, well . . .' Murena frowned at his feet, as if a snake was crawling up his leg. 'Let's just say they wouldn't be too happy. Our problem is, can we trust you? Luckily for you, Pallas and I are giving you a chance to prove your loyalty to Claudius.'

'How do you mean?' Macro asked, his voice low and uncertain.

Murena grinned as the sound of the crowd slowly died away and the heavy drum roll of footsteps echoed through the plaza as people made their way to the exits and flooded out into the streets. The freedman said, 'Since you appear to be a rather effective gladiator trainer, you're going to train Pavo's next opponent. You know the young man's weaknesses. You will train your man to exploit them, so that the mob will see Pavo humiliated. . .'

CHAPTER TEN

A short while later, Macro watched the workers dismantling the temporary stands in the fading light. He shook his head as a cold knot of fear tightened in his guts. Train the next opponent to face Pavo? The notion left a bitter taste in his mouth. Surely the young lad had been through enough, Macro told himself. He gritted his teeth as he watched two slaves struggle to heave the body of Britomaris on to a handcart.

The clean-up operation at the Julian plaza was under way. Groups of servants swept away chipped clay tickets and shards of shattered wine jugs. The crowd had quickly emptied from the stands after the gladiator fight, pouring out into the streets of the Campus Martius. Emperor Claudius and his retinue had swiftly departed and Murena had followed in their wake to tend to official business, detaining the optio at the arena while he made up his mind whether to help the aide to the imperial secretary. Pavo's victory over Britomaris ought to have been a moment of personal pride for Macro. Instead, by defeating Britomaris, he had helped Murena and Pallas, sealing Pavo's fate.

'Bollocks to this,' the optio muttered to himself, kicking a wine cup away in frustration. 'I should be in Germany right now, not bloody Rome.'

'Pah! You ought to be thanking the gods, not cursing them!' announced a Praetorian Guard standing at the entrance to the arena. His comrade to his left smiled thinly. The pair of them had been detailed to keep an eye on Macro until the aide to the imperial secretary returned from his business at the palace. 'You ask me, I reckon you're lucky to have avoided the chop. That's the usual fate for anyone who pisses off an emperor. Claudius is no exception.' He winked at his comrade. 'That reminds me. How's the head?'

Macro reached a hand to the welt at the back of his scalp and snorted in disgust. Blood had matted his hair together in dry clumps. Knocked unconscious by a sodding Praetorian, he thought. A deep sense of humiliation brewed in the pit of his stomach.

'No hard feelings,' the guard chortled. 'Serves you right for sticking your nose where it doesn't belong.'

'You're a disgrace to any uniform, my friend. Same as that slippery Greek turd Murena.'

'What did you say, Optio?' a silvery voice snapped at his back.

Macro spun around. Murena materialised from the shadows of the corridor leading under the western portico and paced slowly towards him, carefully measuring each cautious step as he cast his eyes left and right.

'Nothing,' Macro replied bluntly as Murena stopped and studied his face. The freedman acknowledged the soldier with a polite smile. Then he glared at the amused Praetorians and nodded towards the arena. 'You two. Give the servants a hand.'

The guard on the right looked incredulous. 'That's slaves' work. Not for Praetorians.'

'Your job here is done, soldier. I just gave you both an order.'

'But—'

'Do it, or I'll have you transferred to the Rhine Frontier.'

The guard grunted to his comrade. The pair of them reluctantly shuffled down the corridor towards the arena, grumbling to each other under their breath. Murena calmly swivelled his gaze towards Macro. The imperial aide's curly black hair was ruffled. His grey eyes were bloodshot. A deep frown ran like a ridge across his forehead. He looked stressed, the optio thought.

'This should have been a day to celebrate,' the aide lamented. 'The day that a Roman put an end to that Gallic thug Britomaris.' He shot a disapproving look at the body sprawled on the bed of the handcart. 'Instead Pallas has me running around putting out fires.'

'Spare me the sob story,' the optio replied. 'You've got what you wanted. Pavo won, didn't he? Britomaris is dead. You and Pallas have your precious victory. Old Claudius must be delighted with the pair of you. You don't need me here now.'

79

Murena wrung his hands. He gave the impression of a man wrestling with a terrible dilemma. 'Pavo is still alive, Optio. And he's celebrated by the mob, no less! Gods, some of them are even declaring him to be a true Roman hero!' He wore a pained expression as he went on. 'Can you imagine what Emperor Claudius will think if he hears of Pavo's new fame?'

'I'd have thought it was pretty obvious from the crowds chanting his name,' Macro said. He turned away from the arena and brushed past Murena.

'Where in Hades do you think you're going?' Murena cried.

'The nearest inn,' the soldier thundered as he paced down the corridor towards the marble steps leading out to the street. 'To get blind drunk. I've had enough of your shit for one day.'

'You can't walk away!' Murena barked. 'Not while your work for me is still unfinished.'

Macro felt an icy sweat slither like a snake down his back. Unfinished? Taking orders once from the scheming freedman Murena and the imperial secretary had been bad enough. The prospect of undertaking a second mission for the Greeks filled him with dread.

'Should never have left the Rhine . . .'

The aide hurried after Macro, his shuffling footsteps echoing off the high ceiling. 'If only that fool Britomaris had stabbed Pavo and succeeded in poisoning him!' He threw his hands up in anguish. 'Now I'm afraid you must remain here and help me correct this unfortunate problem.'

'Get someone else to do your dirty work. I'm not interested.'

Murena raised a bushy eyebrow. 'What about that promotion to centurion?'

Macro shrugged. 'I'd rather be an optio on the Rhine than a centurion in Rome.'

'Emperors come and go,' the freedman said. 'Soldiers too. Even men like Pallas and myself must pass on one day. But Rome is permanent. It is here for ever.'

'Oh, for fuck's sake . . .' Macro growled wearily. 'Spare me the patriotism. You're in it for the power and the money. Don't even try and pretend otherwise.'

Murena puffed out his thin chest. 'Whatever you may think, it is the duty of each and every man to serve Rome as best he can. You might disagree, but every decision Pallas and I make is for the greater good.'

'What about Pavo?'

'What about him?'

'It's hardly his fault his father was condemned as a traitor.'

'Titus committed an unforgivable betrayal. Pavo must pay for the crimes of his father. Being lenient on him would merely encourage others to challenge the Emperor's authority. Pallas and I have gone to great lengths to ensure that the new Emperor does not make the same mistakes as his unfortunate nephew Caligula. That includes rooting out enemies of the imperial palace and seeing them punished. Every new dawn that Pavo draws breath insults the Emperor and gives fresh hope to those who would seek to oust Claudius.'

'But you disgraced Titus and dragged his name through the mud,' Macro replied angrily. 'You've condemned his son to death one way or the other. If I were a conspirator, I'd think twice before having a pop at Claudius.'

'It's not as simple as that. Before he was a traitor, Titus was a hero of the legions. His son served as military tribune in the Sixth and was held in high esteem by his men. Father and son come from a proud military tradition. Claudius, on the other hand, has never wielded a sword in his life. He looks weak by comparison.'

Macro said nothing. His darkening expression and clenched jaw spoke volumes.

'I understand you are a little, shall we say, sore about Pavo's fate,' Murena went on. 'But I can assure you he will be properly rewarded for his victory over Britomaris.'

'How so?'

'His son will be spared.'

'Gods! What would you have done if he had lost?'

'Flung Appius off the Tarpeian Rock, naturally.'

Macro shivered. Being hurled from the Tarpeian Rock was a fate traditionally reserved for traitors. But executing entire generations of a family was taking things a little too far, even by Rome's murderous standards. The optio tried to disguise his unease, but Murena saw it immediately and shot him a scathing look. Very little went unnoticed by the aide to the imperial secretary, Macro noted sourly. His slit-like eyes were always on the prowl, his ears always pricked, alert to the slightest detail.

Murena paused for a moment and stared at the optio. 'The Emperor intends to usher in a new Golden Age, stirring memories of the days of Augustus. But first we must stamp out our enemies within Rome itself.'

'Assuming there are any left,' Macro responded drily. 'I'd have thought you would've bumped them all off by now.'

A pained expression slid across the aide's face. 'There will always be enemies. The Emperor is the most powerful person in the world, and a great number of men covet the purple toga and the glory of Rome. Men who are motivated by greed and wealth, rather than the good of the Empire.'

'Unlike you, I suppose,' Macro replied.

'You are implying that Pallas and I do not bear the Emperor's best interests at heart. If that is your attempt at subtlety, Optio, I shudder to think what you consider to be blunt. But you are mistaken. I, like the imperial secretary, am a freedman. We are simply glad to be free of the shackles of servitude. Our gratitude to his imperial majesty should not be underestimated. The real threat is young Pavo.'

'Pavo?' Macro sputtered. 'How in the name of the gods is he a threat? He's been condemned to a ludus!'

'He is a hero to the mob,' Murena countered impatiently. 'In case you are not aware, the Emperor's regime will fall unless he wins the support of the mob. It is no great secret that the man on the street sees Claudius as somewhat distant and aloof. Now they have Pavo to cheer. His growing popularity is . . . maleficent.'

'Maleficent?' Macro frowned.

The aide rolled his eyes. 'Portentous.' Still confronted with a blank look from the optio, Murena tried again. 'I mean threatening.' He sighed. 'My point is, the mob have fond memories of Tiberius, and Titus was well known as Tiberius's right-hand man. Now we have young Pavo reminding people of the Valerius name.

His popularity is an insult and, worse, a threat to the Emperor.'

'As I recall, you were the one who wanted Pavo to fight Britomaris. You must have known the mob would celebrate his good fortune if he triumphed.'

'An outcome we had planned to cut off as soon as it sprouted,' Murena replied with a glare. 'Our error was to trust that hare-brained lout Britomaris to wound Pavo. We do not intend to make the same mistake twice.'

'I'm just a soldier,' Macro protested. 'I kill the enemies of Rome for a living, not its citizens. You want someone to dispose of Pavo in a dark alley, you're better off talking to those idiots.'

He pointed at the pair of Praetorians pottering about in the bowels of the arena, grumbling to each other and shaking their heads. One of the guards nudged his comrade in the chest and they quickly set about looking busy, picking up wine jugs and trinkets and lugging them out of the arena. Murena turned back to Macro.

'You won't escape your obligation to me that easily, Macro. You'll see to it that Pavo is humiliated in the arena – or you'll be enjoying a fine view of the Tarpeian Rock, on the way down . . .'

CHAPTER ELEVEN

A frosty silence hovered between the aide and the soldier. In the weeks he had spent training Pavo at the ludus in Paestum, Macro had developed a fondness for the high-born young gladiator. Although he'd never have admitted it to Pavo, in Macro's opinion the lad had suffered a great deal under the new regime. He felt compelled to plead his case.

'You don't need to murder the boy,' Macro said cagily. 'He's in a ludus, remember. He'll probably be butchered in a year or two anyway. That's how long most fighters last. Even the lucky ones. He can't do you any harm.'

Murena opened his mouth to reply, but hesitated as four servants emerged from the plaza, carrying equipment towards a waiting wagon to be transported back inside the city gates. One of the servants cradled the sword used by Pavo in the fight. Dried blood lacquered the length of the blade. The servant laboured under the weight. Murena waited until the group had paced beyond the steps and reached the wagon before continuing.

'That is not how I see it, Macro. Or indeed Pallas, for that matter. The imperial secretary has decreed that Pavo must die. Which means the order is as good as from Claudius himself. Killing Pavo will leave the Emperor free to focus on rebuilding Rome.' Murena clicked his tongue. He stared at Macro out of the corner of his eye. He had an unsettling habit of studying people in that way, Macro thought to himself.

'Just between you and me,' Murena continued, 'the Emperor's programme of public works will represent a pleasant change of duty. All this shoring up of the new regime is getting rather tiresome.'

'Tell me about it,' Macro grumbled. 'You're forgetting something, though. Pavo is a natural with a sword. The way he saw off Britomaris wasn't just down to training. It takes skill and courage to fight under pressure. Plenty of soldiers are bloody good at the palus but shit themselves at the first sight of a barbarian foaming at the mouth. Pavo didn't. The lad is made of strong stuff.'

'Perhaps. But you know his weaknesses. You can train someone to exploit them.'

'You'll still have to find an opponent,' Macro said. 'Pavo could win against most of the imperial gladiators when the mood suits him.'

'We have already chosen our man,' Murena replied. He paused, and a knowing smile played out across his thin lips. 'Decimus Cominius Denter.'

'Denter?' Macro repeated disbelievingly.

'You're familiar with the name?'

'Who isn't? Denter is a fucking lunatic! Pardon my Gallic. He once bit the nose off his opponent. Beat another gladiator to death with his bare hands. Drinks the blood of his enemies once he's killed them. At least he did while he still fought. He retired ages ago. Bought his freedom after the last spectacle under Caligula.' The soldier shrugged. 'That's what I heard.'

'Pallas has a plan for enticing him out of retirement.'

'Money, I suppose? Great big bloody bags of it.'

Murena glanced up at the sky. Dusk was closing over Rome. 'Time for me to return to the palace. Walk with me, Macro.'

Carefully tended fires were being lit as the frigid night wind buffeted the city. Braziers and torches in the open public spaces bathed the temples and forum in orange. Elsewhere the tiny twinkles of oil lamps pricked out from the gloomy mass of tenement blocks and private villas. Trekking through the streets of Rome at night only reminded the optio of why he hated the place. Beggars and thieves lurked in the shadows, bucketfuls of slops were tossed from tenement windows, and the endless din of drunks shouting and brawling and the cry of hungry infants made a good night's sleep impossible. Give me the Rhine any day of the week, he thought.

Murena grimaced. 'Denter may well have been one of the finest fighters to grace the arena, but retired gladiators are not the most upstanding of Roman citizens. To be frank, he has squandered his substantial earnings on drink and tarts.'

'Sounds like a man after my own heart,' Macro replied with a grin. 'Where is the old boy now? Travelling with some second-rate troupe of gladiators for a few denarii, I suppose?'

'Pompeii, actually. He does the odd bit of training. The lanista of the local gladiator school will help you to find him.'

'Pompeii?' Macro stuck out his bottom lip approvingly. 'I hear the Falernian is the best in all Italia there. Good tarts, too. Don't rip you off. Wouldn't mind living there myself, when I retire.'

'Be careful what you wish for, Optio.' Murena's eyes glowered at the soldier. 'You are to travel there at once and train Denter.' He smiled coldly. 'Although "train" might be putting it rather strongly. Denter was undefeated in over thirty bouts. I doubt there is much you could teach him. Think of yourself as less of a gladiator trainer and more of a minder. Ensuring Denter stays out of the taverns will keep you busy enough. He is one of those degenerate brutes who fritters away his money on drink and the races by day and degrades himself with nightly visits to the brothels. And that's when he isn't getting into scraps with the locals. Your job will be to keep him sober and whip him into shape.'

'Great,' said Macro sullenly. 'So I'm reduced to looking after a drunk.'

'Denter will be suitably motivated to stay clean. His reward will be five thousand sestertii.'

'Five thousand sestertii?' Macro sputtered disbelievingly. 'Why on earth would he fight for that stingy sum? Unless he plans on killing Pavo out of the kindness of his heart.'

Although the amount Murena had mentioned was more than five times the standard legionary pay of nine hundred sestertii a year, Macro was familiar enough with the workings of the arena business to know that it was considerably less than the usual amount used to lure a gladiator out of retirement.

'These are austere times,' Murena said. 'Caligula emptied the imperial coffers. The Emperor does not have a bottomless bag of coins to hand out to scum like Denter.'

'The amount you're offering him is an insult,' Macro countered. 'You know what these gladiators are like. Greedy buggers. Piss money away as fast as they can earn it. Denter would have to be mad to accept.'

Murena shrugged. 'Denter will agree to our terms. Especially when he learns that his opponent is a Valerius.'

'Why? What's that got to do with anything?'

'Before Denter was a gladiator, he was a legionary in the Fifth. It seems he had some minor disagreement with a comrade over accusations of stolen rations. Denter stabbed him twice with his sword. The poor chap was lucky to survive. His cohort was noto-riously undisciplined and the commanding officer sentenced him to six lashes of the whip. But Titus had just assumed the role of legate of the Fifth and brought with him grand ideas of Roman nobility and grace. He ordered that Denter be dishonourably discharged as an example to the other men.'

Macro thumped his chest. 'Denter's a lucky boy. You get caught doing that in the Second and you're for the chop.'

'Nevertheless, his misfortune is a gift from the gods. He under-standably bears a serious grudge towards Titus. His old lanista said he constantly spoke of his hatred for the man. He will jump at the chance for revenge over the son.'

'Where's the fight taking place?'

'The amphitheatre in Paestum. In six weeks' time. The local council were already in the midst of preparing a pitiful spectacle. We will simply take over the administration and bump Pavo to the top of the bill.'

'A nice long time to get him ready, then. No rush at all,' the optio noted wryly. He paused as a thought unravelled itself in his head. 'But why Paestum? Why not Rome? I'd have thought you would want as big an audience as possible to see Pavo stuck like a pig.'

Murena shifted uncomfortably on the balls of his feet.

'Seeing the crowd chant Pavo's name in the Campus Martius is not something we wish to repeat. Far better to risk hosting the spectacle in a sweaty backwater like Paestum. Just get Denter fighting fit, so that he will be certain to triumph over that brat.

With the young man dead, the mob will soon forget his name, and any doubts over Emperor Claudius will be silenced. Cheer up,' Murena added, seeing the dour look on the face of the optio. 'Succeed and you'll get your promotion to centurion.'

'Great,' Macro grumbled. 'But if it's all the same to you, I'd prefer to leg it back to Germania. There are plenty of good gladiator trainers kicking their heels in the imperial ludus. Get one of them to work with your man Denter.' Underneath his desire to return to action, the idea of conspiring against Pavo left a sour taste in the optio's mouth. Even if he couldn't spare Pavo a grisly death, he didn't have to hasten it by teaching another man his weak points.

'Nonsense,' Murena replied with a dismissive wave of his slender hand. 'Pallas and I consider you the perfect choice to train Denter. You tamed Pavo – a tempestuous young man. I think it highly unlikely that your new charge will be any worse.'

Macro choked on a laugh. The aide went on regardless.

'I've arranged for a horse and the appropriate documents for your journey to Pompeii tomorrow at dawn, as well as a modest sum of expenses for your stay in the town. The lanista of the local ludus has organised your accommodation, and you will be permitted use of the training ground next to the barracks to work with Denter.' They had reached a side entrance to the imperial palace and Murena stopped and turned to Macro. 'Now, you must excuse me. There is much planning to do ahead of the fight. Paestum is a rather small arena and a great many dignitaries will wish to be in attendance.'

With that, he turned to leave. He paused when he spotted Macro pursing his lips. 'Something the matter, Optio?'

Macro hesitated briefly. 'I don't understand how you're so sure that Pavo will be humiliated,' he said cautiously. 'I mean, the mob are fawning over the lad. What happens if he puts up a good fight, and the crowd beg for mercy to be shown? I've seen it happen. If the Emperor gives the signal for death, the mood could turn ugly.'

Murena smiled knowingly. 'You say that Pavo is skilled with a sword.'

'Not just skilled,' Macro replied, with a pang of pride in his chest. He had, after all, been the one who'd turned Pavo from a fearless but volatile trainee into an indomitable swordsman. 'He is one of the best I've ever seen.'

'Then the answer is simple. We will take his sword away from him.'

CHAPTER TWELVE

Paestum

'On your feet, you bloody wretch!'

Pavo shook his head as his opponent tapped his wooden sword against the base of his wicker shield. A moment earlier the same sword had thwacked Pavo on the side of his skull and sent him crashing to his hands and knees on the floor of the ludus training ground. Now the metallic taste of blood was fresh in his mouth and a ringing noise filled his ears. He felt the callused palms of his hands scalding against the sun-baked sand. Spitting out a mouthful of blood, he lifted his eyes to his opponent. Amadocus towered over him. From his position on the ground, the young man could see only a pair of gnarled feet with blackened toenails, and bulging veins stretching up the length of his wide legs like the twisted fibres of a catapult. Pavo shook his dazed head clear and made to scrape himself off the ground. The veteran booted sand at his face.

'You fight like a woman, Roman!' Amadocus snarled in a guttural tone that mangled each word of Latin. Pavo blinked the sand out of his eyes as the Thracian snorted. 'Think you're special because you defeated that good-for-nothing Gaul? Fortuna was kissing your arse that day.' He kicked another cloud of sand at Pavo. 'Get up, damn you!'

'Amadocus!' a voice barked from behind Pavo. The veterans and recruits who were huddled in a tight circle around the fighters abruptly stopped cheering and listened to the gladiator instructor. 'This is a training bout, not a fight to the death.' The instructor's lips curled into a cruel smile. 'Let the young man get to his feet, so he may be given a proper beating.'

'Yes, Doctore,' Amadocus grumbled, while fuming through his nostrils. Pavo lifted his eyes a little higher and saw his opponent's giant pectoral muscles heaving up and down, his blistered hand gripping the base of his training sword. Then the Thracian scowled and took a step back. His vast shadow slipped off the young gladiator like a cloak. Amadocus tapped his sword against his wicker shield again.

'Hurry up, Roman,' he grumbled. 'I've been waiting for this chance to humble you ever since you were chosen to fight Britomaris.'

Pavo slowly picked himself off the ground. His leg muscles were taut and stressed from the morning's yard exercises and he fought hard to steady himself. Amadocus stood two paces back, his shield resting at hip height and the tip of his sword pointing at his opponent's throat. His pale face was locked into a scowl. Pavo stole a glance at the gladiator instructor past his shoulder. Calamus stood at the front of the circle of spectators, his arms folded across his bare chest, a withering expression etched across his lacerated face.

'Come on then, you posh little prick!' he sneered. 'What are you waiting for? You slew Britomaris with a single stab. Surely you can stand up to a couple of light knocks from Amadocus.'

Pavo turned back to his opponent. Training-ground fights were normally timid affairs, he reminded himself. Neither gladiator wanted to get injured and risk their shot of glory in the arena. But the Thracian had attacked with a ferocious intensity, and now Pavo felt the hard stares from the twenty volunteers and forty-two veterans of the gladiator school of the house of Gurges as they willed him to lose.

A week had passed since Pavo had returned to Paestum, but already his victory over Britomaris seemed distant. He had returned not to a hero's welcome – as befitted a man who had spared Emperor Claudius's blushes – but to the filthy reality of life in the ludus. The veterans boiled with resentment at his surprise victory, while most of the new recruits loathed him for his privileged background.

Ignoring the hatred swirling around him, Pavo adjusted his

stance and edged cautiously towards Amadocus. His wooden training sword felt heavy in his hand. When he was almost a sword's length from the Thracian, he pushed forward on his right foot, bending his leg at the knee as he lunged at his opponent jerking his training sword upwards. Amadocus had been schooled as a Thracian class of gladiator and used a small curved training shield made of thickly thatched willow stem. It was much smaller than the standard legionary shield and the Thracian had it raised at chest height, leaving his neck exposed. His eyes widened in surprise as he saw the tip of Pavo's sword darting towards his neck. The Thracian twisted sideways to evade the blow. He was too late. There was the dense clunk of weathered ash slamming into human bone as the sword struck Amadocus on the sternum and glanced up and off his collarbone. Badly winded, gasping for air, he bent forward and presented the back of his exposed head to his opponent.

Now Pavo drew a half-step closer. A pained retching sound escaped the Thracian's slack mouth. Pavo hoisted his sword over his prone opponent. With a wrench of his torso, he plunged the sword down at the back of Amadocus's head. The Thracian snarled and in a sharp jolt of movement jerked his shield up to block Pavo's sword. A violent blow shuddered through Pavo's wrist and echoed up his forearm as the Thracian's shield swung in a wide arc, swatting the sword away. Amadocus rumbled with anger as Pavo lost his footing, the momentum of his attack sending him staggering to his left while Amadocus deflected his sword arm to the right. Pavo's shoulder muscles were ripped in opposite directions. He cursed himself for launching a rash attack rather than retreating for cover behind his shield. Then Amadocus slashed his foot-long curved dagger upward. The edge of the wooden blade struck Pavo on his outstretched forearm. Pain flared in his wrist and his fingers eased their grip on his own sword. It dropped to the ground with a heavy thud. As he stooped down to pick it up, Amadocus cut him off with another swipe of his dagger, this time directed at Pavo's stomach. The blow knocked the young gladiator off balance and he stumbled backwards, clutching his guts as nausea swelled in his throat. He looked up and saw

Amadocus charging towards him, his deep-set eyes almost popping out of their sockets with rage.

Pavo shrunk his torso behind his three-foot-long oval shield just as Amadocus jabbed his blade in a quick thrust at his opponent. The shield juddered as the dagger pounded like a hammer on its wooden frame. The veteran started raining down a torrent of hefty blows, grunting with each big swipe of his weapon. There were gasps from the spectators at the ferocity of his attack. Pavo glanced in despair at his discarded sword. He pricked his ears, waiting for the inevitable call from Calamus to stop the fight. But the doctore remained silent. Amadocus struck again, and this time the shield cracked down the middle on impact, spattering Pavo's face with splinters. Pavo retreated towards the edge of the circle. Around the two men a chorus of roars erupted from veterans and recruits, goading the Thracian on.

'Bash his bloody skull in!' a voice screamed behind Pavo.

It sounded close, almost on his shoulder. Pavo quickly glanced round, realising that he had retreated nearly into the spectators. A scrawny Persian man puckered his brow at him. His eyes were different colours and he sported a curly black beard. Pavo knew the man as Orodes, a prisoner of war captured during a Parthian raid into Armenia. Orodes booted Pavo in the back. The blow sent the younger man lurching towards the centre of the circle, and Amadocus's seething mass.

The Thracian wound up for a decisive slash at Pavo's neck. But Pavo ducked his head. Gripping his shield with both hands, he thrust the top edge up towards Amadocus. The move caught the Thracian by surprise. He groaned as the rim smacked up at his chin, his jawbone slamming shut. Before his opponent could come to his senses, Pavo cast his lumbering shield aside and dived towards him. The look of anger on the Thracian's face melted away as he lost his footing and fell backwards with Pavo on top of him. There was a rowdy cheer from the spectators as the two men crashed to the training-ground floor with a crunching thump. At first the big Thracian was stunned. Then he rolled over on top of Pavo, using his immense strength to pin his opponent to the ground. Pavo balled his right hand into a fist and slammed a punch at Amadocus on the bridge of his nose. His knuckles flared with pain. The spectators booed, urging the Thracian to finish off his opponent. Pavo thumped Amadocus a second time. Now blood streamed out of the Thracian's nostrils and splattered across his lips. Enraged, Amadocus thrust out his right arm at Pavo and clamped his fingers around his throat. Now the Thracian smiled cruelly as he slowly crushed his opponent's windpipe. Pavo felt the air trap in his lungs. His eyes bulged inside their sockets. He realised he was going to die.

Suddenly a wooden sword came whooshing down in front of Pavo and struck Amadocus on his head. The Thracian grunted as he fell away, his arms flopping by his sides. Pavo rolled over and gasped with relief as air filled his burning lungs.

'That's enough,' Calamus boomed, thrusting them apart with his sword. The Thracian glowered at Pavo. Two veterans, fellow Thracians who Pavo had seen by his opponent's side in the canteen, stepped forward from the circle. Each one slipped an arm around Amadocus and hauled him to his feet. They began to escort Amadocus away, but the Thracian gestured for them to stop. He turned back to Pavo and scowled.

'This isn't over, Roman.' He spat blood. 'I pray to the gods that we will fight to the death in the arena, and the last thing you see before you visit the Underworld will be my sword plunging into your fucking neck.'

'You two.' Calamus nodded at the other Thracians. 'Take Amadocus to see Achaeus and get him cleaned up. Our lanista insists on paying that Greek physician a king's ransom, so we may as well get some use out of the senile old fool.'

The two Thracians pulled Amadocus away. The circle of spectators hastily parted for the three men, veteran and recruit alike distracted by the sight of Amadocus hobbling towards the medical quarters mumbling curses.

'Right, you lot. Enough pissing about. Get back to training, and the gods help anyone I catch slacking off this afternoon.' For a second none of the men moved. Calamus lashed his short leather whip on the sand, causing one or two of the recruits to flinch. 'That's an order, ladies. This is a ludus, not a fucking Greek debating society.'

There were grumbles and low whispers as the men reluctantly dispersed and trudged towards the opposite ends of the training ground. The recruits headed for the paluses assembled at the southern end of the ground, whilst the veterans gathered to fight in pairs in the shade of the portico at the northern end. Calamus frowned at the dispersing crowd and turned to Pavo.

'Come with me, rich boy,' the doctore growled as he seized him by his left arm and marched him across the training ground.

'Where are you taking me?' Pavo demanded, ignoring the angry looks thrown in his direction from the gladiators.

'The lanista wants you,' Calamus said. 'Don't ask me why. Frankly I couldn't give a fuck about a snivelling little shit like you. You might have fluked that win over Britomaris, but don't think for a second you're worthy of being branded a true gladiator. Not while I have a say on the matter. Mark my words, one of these days Amadocus will have his hands wrapped around your throat again. And next time, I won't save you.'

CHAPTER THIRTEEN

Calamus guided Pavo under the shadow of the portico and up a stone staircase leading to a door with a pair of lightly armed guards positioned either side. The guards stepped aside and Calamus yanked open the hefty door, ushering Pavo down a colonnade with a series of small rooms to the left and a garden to the right adorned with an ornate fountain and sculptures of gladiators striking various poses. Beyond the colonnade a short passage opened on to a wide room with a high ceiling. Pavo spotted Gurges standing beside a shallow pool of rainwater positioned directly beneath an opening in the roof. Reflected light from the pool shimmered across his face. There was a bronze bust mounted on a plinth, and a wooden chest fitted with polished bronze locks. Gurges did not appear to notice Pavo and Calamus at first. He was deep in discussion with a corpulent man dressed in a vast tunic that had the proportions of a sail. His green eyes glinted and he sported a trimmed black beard with a shaved upper lip and dark hair curled in the Greek fashion. Gold rings gleamed on each of his chubby fingers.

'So it's agreed, then,' the corpulent man said. 'Fifty thousand sestertii is the bet. Should your man win, you'll stand to make four hundred thousand sestertii. Lose, and the fifty thousand is mine.' He examined his gold rings and went on, 'I would prefer to have something in writing. It is the custom.'

Gurges chuckled. 'You don't trust me to pay if I lose, Carbo?'

'I am a bookmaker,' Carbo replied tersely, pressing the palms of his hands together in front of his double chin. 'It is in my best interests to be cautious when a client lays down a fairly, shall we say, substantial sum. Naturally, I would never question the integrity of the house of Gurges.'

The lanista chuckled. 'Very well. I'll arrange for the necessary contract to be drawn up. Now, unless there's anything else, I shall see you at the banquet to discuss the other gladiators for the forthcoming show.'

'I look forward to it.'

The lanista signified the end of the conversation, wheeling away from Carbo and acknowledging Calamus with a brisk nod. As Carbo made to leave, he spotted Pavo and stopped. He smiled curiously at the trainee. 'So this is the hero of Rome?' he mused. 'The man who saved the reputation of Emperor Claudius from ruin, eh?'

'That's one way of putting it,' grumbled Calamus.

Carbo stuck out his bottom lip in disappointment. He waddled a couple of paces towards Pavo and paused a moment while he tickled a flabby fold of skin under his chin. 'I must say, you're somewhat slighter than I expected. Mind you, many gladiators have so much muscle on them these days, they can hardly move.'

'The muscle is so they can swing a sword,' Calamus interjected. 'And the layer of fat on top protects their organs when a blade cuts through their flesh and draws blood.'

'Yes, well. Thank you for that, doctore.' Carbo shivered at the thought. He nodded to Pavo. 'You did well to triumph against that savage Britomaris. But I fear you will do even better to survive long against your next opponent.'

'Next opponent?' Pavo asked. His heart thumped inside his chest.

The lanista patted Carbo on the back and the men said their goodbyes. Then Carbo departed, winking at Pavo as he waddled past on his way to the corridor. Another fight, thought Pavo. He offered a silent prayer to the gods that he would at last face Hermes, and achieve the revenge he had craved since the man had beheaded his father in front of the Emperor.

Gurges waved a bony hand at Calamus. 'Leave us, doctore.'

'Yes . . . sir.'

The lanista patiently watched Calamus retreat down the corridor, his hands placed behind his back. At the clunk of the shutting door, he at last turned to Pavo and abruptly perched himself on the ledge of the pool. He crossed his legs in the dainty fashion of the Greeks and said, 'I understand from Calamus that you've been making an enemy of Amadocus.'

Pavo wiped sweat from his face. 'He started it, sir.'

Gurges laughed. 'Ignore him. He's just upset that you're threatening his position within the ludus.' The lanista dipped a hand into the pool and went on, tracing circles in the rainwater, 'You had better get used to the attention. You're the new darling of the mob, Pavo. And you know what that means?'

He was interrupted by a Greek slave entering with a tray of tiny pastries. Pavo felt his empty stomach rumble at the sight of the food. He lived in a state of permanent hunger and thirst, working up a ferocious appetite during the hours spent on the training ground that was hardly sated by the standard fare of barley wheat, bread and the odd cup of vinegared water. The slave hovered at Gurges's side while the lanista picked away at the snacks. Too distraught with hunger to watch Gurges eat, Pavo turned his gaze to the bronze bust. Upon further examination he realised it was a portrait of the lanista. He silently scolded the sculptor for doing such a dishonest job. Gurges's crooked nose had been smoothed out. His balding pate had been generously transformed into a thick head of curly hair. Pavo briefly wondered how a lowly lanista, considered on a par with a brothel madam, managed to live in such splendour.

'I have exciting news for you,' Gurges said. Pavo felt an icy shiver of anticipation crawl up his spine.

'Am I to fight Hermes at last?' he asked.

The lanista burst into laughter. 'Hermes? There's more chance of me shagging a Vestal Virgin than enticing him out of his recent retirement. Besides, he's still recovering from his recent mugging. Word has it a gang of street robbers roughed him up and broke several of his bones. It'll be a while yet before he's fit enough to take to the sands, even assuming that he'd want to step out of retirement.'

Pavo burned with anger. 'But we had a deal. You said if I won you would help me get my fight with Hermes.' His voice rose and trembled with indignation.

'I promised no such thing,' Gurges replied, feigning an insulted look. 'I only said that I'd see what I could do. It so happens that I am still making enquiries. But I'm sure you appreciate that these matters take time. Hermes is a darling of the Emperor. The last time he retired was under Caligula, and it took a great deal of persuading to convince him to return to the arena.'

Gurges rose and paced over to Pavo, licking his fingers clean. His crude manners offended Pavo, who had been educated by his father to believe that conduct and dignity were what separated the Romans from the barbarian hordes at the edges of the Empire. 'Even if the old boy did accept your challenge, it's highly unlikely the Emperor would personally sanction it. The risk of losing Hermes and undermining his own reputation would be too great. My point, dear boy, is that bringing Hermes out of retirement is a costly business. You need to make it worth my while. All you've done so far is cost me money.'

'How do you mean?'

'We are to host a spectacle,' said Gurges, wiping his mouth with the back of his hand. 'Right here, in Paestum. Dignitaries from across the Empire will come to watch the fighters of the house of Gurges. My name will be famous throughout the provinces.'

'Who's the sponsor?' Pavo wondered aloud.

'In theory, Emperor Claudius.' Gurges puffed out his chest with pride and stared into the middle distance, as if looking directly at the Emperor. He turned back to Pavo. 'In practice, me. You see, the Emperor is far too busy cementing his hold on power to handle the daunting task of organising a spectacle for the mob. I kindly offered to take care of matters for him. Claudius will be represented in Paestum by the imperial secretary.'

'Pallas!' Pavo felt a cold, clammy fear grip his bowels. 'He convinced Claudius to execute my father. I pray to the gods daily that he meets a violent end.'

Gurges laughed and said, 'You should be thanking the man, not cursing him. Pallas has kindly chosen you on behalf of the Emperor to top the bill. You'll be fighting against an illustrious name from the past. A talented gladiator by the name of Decimus Cominius Denter.'

'And if I defeat him, I'll fight Hermes?' Pavo asked, his voice tinged with hope.

'One step at a time, young man,' Gurges replied, patting the gladiator on the back as if they were old friends. 'Your next fight will not be straightforward.' The lanista shifted awkwardly on the spot. 'You are to train as a retiarius.'

Pavo felt a stab of anxiety. 'A net fighter?'

'That's right.' Gurges nodded. 'You'll fight with a trident and a net. No shield. Your opponent will fight as a secutor, armed in the traditional way, with a short sword and a legionary shield.'

Pavo bristled with anger. He furrowed his brow. 'There must be some mistake. I'm a swordsman. I learned my trade in the military. I should be fighting as a murmillo or a hoplite, or perhaps a thraex. Any other type of gladiator, in fact. Not with a damn net.'

Gurges stared irritably at the high-born fighter. 'It's not often we get such a grandiose spectacle in Paestum, and Claudius is personally sponsoring the event. You'll fight with a fucking stick if the Emperor demands it.'

'And why should I do what he says?' Pavo replied angrily. 'Claudius and his lackeys confiscated my father's property. I have no inheritance. My parents are dead and buried in unmarked graves and my son is being held hostage in the imperial palace.'

Gurges gently scratched his chin. 'How badly do you want to kill Hermes?'

'It's the only reason I train,' Pavo said, his veins thumping against his temples at the thought of striking down the legendary gladiator.

'I see,' said Gurges quietly. 'Then consider this. You're the slayer of Britomaris. To the mob you're already a hero. They talk of you in taverns and public baths. But that's just one bout. You might just be a flash in the pan. Now, a fight against Denter will be the biggest seen in Paestum for many years. Men and women will flock here from Pompeii and Puteoli, Capri and Capua.' Gurges rubbed his hands gleefully. 'We'll rake it in. We'll sell statuettes and replica swords. I might even charge people to watch you work at the palus.'

Pavo huffed. 'And why should I want to help you get filthy rich?'

'Luring Hermes into the arena will be no easy task. But should you put on a good show for me, we'll have enough of a profit to persuade him to renounce his retirement and accept your challenge.'

Pavo went quiet for a moment as conflicting thoughts swirled inside his head. There was an irrefutable logic to Gurges's plan. Retired gladiators only stepped back into the arena for tens of thousands of sestertii. And Pavo was broke. A voice cautioned him that he would be foolish to trust the lanista, but then what choice did he have if he wanted to face Hermes?

'Do we have a deal?' Gurges asked.

Pavo nodded grudgingly.

'Splendid.' A smile retreated to the corners of the lanista's mouth. 'There is one, ah, slight problem.' He wrung his hands. 'You are undertaking an entirely new style of fighting, and there is no specialist net-fighting trainer in the ludus. Calamus will help you as best he can, but for the most part you're on your own. I'm sure a hungry young man like you will get the hang of it soon enough.'

Pavo's face darkened angrily. 'How am I supposed to learn to fight someone like Denter without getting the proper training?'

Gurges shrugged and reached for another pastry. 'It's a net and a trident. You cast your net over your opponent so that he is entangled. Then you stab him with the trident. How hard can it be?'

Biting his tongue, Pavo turned away from the lanista and stomped back down the corridor with a sinking feeling at his prospects for the coming fight. 'By the gods, how can this day get any worse?' he muttered to himself.

CHAPTER FOURTEEN

A cracking noise rattled the sky as the doctore lashed his leather whip at the recruits.

'By Jupiter's cock!' Calamus boomed at the men practising with wooden swords against their posts at the far end of the training ground. The palus belonging to Bucco stood untouched. Pavo had yet to discover what had happened to his friend, and had privately resigned himself to the likelihood that Calamus had dispatched Bucco to a mine in some far-flung corner of the Empire.

'Is this the best you miserable bastards can do? I think you lot might be the worst recruits I've ever seen. Keep this up, ladies, and you'll all be working in the mines before the year is out.'

The recruits increased their pace, sweating away under the piercing gaze of the doctore despite the cold of the early morning. Some gladiators were desperate to please the trainer and win an opportunity to fight in the arena. Others went through the motions, hoping to escape the wrath of Calamus and delay their appointment with the sword. Pavo busied himself with stabbing his palus with a fishing trident acquired from the armoury. Two weeks had passed since Calamus had first introduced him to his new weapons. Since then, Pavo had been left to train alone. After long hours of wielding the net and attacking the palus with the trident, he was still no closer to truly mastering the technique of a retiarius. The net seemed an entirely impractical device. Denter could simply dodge it, or cut himself free if caught. And then Pavo would be defending himself against a heavily armed gladiator with nothing more than a trident and a dagger.

He quelled the anxiety rising in his throat and considered the other recruits slogging away at their individual paluses. They wielded wooden swords of various lengths and styles. Some grasped legionary-style swords. Others trained with spears and short swords, depending on the gladiator type they had been selected for. During the first morning of training the doctore had explained to the recruits that the style of fighter they would eventually become was decided by the lanista, on Calamus's advice. Once assigned, the recruits were trained by specialist instructors. A heavyset man with a scar running across his shoulders instructed the hoplite fighters, while a wiry, nimble comrade oversaw the provocators. Specialising in a particular type of combat meant that each man was another step closer towards his first appearance in the arena. They were all aware that if they did well in training, they were more likely to be paired with a weaker opponent on their first appearance, since it was the worst-kept secret among the gladiator schools that lanistas used the early bouts to get rid of the less able recruits by pitching them against promising young fighters, who in turn would curry favour with the mob by slaughtering their mismatched opponent.

The posts were arranged in two wide rows to give each man ample room to perform a series of stabs, lunges and thrusts at the various points representing the human body, and each had painted a crude face atop his palus. One or two of the new recruits had improved noticeably since Pavo had left to train separately with Macro. Although they had yet to make their debuts in the arena, they now attacked their paluses with powerful, coordinated move-ments, constantly shifting on the balls of their feet as the doctore had instructed. Their brows were furrowed in deep concentration. Their enlarged abdominal muscles and pectorals glistened with sweat. The climate in Paestum was wet and swampy even this late in the year, and Pavo found it difficult to breathe.

'You!' Calamus boomed at Pavo, pointing him out with a gnarled finger. 'If I catch you slacking again, I swear to the gods you'll spend the next week in solitary confinement.'

'Yes, Doctore.'

The instructor tucked his thumbs into the metal belt that was strapped to his waist above his loincloth. 'Perhaps you think you've got time to stand around picking your nose. Perhaps you think you don't need to train; that just because you chalked up one lucky win in the arena, that gives you the right to nod off.'

'No, sir,' Pavo replied.

'You're getting too big for your boots, Pavo. You might have had your head up Fortuna's arse when you fought Britomaris, but Denter is twice the gladiator that barbarian ever was.' The doctore smirked at Pavo and gestured to the trident. 'Since you clearly rate yourself, perhaps you'd care to show us all how to fight using that bloody thing.'

The other men stopped to watch Pavo. Taking a deep breath, the recruit scooped up the net in his left hand, clutching the trident in his right. He sensed Calamus's steely gaze burning his back.

Pavo was poised to attack the palus when a chubby figure with a prominent paunch drooping over his loincloth emerged from the shadows of the east-facing porticoes. His cropped hair was unkempt and he lumbered across the sand towards the recruits. A moment later Calamus caught sight of him.

'Well, stuff me in a sack and cast me off the Tarpeian Rock,' the doctore said in a cutting tone. 'Look who returns to grace us with his fucking presence. Manius Salvius Bucco.' Raising his voice, he boomed at the figure, 'Hurry it up, fatso! We don't have all day.'

As Bucco drew towards the recruits, Pavo could see that he sported several bruises on his arms, legs and face. His lips were purpled and his jaw was swollen. He grimaced with every pained stride he took across the training ground before stopping at the palus to the right of Pavo. A river of sweat glistened on his forehead.

'Bucco!' Pavo murmured. 'Where in Hades have you been?'

'In the infirmary. Long story. I'll explain later.' Bucco paused to catch his breath. 'I thought you'd sodded off to Rome for good. The ludus is no place for a high-born lad like you.'

Pavo smiled, thankful to see a friendly face at last. 'How could I resist the lure of the house of Gurges?' he said drolly. 'Delicious food, wonderful sleeping quarters and charming company.'

Bucco laughed. Then he winced with pain and placed a hand to his sore ribcage.

'Something funny, Bucco?' Calamus rasped.

'No, sir,' Bucco replied soberly.

'Achaeus has declared you fit to leave the infirmary, I see.' The doctore examined the volunteer from head to toe. The dark look on his face suggested he did not like what he saw. 'The old man must be thick as well as blind. Well, you're just in time to see Pavo demonstrate how to use a trident.'

Wielding the trident in an overhand grip at the middle point of the shaft, Pavo yanked his right arm back so that the three wooden tines were parallel with his shoulder. Then he thrust the trident at the palus, driving it at the throat of the post with an angry shout. The tines thwacked weakly against the wood.

'Fuck me, Pavo,' the doctore said curtly. 'I've seen some dross in my time, but you really are taking the piss. Call that a bloody stab? The only thing your opponent might die of is laughter.'

Pavo lowered his head in bitter disappointment. The size and weight of the trident conspired against him. No matter how he gripped it, he couldn't seem to generate enough thrust to land a killer blow. And the tines were too short to cause any real damage. Each measured roughly the same length as an index finger. He doubted they would be able to penetrate deep enough through bone and muscle to puncture vital organs.

Calamus stormed past the wooden posts and stopped directly in front of the recruit, working his features into a rabid snarl. 'You're in trouble, Pavo. Big trouble.'

Pavo knew better than to rise to the bait. He stared at the horizon while the doctore fumed at him through his tunnel-like nostrils. Calamus edged closer. He dropped his voice to a hiss as he leaned forward.

'Denter might be a drunkard, but he was one of the finest gladiators who ever graced the arena. A scrawny pipsqueak like you isn't fit to wipe his arse. This net and trident won't save you from what's coming. Thousands of people are going to flock to the arena. And you know what they're going to see? Denter disembowelling you. You'll be joining your old man in the Underworld before the mob have had a chance to warm their seats.'

Calamus wheeled away from Pavo in disgust. He inspected the sundial in the middle of the training ground. A small spot of light hovered at the halfway point on the truncated surface of the dial. 'Break for lunch, ladies. Before the rest of you make me as sick as Pavo.'

Propping their training swords against their paluses, the recruits plodded over to the canteen for a modest lunch. The doctore stopped on the half-turn as he caught sight of Bucco. His hands tensed against the leather strands of his whip. 'I suppose you're ready to return to training.'

Bucco puffed out his chest. 'Yes, sir.'

'You don't look ready to me, Bucco. You know what you look like to me?'

'No, sir.'

'A two-pound shit stuffed into a one-pound bag. I hear the gold mines in Dacia are in need of more men. Could be the ideal place for you, fatso. Horrible conditions down there, mind. Constant risk of floods and falling rocks. Tunnels tighter than a Vestal Virgin's privates. You'd get stuck.'

Calamus jabbed Bucco in the belly with the grip end of his short whip. The volunteer gulped loudly. 'You're an embarrassment to this ludus,' he went on. 'If you think I'm going to risk an armpit-plucker like you in the arena, shitting all over the good name of the house of Gurges, you've got another think coming.'

'Do you mean that I'm not to fight at the games, sir?' Bucco asked hopefully. 'I could rake the sand, sir, or prepare food and drink for the men. I'm a good cook. The secret is always to add lots of garum sauce.'

'No, fatso. It's the mines for you,' Calamus said. He paused, and his severe eyes beamed with wicked intent. 'On second thoughts, I've got a much better job. One that involves making a complete fool of yourself. A toga-lifting clown like you will feel right at home.'

'Really? What is it, sir?'

'You'll find out soon enough,' the doctore laughed. Bucco looked puzzled as Calamus turned his back on the recruits and paced across the ludus towards the assembled veterans.

Now that they were alone, Pavo approached Bucco and nodded at his bruises.

'What happened to you?'

Bucco looked away. 'I got into a spot of bother with Carbo.'

Pavo frowned. 'Carbo? I've heard that name before.' He recalled his meeting with the lanista. 'He was talking to Gurges. Something to do with a wager on the games.'

'Spurius Gratius Carbo,' Bucco said. A frown weighed heavily on his forehead. 'He's the bookie I was telling you about.'

Pavo felt pressure build between his ears as he recalled the nights spent listening to his cellmate ruing his misfortune with the dice. Bucco had travelled from his home in Ostia to Paestum in the hope of borrowing money from a distant relative to cover his debts. But the relative had been long since removed from Paestum and Bucco had drowned his sorrows at a local tavern, where he'd started talking with a gladiator recruiter from the local ludus. The money on the table – two thousand sestertii upon signing the contract and a further two thousand at the end of his two-year service, together with winnings on top for each victory he notched up – seemed too good to be true. However, Bucco did not plan to pay off his debts with victories earned in blood.

Pavo fumed. He frowned at Bucco's injuries. 'Carbo did this to you?' he asked doubtfully. 'He didn't strike me as the strong type.'

'Not Carbo.' Bucco winced again and put a hand to the small of his back. 'His cronies. He employs ex-gladiators as bodyguards.' Tears welled in Bucco's eyes. He hesitated to go on. 'I'm sorry, Pavo. I placed a bet on your fight with Britomaris.'

'I see,' Pavo said, confused.

'I don't think you do.' He hesitated, kicking the foot of his post despondently. Then his eyes met Pavo's and he said, 'I bet on you to lose.'

Pavo's entire body jolted. He took a shaky step back from Bucco. His forearms trembled. He fought a strong urge to strike Bucco and dug his fingernails painfully into the palms of his hands.

'Carbo talked me into it,' the volunteer protested. 'I'm sorry, Pavo. I wasn't thinking.'

'There's a surprise,' Pavo murmured through clenched jaws.

'I only made the bet because Carbo offered me stupid odds,' Bucco sniffed. His swollen cheeks were now smeared with tears. 'After your victory, I didn't have the money to pay off my debt when Carbo came calling. He got one of his cronies to beat me up. He told me to come up with the money by the end of the month or else.' His shoulders sagged. 'You have to help me, Pavo.'

'Oh yes, I'll get you out of the giant hole you've dug yourself,' Pavo said scornfully. 'Then you can squander your winnings on another stupid bet with Carbo. Thank you, but no. You're on your own this time, Bucco.'

'I'm not asking you to help *me*,' the volunteer said softly. 'I'm asking for the sake of my family.'

'What in Hades do you mean?' Anger constricted Pavo's neck muscles and made his voice scratchy and stiff. It took a considerable effort for Bucco to raise his anxious head to look at his friend. His eyes were moist and his lips quivered with fear.

'They're gone,' he said. 'Carbo took them. My wife Clodia and my little boys, Papirius and Salonius. Kidnapped them from my home. He said if I couldn't pay, he'd sell them into slavery. He's given me a week to raise the money, but I don't have it. You've got to help me get them back.'

Pavo closed his eyes. Although he was furious with Bucco for wagering money on him to fail against Britomaris, the thought of the man's family suffering for his folly forced Pavo to stifle his resentment. He knew the pain of losing loved ones. A voice scratched at the base of his skull telling him that although it was too late to save his own family, he could help save another. He took a deep breath, swallowed his anger, and opened his eyes. Bucco stared expectantly at him.

'Fine,' Pavo said at last. 'I'll help. But I'm only doing this for your family.'

'Thanks, Pavo. You're a good friend.'

The gladiator raised a palm. 'Save the thanks for when Clodia and your boys are free.'

'What are you going to do?' Bucco asked tentatively.

'Have a word with Carbo and tell him to release them. And

if that doesn't work, I'll wrap my fingers around his fat throat and choke him until he gives up the location of your wife and children.'

Bucco pursed his lips. 'What if he won't tell you?'

'If you have a better plan, Bucco, feel free to share it.'

'Sorry.' Bucco contemplated his feet. 'I'm grateful for your help, really. I just want my family back.' His face reddened with shame. 'I swear to Venus, I'll never gamble again!'

Pavo grunted and rubbed his jaw. 'Do you have someone on the outside? Someone who could get to your family if I found out where they're being held?'

'I think so,' Bucco said. 'An old mucker of mine called Umbrenus. He's a merchant in Puteoli.'

'Be ready to pass a message on to him,' Pavo warned. 'Once I've confronted Carbo, they won't be safe. Umbrenus will have to reach them before Carbo has a chance to sell them on. I take it Carbo is a regular visitor to the ludus? He is a bookie, after all. His trade depends entirely on him judging the form of gladiators for upcoming matches and scamming the public.'

Bucco nodded. 'He comes once a week. Not just to watch. To collect. Half the men in the school have accounts with him. Most of them are in debt, like me. Slaving away at the palus while he profits from other people's misery!' He thumped a plump fist into the palm of his hand.

'When is he coming next?'

'Tomorrow,' said Bucco. 'At dawn.'

CHAPTER FIFTEEN

Darkness lingered like a shroud over the training ground early the next morning. Pavo had been awake most of the night, listening to the horrific sound of a new recruit enduring torturous initiation rituals in a nearby cell. His window overlooked the western side of the ludus, giving him the perfect view of the main entrance to the school. Four heavily armed guards manned the wrought-iron gates day and night. Beyond the ludus Pavo could see a road leading towards the centre of Paestum. The forum glimmered faintly under the soft moonlight. As dawn appeared over the horizon, he permitted himself a grisly thought. He would die in the arena, one way or the other. The Emperor would never allow him to go free, and the strict social mores of Rome dictated that once a man fell into the infamy of life as a gladiator, he could never regain his former status among the aristocracy. His old life was finished. His only purpose was to survive in the arena long enough to slay Hermes, and restore the stained reputation of his family. He resolved not to let anyone – Denter, Murena, Pallas or Carbo – stand in his way. And if they did, he would make them pay.

'Rise and shine, ladies!' Calamus thundered from the far end of the cell block. There was a collective groan from the other recruits as they slowly rose from their slumbers. Pavo heard Calamus marching down the corridor, his footsteps accompanied by a resounding clang as he banged the stem of his whip against each of the cell doors. 'Last man out of his cell goes without rations!' he yelled. His voice grew louder as he neared Pavo's cell. The doctore stopped in front of him. Ignoring Pavo, he directed a venomous stare at the still-snoring Bucco. 'Get up, fatso!' he exhorted, prodding him with his whip through the cell door. 'So help me, gods, I've taken shits that show more signs of life than this lazy bugger.'

After a paltry breakfast of a cup of warm water, Calamus put the trainees through their paces with a series of warm-up exercises, beginning with five circuits of the ludus at a moderate jogging speed followed by twelve sets of twenty reps of ball throws, where the men stood opposite one other in pairs and chucked a weighted pig's bladder at their partner's midriff. At the usual hour Calamus ordered the men to break while he discussed tactics with the specialist coaches. Pavo was still bitter with Bucco for betting against him and he slammed his pig's bladder at the volunteer with a degree of force. Badly winded, Bucco doubled up in pain.

'Bucco!' A familiar high-pitched voice sounded behind Pavo. 'Demonstrating your famous warrior instincts, are you?' Pavo spun around to see Carbo standing beside the sundial, his hands folded behind his back. He appeared to be alone, trusting his safety to the men guarding the household of the lanista. 'My dear friend Gurges must have been desperate, to accept a man of such limited ability into his glorious ludus.'

Bucco straightened his back, rubbing his sore paunch. Carbo nodded to the other recruits. The eighteen men made their way towards the paluses to resume their training. Carbo dismissed Pavo with a wave of his bloated gold-fingered hand. 'You may leave us, young man. I wish to discuss a private matter with Bucco.'

Pavo stood his ground. 'I'm his friend. He told me you kidnapped his family. Now look here. Bucco may owe you money, but the debt is between him and you. Clodia and the boys don't deserve any part of this. Let them go.'

Carbo grinned at Bucco. 'Prickly one, isn't he?' Then he let out a weary sigh, as if he had heard the same argument many times before, and narrowed his eyes at the training ground. 'Perhaps we might discuss things somewhere more secluded,' he continued, angling his head at the balcony above the porticoes. Pavo knew it was not unusual to see Gurges leaning over the balustrade surveying his gladiators. 'One never knows who is watching out here in the open.'

They followed the bookie into a cramped and dimly lit

passageway leading under the porticoes on the east side of the training ground, and turned right into the canteen, which was empty at this time of day. Carbo shuffled in ahead of Pavo and Bucco and propped his considerable girth on the edge of a long trestle table. His skin had reddened from exhaustion and his forehead was heavily beaded with sweat.

'I am a busy man, Pavo,' he said, wiping his brow. 'So I'll get right to the point. Bucco owes me the princely sum of two thousand sestertii.' He frowned at a blood spot on his tunic. 'You are aware that your so-called friend bet on you to lose against Britomaris?'

'Just get on with it,' Pavo said through gritted teeth.

'Since Bucco does not have the money, I have seized his assets, as is my right as a debtor. Being a destitute gambler enrolled in a gladiator school with no property to speak of, he has only three saleable assets. Namely his wife and the two boys.'

Pavo clenched his jaw and stepped into Carbo's face. 'Give him more time to pay. He'll be fighting in the arena soon enough.'

'Have you seen him with a sword?' Carbo sniffed. 'Bucco couldn't fight his way out of a wet sack. His first fight will also be his last.'

Pavo shook his head. 'I'm not here to argue how much he owes,' he said tersely, 'or how he intends to pay you back. I'm here about his family. They're innocent. Leave them out of your dispute.'

'Or what?' Carbo scoffed. 'You're not exactly in a position to issue threats, boy. You forget your station. You're not the son of a respected legate any more. You're just a high-born brat fallen into infamy. No better than a common slave.'

Pavo glared at Carbo. He balled his hands into fists. 'I'll ask you one more time. Release his family at once,' he seethed.

'Let me see,' Carbo replied scathingly as he stroked his drooping chin. He appeared remarkably calm, Pavo thought, given that he was facing a pair of gladiators. Even if one of them was Bucco. 'My answer is no. Bucco cannot pay in coin, so he must pay in flesh. Those are the rules. Besides, Clodia will make a nice bit of cunny, and the boys will fetch a good price at market.'

Carbo tried to push past Pavo. The young fighter blocked his way. Then the bookie flashed a sinister smile and levelled his eyes at a spot past Pavo's shoulder. Footsteps sounded at his back. Pavo looked towards the door. A pair of tall, burly Spaniards blocked the doorway. Their shoulder and back muscles were so large they blotted out the light in the corridor. Both men bore the branded mark of the owner of another gladiator school.

'Allow me to introduce Priscus and Verus,' Carbo said. He nodded at the two men in turn. Priscus cracked his knuckles. 'Formerly champions of the arena in Capua. Now my bodyguards.'

A cold sweat gripped Pavo. He shot a withering look at Bucco as he backed away from the door. 'You didn't say anything about bodyguards,' he muttered.

'Sorry,' Bucco replied quietly, lowering his chin an inch. 'I didn't know.'

'Priscus, Verus,' Carbo ordered with a deft flick of his wrist. 'Teach this brat a lesson.'

Priscus came at Pavo first. He led with his right foot, shaping to unleash a devastating right hook. In a blur of motion Pavo ducked to his right and dropped his left shoulder, stepping out of the way of the balled fist arrowing towards his jaw. As Priscus swiped at thin air, the young man sank to his knees and grabbed the nearest stool with both hands, then sprang upright. At the same time he swung the stool with all his strength. There was a solid crunch as it crashed into Priscus's chin. The Spaniard let out a low grunt, his jaw slamming into the roof of his skull.

Priscus tottered backwards a step. He shook his head clear and charged at Pavo again. This time Pavo swung in the opposite direction, raising the stool from beside his left thigh up and across his right shoulder. Priscus stumbled into its path. His arms went limp by his sides as the edge of the stool thunked against his cheekbone. He fell away, his eyes rolling into the back of his head, and landed in a heap next to the door.

Now Verus tried his luck. The second bodyguard had a gargantuan amount of muscle loaded on to his tall, wide frame. He charged over the body of his stricken comrade and bared his sharpened teeth at Pavo. With outstretched hands he lunged at

113

the legate's son and sent him tumbling to the ground, the stool dropping from his grasp. Pavo swiped a boot at Verus, stopping the bodyguard and giving himself time to scramble to his feet. He blinked and saw Verus tramping towards him. Bucco tried to block his path but the bodyguard roared hoarsely and elbowed him out of the way. Verus charged at Pavo, his gigantic fists swinging madly in front of him.

The gladiator seized a broom from a rack on the wall next to the door. Then he whirled back around to face Verus. The ground shook with the thunderous pounding of the bodyguard's boots. As a punch flew towards his exposed chest, Pavo dropped to a crouch and jabbed the shaft of the broom at Verus in a powerful thrust. The bodyguard had just enough time to register a look of horror as the blunt grip plunged towards his midriff and struck him on the groin. He keeled over, gasping in agony, his shovel-like hands pawing at his manhood. Without hesitation Pavo tilted the broom handle up a notch and swung it in a furious arc at the side of the bodyguard's head. The sturdy wooden shaft cracked into his temple. The bodyguard's head jolted sharply to the right, his neck muscles shuddering with tension. Then it snapped back to its natural position, and Verus fell to his knees, choking and gasping and groaning. Pavo tossed the broom aside and watched the second bodyguard slump to the ground. The blood was rushing in his ears, his heart tapping frantically against his breastplate.

'Pavo, look out!' Bucco shouted.

As Pavo glanced across his shoulder at Bucco he caught something gleaming to his right. Spinning fully around, he came face to face with Carbo. He went very still as the bookie pressed the tip of a dagger to his throat. Carbo fumed at Pavo through his pinched nostrils. For a moment he looked poised to plunge the dagger into the young man's neck. Then he smiled from the corner of his mouth.

'You surprise me, young man,' he said. 'You may surprise someone else too.'

Pavo glanced calmly at the dagger the bookie was holding. The tip glinted lethally in the murky gloom. 'What do you mean?'

'I had dismissed you as a one-off, as Gurges and the doctore have done. Gods know, I've seen plenty of gladiators win a surprise victory and come unstuck on their second appearance.' Carbo flicked his eyes to the pair of bodyguards groaning and writhing in pain on the ground. 'But you just took out two of my best men.'

'Gladiators get old very quickly,' Pavo said.

A smile swelled across the bookie's flabby jowls as he went on, 'If there's one thing I've learned in all my years watching men shed blood in the arena, it's this. Being a gladiator isn't just about physical strength. It's about thinking on your feet. You, young man . . . you show admirable resourcefulness when your back is against the wall.'

'Blame it on my childhood. I grew up in legionary camps,' Pavo said. 'I learned nothing from books or tutors. Soldiers taught me everything I know.'

'Interesting.' The bookie dragged the tip of the dagger up Pavo's neck, as if giving him a shave. 'However, some things cannot be taught. Such as fearlessness when faced with the sharp end of a blade.' He traced the dagger up to Pavo's Adam's apple. 'You didn't flinch when you saw the dagger. You didn't even blink. You cannot teach a man how to forget fear. It is a rare quality, and I have witnessed only one other man who never shuddered at the sight of raw steel. Perhaps you have heard of him? His name is Hermes.'

Pavo stirred at the mention of his bitter enemy. His expression remained grim. 'Tell me where you're keeping the family.'

Carbo laughed as he raised the dagger, the tip dancing between Pavo's eyes. 'It's not that simple. I'm afraid your friend owes me a great deal of money. And he's not the only one indebted to me. In order to run a profitable business, a bookmaker must strictly enforce the obligations of his clients, no?'

'Get to your point,' Pavo said.

'I cannot release the family now, but nor will I sell them into slavery. Not yet, at least. Instead, I propose a deal.'

'What kind of deal?' Bucco asked.

'Not with you,' Carbo snapped. He winked at Pavo. 'With the young hero of the arena. Seeing you dispose of Priscus and Verus makes me think you have a better chance against Denter than everyone else believes. Though the mob will back you, informed opinion suggests that Denter will carve you up like roast mutton.'

Pavo grunted. 'Denter is a washed-up drunk.'

'He used to be.' Carbo admired his dagger for a moment. 'But I have it on good authority that he is sober and clean and training hard in preparation for the fight. The man training him is a soldier, I believe.' He shrugged. 'And you fight with inferior weapons. Even half-fit, Denter would pose you serious problems.'

'But you would back me to win?'

Carbo let his smile melt into his sagging, porous cheeks. 'I wouldn't go that far. But I think you have a decent chance. Gurges, in particular, has staked heavily on a Denter victory.'

'The lanista bet against me?' Pavo said as a puzzled look unfolded on his face.

'Rather the trend, it appears,' Carbo replied acerbically. He glanced at Bucco. 'You really ought to keep better company, young man. My point is, a lot of money has been placed on Denter. If you win, I will make myself a handsome margin.' He placed a finger carefully to his bottom lip. 'Perhaps then I could be persuaded to clear the debt with Bucco and release his family.'

'Swear to the gods you'll set them free,' Pavo demanded.

'We have a deal,' Carbo replied, retracting the dagger and secreting it under his tunic. 'You had better return to training. Take it from me, boy, there's plenty of work for you to do. You might have raw talent, but Denter has never lost in his long career.'

'There's a first time for everything,' Pavo said.

Carbo responded with a snort. 'Don't get too cocky. You only have a matter of weeks before the fight.' The bookie clamped his lips. 'A final word of warning. Denter is notorious for using dirty tricks at the banquet for the gladiators the night before the games begin. The fool once ripped out a tooth in front of his opponent. To show the man he didn't care about pain, you see. Whatever antics he tries against you at the banquet, don't let him get to you.'

With that, Carbo lumbered towards the door. He stopped by the prone bodies of his two guards and booted one of them in the stomach. 'Priscus! Verus!' he screeched, clapping his hands. 'On your feet!'

The two groggy bodyguards shot evil looks at Pavo as they picked themselves off the floor. They trailed behind Carbo as he lumbered out of the canteen and together they disappeared into the darkness of the corridor. As Pavo watched them slink away, Bucco appeared by his side.

'Bloody hell.' He puffed his fat cheeks. 'Denter sounds like a right vicious bastard.'

'Thanks for the vote of confidence, Bucco.'

'I didn't mean that. It just sounds like it's going to be a seriously tough fight. I'm sorry, Pavo. If there was some other way I could get Clodia and the boys back, I'd do it.'

In truth, nothing Bucco said could make Pavo feel more disheartened about his prospects against Denter than he already did. Thoughts of the looming fight filled him with a sense of dread. The previous night he'd believed his opponent would be a dishevelled former gladiator. Now he had to confront a different reality. He would be coming up against a highly motivated opponent with a string of notable victories under his belt. Worse, it wasn't only his own life that depended on the outcome. The lives of Clodia and two boys were in his hands, and quite possibly Bucco's as well. The responsibility weighed heavily on Pavo's shoulders, and as he departed the canteen and headed back to the training ground, the words of the bookie resonated inside his head. A drunk, wild Denter would prove a tricky but beatable opponent, even though Pavo would be hampered by his weapons of a net and trident. But a sober Denter, motivated by rage and trained by a soldier, would be a formidable foe.

Pavo prayed to the gods that Carbo was wrong.

CHAPTER SIXTEEN

A mild breeze drifted over the crowd as Pavo and the other recruits and veterans stood in a line at the southern end of the forum square under the watchful glare of a dozen heavily armed guards from the local barracks. The gladiators were bare-chested and wore plain linen loincloths. They would not have a chance to brandish their weapons and shields until they set foot in the arena. A flock of onlookers had crammed into the surrounding streets to inspect them at the open-air banquet.

The crowd was far bigger than Pavo had expected. People peered out of the first-floor windows of the taverns and shops arranged to the north. Others jostled for the best view from the heightened steps of a nearby modest theatre. All of them looked at the gladiators with a mixture of fear and awe. Pavo had not ventured outside the ludus for six weeks, and had been shielded from the build-up to the games within the walls of the school. Now he witnessed first-hand the excitement trembling on the faces of the crowd. Women fanned themselves as they ogled the gladiators' oiled, muscular torsos. Children fought with toy swords. Half a dozen stalls had been set up around the square for fans to purchase carved miniature statuettes of their favourite fighters, as well as necklaces and various trinkets. Another sold copies of the programme for the following afternoon's bouts. All the while the smell of grilled pork wafted through the air as merchants hawked small sausages to the hungry, impatient crowd.

Pavo watched the sun sink behind the horizon. In the middle distance he spotted the ludus, situated on rising ground amid the entertainment quarter to the north of the forum. The arena stood to the right. Its stone exterior glowed a pale hue in the dying embers of late autumn. A dozen silhouettes laboured near the top row of the seating area. They were busy mounting linen awnings in preparation for the following day. A cracking roar shook through the sky as the workers flogged the awning, flattening the linen sheet before attaching it to poles and crossbeams fixed to the top of the arena.

'Look at that lot,' said Bucco grimly. 'There must be a thousand people come here to gawk at us. Maybe more.' His usually cheerful voice was now stifled with fear and it provoked a pang of anxiety in Pavo. He had never attended a gladiatorial banquet before, but he understood that it was customary to host them in the open. Tradition dictated that it was a chance for the gladiators to publicly express their stoicism in the face of impending doom. The open-air feast also had the added effect of generating enthusiasm among the mob ahead of the fight. Pavo watched a crowd of men descend on Carbo to fritter away their hard-earned money.

'At least we get some grub out of it,' Bucco said sourly, pointing out the trestle tables being set up in the middle of the forum square. 'Funnily enough, I don't feel hungry.'

His tone surprised Pavo. Normally Bucco would be licking his lips at the thought of a slap-up meal, but his appetite had deserted him at the thought that the fate of his family hung in the balance. Pavo glanced sympathetically at his friend. He was gripped by the same feeling, as if a horde of mice were scurrying around his guts.

Pavo snorted as slaves laid out trays of food on the tables for all to see. There were countless bowls of freshly cut lettuce and plates of salted tuna garnished with quails' eggs, along with lumps of ripened cheese and shellfish and raw vegetables. Silver goblets were topped up with sweetened wine from large jugs. Further trays of stuffed fowl, sow's udders and ox tongues were also brought out. The feast made Pavo feel sick, despite the ravenous hunger in his belly. Such extravagant foods had been a staple of his child-hood when his father had enjoyed the worship of the Fifth Legion, respected and feared in equal measure by the tight-lipped men of the Senate. Each tray of food reminded him of a happier time, of a life he would never be able to return to. He looked away before the rumbling in his stomach grew irresistible.

'Makes you wonder why they're laying on all this food,' Bucco mused, scratching his elbow. 'We have to train eight hours a day on a diet of stale bread and gruel, and *now* they decide to give us a proper feast.' He shook his head at the logic.

'They treat us well today because they expect us to perish tomorrow. Romans like their condemned men to die on a full belly,' Pavo growled. He shook his head. 'Anyway, you still haven't told me about your role at the games.'

The thought tickled Bucco and his mood lightened somewhat at the news he had kept back from his friend. He patted his considerable paunch and a pained smile crossed his lips as he declared, 'You're looking at the new comedy act. The doctore reckons I'm a natural at making people laugh.'

Seeing the look of dismay on Pavo's face, he went on, 'Oh, it's not so bad. I get to provide a spot of light entertainment for the mob between fights. Better yet,' the volunteer tapped the side of his nose, 'I won't get chopped up by some battle-hardened Syrian tomorrow.'

Pavo studied his friend. 'You're in good cheer.'

Bucco wedged his thumbs down the front of his loincloth and lifted his chin defiantly at the crowd. 'Comes with the territory, my friend. When you're born in the gutter, there's no point bleating about your lot in life. You've just got to get on with it, haven't you? Anyway, I wouldn't change places with a high-born lad like you for all the Falernian in Campania. All that scheming and having to watch your back. From what I can tell, you posh lads get very rich, and then you end up exiled, condemned to a ludus or worse, butchered in some back alley in Rome by a squad of Praetorians. Give me the simple life any day.'

'How very noble of you, Bucco. Perhaps you'd care to fight Denter yourself and use the winnings to pay off your debts to Carbo, Gurges and any other unfortunate soul you happen to owe money to.'

Bucco fell silent.

'No,' Pavo went on. 'I rather thought not.'

With a heavy sigh, Pavo searched the forum for Gurges. He found the lanista mingling with the other dignitaries in attendance on the marble steps of the public hall to the rear of the square. Servants hovered around the area, presenting trays of figs, olives, dates and other appetisers. Gurges stood to the side of the main group of dignitaries, Pavo saw. He was in conference with a tall, dark man with sculpted cheekbones and smoothly shaven skin.

'Who's that good-looking bloke with Gurges?' Bucco asked.

'Pallas,' Pavo muttered darkly, recognising the man with a start.

The crowd hushed. Pavo and Bucco faced forward as a squat man stepped out in front of the trestle tables and climbed on to a temporary wooden platform that had been erected in the square. The man cleared his throat.

'Gods, the herald,' Bucco grumbled. 'Let's hope this old fool doesn't blather on like the ones back in Ostia.'

Pavo glared at his friend. Men and women at the back of the crowd pricked their ears. Silence descended over the forum.

'His imperial majesty, Emperor Claudius, is proud to announce a unique spectacle for the people of Paestum,' the herald declared in a gravelly voice that carried over the heads of the crowd and resonated through the streets.

A cold sweat gripped Pavo as he realised that his victory over Britomaris had only helped consolidate Pallas's position of trust within the imperial household. Claudius might hold the title of emperor, he reflected glumly, but the true power lay with Pallas and his lackey Murena. Typical of my luck, he thought bitterly. I've made enemies of the most powerful men in Rome.

The herald went on, 'A day of spectacular gladiator fights will take place at the arena tomorrow, sponsored by the Emperor, represented in person by the imperial secretary, Marcus Antonius Pallas.'

Pavo looked back at the freedman. He waved at the crowd, milking the applause. Beside him Murena whispered something into his ear. Pallas sneered.

'The morning will see executions!'

The crowd cheered as the herald gestured to a ragged line of condemned men standing to the right of the gladiators. Chains were clamped around their gaunt wrists and ankles. Their skeletal, bearded faces were shorn of hope. One or two of the simpler souls had ravenous looks in their eyes as they watched the slaves carry yet more trays of food over to the tables.

'In the afternoon there will be twenty pairs of fights,' the herald bellowed, to another raucous chorus of approval from the mob. 'The main attraction will feature two legends of the arena fighting to the death.' He gestured to Pavo and the doctore to step forward from the line of gladiators. 'First, the challenger. I present to you the son of a treasonous legate and the gladiator who defeated the scourge of Rome, Britomaris . . . Marcus Valerius Pavo.'

The crowd erupted into riotous applause as Calamus escorted Pavo towards the middle of the square. He climbed on to the wooden platform, with the doctore, as his trainer, standing to one side. The cheers swelled. Men shouted themselves hoarse in cele- bration of their new hero. Women elbowed their way to the front of the crowd and ogled him. The scene momentarily overwhelmed Pavo before the nagging anxieties of his predicament returned to his thoughts. Despite his efforts to master the technique of a retiarius, he still felt far more confident with a sword in his hand. He was untested in combat with his new weapons. A pang of regret hit him, and he secretly wished that he had Optio Macro by his side for his match against Denter. Despite their differences, Pavo and Macro had shared a mutual understanding of swords- manship and a common hatred for the bureaucracy and infighting that festered within the heart of Rome.

A gang of boisterous men loitering outside a tavern broke into drunken chants. 'Meat hooks for Pavo!' they sang, raising jugs of wine in the air. 'Meat hooks for Pavo! Oh, they'll be dragging you out with a meat hook!'

'Charming folk,' said Pavo.

'Hooligans from Pompeii,' Calamus retorted. 'I've seen them in the arena down that way a few times. They worship Denter. Of course, they don't really go to watch the fight. They just get pissed and beat up locals. Take no notice of them.'

Pavo looked back at the gladiators. Amadocus was working his bruised features into knots of rage at the adulation being bestowed on the younger fighter. Pavo looked ahead as the herald swept a hand in an arc in front of his chest. The mob hushed.

'And who will Pavo face tomorrow?' The herald projected his voice further to make himself heard above the hooligans. He left the question hanging on his lips for a moment, until he had whipped the crowd into a frenzy of anticipation. Then he continued: 'Winner of forty-nine bouts in the arena. Conqueror of Felix the Fearless. Destroyer of Niger the Thracian. I give you the pride of Pompeii. Decimus . . . Cominius . . . Denter!'

The crowd parted to the west. Pavo focused on a figure disgorging from the mob and got his first look at Denter.

'Oh, shit,' he muttered under his breath.

One look at his opponent confirmed Carbo's warning that Denter had been training flat out. Despite his relatively slender physique, he possessed sharply defined muscles on his arms and shoulders and a chiselled chest. Pavo had never seen Denter fight in the flesh, but from his body shape he supposed that the gladiator cut an agile figure on the sand.

He looked on intently as Denter pumped a clenched fist in the air and strode towards the platform. A chorus of boos and jeers greeted him, broken by delirious roars from the hooligans. Denter stopped. Turning to confront the crowd, he clutched his manhood and made a lewd gesture in their direction, prompting a frenzied wave of obscenities. A second figure shoved the gladiator through the baying crowd. Pavo presumed this was Denter's trainer. He craned his neck to get a better look at the man. But his view was obscured by outstretched arms from the mob clawing angrily at Denter. The second figure hurried his charge to the platform just as the mood among the crowd started to turn poisonous. With a final shunt the gladiator stumbled forward, to the obvious displeasure of the herald, and clambered on to the platform to hoots of approval from the Pompeiians.

Up close Denter had an intimidating presence. Crazed eyes bore down on Pavo from above a thickly bearded face. Tattoos tapered from his neck down to his forearms. Breathing heavily through his nostrils, he closed in on Pavo so that the pair were standing toe to toe. Then the veteran lowered his chin an inch and stared at Pavo down the length of his thin nose. His breath reeked of sickly-sweet wine. Beyond his opponent's shoulder, Pavo spotted one of the hooligans painting an offensive slogan across the front of a tavern.

'So you're the great Marcus Valerius Pavo,' Denter slurred. 'You don't look like much.' A grin broke out on his face. 'Then again, your old man Titus was a fucking coward.'

'He was a respected legate,' Pavo stated proudly. 'He was no coward.'

Denter screwed up his face in disgust. 'He was a tight-fisted bastard! Never let us plunder anything worth a damn. I only joined the bloody legion so I could get some loot, murder a few Gauls and rape a few tarts. Then Titus came along lecturing us about honour and duty. Pah! All that talk didn't stop your old man being gutted.'

'He was murdered,' Pavo said sullenly. 'By Hermes. In the arena.'

'I don't care if Jupiter himself did the deed,' Denter blasted. 'I just wish I'd the chance to carve up the stuck-up old fool. Titus booted me out of the legion. He forced me into this career, living for years among slaves and foreign scum. I'd have loved to watch him die. When the Emperor asked me to butcher Titus's son, I happily accepted. Get ready to join your gutless old man in the Underworld.'

Pavo looked away again and got a clear look at Denter's trainer. A hot streak of anger pumped through his veins as Denter began flexing his muscles at the crowd.

'I don't believe it,' Pavo seethed. 'It can't be him. It can't be!'

'Look at me, you little shit,' Denter said.

But Pavo blanked Denter. He simply stared at the trainer stationed at the foot of the platform, muttering his name under his breath.

'Macro . . .'

CHAPTER SEVENTEEN

A chill ran up Pavo's spine at the sight of the soldier. A contrite expression flashed across the optio's face. Then Macro shook his head firmly and resolved his features into a stern look, acknowledging Pavo with a brief nod. Pavo had not seen Macro since that fateful afternoon in the Julian plaza, and the sight of him now pricked the gladiator with a mixture of shock and suspicion.

'What are you doing here?' he hissed.

'What does it look like?' The optio cocked his head at Denter. 'Training this old sweat.'

'You traitor!' Pavo exploded with fury. 'I trusted you to help me defeat Britomaris and now you conspire against me?'

Macro started to protest. He was cut short by a scuffle breaking out in the crowd as the hooligans and local supporters of Pavo clashed outside the tavern. There was the piercing sound of clay shattering when one of the Pompeiians threw a jug at the mob. The herald raced through the rest of his announcement, striving to make himself heard above the fracas. Some of the Pompeiians traded punches with the crowd. Their comrades hooted and hollered. A flustered Pallas signalled to the sparse number of men from the urban watch, who quickly intervened, separating the fighters and moving the Pompeiians on.

The doctore marched to the front of the line of gladiators and clapped his hands.

'Right, then, ladies,' he said. 'Time to eat.'

The men began hurrying towards the benches. Calamus immediately raised a palm. Groaning, they halted.

'Now remember what I said. Don't go stuffing your bellies. Eat a little, not a lot. I don't want to see any of you shitting out your guts when you step on to the sand.' Calamus shot a look of contempt at the condemned criminals. 'Leave the pigging out to those sorry bastards. It's their last night before they tramp off to the Underworld. The rest of you have a chance of walking out alive. Some of you, anyway.' Calamus looked at Pavo as he uttered the last words, and laughed.

Pavo took up his spot on the bench in a daze. The condemned men gathered meekly around a separate table, their chins tucked closely to their chests as they picked at the food on their plates in morbid silence. Half of the crowd stayed to watch the gladiators eat what would for some be their last meal. Others turned their attention to the goods on offer at the stalls, or departed to debate the upcoming games over a jug of cheap wine in the nearest tavern. Bucco plonked himself next to Pavo and looked half-heartedly at a tray of dainty pastries. His normally voracious appetite had deserted him. He slid a tray of shellfish across to his companion.

'You'd better eat something,' he implored. 'You don't want to fight Denter on an empty stomach.'

'I'm not hungry,' Pavo replied pithily.

'Makes two of us, then,' Bucco muttered as he stared at his feet.

'What's the matter, Roman?' a glottal voice spat from further down the table. Pavo leaned forward to see Amadocus gorging on a bowl of sausages. Morsels of meat spilled down his front. He jerked his head in the direction of Macro. 'Upset that your boyfriend has found a new lover?'

Pavo did not reply. Privately he was crestfallen at the thought of Macro training Denter. He struggled to fathom why the optio would help seal the fate of someone who had been wronged by the imperial palace. He made a silent plea to the gods to curse Macro.

A sudden burst of angry shouts broke out at the next table. Pavo awoke from his daydream and looked across to see Denter throwing Orodes to the ground and casually dropping into his spot at the bench. The other gladiators at the table stared at him in silence.

'What do you think you're doing?' Orodes snapped as he scraped himself off the ground.

Denter grabbed a fistful of shellfish and shovelled them ravenously into his mouth. He washed down the mouthful with a loud slurp of wine and let out a monstrous belch. 'You were in my seat, Persian.'

Anger rumbled in Orodes's throat. He stood behind Denter and waited for him to move. But the veteran kept piling more food on his plate and swigging from the wine. Orodes stared coldly at the back of Denter's head. Denter polished off the wine and slammed the cup on the table. In a blink, Orodes snatched the cup, hoisting it like a trophy above his head, and brought it crashing down on top of Denter's skull. The sound of shattering pottery pierced the air. Denter froze. A wild smile formed on his lips as wine mixed with blood from his head wound and soaked his beard. He licked the mixture off his bottom lip. Then he slowly rose from the bench and turned to face Orodes. The Persian gulped with abject fear. His eyes widened with the realisation that striking Denter had been a terrible mistake.

In a sudden burst of anger, Denter charged at Orodes and wrapped his long arms around his neck. The other gladiators looked on in shock as Denter twisted the Persian's head at an angle and clamped his teeth around his ear. Orodes howled in agony. Denter chewed on the ear for several painful moments. Then he ripped his head away in a furious grunt. Orodes squealed like a boiled rat as the ear was torn from his head. Blood sprayed the trays of food on the table. Denter spat mangled skin and cartilage from his mouth, his chin awash with blood, and let out a chilling roar.

'Carbo was right,' Bucco said. 'Denter really is crazy.'

Two guards stormed towards Denter. A savage grin formed on the gladiator's lips. The others shuffled back as Denter lowered to a crouch in front of the abandoned table, securing his palms against the edge. Springing upright, he tipped the table on to its side, then released his grip so it came crashing down at the onrushing guards. There was a cacophony of noise as an assortment of jugs and cups and trays smashed on the ground. The two guards scrambled to get out of the way as the table pounded down on top of them. The thud of wood against the paved ground was accompanied by the distinct crack of shattering ribcages. A third guard attacked Denter from across the forum, slashing his sword wildly. The blade hacked across Denter's back and drew a howl of pain from the veteran. He clasped a hand to his back as another six guards swooped over their fallen comrades and surrounded him. Denter pumped a fist defiantly at the sky, much to the delight of the hooligans being marched away from the square. Then he disappeared behind a whirlwind of armour and swords. After a brief struggle, the guards wrestled him to the ground.

'That's it!' Gurges fumed, his face stitched with rage. 'The banquet is over! You!' The lanista jabbed a bony finger at the chest of the nearest guard. 'Round up the gladiators. I want them escorted back to the ludus at once. Condemned criminals are to return to jail for the night.'

The guards snapped into action, roughly hauling the gladiators to their bare feet and marching them into a ragged line. Bucco staggered into place as Pavo spied Gurges returning to the imperial secretary, his head hung low and his palms clasped humbly in front of him. Although Pavo was out of earshot, the tone of the lanista's voice told the young gladiator that he was in the middle of a grovelling apology. The freedman looked unimpressed. Murena, Pavo noticed, had quietly slipped away from Pallas's side to seek out Macro.

A guard grasped Pavo by the forearm and shifted him into line behind Bucco. The volunteer cast a final despondent look at the feast left on the trestle tables. Then the guards marched the gladiators out of the square and back to the ludus.

Macro watched Pavo and the other gladiators tramp out of the forum. The mob lingered, captivated by the abrupt outbreak of violence. The optio stared at Denter. His charge remained pinned to the ground by the guards. A pair of servants helped Orodes to his feet. Gurges instructed them to escort the wounded Persian to the ludus infirmary. The optio stared at the severed ear lying on the ground amid the scattered olives and breads and shards of shattered clay cups. He looked up to see Murena picking his way across the carnage.

'What in Hades was that about?' the aide rasped. His eyes were narrow and sharp like the teeth of a wolf. 'We had a deal, Optio. You were supposed to keep Denter sober until after his fight with Pavo.'

'And I would have kept my word if you hadn't invited him along to the banquet,' Macro countered with a snort and a hard glare. 'I've been minding that lunatic for six long weeks, but I can't watch him every hour of the day. My back was turned for a minute. Next thing I know, some lads are buying him rounds in the tavern. If we hadn't had to bother with all this pomp and ceremony, Denter would be tucked up in bed now, sober as a state funeral.'

Murena flashed a scolding look at the soldier.

'I don't tell you how to do your job, Optio. Don't tell me how to do mine.'

Macro shrugged. 'Just saying.'

Two guards dragged Denter to his feet and slipped their arms across his shoulders. His eyes were glazed and heavily lidded. Drool slobbered from his slack lips and dribbled down his chest. He mumbled something incoherent about Titus. Macro and Murena watched the guards manhandle him away from the square. Macro yawned.

'Well, that's his chances of winning fucked,' the optio announced.

'Not necessarily,' Murena replied.

'What do you mean?' Macro scoffed. 'The man's out of his skull. He'll not recover in time for tomorrow. And look at that.' He pointed to the injury inflicted by the guard. Blood puckered out of a crescent-shaped gash running the length of his back. Macro had seen plenty of wounds in his years in the Second Legion, and he could instantly discern that it was not deep enough to be fatal. Which is why we stab instead of slash in the military, he reminded himself. But it would still require treatment, and in the meantime Denter would find his movement severely restricted.

'The idiot will be lucky if he can hold his bloody sword straight,' the optio concluded.

Murena laughed. It was a cagey laugh and one that Macro had heard before, shortly after Pavo had conquered Britomaris, when the optio had learned of the plot by the aide to poison the young man. Now the hairs on Macro's neck bristled.

'It's taken care of, Optio.'

'What have you done?' Macro hissed at the aide, fighting an urge to break his spindly neck.

Murena waved a hand at Gurges. The lanista nodded and scurried towards his waiting litter. 'Let's just say that Denter won't be the only one finding it difficult in the arena tomorrow.'

Macro frowned. 'Suit yourself. But I'd be wary of Pavo losing, if I were you.'

Murena looked sharply at the soldier. 'Why?'

'That lot, for starters.' Macro jerked a thumb at the Pompeiians. The thinly spread guards were struggling to move the gang on. Their number had doubled in size and their mood had grown openly hostile. 'More of them are on the way. From what I hear, the fans from Pompeii travel in large numbers.'

Murena smiled weakly at the hooligans. 'I hardly think a few fist fights between rival gladiator fans are cause for concern, Optio.'

'It's not them you should be worried about.' Macro folded his arms stiffly across his chest and nodded at the overturned trestle table. 'The mob loves Pavo. They won't want to see their hero getting chopped down, and they won't like a bunch of nutters from Pompeii crowing about it. You think the mood was ugly today, wait until you see what they're like tomorrow.'

CHAPTER EIGHTEEN

The roar of the crowd trembled through the arena and shook the building to its foundations.

'No mercy for Mesonius!' the crowd yelled in unison. 'Kill the murmillo!'

The arena shuddered again as the crowd gave full throat to its bloodlust. Pavo felt sick. The air in the tunnel was laden with the stench of sweat and vomit. Hysterical screams emanated from the makeshift infirmary. Since Pavo topped the programme, his fight against Denter would be the last contest of the day's schedule. He had spent the afternoon listening to the shrill clash of metal, the roar of the mob and the howls of men being operated on by Achaeus. The closer he edged towards his fight, the more the passage of time seemed to stretch out, straining his nerves to the limit.

He steadied his breathing and focused on the task in front of him. He watched Calamus and waited for the signal to enter the arena. The doctore stood with his back to Pavo as he looked on at the action unfolding beyond the gates at the mouth of the tunnel. Two guards manned either side of the gates, their hands resting on the pommels of their swords. Six more were positioned at equal intervals down the length of the tunnel. They had kept a watchful eye over the men throughout the day. With good reason, Pavo thought. The moment before he stepped out to face death was the only time when Rome trusted a gladiator with a sharpened blade.

The crowd hushed. The herald's voice resonated through the passageways as he formally announced the next pairing of gladiators.

'It's time,' Calamus growled.

A chill clamped around the back of Pavo's neck. Two orderlies hurried down the tunnel from the armoury. One of them clutched Pavo's weapons, the net slung over his shoulder while his hands gripped the trident and dagger. The second orderly carried the keys to the armoury, as well as a large clay cup. Accepting the weapons, Pavo dumped the net by his feet, tied the dagger to his belt, and concentrated on testing the balance of the trident.

Calamus turned away from the gate. He seemed amused at Pavo's tense expression. 'Don't look so glum, boy. Most of the recruits die on first appearance. You did well to make it this far.'

Pavo clamped his jaws shut and turned his attention to the net. The rope was made of soft flax fibres spun together in yarn and twisted into thin strands. It was round and wide enough to trap a large man underneath, with small meshes to make it harder for the ensnared gladiator to escape. Sharpened lead pellets were fixed to the edges of the net to make it easier to cast. Although Pavo felt terribly naked without a helmet or a shield, he would not be hampered by the weight of the equipment. Aside from the trident and net, he wore guards on his left arm and leg, with a shoulder guard mounted above his right arm padding to provide extra protection to his net-throwing arm and a flared tip on the shoulder guard for shielding his head behind should Denter aim for the jugular.

Pavo was securing the loop on the corner of the net around his left wrist when an orderly shoved the clay cup in front of his face. He lowered his gaze and a felt an instant wave of nausea hit him. The cup was brimming with a lumpy liquid the colour of coal and sprinkled with grey flakes. The smell clogged Pavo's nostrils. He choked back the nausea rising in his throat.

'Gods!' He looked horrified. 'What foul brew is this?'

'Standard pre-fight concoction, courtesy of Achaeus,' Calamus answered matter-of-factly for the orderly. 'It's got a secret ingredient in it. Helps you keep your nerves in the arena. Drink up, lad.'

Pavo frowned at the cup. 'I'd rather not.'

The doctore turned to face Pavo. 'You little shit,' he said, his voice coarse and sharp, like a blade slicing through fabric. 'Still think there's one set of rules for you and one for everyone else, eh? Give me that!' He snatched the cup from the orderly. Drops of the liquid spilled over the rim and slopped on to his fingers.

'Drink!' he insisted.

Pavo wrinkled his nose. Just looking at the cup made him queasy. 'Thanks, but I'll pass.'

'Drink. That's an order!' Calamus snapped. Spittle flecked Pavo across the cheek. The doctore snatched the trident and thrust the cup at the gladiator. Pavo took a deep breath, clamped his eyes shut and poured the mixture into his mouth. He swallowed nervously. He could feel his stomach squirming with the inclination to retch. As the liquid slithered down his throat, he was left with an acrid taste in his mouth. Then he leaned forward, pressing his palms against the wall, and dry-heaved as he fought his desire to puke. The wall shuddered with the movements of the crowd above. Pavo could hear the doctore's laugh ringing in his ears as he spat out bitter lumps of the drink. Wiping his mouth clean, he stood upright and flashed a look of withering contempt at Calamus. He could feel the concoction sloshing around in his guts.

'How's that?' The doctore grinned. 'Better?'

'Worse,' Pavo groaned. 'What in Hades is in it?'

'Animal ashes, charred roots and fish guts mixed with vinegared water.' Calamus grinned broadly. 'The taste of victory, that is.'

The orderlies slipped away. The screams abated. Pavo looked back down the tunnel and searched for a friendly face. But Bucco had retired to the ludus after his lunchtime comedy fight with a dwarf, together with the victorious gladiators. Even though he had the doctore and half a dozen others for company, Pavo felt very alone.

'Right then.' Calamus slapped his charge on the shoulder. 'Off you go.'

The doctore shoved the trident at Pavo's chest. The young man clasped it in his right hand, with his left gripping the rolled-up net. Behind Calamus the gates creaked as the guards cranked them open to a terrific wall of noise from the crowd. Pavo brushed past the doctore and strode up the passage towards Denter, thinking that Calamus would not be shedding any tears if he died.

He emerged into the arena, blinking in the glare of the late autumn sun. His ears were assaulted by the terrible din echoing from all sides. A faintly stale stench of spilled blood lingered in the air. Dark stains tarnished the glittering sand. Pavo shielded his eyes. Yesterday's gently fluttering breeze had dissipated. Now the atmosphere in the arena was muggy, with the massed ranks of spectators packed tightly inside the amphitheatre and the air thick with blood and sweat. Cold beads of sweat trickled down Pavo's back. The heat of the arena smothered him. His mouth was salty from the charcoal drink and he craved a sip of water.

Trumpets blared. The roar of the crowd reached a new crescendo and Pavo sensed ten thousand necks craning to get a look at him as he paced towards the middle of the arena. Spectators had squeezed in shoulder to shoulder. The capacity crowd throbbed with excitement and anticipation. Pavo ran his eyes across the galleries. The arena in Paestum had four levels, with a steep balbic set at the foot of the lowest gallery to act as a parapet and protect the aristocrats from the bloodletting that took place in the arena. A short step up from the balbic stood the podium. The place reserved for the Emperor had been left unoccupied in a nod to his ultimate sponsorship of the spectacle. Murena and Pallas sat either side of the empty seat. Gurges had managed to secure a place in the gallery immediately behind the freedmen. The lanista was dressed in his ceremonial outfit of an off-white woollen toga cumbersomely draped over his slight figure. Shadows wavered across the dignitaries from the awnings flapping above the arena. Gurges had skimped on the size of the awnings, Pavo realised. The sheets provided relief only for the dignitaries assembled at the podium and the surrounding galleries.

'Oi, fisherman! Catch me a sardine!' a voice shouted from a section of the gallery above the tunnel. A chorus of laughter rippled through the crowd. Pavo turned to face the spectator. He was a savagely fat man. His face was blasted red by the sun and the jug of wine in his hands. He stood up from his seat and shook his fist at Pavo. 'Denter is going to have your guts for supper.'

Pavo recognised the man from the gang of Pompeiians at the banquet the previous day. With a start he realised that entire galleries were taken up by Denter's supporters. Their number had swelled to fill a quarter of the arena. Despite being outnumbered, they quickly set about stoking tension between the rival supporters, drowning out the locals with a string of rhyming chants that detailed the sexual proclivities of Paestum's women. Towards the highest tier of seats several drunken Pompeiians stood up and bared their hairy backsides to Pavo in unison.

The umpire tapped his foot impatiently in the middle of the arena. Gritting his teeth, Pavo tried to clear his mind of all distractions. An image of Hermes loomed large in his mind, reminding him of his purpose. He paced towards the umpire with renewed vigour, determined to triumph over Denter.

A wave of boos from three-quarters of the arena announced the entrance of his opponent. Denter stormed out of the opposite tunnel and half ran across the sand towards Pavo and the umpire. Boisterous cheers erupted from the hooligans. Pavo focused on the veteran as he drew nearer. Then Denter lowered his legionary shield a notch and Pavo felt the blood freeze in his veins as he saw a coat of ringmail protecting his opponent's torso. Gasps broke out among the mob. Pavo had been to many fights at the Statilius Taurus arena in Rome, but he had never heard of a gladiator fighting with such heavy protection. He lifted his eyes to the podium. Pallas and Murena swapped knowing glances. Gurges smirked. Around them dignitaries squirmed in their seats at this crude manipulation of the odds in favour of Denter.

'Those filthy Greeks,' Pavo muttered under his breath. 'They deceived me.'

The umpire signalled with his stick for the fight to commence.

Both men held their ground for a moment. Denter carried the weight of his armour easily. As well as the ringmail coat, he had been equipped with metal arm and leg greaves supported with padded guards, and his head was completely encased inside a smooth, brimless metal helmet. A pair of small eyeholes afforded him a limited view of the arena. The helmet gave the veteran a terrifying appearance. Both men breathed hard in the sweltering heat. Pavo was already drenched in sweat and he had yet to launch an attack.

The umpire scampered out of the way as Denter made the first move, hoisting his large rectangular shield to his chest and edging towards Pavo. A symbol of Fortuna had been painted on the calf-skin cover of the shield. The gladiators were separated by a distance a little greater than the length of a legionary javelin. Pavo kept his opponent at bay by holding the trident in an underarm grip with the weathered-ash shaft resting on the underside of his forearm. He would have preferred a two-handed grip to put more force into each thrust, but the coiled net in his left hand forced him to fight one-handed. He kept the tines angled at waist height, allowing him to attack Denter's upper torso or legs in rapid succession. He continued patiently circling his opponent. The Pompeiians urged Denter to attack. He snarled his rage and with a fierce snort charged at Pavo, shifting his weight on to his right foot and angling the point of his short sword at his opponent's bare chest.

Pavo jumped back from the attack and in a beat sidestepped to the left, swiftly circling his opponent and thrusting his trident at Denter's exposed groin. At the very last moment the veteran swung around and became aware of the tines driving at his mid-section. He let out a harsh roar as he deflected the trident with a rugged swipe of his shield. Pavo felt his elbow lock into position as the weapon arrowed harmlessly towards the sky. The weight and momentum of the trident dragged on Pavo and he lurched forward and abruptly found himself within range of Denter's short sword. With a neat flick of the wrist the veteran jerked his arm up and slammed the base of his sword into Pavo's temple. An ear-shattering noise ripped through his skull and a burst of white flashed before his eyes.

Denter came at Pavo again. The young gladiator stumbled backwards, his head ringing and his legs swaying. Blotches of colour floated across his line of sight. He moved away from his opponent as swiftly as he could, thankful that he wasn't bogged down under a full complement of armour like Denter. For every one step his opponent took, Pavo took two. He rapidly retreated and in four steps had cleared himself out of stabbing range. Denter held back, gathering his breath for a renewed attack. Pavo shaped to manoeuvre to the side.

'What the . . .'

Pavo froze in horror. He looked down at his feet as the feeling drained from his legs. It was as if someone had severed him at the torso. For a moment he faltered on the spot, clinging to his trident for support. His lips tingled. His cheeks numbed. The blotches in his vision multiplied. Gradually he felt a loss of sensation in every part of his body. To audible gasps among the crowd, he sank despairingly to his knees. The umpire flashed a questioning glance at the young fighter. Gripping his trident for dear life, Pavo tried to utter a warning of distress, begging the umpire to call off the fight. But an invisible noose had tightened around his neck. His breath felt as if it was trapped in his throat, and when he tried to speak, only a croak escaped from his cold lips.

A chill disquiet descended over the arena. The crowd became openly hostile as they realised that their hero was doomed. Pavo collapsed on to his front, dimly aware of the murmurs of discontent spreading like a fire through the upper galleries. Enfeebled, he lifted his eyes to see Denter charging at him, dragging his sword by his side, the tip cutting a line through the hot sand.

Denter angled his head at the podium for the signal to execute his vanquished rival. Pavo couldn't make out Pallas and Murena. Everything had blurred. The crowd was a smudge of coloured tunics. The men at the podium were a row of white blotches. Spectators pleaded for Pavo to be spared. The hooligans cheered for him to be put to the sword.

'Time to die,' Denter said, his voice muffled behind the metal of his helmet. The black, dull eyeholes stared cruelly at Pavo. 'I'm going to cut off your head. Just like Hermes did to your father.'

'Go to Hades,' Pavo whispered.

Denter raised the sword above his head with both hands wrapped around the pommel.

But at the last minute he hesitated. Pavo glanced up, wondering why Pallas had not given the signal. Something had caught the attention of both Denter and the umpire. Pavo rolled his eyes in the same direction. He was stunned to see spectators clashing in the galleries. Pompeiians and locals traded blows, hurling cups and jugs at each other. A darkly featured youngster grappled with an elderly local and tipped him over the side of the gallery. The man crashed amid the dignitaries, whose wives shrieked at the tops of their voices. More Pompeiians began clambering into adjacent sections populated by local supporters loyal to Pavo. The Pompeiians laid into the crowd with their fists. A few of the guards attempted to intervene but they were brushed aside by locals and Pompeiians alike, and soon the violence had spilled across to every part of the arena. Pavo's vision slowly returned. He caught sight of Pallas shooting to his feet, his lips pressed together in a thin line as he chopped his hand at the umpire.

'Oh gods,' said the umpire, inserting himself between Pavo and a livid Denter. 'The fight is postponed! Orders of the sponsor. Return to the tunnels.' He flinched as a shower of jugs and cups rained down on the gladiators and shattered on the ground. 'Now!'

CHAPTER NINETEEN

P avo watched the violence unfolding in the crowd as two orderlies dragged him towards the tunnel. The umpire thrust Denter
back towards the opposite arena entrance as hordes of spectators left
their seats in a desperate hurry, abandoning the cushions they had
brought to make the stone seats more comfortable. They stampeded
towards the exits leading down into the street, shoving fellow citizens to the floor in their mad rush to escape. But they found their
progress blocked on the steps of the gallery exits by pockets of
guards, who had panicked at the sudden mass of humanity surging
towards them and had taken to randomly slashing at the civilians
in front of them. The orderlies dumped Pavo in the mouth of the
tunnel, and the gladiator experienced a chilling fear clamp around
his neck as he realised it was only a matter of time before the guards
were overwhelmed by the sheer size and desperation of the crowd.

A cloud of dust and mortar poured down from the arched
ceiling and choked Pavo. He coughed violently. Tears welled in
his eyes as he hacked up a lungful of hot dust and slumped against
the wall. His hands and feet tingled as feeling slowly returned to
his deadened limbs.

'Hard to please, that lot,' a gruff voice said. 'The mob.'

Pavo was conscious of a form emerging from further down
the corridor. The figure stopped next to him and crouched. Pavo
adjusted his eyes to the dark and saw the grizzled features of
Macro staring back at him.

'What are you doing here?' Pavo responded weakly. His throat
felt as if it had shrunk to the width of a reed and he struggled
to utter every word.

'Orders of those two bloody freedmen.' The optio jerked a
thumb towards the galleries and sucked his teeth.

139

'I suppose they ordered you to train Denter too,' Pavo responded tartly.

'They did, as it happens.' Macro rose to his feet and frowned as the shouts of the Pompeiians spilled down from the galleries. 'Roping you into a fight with that drunken madman was their brilliant idea. They only travelled down here to celebrate your death.'

'I knew it!' Pavo gritted his teeth. 'They kitted me out as a retiarius and sent me to face a legend of the arena clad in armour from head to toe. I never had a chance.'

'If it's any consolation, the mob are just as pissed off. That's what sparked the riot out there. Pallas had to interrupt the fight. If the violence spills into the streets, there'll be blood on his hands. And the Emperor's, since he's sponsoring the event.' Macro sighed as a spectator was hurled down from the upper gallery and crumpled into a heap on the arena floor. Servants rushed over to tend to the bloodied victim. 'Tell you what,' the optio grumbled. 'If that pair are supposed to be the best advisers Claudius has got, then we're all fucked.'

The comment drew the hint of a smile to Pavo's lips. Macro glanced over his shoulder. Pavo suppressed his smile before the optio could see it. 'Pallas and Murena are snakes, but they're no more rotten than half the officials in Rome. They don't give a shit about the mob. They're only in it for themselves.' He hardened his gaze at Macro. 'And what about you, Optio? How did you stand to profit, if Denter won today?'

Macro looked with surprise at Pavo for a moment, then clamped his lips. 'I had no choice, lad. Pallas and Murena forced me to do their bidding. If I refused, they would've thrown me from the Tarpeian Rock.' He shook his head slowly. 'All their scheming makes my bloody head reel.'

'Business as usual in Rome, then.' Pavo looked away from Macro. 'You conspired against me.'

'Bollocks, lad!' Macro grunted testily. 'I'm not your enemy here. It's those stylus-pushing Greeks.'

Pavo turned back to the optio. Macro stared at him.

'You're not the only one getting shat on by the imperial

household.' The optio ground his right fist into the palm of his left hand. 'I won a medal for killing a bunch of wild Germans, and what did I get in return? No tarts or gold. Just a back-handed thank you from an imperial arse-licker and a job trawling the taverns and brothels of Pompeii, keeping a drunken old gladiator out of trouble.'

'Sounds like your ideal mission,' Pavo snorted derisively.

'Ideal pain in the arse, more like. Truth is, I'm glad to be out of Pompeii. It's a pleasant little town but no place for a soldier. Nothing ever happens there and never will. I didn't like the idea of helping a pair of imperial snakes plot against a decent lad.'

Pavo tilted his head in puzzlement at the optio. 'You mean me?'

Macro nodded. 'You're quite the thorn in the Emperor's side, boy. But you know what? As long as the crowd are chanting your name, Claudius and his freedmen can't lay a finger on you.'

Pavo pursed his lips. 'Pallas and Murena hold sway over the Emperor,' he said softly. 'They do as they please. No one is untouchable in Rome these days, Optio. Look how they've treated you, a newly decorated hero of the Empire.'

'Don't I bloody well know it.' Macro considered the trident and net the orderlies had placed next to Pavo. 'But you're wrong about one thing. Pallas and Murena need the support of the mob. Murena said so himself. Without the people, Claudius's regime won't last long.'

Pavo blinked. 'So?'

'Listen to that lot.' Macro rolled his eyes and nodded to the arena. The sound of the fighting had died away, drowned out by the rhythmic chant of Pavo's name. 'They're not completely thick. They can see the odds have been stacked against you, and they don't like to see Rome humiliate its heroes.' The optio averted his gaze. 'Not publicly, anyway. Your old man was guilty of treason. This is different. The mob's on your side.'

Pavo grimaced. Macro had a point, he conceded. Control of the mob was more powerful than any ancestral tree or official title. Emperors since the days of Caesar had arranged gladiatorial combats to win the support of the mob, and now the same trick

141

had come back to haunt Pallas and Murena. The young gladiator smiled at the thought of the freedmen breaking out in a cold sweat up in the podium. He now found he could move his legs, albeit clumsily.

'Go out there and win,' Macro urged.

'Win?' Pavo mumbled sarcastically. 'I can hardly stand up!'

Macro cleared his throat and made a pained face. 'They put something in your drink,' he admitted. 'Murena told me shortly before ordering me down here. He bribed Gurges. Achaeus added a potion to the usual brew to slow you down. The effects wear off quickly enough, I'm told. You'll soon be back to your usual cheerful self.'

Pavo felt a surge of rage sweep through his veins as he thought back to the cup of foul liquid the doctore had forced him to swallow. 'They have no shame, those Greeks . . . Bastards.'

'Sod them,' Macro snapped. 'If you don't go out there and sort out Denter, then we're all in trouble. The guards are keeping the mob in check, but there's only a few of them and they won't hold for long. If they fall, we're looking at a full-blown riot.'

Pavo growled through clenched teeth at his predicament. 'So either I triumph over Denter and save the skins of the two men who ordered the death of my father and have conspired to kill me off, or I fail and cause their downfall, at the expense of count-less lost lives and the ruin of an entire city.'

Macro nodded. 'That's about the size of it, lad.' He pursed his lips and smiled stiffly. He had thought about informing Pavo that Pallas had threatened to execute both the optio and the gladiator if they failed to quell the growing public unrest. Macro had listened ashen-faced to Murena, stunned at how quickly and brutally the mood could change. Two months after being decorated a hero, he was facing the prospect of a crucifixion along the Appian Way. But he bit his tongue. Pavo had plenty on his plate already, he reminded himself. No point shovelling more worry on top. Besides, Macro wanted him to confront Denter with renewed purpose, not a bellyful of anxiety.

Pavo examined the ground. 'Not much of a choice.'

'It never is, in my experience,' the optio replied grimly.

'To Hades with Rome,' Pavo grumbled darkly. 'When this is all over, if I somehow manage to survive, I will leave the city and get as far away as possible from its dark soul.' He stiffened his neck. 'The frontier with Parthia, perhaps.'

'Rather you than me,' Macro replied sarcastically. 'I hear that's a proper shithole.' He slapped Pavo heartily on the shoulder, quelling the sense of dread writhing in his bowels at the thought of being crucified. 'Well, there's nothing for it now but to knuckle down and get the job done. Come on, lad. On your feet.'

Pavo squinted at the arena. Servants worked quickly to clear away the debris that had been thrown into the grounds. 'I'm not sure I can beat Denter,' he said. 'That man doesn't know fear.'

'Bollocks.' Macro chuckled. 'Denter isn't a patch on you. He's just a thug.' He looked at Pavo with a glimmer in his eye. 'Do you know why he won so many fights?'

Pavo shrugged. 'Because he's good with a sword?'

'Because he's already won the battle before he steps out on to the sand.'

Pavo looked at Macro quizzically. 'How do you mean?'

'He frightens his opponents. All that rubbish about ripping out his own teeth at the banquets? It's scare tactics. The German tribes along the Rhine are the same. Soldiers in camp swap horror stories about them over supper. When the time comes to face them in battle, some of the lads have surrendered before the first arrow has been shot. Denter is just trying to bully you, lad.'

Pavo shrugged. He wanted to believe Macro, but the daunting record of his opponent made him hesitant.

The optio pressed on, his voice rising with conviction. 'Think about it. Pallas and Murena clad Denter in armour from head to bloody toe. They're scared of you, Pavo. And you know why?' Pavo shook his head. Macro puffed out his chest in pride. 'Because you have the ability to beat him. I know it. I've seen what you are capable of.'

Macro surprised himself with the compassion in his voice. He was an old-fashioned soldier at heart, not one given to moments of sympathy. He'd lived a hard life on the outposts of the Empire, keeping the barbarian hordes at bay, and kindness was in short supply. But Pavo had been through plenty, in his eyes. He did not deserve to fall to a thug like Denter.

'With a sword, I might have a chance,' Pavo conceded. 'But with these . . .?' He waved a hand at the trident and net, sighing wearily as his voice trailed with uncertainty.

'Funny you should say that.' The optio bent down to the net and pricked his thumb on the tip of a lead pellet, testing its sharpness. He looked back to Pavo and beamed. 'I've been thinking about your weapons. And I've got a plan . . .'

Denter was already parading around the arena when Pavo emerged from the tunnel to a chaotic wave of noise. The servants had cleared the arena and the veteran stood freely in the middle, pumping his clenched fist at a section of the crowd in an effort to wind them up even more. Pavo looked up at the galleries. Guards stood menacingly at the exits, ready to pounce on any troublemakers trying to stir up further violence. Denter's supporters and local people clutched their blood-streaked faces. Servants dragged the limp corpses of several men towards the gallery steps. Order was restored to the crowd as the herald announced the return of the two gladiators to the stage. Pavo swallowed hard and slogged towards his opponent with great difficulty. He still felt listless from the effects of the potion-laced drink. A thick fog had settled behind his eyes.

He stopped a short distance from Denter. He stared at his opponent and thought once more of the revenge he had vowed to take on Hermes.

'Come back for more, have you?' Denter growled through his helmet. 'Ha! The crowd won't save you this time, you spineless shit.'

The umpire signalled for the bout to resume.

Pavo tensed his muscles as Denter burst at him, a grating snarl sounding inside his brimless helmet. Jolted into action, Pavo hoisted his trident towards his opponent's exposed mid-section and directed the tines towards his intricately detailed loincloth. But his movements were still slow and heavy and the trident felt unwieldy in his grasp. Denter batted it away with a quick downward thrust of his shield. Pavo felt his heart sink as the tines plunged into the sand. Now Denter hammered his shield into the ground, trapping the trident under its iron rim. Pavo unsuccessfully tried to wrench it free. Letting out a roar, Denter raised his sword high above his helmet and swung the blade down at the trident. With a distinct crack the sword hacked through the shaft, detaching the iron shank and tines from the splintered handle.

Pavo relinquished his grip on the broken weapon and backtracked away from the middle of the arena. Now Denter hefted up his shield and chased down his opponent. The veteran's blood was up. Pavo could discern his heavy breathing through his helmet as he smelled the imminent defeat of the young challenger.

'Stand your ground, you little shit!' Denter rasped. 'Victory is mine!'

Pavo edged back a little further. The local people in the crowd heckled Denter as he closed in on his opponent. Some of the spectators rose from their stone seats and waved strips of white cloth at their rivals from Pompeii. Pavo sensed the mood turning among the fractious mob. Denter charged at him, spurred on by the roars from the Pompeiians, and emboldened by the fact that his rival had lost his main weapon. He dropped his shield to his side and thrust his sword at Pavo's bare chest. The younger gladiator lumbered to the left in a frantic bid to avoid being cut. But he was too slow and Denter caught him on the left shoulder, the tip of his sword skewering Pavo's joint. Some of the spectators screamed as the blow struck. The Pompeiians whooped with delight. Pavo felt a burning pain explode in his shoulder muscles. Denter gave the sword a twist, dicing tendon and cartilage, sending another sickening wave of agony through Pavo. Nausea tickled his throat. He braced his jaws shut as Denter ripped the blade free. Hot blood gushed out of his wound and splattered the sand.

Clenching his teeth, Pavo resisted the urge to clamp a hand to his injured shoulder. Denter milked the applause from his supporters and prepared to cut down his opponent with another blow. The young man gasped. He shut out the noise and the pain and the looks of Pallas and Murena in the podium, and focused instead on the advice Macro had conveyed to him in the tunnel.

Gripping the bulk of the net in his trembling right hand, he wielded its coiled length in his left hand in the manner of a drill instructor preparing to mete out punishment with a whip. The lead pellets at the edges were bunched together at the end to form a series of sharp teeth. Pavo whirled his wrist in a circular motion, building up momentum in the coiled end of the rope. Denter paused, his sword hanging in front of him, blood dripping from the tip. Pavo flicked his wrist forward and lashed th net at his opponent. It arced in front of him below waist height and lacerated Denter's right leg, the numerous lead pellets hooking into the ample flesh of his thigh. Then he ripped the net across and a hollow scream erupted from inside Denter's helmet as the pellets ripped off chunks of flesh. The veteran stumbled back and dropped his sword as he struggled to retain his balance. Bright-red blood streamed thickly from the torn flesh of his leg.

Retrieving the coiled length of the net with a jerk of his pained right arm, Pavo lashed in the opposite direction. The pellets sank into Denter's other leg, prompting another wild howl of agony as Pavo yanked it free, tearing off more strips of flesh. Denter sank to his knees on the sand. Both his legs were drenched in blood. The crowd roared Pavo on as he cast the net over Denter's head and encircled the stricken veteran, wrapping it around him so that his arms were constricted. Then he released the net. Denter tried rolling towards his abandoned sword. But Pavo darted over to the weapon and scooped it up to another chorus of cheers from the spectators. The Pompeiians had fallen deadly silent. They looked sheepishly down at their fallen hero and shook their heads mournfully.

Pavo booted Denter in the back and sent him crashing to the ground. Then he glanced up at the podium. The imperial secretary and his aide looked profoundly relieved. Pallas straightened a wrinkle in his toga and gave Pavo the thumb. The crowd roared itself hoarse. In the gallery above the freedmen, Gurges stared at Denter with horror. Then he hurried out of his seat and bolted for the nearest exit, elbowing his way past the guards.

Pavo pulled his net off Denter to allow his opponent to rise to his knees and accept his fate with a measure of dignity. But instead Denter hurled himself at Pavo. It was a desperate lunge, and Pavo cut him down with a stab to his right arm. The blade tore through his bicep and the pain threw Denter off balance and sent him stumbling to the ground. The spectators whistled and jeered at the outrageous behaviour of the veteran. Now Pavo stood over him and held the sword above his head, poised to plunge it into the back of Denter's neck. His arm muscles tensed. He looked down and considered his defeated opponent with a mixture of pity and contempt.

'Son of a fucking traitor,' Denter sneered, his voice laced with venom. 'Son of a cowardly, gutless—'

Pavo drove the sword down in a fell swoop. The tip pierced the back of Denter's neck. The fallen gladiator briefly spasmed as the blade cut through his spine. Then he stilled, and the umpire raised Pavo's wounded arm in victory. The crowd erupted with joy.

The dust had settled and Paestum brooded under a velvet night sky as Macro was escorted to the makeshift infirmary by guards from the local barracks. The arena was deserted now, as the supporters had flocked to the taverns and brothels to toast a local victory against their hated rivals from Pompeii. The town had been relatively peaceful, by all accounts, and Macro was greatly relieved to have escaped a riot. In his mind barbarians thirsting for your blood were one thing, but warring Romans unsettled him. The smell of death permeated the corridor leading towards the infirmary. Like mouldy cheese, thought the optio. Another reminder of why he avoided field hospitals at all costs.

He found Pavo lying on a straw mat, lost in thought as he stared at the ceiling. His right shoulder had been dressed by a nurse. The bowls of blood-tinged water and trays of used surgical instruments were all that remained of the day's work, much to Macro's relief. Pavo turned at the sight of the soldier entering the infirmary and smiled weakly through the throbbing pain of his wound.

'That worked out all right in the end, then,' Macro announced. He tried to sound cheerful but the words came out weary and

147

flat. He was merely relieved to have avoided a grisly death at the hands of the imperial secretary and his aide. Gladiator bouts were a lot more difficult to watch when your own life rested on the outcome, Macro thought.

'Oh yes,' Pavo replied, affecting a mock-cheerful tone. 'Honestly, I don't know why I grumble about the life of a gladiator. You only have to avert widespread rioting and looting, save the skins of a couple of imperial rats and help free the family of a friend threatened with being sold into slavery. But other than that, this fighting business is easy.'

'All right, it got a bit hairy out there, lad,' Macro conceded. 'But there is a bright side to your victory.'

Pavo screwed up his face at the optio. 'Really? And what do you suppose that is?' he asked coldy. 'The noblemen of Paestum can sleep easily in their beds tonight, thankful that their fellow citizens haven't ransacked the whole city? Or perhaps I should celebrate the fact that Pallas and Murena escaped causing the Emperor huge embarrassment by allowing a riot to break out at an event he sponsored?'

Something in the optio's expression intrigued Pavo. Macro folded his arms across his chest. 'There's more, lad. You're not a gladiator at the house of Gurges any longer.'

Pavo frowned. 'What are you talking about?'

'He wagered a fortune on Denter winning today.' Macro shook his head and grinned. 'Placed it all with some bookie called Carbo. Gurges has lost everything. He's bankrupt. He's had to sell off his gladiators just to pay his other debts.'

'Thank the gods . . .' Pavo said, closing his eyes. His triumph had not been in vain. Newly enriched with the proceeds from Denter's defeat, Carbo would release Clodia and the boys. And with the ludus being disbanded and only promising gladiators possessing any resale value, there was even a chance that Bucco might be reunited with his family after all. A smile was poised to break out on Pavo's face when another thought nudged him. He opened his eyes and cocked his chin at Macro.

'But if the gladiators have been sold off – who owns me now?'

'I do,' a sly voice behind them said.

Macro and Pavo turned their heads and saw Murena standing at the infirmary entrance. Pavo felt his muscles tense across his chest and tried to sit up on his straw mat to confront the imperial aide, but his wound flared and he leaned back again, wincing in pain.

'What are you talking about?' Macro snapped at Murena.

A flame flickered in the eyes of the freedman as he folded his hands behind his back. 'Gurges has been forced to sell his assets to the highest bidder. In this case, the imperial palace.' His thin lips strained into a grin. His eyes flicked from the enraged optio to the aghast gladiator. 'Smile, Pavo. You're now enrolled in the imperial ludus in Capua.'

For a moment Pavo lost the power of speech.

'You're probably wondering why.'

Macro and Pavo exchanged troubled glances. Murena stepped into the infirmary and brushed past the optio. He paced to a table and ran his hands over an array of blood-encrusted surgical instruments laid out on a tray.

'It's very simple,' he said. 'Today we saw the power of the mob. Thankfully, that uncouth multitude are too slow to grasp their own influence. Otherwise they might chase us out of the palace and run the place themselves.' He picked up a pair of bronze forceps and admired them under the flicker of an oil lamp. 'In the country of my birth, we would call that a democracy.'

'Sounds shit,' said Macro.

Murena gently reset the forceps on the tray. 'For once, Optio, I find myself agreeing with you.' His eyes lingered on the array of bone levers and tile cauteries and speculums in front of him. Then he sighed and turned away from the tray. 'The plebs worship you, Pavo. And since we need the support of the mob to cement the regime of his imperial majesty, your sudden celebrity, distasteful though it may be, has given me an idea.'

'What idea?' Pavo felt a cold lump lodge at the back of his throat. The hairs on the back of his neck prickled.

'In a moment.' Murena fixed his ruthless gaze on Macro. 'First, the optio and I must settle our affairs.'

'About bloody time,' Macro grumbled. 'Let's get this over with.

I've put up with enough bollocks from you and Pallas. I'm actually starting to miss the Rhine.'

'You'll have to get used to the feeling,' snapped Murena. 'You have more pressing business to attend to, Optio.'

Macro folded his arms and snorted. 'Such as?'

'Such as preparing your papers for your journey to Capua,' Murena retorted with barely disguised delight. 'As you may or may not have heard, the imperial lanista met a rather gruesome end when his bodyguard crushed his skull. The price he had to pay for getting too big for his own boots. We need a lanista to administer the school.' The aide raised a hand to Macro's darkening face. 'The position is not up for discussion, Optio. It's only a temporary appointment, until we have a chance to find someone more, shall we say, palatable than the previous lanista. Besides, you seem to know your stuff. You've succeeded in guiding Pavo in two very different types of fighting.'

Anger tightened its grip around Macro's neck. He felt his stomach muscles churn and his jaws harden. He was about to launch himself at the aide when a pair of hands clamped on either bicep. The optio resisted as two guards grappled with him and dragged him towards the exit.

'What about my promotion?' he thundered.

'Off the table, I'm afraid. And the reward that goes with it. The riots have caused significant damage to the arena. It will cost the Emperor a great deal of money to repair. He will not be pleased with you, Optio. Consider yourself lucky to have avoided a long walk off the Tarpeian Rock.'

'But the riots were your fault!' Macro felt his pulse thumping at the side of his head, overcome with rage at the aide's scheming. 'I'm not to blame!'

Murena ignored him and with a dismissive wave of his hand gestured for the guards to haul Macro out of the infirmary. The aide sighed deeply as the soldier's protests echoed down the corridor.

'Now then, where were we?' He clicked his tongue. 'Ah, yes! Our plans for your glorious future in the arena.'

Pavo watched the guards drag Macro away and turned back to

Murena. 'Plans?' he said pithily. 'I thought you wanted me dead.'

The aide flashed a look of mock horror at Pavo, as if offended that the idea had ever crossed his mind. Then he folded his hands in front of his lap. 'The mob has spared you, young man. That is a judgement that even the Emperor cannot overrule. We must not do anything to infuriate the mob during this delicate period.'

'I'm done winning fights for Claudius,' Pavo replied. 'I don't see why I should help the Emperor to keep the peace.'

Murena furrowed his brow. 'This is what is going to happen. You will be branded with the mark of the imperial school. That mark will declare you to be the personal property of his imperial majesty, Emperor Claudius. It will be a tacit display of your support for our regime, and your rejection of Titus's misguided principles. You shall wear it with pride.'

'You must be joking!' Pavo faltered. 'I would never betray my father.'

'Oh, but you will, my boy . . . if you want to fight Hermes.'

A triumphant smile threatened to cross the aide's lips before he checked himself and cleared his throat. His eyes gleamed in the jittery reflection of the oil lamp. Pavo blinked at Murena. His pulse quickened at the thought of finally confronting his nemesis.

'Hermes?' he uttered uneasily.

'Why, yes.' Murena permitted himself to smile now. He appeared very pleased with himself, Pavo thought. 'I believe it is your wish to fight the man who killed your father – or am I mistaken?'

'No, no!' Pavo replied, far too quickly. 'I want nothing more than to see Hermes bleed.' He looked at the ground and tried to swallow the lump in his throat. 'But I thought he had retired?'

The aide grinned and shook his head. 'Hermes has requested that he come out of retirement. The Emperor has agreed. It seems you shall have your wish at last.'

CHAPTER TWENTY

Capua, three weeks later

Pavo was awoken in the middle of the night by a swift kick to the ribs.

'Get up, you worthless shit!'

The young gladiator winced as he stirred and rolled on to his back. Squinting in the gloom, he saw an armed guard towering over him, with a second guard stooped further back in the entrance to his cramped cell. Pavo touched a hand to his pained ribs and shook his head clear.

'What's going on?' he croaked.

'Murena wants a word,' the nearest guard barked. 'On your feet.'

'That Greek snake,' Pavo muttered darkly. 'What does he want with me now?'

'Fuck should I know?' the guard snarled, seizing Pavo by the arm and yanking him to his feet. 'Now hurry up! Murena doesn't like to be kept waiting.'

Pavo was too groggy and confused to protest. The guards manhandled him out of the dormitory and dragged him through the ludus gates. A wintry wind swept over the landscape as they marched the young gladiator down the road towards Capua and a cluster of lights flickered on a distant hill. Pavo made out the dim shape of a villa perched on the slope of the hill. The guards shoved him in the direction of the villa. The young gladiator moved awkwardly, his leg muscles aching under the leaden weight of the chains clamped to his wrists and ankles. The sutured wound on his left shoulder throbbed dully. The guards paced warily alongside him. He noted from their uniform of plain white togas over their tunics that they were Praetorian Guards.

'So you're the famous Marcus Valerius Pavo, eh?' the guard to his left scoffed. 'Champion of the arena. Hard to believe. Posh twat such as yourself.'

'Perhaps you're right,' Pavo replied drily. 'Perhaps I am too high-born to be a champion gladiator. But you two seem to be scared of me, since you're both keeping a hand on your swords, even though I'm unarmed and bound in chains.'

The guard scowled at him. 'Think you're tough? Bollocks!' he spat. 'Fucking gladiators, always showing off. Just you wait, lad. You'll get cut down in the arena and slung into a grave pit like every gladiator with a big mouth. You won't look so clever then.'

Pavo was too disheartened to reply. Quartz glinted between the stones lining the paved road, reflecting the pale moonlight. He felt a deep unease in his guts as they drew close to the villa. Ever since his transfer from Paestum to the imperial ludus, he had been living in fear that Murena and Pallas would seek to dispose of him sooner rather than later.

He feared that moment had now arrived.

The small party reached the villa as the night sky faded and dawn glimmered coolly on the horizon. The imposing structure was bordered by a sprawling olive grove. A train of luxury horse-drawn wagons rested in front of the entrance, slaves groaning as they carried baggage off the wagon beds and lugged the heavy loads towards the villa. Porticoes lined the front of the property, rising in tiers to an ornamental balcony two storeys above, where Pavo supposed wealthy guests might catch a gentle breeze on a hot summer's night. Two Praetorians stood on duty at the entrance to the villa. One of them blocked the path of Pavo and the guards while his comrade stepped forward.

'Password?' the Praetorian asked.

'Flamingo,' Pavo's guard replied.

'What's your business here?'

'The aide to the imperial secretary sent for this one.' The guard pointed to Pavo.

Stepping back, the Praetorian waved Pavo and his escort through.

Pavo baulked as he stepped into the villa. Memories of child-hood summers spent at the family's villa at Antium came flooding back to him as the guards led him down the entrance passage at a brisk pace. They hurried through a garishly coloured vestibule leading to a wide central hallway with elaborate frescoes decorating the walls and an intricate mosaic sparkling on the floor under the flicker of several ornate torches. Waves of heat rose up from the hypocaust floor, warming the gladiator's frozen feet.

At the end of the hallway the guards ushered him into a large study. Scrolls and books were arranged on honeycombed shelves to the left. An oak desk littered with papyrus scrolls and wax tablets occupied the centre of the room, with a tall window behind it overlooking a sprawling vineyard. Murena sat behind the desk. The aide to the imperial secretary frowned in deep concentration at a scroll and for a moment appeared not to notice the prisoner and his escort. Finally he looked up at the young gladiator and grinned.

'Ah! Marcus Valerius Pavo,' he announced, setting aside the scroll and clasping his bony hands. 'Tell me, how are you enjoying your new position as First Sword?'

Pavo grunted. He'd been proclaimed First Sword upon his arrival at the imperial ludus in Capua. It was the title given to the leading fighter of the imperial gladiators, and the news had surprised him. A gladiator elevated to First Sword after just two fights was unheard of. But his shock quickly turned to unease. Although the title afforded him some privileges, such as having his own private cell and cooked meat and vegetables at mealtimes instead of the usual fare of barley gruel, it also made him a target for the other fighters. Many of the men in the ludus had been captured by legions in battle, or were impoverished slaves. As the son of a Roman nobleman and a former military tribune in the Sixth Legion, Pavo was already loathed by those same gladiators. Being named First Sword had only further estranged him from the brotherhood. He viewed the title as more of a curse than a blessing.

Murena nodded to the guards. 'You may go.' He watched them retreat down the hall. Then he cleared his throat and looked back to the young gladiator. 'I won't keep you for long. I have several pressing matters to attend to before his imperial majesty arrives.'

'Claudius is on his way here?' Pavo asked, tension rising in his throat.

'In a few days' time. The Emperor is currently inspecting the naval base at Puteoli. Afterwards he wishes to cast his eye over his troupe of imperial gladiators ahead of the forthcoming games.'

'Games?' Pavo asked.

'I will come to that shortly. Pallas has asked me to travel ahead of the Emperor and prepare the estate for his arrival, as well as sort through the affairs of the unfortunate previous owner of this quite splendid villa, a treacherous senator who thought he could outwit Claudius.'

There was a sinister gleam in the aide's eye that made Pavo shudder.

'The senator paid the price for his treachery and his estate was confiscated after his death. The chap had rather a lot of properties and assets. I have to say, sorting through it all is rather tiresome.'

'Just tell me what it is that you want,' the young gladiator said through gritted teeth.

Murena studied Pavo with a look of a hunter trapping a wild animal.

'I wonder if you have reconsidered my generous offer?'

Pavo instinctively balled his hands into fists. 'There's nothing to consider,' he replied. 'Claudius is my sworn enemy. As are you and that other backstabbing Greek bastard, Pallas.'

Murena stared at Pavo with barely concealed rage.

'Your insolence will not be tolerated! I purchased you from that spendthrift lanista in Paestum on behalf of the imperial treasury. You serve Claudius now. And as a representative of his imperial majesty, you will treat me with the same courtesy and respect as if you were speaking with the Emperor himself!'

'I'll regard you as exactly what you are,' Pavo replied bitterly. 'A devious Greek who does the bidding of a slobbering old fool in a purple toga.'

The imperial freedman opened his mouth to respond, but quickly checked himself. 'No, have your fun. Call me whatever names amuse you. Nothing changes the fact that you belong to me now, and shall do as I please.'

Pavo stared silently at the aide.

'There is another reason I sent for you,' Murena continued. 'Since we last spoke, the situation has changed.'

'What do you mean?' Pavo asked.

'The Empire is in danger, and we need your help to save it.'

The young gladiator looked puzzled as Murena went on.

'What I am about to tell you is strictly between us. There is a secret network of traitors operating within the walls of Rome. Not the usual drooling old fools in the Senate. This is a much more dangerous group. They call themselves the Liberators. They are determined to overthrow Claudius and return Rome to the dark days of the Republic.'

'Perish the thought,' Pavo replied tonelessly.

'More important things are at stake here than your disagreement with Claudius,' Murena snapped. His voice was laced with fear, thought Pavo. 'The Liberators pose a serious threat to the future stability of Rome. We must crush the group before they have a chance to establish a groundswell of support against the Emperor.' The aide offered Pavo a terse smile. 'Which brings me to the subject of the games to be held at the Statilius Taurus amphitheatre next month.'

Pavo digested the news impassively. Announcing a spectacular series of games was nothing new. It had been something of a tradition for newly crowned emperors ever since Augustus had begun hosting gladiator fights purely for the purpose of entertaining the restless mob.

'Claudius intends to make an announcement at the games. Livia is to be deified.'

'She's to become a god?' Pavo muttered in astonishment.

'Indeed. Claudius has wished for some time to deify his grandmother. Her deification will emphasise the divine lineage stretching from Augustus down to Tiberius and Claudius, arousing memories of the Golden Age.'

'Sounds like a cynical tactic to win the approval of the mob.'

'This is Rome. Of course it's cynical.' Murena looked pleased with himself. 'Dignitaries from across the Empire will be in attendance to witness the chariot races at the Campus Martius and processions through the Forum. In the arena, a morning beast-hunt featuring elephants and tigers will be followed by the usual crucifixions and floggings. In the afternoon, you and the other imperial gladiators will take to the sand.' He pursed his lips. 'When you enter the arena, you are to bow before his imperial majesty in front of the mob and pledge your undying allegiance to the regime.'

'Never!' Pavo raged. 'I won't sully the legacy of my father. Besides, what difference would a public display from me make, if the Liberators are Hades-bent on overthrowing Claudius?'

'You underestimate your reputation. The Liberators have big plans for you. They consider you well placed to be sympathetic to their aims.'

'How do you know?'

'We had a spy in their ranks. Sadly, his identity was unmasked, and the poor officer suffered a quite violent death.' Murena rolled his tongue around his gums, as if trying to dislodge a scrap of food. 'My point is, the Liberators need a spokesman. A role model, if you like. They admired Titus for his outspoken republican views, and as his only son and heir you represent the same sentiment. The Liberators are convinced that you are ripe to recruit to their cause – a popular figure to win over the common man.'

The aide drummed his fingers thoughtfully on the desk.

'We will beat the Liberators at their own game,' he said. 'They need the mob as badly as Claudius does, if they are serious in their intention to return Rome to a republic. With your show of support, the mob will back Claudius. Not even the Liberators are foolish enough to act against the wishes of the masses.'

Pavo shook his head in protest. 'I'm one man. There are count-less other gladiators who have been more popular than me. Felix the Destroyer, Triumphus the Terrible . . . even Hermes.' He clenched his jaw. 'I don't hold such sway over the mob.'

Murena raised an eyebrow. 'Not yet, perhaps.'

An icy feeling struck the young gladiator on the nape of his neck.

'Why else do you think I promoted you to First Sword?' asked Murena.

Pavo shrugged.

'Because you're a class apart from the likes of Felix and Triumphus. You're the classic Roman hero and son of a successful military leader. Not some barbaric milk-drinking Thracian who barely speaks a word of Latin. You're the first home-grown champion of the arena. And as First Sword, you are well on your way to becoming the most celebrated gladiator Rome has ever seen, with the power to influence the mob more than anyone other than the Emperor.'

Pavo folded his arms across his chest. 'My decision is final. I won't help you.'

Murena studied the gladiator. A pallid smile crept across his thin lips. 'Endorse the Emperor, and I'll ensure that your next fight is the one you have waited for all this time. Your match in the arena will be against Hermes.'

'So you say,' Pavo sniffed. 'What's to stop you from simply bumping me off once I throw my weight behind Claudius?'

The aide feigned a look of surprise. 'You will have to trust me.'

Pavo was incredulous. 'First you tried to poison me. Then you had me drugged for my fight against Denter. Now you expect me to believe that you and Pallas would honour any sort of deal?'

Murena compressed his lips.

'No,' Pavo said through gritted teeth. 'I won't endorse the Emperor, no matter how much you might try to sway me.'

'As you wish,' Murena replied, breathing loudly through his nostrils. 'Then I suggest you return to the ludus and prepare for the games. If you won't help us defeat the Liberators, then you leave me no choice but to make an example of you to the mob. You will be crucified upon the charge of treachery to Rome . . . after Appius is thrown to the beasts before your eyes.'

Pavo squeezed his eyes shut and mouthed a silent prayer to Fortuna and Jupiter that he would one day get his chance for vengeance on Pallas and Murena.

The aide clapped his hands loudly. 'Now, if you'll excuse me, I must return to the business at hand. Guards!'

He waved Pavo away and returned his attention to the stack of scrolls and wax tablets. Footsteps echoed down the corridor as the guards returned to the study. They were about to haul Pavo outside when Murena suddenly remembered something and motioned for them to halt.

'Oh, and before I forget,' he said to Pavo, 'send my regards to your lanista, won't you?' He smiled faintly. 'I'm sure Macro will have whipped the men into good shape by the time Claudius arrives.'

CHAPTER TWENTY-ONE

M acro settled his piercing gaze over the ludus training ground and shook his head in disgust.

'Lanista of a bloody ludus,' he muttered under his breath. 'I'll never live this day down with the boys in the Second Legion.'

He grunted as the gladiators trudged towards him at the end of their afternoon training session at the wooden training posts in the shadow of the two-storey dormitory block that dominated the ludus, and prepared to deliver his first address to the gladiators as the new imperial lanista. It was not a task he approached with much enthusiasm. Macro had arrived at the ludus earlier that morning in a foul mood. He had reacted badly to news of his appointment as the temporary lanista. Although he enjoyed a good gladiator show as much as the next Roman, he held a dim view of the gladiators themselves. His estimation of lanistas was even poorer. At least the gladiators fought with honest steel, Macro privately conceded, whereas the lanistas were greedy profiteers who grew wealthy from the killing of slaves and condemned criminals.

A burly, squat man with a heavily scarred leg stood at his shoulder, tightly gripping a short leather whip.

'It's not all bad, sir. At least we get to beat the shit out of scum.'

Manius Ovidius Aculeo held the title of newly appointed gladiator trainer to the ludus. Macro had been introduced to him after arriving at dawn in Capua. The optio's departure from Paestum had been delayed whilst he waited for his papers to be drawn up. Plenty of work required his attention upon his arrival, and the morning had been a blur of introductions followed by a meeting with the clerks and a review of the parlous financial state of the ludus. He had barely had time to pause and catch his breath.

'There are worse jobs to have,' Aculeo went on. 'Imperial lanista is a bloody big deal. You're in charge of Claudius's personal troupe of gladiators. There's plenty in Rome who'd scratch their eyes out to be in your boots.'

Macro shook his head. 'I wasn't born to nursemaid a bunch of muscle-bound glory-hunters.'

'*Imperial* gladiators, sir,' Aculeo pointed out. 'Hand-picked by the Emperor from the thousands of fighters from across the length and breadth of the Empire.' The doctore waved a hand at the men forming a thin line across the training-ground sand, under the watchful eyes of a handful of armed guards. 'This lot are the best swordsmen around. Apart from the gladiators at the main imperial ludus in Rome, I suppose.'

'Bollocks!' Macro spat. 'These men might work the crowd up with all their chest-thumping and swashbuckling, but stick 'em on the Rhine Frontier to face a horde of barbarians foaming at the mouth and they'd soon come unstuck.'

The doctore chuckled and shook his head. 'Sorry, sir, but I beg to disagree. The legions ain't what they used to be. I was a drill instructor in the Thirteenth once. When I joined up, a man would be flogged for so much as looking at some Syrian tart. Times have changed. The legions are too soft these days by half.'

Macro bit his tongue, resisting the temptation to remind Aculeo that there was a world of difference between the Thirteenth Legion and the Second. Murena had briefed the optio on the new doctore shortly before he departed Paestum. He'd been told that Aculeo had been discharged from the military after acquiring a reputation for being rather too enthusiastic with the application of his vine stick, provoking the men almost to the point of mutiny. Macro made a mental note to keep a close eye on the new doctore. The last thing he needed was a vindictive trainer venting his frustrations on the gladiators. There were more than enough problems to keep him busy as things stood. The previous lanista, Gaius Salonius Corvus, had been more interested in the trappings of wealth than managing a ludus, and training under his leadership had been lax. Macro felt the burden of the task ahead weighing on his shoulders like a heavy marching yoke.

Now the last of the gladiators assembled. Macro cast his eyes over the ludus as Aculeo ordered the men into formation. To his left stood the wooden training posts. On his right was the practice arena, a replica of the much larger arena in Capua, constructed from wood and with galleries capable of seating an audience of over two hundred. Two guards were stationed at a guard post south of the training arena, to the side of the main entrance to the ludus, an impressive structure with an intricately decorated arch above the gate bearing the reassuring symbol of the god Securitas. A series of guardrooms were built either side of the arch, along with solitary confinement cells for ill-disciplined gladiators. A portcullis sealed the mouth of the gate, along with an outer door which had a locking bar on the outside. Two additional guards were stationed by the outer door at all times. They were only permitted to open the door when the regular supply wagons arrived bearing food and wine for the ludus. The only other entrance was through the main doors at the front of the lanista's quarters. If nothing else, the place seemed reasonably secure.

Aculeo called the men to attention. The gladiators slowly formed into ten fairly orderly lines of twelve. Stiffening his neck, the optio reasoned that since he was in charge for the foreseeable future, he may as well make a good fist of his command. If nothing else, it might sharpen his leadership skills.

Taking a deep breath, he addressed the men.

'I am Lucius Cornelius Macro, optio of the Second Legion, decorated hero of Rome!' His naturally gruff voice boomed across the training ground. 'Ladies, I am your new lanista. You will all address me as "sir", understand?'

The gladiators stared at Macro in leaden silence.

'I can't hear you!' the optio thundered. 'I said, do you understand?'

'Yes, sir,' the gladiators replied meekly.

'Louder!'

'YES, SIR!' they bellowed in unison.

Macro nodded. 'That's better.'

He surveyed the gladiators with a sinking feeling in his guts. Many of the men were in poor condition. Some were slack-muscled and overweight. Quite a few sported prominent paunches or double chins. Not for the first time, Macro found himself cursing the prized decoration he'd been awarded. That decoration had brought him nothing but trouble. Biting back on his unease, he went on.

'Your previous lanista, Gaius Salonius Corvus, left this ludus in a right bloody mess. It's up to me to sort it out. That includes you lot. And speaking frankly, what I am looking at now makes me want to vomit.'

The gladiators looked surly.

'You're supposed to be the most feared swordsmen in the Empire. But an Egyptian beggar would strike more fear into the heart of a Roman soldier than any of you miserable bastards. If I had things my way, I'd pack the lot of you off to the mines. Unfortunately, I'm stuck with you. A great festival of games is scheduled to take place a month from now, when you will be pitted against your comrades from the imperial ludus in Rome.'

Macro paused as the gladiators absorbed the news with a degree of unrest. The announcement of forthcoming games always prompted a mixed response, he reflected, in a way that reminded him of soldiers greeting news of an imminent battle. There was excitement at a welcome break in the monotonous routine of training and drills, but also despair that some of them would soon shuffle over to the afterlife.

'As imperial gladiators, I expect you to put on a good show for the Emperor. Corvus might have been happy to let you lose against the boys from Rome. But I didn't travel all the way up here just to watch you be defeated. Lads, we are going to beat those noisy upstarts from the Roman ludus. If we want to win, there's going to have to be some big changes around here.'

Macro paused again. Many of the veteran gladiators appeared unconvinced by his bold words. While the gladiators bore plenty of scars from the arena, they had grown attached to the comforts of life under their old master, and were understandably appre-hensive about the prospect of hard training.

'I have personally slaughtered enough barbarians to half fill this ludus. The secret to Roman warfare isn't our weapons or the so-called leadership skills of our generals, thank the gods. It's our drills.' Macro thumped a fist against his chest. 'We drill day and night. We drill until our arms ache and we can hardly stand. We drill in our fucking sleep. That's what we're going to do, ladies. From now until the day of the games there will be twice-daily training sessions.' He gestured to Aculeo. 'This is your new doctore. He's also a military man through and through. He will help to instil legionary discipline in each and every one of you.'

There were grumbles from the throng of gladiators. Several directed evil glares at the doctore. Aculeo merely puffed out his chest in pride, oblivious of the venomous reception from the men.

'The doctore will take training from dawn until noon,' Macro continued. 'After a short rest you'll work at the paluses with the specialist coaches. By the end of each day you will be hurting worse than you have ever done in your pathetic lives. By the end of the month, you'll have muscles in places you didn't even know you had places. Then you'll train some more. Am I understood?'

'Here, what about our bounty?' one of the men asked.

'Too bloody right!' another added. 'We still haven't received our share of the winnings from the previous fights! Some of us have wives and children to feed on the outside.'

Macro knitted his brow. 'Blame that selfish turd Corvus. He left this ludus without an amphora to piss in. There's no money to be had, so you'll have to make do without the bounty for a while.'

Groans and murmurs of discontent erupted among the gladiators.

'That can't be true,' the first gladiator insisted. He was a pale man whose upper body was covered in tattoos. 'Corvus rented us out as bodyguards. He was raking it in. There must be some money to share around.'

'Corvus rented you out to pay his debts,' Macro replied coldly. 'That's why the Emperor had him bumped off. He left the ludus penniless. End of discussion.'

The gladiators exchanged angry looks. Macro sympathised with their grievance up to a point. Comparatively few gladiators achieved freedom by winning the rudis, the wooden sword awarded for triumphant gladiators at spectacular events. For most, their only real hope was to earn enough prize money to eventually buy out their contract with the lanista. A lower share of the winnings meant that a gladiator would need to survive more fights in order to purchase his freedom. Macro sensed the mood turning ugly. He silenced the protests with an abrupt wave of his hand. What he had to say next would undoubtedly provoke an acrimonious reaction.

'While we're on the subject of Corvus, I understand he permitted you lot cheap wine at supper and, gods forbid, even let you entertain tarts at night. Under my leadership, army rules will apply. No more wine. Anyone trying to smuggle a tart into their cells will be taken out to the training ground and given thirty lashes.'

'No wine?' one gladiator asked despairingly.

'Not even a bit of fresh cunny?' another shouted.

'Plenty of that waiting for you in the afterlife,' Macro replied.

'That's not fair! You can't just take away our privileges like that. We're imperial fighters, us lot. We deserve what Corvus promised us.'

'Corvus is dead!' Macro thundered. 'I'm the lanista. And you had better fall into line. That goes for each and every one of you miserable bastards. The next man to speak out will get twenty lashes.'

Satisfied that he had settled the argument, Macro wheeled away, gesturing to Aculeo to begin the day's training-ground exercises – twenty laps of the ludus followed by excruciating sets of press-ups, sit-ups and star jumps. He stopped dead at the sound of applause coming from somewhere within the massed ranks of gladiators.

'What a fine speech, Roman,' a voice rasped.

'Who said that?' Macro bellowed, turning back to the men.

The line of gladiators slowly parted to reveal a tall, well-built man with enlarged chest and shoulder muscles. He looked to be fitter than most of his peers. He struck Macro as a disciplined but serious sort of fellow. Judging from his straggly beard and the loose, flowing dark hair hanging down past his shoulders, Macro presumed he hailed from the barbaric lands to the east of Rome. A scar on his upper lip locked his mouth into a permanent scowl.

'You!' Macro shouted. 'Name!'

'Bato.' The gladiator smirked at Macro. The men around him looked at him with a mixture of awe and fear. 'I know your kind, Roman. I killed many soldiers like you on the field of battle in Thrace.'

Macro chuckled. 'Didn't stop you from getting captured and thrown into a ludus, I see.'

Bato glared back. 'How perceptive of you. True, I am in bondage, with many of my brothers.' He acknowledged a group of men standing at his broad shoulders. 'But I fought bravely, as an honourable warrior and the proud leader of my tribe. Not like you Romans, hiding behind your shields like women.'

Macro stared hard at the gladiator. 'You can comfort yourself with that thought tonight while you're picking cockroaches out of your gruel and I'm treating myself to a cup of Falernian.'

The gladiator scowled. Macro balled his right hand into a fist and punched the man in the guts. There was a sharp draw of breath as the blow winded Bato and he doubled up in agony.

'Speak out of turn again and I'll have you on half-rations for a month.'

Macro turned to leave.

'That's right,' said the gladiator, fighting to catch his breath. 'Walk away.'

The optio spun back round. Bato flashed an evil stare and addressed the other gladiators between sharp breaths.

'We didn't triumph in the arena, defeat countless opponents, spill blood and fight our way to become imperial gladiators just so this halfwit soldier could push us around. Down with the lanista! I say we take what is rightfully ours!'

A pocket of the men cheered Bato. In a burst of anger, Aculeo lashed out with his whip, striking the sand at the feet of the gladiator. Bato stared back at him, his face shading white with rage.

'Doctore,' Macro ordered. 'Lash this man at the post.'

'Roman scum!' Bato roared. The cheers among the other gladiators swelled.

'Make it thirty lashes.'

'I spit on you!'

'Forty!' Macro boomed above a deafening chorus of support.

'Yes, sir.'

Aculeo stepped forward, smacking his lips at the prospect of inflicting severe pain on the Thracian. He grabbed hold of Bato with a firm grip and started dragging him away. The armed guards scattered around the training ground exchanged anxious looks, their lack of training and battle experience telling in their hesitant faces and the nervous twitches of their hands. Macro knew a poor soldier when he saw one, and a brief look at the garrison guards told him that they were no match for the men of the Second Legion. The guards watched the Thracian uneasily as he screamed his defiance, echoed by his comrades.

'You haven't heard the last of me, Roman!' Bato roared as two more guards rushed to the doctore's aid in an attempt to subdue him. 'I'll make you regret the day you set foot in this ludus!'

CHAPTER TWENTY-TWO

A tense mood hung over the ludus as the gladiators toiled at the training posts. Pavo practised with his sword, a lead weight in his heart. Six days had passed since his meeting with Murena, and the young gladiator had sunk deeper into a pit of anguish with each passing day. His journey had come to a premature end, he reflected. There would be no vengeance over Hermes. No freedom for his son Appius. The humiliation and sense of injustice at his misfortune burned deeply in his heart, and for a fleeting moment he wished he had lost against Denter and perished in the arena, bringing an end to his misery.

He shook his head, angry with himself for permitting such black thoughts. The compulsive desire for revenge pounded between his temples. He thought of the promise he had made on his father's grave to kill Hermes. He'd sworn that he would not rest until the blood flowed freely from Hermes's neck. But unless he agreed to publicly support Claudius, he would not have the chance to fight his nemesis. In his weaker moments, Pavo weighed up the notion of offering his endorsement to the Emperor and asking Murena to overturn his decision. No, he told himself with a firm shake of his head. He would not give in. If he had to be executed in order to save the name of his family, so be it. Better to die with his pride and dignity intact than live a life of disgrace and condemn his son to a pitiful existence as a slave.

He stopped to catch his breath, muttering under his breath at the harsh training regime Aculeo had forced upon the men. They were not allowed to stop even for a brief moment during the earlier runs. Some had collapsed with exhaustion at the end. Blinking sweat out of his eyes, Pavo noticed Bato speaking furtively to several of his fellow Thracians.

'Pavo! What in the name of the gods are you doing?' The doctore stomped over to the young gladiator and prodded him in the stomach with his whip. 'This is a ludus for gladiators, not Greeks! If you wanted to stand around all day gazing into thin air, you should've gone to Athens.'

'Sir, I was just—'

'Shut up!' The veins on the doctore's thick neck protruded like tensed rope. His eyes bulged with hatred. 'Just because you're First Sword doesn't mean you can slack off in training. You're no different to everyone else in this ludus. You might think you're special, but to me you're just a slave with a fucking sword.'

'I meant no offence.'

'You offended me the moment you were born.' Pavo raised his eyes to meet the doctore's bone-chilling glare. 'I hate high-born officers almost as much as I hate showboating gladiators. And you are unfortunate enough to be both. You know what that means?'

'No, sir.'

'It means I hate you twice as much as any of the other scum in this ludus.'

'Permission to speak freely, sir.'

'No. You're a gladiator, Pavo. You don't speak freely. You do as you're bloody well told. You shit when I say you shit and you speak when I tell you to speak. Are we clear?'

Pavo bit his tongue. 'Yes . . . sir.'

'Right.' Aculeo took a breath and bellowed, 'Take a break! Make it quick! I want to see every sorry one of you back on the sand at the double-quick!'

Pavo fell into line with the other men pacing towards the canteen, his mood bleak. He was surprised to find himself yearning for his old ludus in Paestum. At least there he'd had a friend in Bucco. Now his premature appointment to First Sword had incurred the wrath of the other gladiators, and no one wanted to be associated with him. Even Macro, his former mentor, had distanced himself.

Entering the canteen at the southern end of the ludus, Pavo joined the orderly queue under the watchful eye of the guards. The gladiators lined up broodingly, accepting their bowls of gruel mixed with animal fat and gristle. Pavo received a plate of grilled sausages and steamed vegetables, as was his privilege as First Sword. He searched for a free place at one of the trestle tables. But the gladiators already seated at the table eyed him as he drew near and began shuffling along the wooden bench, filling up the empty space.

'This one's taken, Roman,' one of the men said sourly.

Pavo turned to another free spot at the end of a table. A gladiator at the next seat placed his hand on the spot and stared coldly at Pavo.

'Taken,' he said.

Sighing, the young gladiator turned to a table located at the far end of the canteen. A veteran sat alone, stirring his gruel with a craggy finger. He offered no protest as Pavo eased on to the bench on the opposite side of the trestle table. The wizened old fighter merely raised his bowl to his lips and sipped his gruel.

'By the gods, this is revolting!' He grimaced. 'It's bad enough they don't pay us the bounty we are due and take away our wine and whores. Now they insist on feeding us slops unfit for animals!' He pushed his bowl away despondently, then looked up at Pavo and considered the young gladiator. 'So you're the new First Sword, eh?'

Pavo nodded.

'Enjoy it while it lasts,' the veteran said. 'I was a young champion like you once. Had the world at my feet. Gladiators feared my name. Women promised me every sexual favour under the sun during my fights. Some of the men too. Greeks, usually. I had it all.'

'What happened?' Pavo asked.

'That bastard Corvus told me he'd give me my freedom after I turned thirty. He went back on his word and I tried to escape. But Corvus got wind of the plan and the guards caught me crawling through the sewers.'

'Isn't that normally an offence punishable by death?'

The veteran grunted. 'Corvus was a greedy shit. He wouldn't kill a gladiator he could still make a few denarii off of. He condemned me to life in the ludus.'

Pavo felt a pang of pity for the veteran. He slid his plate across. 'Here. Have mine.'

The veteran ogled the feast of cooked meat and vegetables. He smacked his lips and reached out to grab a sausage smeared with honey, then hesitated. 'Are you sure, lad?'

Pavo nodded. 'I'm not hungry.'

The veteran shrugged and started to shovel food into his mouth, making appreciative noises as he washed the sausages down with a thirsty slurp of vinegared wine. After wolfing down the vegetables, he let out a loud belch. Then he wiped his lips with the back of his hand and glanced furtively over his shoulder.

'A word to the wise. Watch your back. There's trouble brewing, and you'd do well not to be caught up in it.'

'What do you mean?' Pavo asked cautiously.

'The ludus is split down the middle.' The veteran pointed with a greasy finger to the two sets of gladiators sitting at the trestle tables either side of the canteen. 'On the left, you have the Thracians, under Bato. He's pissed off with you being named First Sword. That used to be his title.'

'Great,' Pavo noted wryly. 'I seem to be in the habit of making enemies of late.'

The veteran shook his head. 'On the right, you've got your Celts. Fucking animals. They have a long-standing feud with the Thracians. The two tribes sit at separate tables and train separately. They even sleep in separate parts of the cell block.'

'They hate each other?'

'Hate is putting it mildly.' The veteran scratched his cheek. 'They'd rip each other's throats out if they were given half a bloody chance. One of the Celts butchered Bato's brother in training a while back. The Celts claimed it was accidental. Bato believes they deliberately set out to murder his brother. There's been bad blood between the two camps ever since.'

A powerful feeling of loneliness struck Pavo. As First Sword and a fallen aristocrat, he had been shunned by the other gladiators. The rivalries bubbling under the surface of the ludus, so obvious to the veteran, were a surprise to the young gladiator.

'You spoke of trouble. What do you think is going to happen?' he asked.

The veteran leaned across the table and dropped his voice to a whisper. 'I've heard rumours that Bato is planning something big. Whatever it is, he'd want to take revenge on the Celts first. Carve the lot of them up. You know what Thracians are like. Long memories. But if Bato sees fit to stir things up round here, most of the men in the ludus will follow his lead.'

He became silent as a shadow fell across the trestle table.

'Well, well! Look who's decided to grace us with his presence.'

The veteran lowered his head at the voice coming from behind Pavo. The young gladiator turned casually. Bato glowered at him, his nostrils flared with anger.

'Do me a favour. Two fights, and you get awarded First Sword? That's bollocks, that is.'

A gigantic gladiator towered by his side. He was shaven-headed and pale as chalk, with a reddish scar running down his chest to his groin. Bato noticed Pavo staring at the man at his side and laughed.

'This is my bodyguard, Duras. He has the hardest punch in all of Thrace. Duras used to kill Roman scum with his bare hands. Once punched a man so hard his head exploded. Isn't that right, Duras?'

The bodyguard grunted his assent.

Bato looked with contempt at Pavo. 'You might carry the title of First Sword, but every man in this ludus knows I'm the true champion. I should be the one getting all the glory and the fame. Tarts screaming my name. The only reason you're even here is because the Emperor appointed that short-arsed army officer, your pal, as lanista.'

'He's not my friend,' Pavo muttered.

'You're both Romans. That makes you both enemies of mine.'

Pavo stood up to leave the canteen. Duras thrust his palm at the young gladiator, shoving him back against the table edge. Something snapped inside Pavo. He grabbed the empty clay plate to his side and shot forward, swinging it at the bodyguard. Duras grunted as it shattered against the side of his skull. Bato leapt back as clay shards clattered across the canteen floor. Duras bared his teeth. Working his thick fingers into a bunched fist, the body-guard punched Pavo in the solar plexus. The blow stunned the young gladiator and sent him stumbling back.

Catching his breath as he regained his balance, Pavo bolted forward in a flash, slamming into Bato head first. Duras looked on in disbelief as Bato gasped, his face purpling as a rush of air shot out of his mouth. He fell backwards, tripping over an upturned bench and collapsing on his back with Pavo on top of him. The other gladiators watched with stunned looks on their faces as Pavo slammed his knuckles against Bato's nose. He shaped to punch again. This time a pair of hands clasped his wrists, wrenching him away from Bato. The young gladiator spun round, ready to punch the bodyguard. Then he saw the face staring back at him and reluctantly relaxed his fist.

'What's going on here?' Macro boomed.

Pavo grimaced. 'Sir, I can explain—'

'I've had enough of you, rich boy! You're nothing but trouble. It follows you around like a bad smell.' The optio looked at Bato. The floored Thracian cupped his blood-spattered nose and groaned.

Just then the doctore came crashing into the canteen. Beads of sweat lined his brow and he gripped the short whip in both hands. He flicked his menacing eyes from Bato to Pavo.

'Making new friends, are we?'

'That Roman shit hit me first,' Bato said in a nasal tone. 'Came at me for no good reason.'

'True?' Macro asked Pavo.

Before the young gladiator could reply, Bato waved a hand at Duras and the other Thracians. 'Ask any of them.'

The men conversed in their native tongue, then looked to Macro and nodded in broad agreement. The optio stiffened his lips.

'Well that settles it, Pavo. You'll have to be disciplined.'

'But Macro – I mean, sir . . .'

'No buts! As First Sword you're expected to set an example to the other men.' Macro jerked his head at the imperial gladiators.

'What do you think that lot will do if they see you escaping punishment? It'll damage morale. And we can't have that, now can we?'

'No, sir.'

'Those are the rules. There can be no exceptions. Aculeo?'

'Sir?' the doctore answered.

'Punish this man as you see fit.'

The doctore flashed a cruel grin at Macro. 'With pleasure, sir.'

Macro glowered at Pavo. 'Now piss off out of my sight.'

A deep resentment stirred in the young gladiator towards Macro. Despite their differences, he had developed a close bond with the optio. The two men had both fought for Rome with distinction, and had an appreciation of the fine art of soldiering. They were united by their shared hatred for Pallas and Murena. Now the optio was treating him like an errant slave, cold and distant and aloof. Stung by a sense of betrayal, Pavo followed Aculeo out of the canteen. He began trudging towards the training posts, bracing himself for the terrible pain that awaited him at the end of the doctore's whip. Aculeo stopped in his tracks and planted his hands on his hips.

'Where do you think you're going?' he asked.

Pavo frowned. 'To the palus, sir. To be lashed.'

'I'm not going to lash you,' Aculeo replied with a hearty chuckle. 'That'd be far too easy! No. A high-born lad such as yourself deserves a special punishment.' He pointed to a building situated at the north-east corner of the ludus. 'You're on latrine duty, Pavo. The drains are blocked again, thanks to bloody Corvus. Do what you can to unblock them, eh?'

'I shall do no such thing!' Pavo retorted indignantly. 'That's slave's work.'

Aculeo cupped a hand to his ear. 'Hear that, Pavo?'

'Hear what?'

The doctore grinned. 'That's the sound of me giving a shit.'

Still grinning, he turned away and began marching towards the latrines. Pavo glumly followed him under the porticoes and down a dimly lit corridor, simmering with outrage at having to do a job he considered beneath him. The whiff of perfumed oil wicks coming from the baths could not stifle the fetid smell of human waste emanating from the latrines. The two smells merged into a pungent, putrid stench that violated Pavo's nostrils and had him fighting his gag reflex.

Aculeo paused by the entrance to the latrines, blocking Pavo's route.

'Not yet, lad,' he said. 'I've got some business to take care of first.'

He winked at Pavo and ducked inside, leaving the young gladiator to loiter amid the shadows, listening to the strains and groans of the doctore as he relieved himself. A short while later Aculeo emerged, hefting up the belt strapped above his loincloth. A noxious stench followed him like a cloud. Pavo pinched his nostrils in disgust.

'Ahhh!' Aculeo patted his belly. 'That was a particularly good shit. Happy Saturnalia, Pavo.'

The paved floor of the filthy latrine was soiled with faeces and the doctore had been careful to foul the water trench cut into the foot of the toilet bench, dirtying the only source of clean water. Aculeo whistled as he set off down the corridor. After a few paces he stopped and turned back to Pavo.

'It, ah, got a bit hairy in there. Must have been all that cake and wine I had for dessert last night. Make sure you give everything a hard scrub, there's a good lad. I want to see that latrine spotless when you're done. Brush and all.'

Pavo gritted his teeth. 'Yes . . . sir.'

It was late afternoon by the time Pavo finished cleaning the latrine. He staggered out with his hands caked in foulness, his stomach heaving and his head ringing with anger at his treatment. Never in all his life had he felt so insulted. He cursed Macro too, and Murena for condemning him to live among barbarians and slaves. He lumbered down the long corridor towards the baths, a leaden despair clouding his thoughts. Cleaning out latrines was in some ways a greater shame than his imminent crucifixion. It served as a painful reminder of the utter depths to which he had sunk.

He entered the changing room, grateful for a few moments'

peace. The distant shouts of the doctore resonated from the training ground, ordering the men to retire to their cells after the end of their afternoon training programme. Pavo decided to remain alone with his melancholic thoughts. He had no wish to surround himself with rowdy gladiators. Setting his loincloth and belt in a neatly folded pile, he crossed under the ornate stucco reliefs and headed towards the hot room. A wave of heat washed over him as he approached the entrance, warming his skin.

A voice pricked his ears.

'We need more weapons. This isn't enough.'

The voice came from inside the hot room. Pavo crept towards the doorway, trapping his breath in his throat. He craned his neck and peeked round the entrance. Inside he spied half a dozen gladiators standing soberly in a semicircle in the middle of the room. He had seen the men before, seated among the Thracians in the canteen. To his astonishment, he spotted an array of make-shift weapons arranged on the mosaic floor at their feet. There were clay shards taken from shattered plates and cups, wooden training swords which had been sharpened at the tips in the fashion of palisade stakes, and a collection of short sticks with rusted nails hammered through them.

'What about the infirmary?' another gladiator suggested.

'Scalpels and needles?' a third asked. 'Against guards armed with swords and spears?'

'We only need to rush 'em and get the keys,' the first gladiator countered. He rubbed his hands in anticipation. 'Once we've released the other men from the cells, getting our hands on some proper weapons won't be a problem. Then we'll overpower the guards, loot the ludus and make our escape.' The man had a sinister gleam in his eyes as he added, 'Not before we've taken care of those bloody Celts, of course.'

'Once we're in the hills, those Roman fucks will never catch us,' the second gladiator said. 'We'll be free to take what we want. There'll be wine and cunny for us all!'

The first gladiator thumped his fist against the wall. 'Bato is right. That bloody lanista reckons he has the run of the ludus. Well he's wrong. He's denied us our bounty and privileges. If we

176

aren't given what we're owed, there's nothing for it but to take it ourselves. Tell you what, boys. We'll earn more working as a brigand unit than we have ever done fighting in the arena!'

The gladiators growled in excitable agreement. The first man nodded to one of his comrades. 'Go to the infirmary. Pretend to Kallinos you have some vague illness. Steal what you can. Go now. We don't have much time. Bato says we must act today.'

The gladiator hurried towards the door. In a blind panic, Pavo spun round to escape from the baths.

'Going somewhere, Roman?' Duras asked in a thick, slow voice, his stale breath filling Pavo's nostrils.

Pavo stood rooted to the spot, his path blocked by the giant bodyguard, fear burning in his throat as the blood drained from his head. Despite the heat emanating from the hot room behind him, he was suddenly very cold.

'You're plotting to escape,' he said quietly.

Duras laughed deep in his chest. His colossal pectoral muscles rippled as he leaned in to Pavo and narrowed his pit-like eyes to slits. 'Suppose we are, Roman. What are you going to do about it? Report us to the fucking lanista?'

'You mean Macro? If you have a legitimate grievance, I suggest you discuss the matter with him.'

'He's a Roman cunt, just like you. I have a better idea. When we've finished cutting up the guards, and those fucking Celts, we'll sling you and the lanista in the same grave.'

Pavo took a deep breath. He heard the patter of footsteps at his back. He turned to see the six gladiators from the hot room closing round him. The man in the middle brandished one of the sticks covered in rusty nails, tapping the tip of the weapon against the palm of his hand. Pavo realised he had no way of escaping the Thracians. They had him cornered. He turned back to Duras.

'Perhaps I can join your rebellion?' He struggled to sound convincing.

Duras smirked as he glanced at the other men. 'A stuck-up Roman siding with us Thracians? Bato would never stand for it.

Nah! Far better to beat you to death right now. Bato planned on killing you anyway.'

'You don't have to do this. I won't betray you.' Pavo felt anxiety rise in his throat.

Duras cracked his knuckles. 'We have a problem. You overheard our plan. We can't trust you not to go running to the lanista, and there's no place in our ranks for a fucking Roman . . .'

Pavo's bowels knotted and he took a step back from Duras, only to bump into the other Thracian gladiators. He tried to duck away to the side, but the bodyguard reacted quickly, wrapping his arms round him and locking his hands round his wrists, gripping the young gladiator in a suffocating hold. Pavo writhed free as the gladiator wielding the stick lifted his weapon above his head, bringing it crashing down against the side of his skull. A piercing sound rang through his ears as the stick clattered into his jaw, drawing hot blood from his cheek. The gladiator swung at him again, disorientating him, while the other gladiators swooped over him, raining a flurry of punches and kicks down on him. He felt sick. Pain burst through his chest as an attacker drove his fist into him. He stopped struggling. Duras released his grip. Pavo collapsed. His face slapped painfully against the marble floor. He was dimly conscious of Duras kneeling beside him, smiling manically from ear to ear. Pavo tried to scrape himself off the floor. A sharp pain flared between his ribs, forcing him to abandon the attempt. Then the giant Thracian placed a bare foot on his chest, pinning him to the ground. The other gladiators surrounded him.

'Got you now, rich boy,' Duras hissed.

Pavo closed his eyes and prepared to die.

CHAPTER TWENTY-THREE

That afternoon Macro undertook a thorough inspection of the ludus's facilities. Accompanied by a clerk, he cast a shrewd eye over the infirmary, baths, latrines, canteen, guards' quarters and armoury, as well as the large two-storey dormitory housing the gladiators two to a cell. The scale of work needed was daunting, but he was determined to make whatever repairs his measly budget permitted. The men needed new training equipment, vital if the optio was going to whip the fighters into decent shape ahead of the forthcoming games. He also reasoned that repairs to the latrines and general upkeep of the cells would improve morale among the men and silence some of the grumbles on the training ground. To fund the work, the previous day Macro had approved the sale of three gladiators to the lanista of a private ludus to the west of Capua. Although sales of imperial stock were theoretically forbidden, the practice had become commonplace under the debt-ridden reign of Caligula, the previous emperor, and Murena had granted Macro special dispensation to sell off excess stock to secure the immediate financial future of the ludus. The sale of three seasoned German provocators had raised 15,000 sestertii each, a staggering sum in comparison to Macro's legionary wage of 900 sestertii per annum.

Even so, most of the income had already been accounted for. Corvus had racked up substantial debts with the local merchants charged with supplying the ludus with victuals. In addition, the administrative staff and guards were owed several months' pay. That would eat up the lion's share of the windfall, with Macro earmarking the remaining sum for the long-overdue maintenance work. After all that expenditure, there would be a small sum left in the coffers to cover any medical bills for gladiators who suffered injuries in the build-up to the games. The sums involved in running a ludus horrified the optio. He privately wondered how lanistas ever managed to turn a profit.

Macro made his way from building to building, pointing out repairs and improvements to be made, which the clerk inscribed on a wax tablet. At the armoury, he stopped to inspect the wrought-iron gate. The air was dusty and rich with the tang of metal. Oil lamps flickered in the corridor. The sharpened tips of swords, spears and daggers glinted menacingly in the gloom. The jambs either side of the gate were surmounted by a crude arch engraved with various gladiator types engaged in battle. Macro grabbed hold of one of the gate bars and tugged at it. The gate groaned on its hinges.

'This lock is fucked,' he sighed to the clerk. 'Any old fool could break in.'

'Yes, sir.'

The meek reply irritated Macro. He'd awoken early that morning with a throbbing hangover, having ended the previous day with an exploration of Corvus's wine store. His predecessor had been quite the connoisseur. The cellar underneath the lanista's quarters was well stocked with Falernian and Caucinian, and even had a couple of amphoras filled to the brim with the finest Faustian. It wasn't hard to see how Corvus had squandered his wealth. Although the quality of the wine was high, Macro hankered for a skinful of the cheap stuff sold at market stalls near the legionary camp on the Rhine. Soon, he reassured himself, he would be relieved of his duties at the ludus and return to action.

He rounded on the clerk. 'This gate is all that separates a hundred and twenty angry gladiators from enough weapons to arm an entire fucking cohort. Now, I'm assuming you remember the story of how that evil bastard Spartacus and his bandits chopped up half of Campania?'

The clerk hung his head in shame. 'Yes, sir.'

Macro nodded tersely. 'Then you'll also know that after Crassus and his legions gave that shit-stirring Thracian a good kicking, strict laws were passed about when and where gladiators could wield a sharpened bit of steel.'

'Of course, sir,' the clerk replied helpfully, shifting on his feet.

'The only time a gladiator gets to use a real sword is when he's about to step out into the arena. Not in his cell, not while he's having a shit, and not on the training ground. Swords are to be kept strictly under lock and key at all times in the ludus. Not left behind a bit of rusting iron. Are we clear?'

'Yes, sir.'

Macro cast a heated glance at the armoury. 'By this time tomorrow this lock had better be replaced and security of the armoury tighter than a Vestal Virgin's cunny. Otherwise I'll make sure you get nailed to a cross. Understood?'

The clerk gulped loudly. 'Understood, sir.'

'Good.' Macro grunted and turned away.

As he marched back to his quarters, he felt a sense of shame at having to use the clerk for the administrative side of the business of managing the ludus. He did not have much choice in the matter, since he could not read or write. His illiteracy was one of his few regrets. As a young boy in Ostia, he'd been taught to identify a handful of letters and numbers, but whole sentences proved impossible and he had never sought to develop his ability. As a soldier, he'd seen no need for it – until he had learned that literacy was a prerequisite for promotion to the rank of centurion. The notion that his illiteracy might prevent him from rising through the ranks festered in his guts, and he resolved to learn his letters and numbers before one of the officers in the legions discovered his secret. Now that he was on the cusp of reaching the rank of centurion, he knew he would have to do something about it soon.

He entered a large rectangular room at the entrance to the lanista's quarters from the east-facing porticoes. The wan twinkle of lamps revealed vividly coloured frescoes adorning the walls. Sunlight cascaded through an opening in the roof and glistened on the surface of a shallow pool filled with rainwater. A set of stone stairs led down to the basement to the right. In front of the pool was an ornamental desk decorated with ivory and bronze, laden with papyrus scrolls and wax tablets. Macro stopped when he noticed a figure pacing nervously up and down the room, muttering under his breath. He was a willowy man with greying locks and a compressed mouth, as if cut with the point of a knife. He wore an off-white tunic and a ceremonial crimson cape fastened at the left shoulder with a clasp. A large chain of dormitory cell keys dangled from his belt. The optio recognised the man as the commander of the ludus garrison.

Macro cleared his throat. The commander glanced up and, seeing Macro, abruptly halted.

'Ah, the imperial lanista,' Quintus Tullius Macer intoned in a high-pitched voice. 'Just the man I was looking for. I want a word with you.' He flicked his eyes to the clerk. 'In private, please.'

Macro nodded to the clerk. 'Dismissed.'

As the clerk departed down a corridor into a side room, the commander of the guard straightened his back and folded his arms across his chest in a defensive posture. He studied the optio for a moment.

'You are making a grave mistake in the way you're running the ludus, Macro.'

Macro snorted his contempt. 'That's "sir" to you.'

The commander huffed. 'I am an officer in the Praetorian Guard. I don't have to address you as "sir".'

Macro rounded on Macer. 'You're on secondment from the guard. Inside this ludus, I am the sole voice of authority, and you had better start addressing me as such. Are we clear?'

Macer glared at the optio. 'As you wish . . . sir. But my protest stands. If you persist with implementing harsh measures over the gladiators, you will drive the imperial ludus to ruin.'

'Harsh measures?' Macro looked at the commander in disbelief. 'Good old-fashioned legionary discipline, I call it. Something the men under your command could do with, Macer.'

'My guards are perfectly capable of defending this ludus, sir.'

Macro snorted derisively. 'I've spent fourteen years as a soldier. I can tell the quality of a fighting man. There's more chance of Neptune himself jumping out of the Tiber than your guards winning a scrap.'

Macer continued to stare implacably at the optio. He had an officious air about him that reminded Macro of the staff officers in the legions. He took an immediate dislike to the man.

'This is not a legionary camp. This is the imperial ludus, sir,' Macer continued. 'We do things differently here. It would behove you to accept that simple fact, as Corvus did.'

'Behove, eh? Speak in simple Latin, man! This isn't a bloody poetry circle.'

Macer twisted his lips in resentment. 'Yes . . . sir. I mean, we must tread carefully with the gladiators. Bato is a noble chief of a warrior tribe. He is not some insolent scum from the Aventine who just happens to wear a legionary uniform and a sword. You must treat him with respect.'

Macro exploded with rage. 'Respect? Fuck off! That Thracian tosser threw down a direct challenge to my authority. Disobedience is not tolerated in the legions, and I won't tolerate it from you either.'

'Be that as it may, you have picked a fight with the wrong man.'

'Bato is a troublemaker. I've seen dozens of soldiers like him. Bad apples. They need discipline. Give him a few good lashes of the whip and a week on half-rations and he'll soon fall into line.'

Macer shook his head. 'I fear not. Bato is no ordinary gladiator, sir. He used to be the First Sword at the ludus until that new chap, Marcus Valerius Pavo, was installed in his place. Pavo's appointment has pissed Bato off.'

Macro shrugged. 'He'll have plenty of time to calm down once Aculeo has finished flogging him.'

Macer clamped his lips shut for a moment, venting his anger through his nostrils.

'The problem is not restricted to Bato. It runs deeper than one man. You see, when Bato was captured, many of the men in his tribe were taken prisoner alongside him. Since they were all exceptionally good fighters, they were transferred en masse to the imperial ludus.'

Macro's face shaded red with anger. 'How many followers are we talking about?'

'Nearly half the men in the ludus, sir.'

'You mean to say that we have a ludus stocked full of prisoners of war itching for revenge against their Roman captors?'

Macer gave a brief nod of his head. After an uncomfortable pause he looked up at Macro. Fear gleamed in his eyes. 'If you push Bato too hard, his men will rebel against your authority. There are a hundred and twenty gladiators within these walls, sir, and only sixteen guards under my command. The Thracian is a simple creature, and he will abide by the conditions of his imprisonment so long as he has wine and women and money. By depriving these men of their privileges, you have laid down a challenge. I fear we will all pay a heavy price for your actions.'

Macro considered the commander with open contempt. He was about to reprimand him when the sound of heavy footsteps cut him off. Spinning round, he saw Aculeo hurrying up the marble steps, gesturing frantically.

'Sir!' the doctore shouted breathlessly. 'Sir, you must come with me at once!'

Macro stiffened at the look of alarm in the trainer's eyes.

'What are you talking about?' he asked impatiently. 'Speak, man!'

Aculeo paused to catch his breath. 'It's the gladiators,' he began throatily. 'Sir, I'm afraid we've got a problem.'

Macro rolled his eyes. 'Don't tell me. Pavo again?' He clicked his tongue. 'That boy is more trouble than he's worth.'

'No, sir,' the doctore gasped. He looked from Macro to Macer. 'It's Bato and his men.'

Macro choked at the doctore's words. 'What have they done?'

'They're refusing to return to their cells, sir.'

Grey clouds smothered the darkening sky as Macro, Macer and Aculeo strode out from under the east-facing porticoes and marched across the training ground. A crisp breeze fluttered across the ludus, and the optio was momentarily reminded of the rain-lashed frontier of the Rhine.

'If only I was so lucky,' he muttered under his breath.

'What's that, sir?' Aculeo asked.

'Nothing,' Macro grumbled.

Shutting out the piercing headache at the front of his skull, he saw a pair of orderlies unloading amphoras from a supply wagon stationed in front of the main entrance. The outer gate had been opened and the portcullis was raised, the iron spikes fixed to the bottom of the oak bars gleaming dully in the gloom. With a heavy grunt Macro swivelled his incensed gaze towards the training posts to the north. There he spotted the troupe of gladiators. He stopped a short distance from the men. Their wooden swords and wicker shields were scattered on the sand at their bare feet in a show of dissent. The gladiators themselves were strangely calm, Macro thought. Their arms were folded across their chests and they stared at him with a cold-blooded defiance that unsettled him. Bato stood at the training post nearest to the guards. His hands were bunched into tight fists at his sides.

A squad of armed guards formed a semicircle round the gladiators. They wore legionary-type uniforms of red tunics under iron cuirasses and sword belts over their shoulders. Their cuirasses were battered and their hobnailed sandals were badly in need of repair. They rested their hands nervously on the pommels of their swords, their legionary-issue shields raised to their chests. One or two of them looked towards Macer for guidance. The commander offered no leadership to his men, Macro thought with disgust. He merely pursed his lips, his eyelids twitching as he tried to shy away from the confrontation.

'What in Hades is going on here?' Macro demanded, turning away from the commander to face the guards and resting his hands on his hips.

'I ordered the men to return to their cells,' one of the guards reported, 'but they won't obey.'

Macro counted the gladiators. 'There are eighteen men here, lad. Where's the rest of 'em?'

'Returned to their cells, sir. We cut short their supper. Thought it best to lock them up, given this protest.'

'What about the other guards?'

'Patrolling the ludus, sir. We've got one gladiator unaccounted for.'

'Who is it?'

'Pavo, sir.'

The imperial lanista felt a tinge of regret at making an example of Pavo in front of the other men at the canteen. Perhaps he had been too harsh on the young lad. But he instantly dismissed Pavo from his thoughts. There could be no special treatment for the young man. Whatever sympathy he had for Pavo was tempered by the fact that he always seemed to be getting himself into some kind of strife. Macro turned to the line of gladiators.

'Right, you lot, that's enough. Return to your cells this instant, or I'll have the lot of you on half-rations for a week.' He fixed his gaze on Bato. 'I suppose you're the ringleader?'

Bato bowed mockingly. 'I am but the mouthpiece of the down-trodden.'

'Bollocks! I should've known you were up to no good.' Macro looked away from the Thracian and addressed the other gladiators. 'Here's my one and only offer. Whoever stops this foolish protest now will be spared punishment. There's no reason to follow this idiot into the mines.'

'We want our wine!' one of the gladiators heckled.

'And our cunny!' Duras joined in.

'Death to the Romans!' a voice from the back taunted.

Macro looked hard at Bato. He resisted a powerful urge to beat up the Thracian for challenging his authority but forced himself to hold back, conscious of the fact that the ludus guards and their weak-willed commander could not be relied upon to deal with the other gladiators.

'Now look here. I'm the lanista. I set the rules. You bloody well follow them, got it?'

'Fuck your rules!' Duras chanted. 'Fuck the ludus!'

Bato chuckled as he gestured at the gladiators. 'You see, Roman. You're wasting your breath. The men are all sworn to me. We have made our position clear. We will not cooperate with you until our privileges are restored and our bounty is paid.'

'Tough shit. I told you before, there's no money.'

A knowing smile tickled the Thracian's lips. 'A barefaced lie, Roman. I know that you acquired the princely sum of forty-five thousand sestertii from the sale of three men. That's ample funds with which to pay off what me and my men are owed.' Bato extended his palm. 'Hand it over.'

'Piss off! That money is already accounted for. There are more pressing debts to settle than your fucking prize money.'

'I am trying to be reasonable, Optio. This is your last chance to save the ludus.'

Macro glared at the Thracian. 'Back down now, or I'll have every man here crucified, so help me.'

Bato sneered. 'You can threaten us all you like, Roman. It will get you nowhere. We want our privileges and our money. And let me see . . .' The Thracian paused, stroking his chin. 'Yes, we would like to negotiate a higher percentage for future victories in the arena. I think an increase to seventy-five per cent of the winning fees sounds like a good deal. What do you think, boys?'

The other Thracians cheered in agreement. Macro breathed furiously through his nostrils, his temper darkening with each passing moment. 'If you think I'm going to give in to some rabble-rousing savage, you've got another think coming.'

'As you wish. But we shall not cooperate until you agree to our demands.' Bato folded his arms. 'Your move, Roman.'

Macer pulled the optio to one side until they were out of earshot of the gladiators. Lowering his shrill voice, the commander said, 'We should negotiate. Give them what they want. No need for any bloodshed, sir.'

Macro clenched his jaw and looked at the commander in disgust. 'I won't negotiate with a bunch of thugs. Besides, if I agree to their demands, the imperial secretary and his aide will go through the roof. This ludus is already on the brink. We can't afford to hand over most of the winnings to Bato and his mob just because they're not happy.'

Macer fell silent. From the corner of his eye Macro spied a violent rage brewing in Aculeo. Now the doctore stepped forward and struck his whip at Bato. Macer winced at the distinct crack of leather tearing off strips of raw flesh. But the Thracian did not blink. Enraged, Aculeo stepped closer. Blood gushed down the gladiator's chiselled torso. The doctore hocked up phlegm in the back of his throat and spat into the Thracian's face.

'You'll get back to your cell now, scum, or I'll whip you so hard you'll be in the infirmary for the next month.'

Bato hardened his stare at Aculeo, the saliva slithering down his nose.

'Fucking Thracians,' Aculeo growled.

Bato launched his balled right hand at Aculeo, aiming for the neck, dropping his right shoulder and bringing his hand round in a wide arc. As he did so, Macro glimpsed a dark object jutting out of the underside of Bato's fist. Fear burned in his throat as he realised that the gladiator was gripping a clay shard. The doctore's eyes widened abruptly as he was struck. The whip fell from his hands. He looked dumbly down as Bato slashed the clay shard across his throat. There was a ripping sound as the shard cut through soft flesh. Blood flowed freely out of the wound. Bato wrenched the shard away, and hot blood splashed over the doctore's chin and trickled down his chest. He staggered backwards and collapsed in a heap on the sand. The guards drew their swords. At the same instant the other gladiators pulled out weapons concealed under their belts and loincloths. Macer visibly shrivelled, taking a step backwards and glancing uncertainly at his men as all hell broke loose.

'Kill them!' Bato roared, pumping his blood-coated fist in the air. 'KILL THEM ALL!'

CHAPTER TWENTY-FOUR

The seven guards were too stunned to react as the gladiators charged them. The nearest gladiator, a broad-shouldered Thracian with a hairy chest, lunged at Macer, yelling at the top of his hoarse voice. The commander lost his nerve and began blindly slashing at the gladiator, his sword trembling in his limp-wristed grip, a look of sheer terror on his face. Macro turned to the guards. An unfamiliar feeling of vulnerability struck him. Unlike them, he had no weapon, having left his sword in the lanista's quarters.

'Hold your ground!' he barked at the top of his voice.

He looked back to the paluses just in time to spot Duras hurtling towards him, teeth bared, eyes blazing with fury. He gripped a sharpened stake in his right hand and plunged the tip at Macro, driving it towards his chest. Macro instinctively parried the thrust with a forceful swipe of his right hand. There was a dull slap as his forearm connected with the gladiator's bicep. Now Macro dropped his shoulder and slammed into the gladiator, sending the man stumbling backwards and crashing to the sand. He snatched up Duras's stake. A blur of colour to the right seized his attention. A pair of unarmed gladiators were storming towards him.

'Come on!' Macro goaded, shaking his stake at them. 'Which one of you bastards wants it first?'

The gladiators swapped a quick look. Then they both charged at Macro, swinging their fists above their heads. Macro easily deflected their sluggish blows. Pouncing at the gladiator on his right, the optio drove his stake into the man's neck. A look of agony contorted the Thracian's face. He made a savage gargling sound, pawing desperately at his throat as Macro tore the stake free. A fist hammered the optio in the right side of the stomach as the second gladiator attacked him. Blocking out the pain, Macro turned to face the man, twisting at the waist and lowering his left shoulder. With his feet planted firmly on the sand, he skewered the gladiator in his exposed abdomen. The man howled in agony. Macro ripped out the stake and glanced up. The guards had backed up to the east-facing porticoes, crouching behind their large shields as the gladiators swarmed at them. Staying hunched, they tentatively stabbed and sliced at thin air with their short swords in an attempt to keep the Thracians at bay. The bodies of two gladiators lay sprawled at their feet.

Macro thought quickly. Although the guards had superior weaponry compared to the clay shards, surgical blades and lengths of wood in the hands of the gladiators, they were taken aback by the wild fervour in the eyes of the men. The gladiators threw themselves at the guards, foaming at the mouth as they roared battle cries in their native tongue. In turn the guards hacked frantically at the charging gladiators. The air quickly filled with the crunching thud of metal against flesh.

One gladiator leapt forward at one of the guards foolish enough to lower his shield and jabbed him in the neck repeatedly with a scalpel. The guard thrashed from side to side as the life spurted out of him. Sensing that the situation was turning desperate, Macro darted forward, his sandals pounding on the parched sand, and hammered his fist into the face of a gladiator attempting to flank the guards. The Thracian's expression registered dumb shock, eyes blinking as his head snapped back.

Now a bearish gladiator slashed wildly at Macro with a clay shard. Macro easily ducked the attack and piked his wooden stake into the man's thigh. Grabbing the legionary sword and shield from the slain guard, he sprang forward on the balls of his feet, rushing over the corpse and crunching his shield into the nearest gladiator, then cutting up with the sword and sinking the blade into the man's armpit. The gladiator growled angrily, staggering back as the blood coursed from his gaping wound. Lowering his sword to hip level, Macro now thrust at a second gladiator, managing to stab the man in his chest with a solid angled drive.

Then he flicked his wrist, giving the blade a good twist and grinding up the gladiator's bowels, drawing a terrified squeal of pain from the man as he collapsed to the sand.

'Stick it to 'em!' Macro yelled to the guards. 'Cut every one of 'em down!'

The men began pressing forward, hunched behind their shields, inspired by the courageous actions of the optio. Slowly they regained the advantage, savagely attacking the poorly armed gladiators. Sword points glinted. Several gladiators continued their attack but their resistance soon crumpled as their makeshift weapons proved no match for their opponents' swords. There was a ferocious roar as the guards pushed forward again, thrusting at the gladiators, stabbing at the mass of exposed torsos with ruthless abandon. The screams of the gladiators were swiftly replaced by the groans and strains of the attacking guards, and the frenzied thunk of swords slamming into bone. Suddenly the surviving gladiators retreated towards the training posts, looking on with dismay as their comrades disappeared under a hail of sword tips and a cloud of dust. Macro did not have time to congratulate himself. He searched frantically around the training ground for Bato.

A rush of motion ahead seized his attention. Duras had cornered Macer. The bodyguard wrenched the shield away from the commander's feeble grip and tossed it aside as if it was made of papyrus. Macer screamed as he retreated from the gladiator, a terrified look stitched into his lax features. Duras roared throatily, diving at Macer. The commander jumped back with fear, slipping on disembowelled entrails and landing on his backside. There was a distinct jingle as the dormitory cell keys tumbled from his belt and landed just out of reach. Duras watched Macer scrabble away on his hands and knees, abandoning the keys, Macro looking on helplessly as the bodyguard bent his enormous frame at the waist and scooped the keys off the ground, chucking them to Bato.

'Bugger it!' Macro grumbled.

He raced towards Bato. The Thracian turned to face him, calmly standing his ground, wielding a wooden training sword which he twirled in his hand as Macro charged at him. His lightning-fast gladiator reflexes caught the optio by surprise. There was a flash of shadow as the wooden blade whacked Macro on the side of his head. He fell to one knee and tried to clear his head of the dizzying sensation. Bato lunged again, bringing the wooden sword down over Macro's head as if chopping with an axe. Macro's combat instincts kicked in, and he rolled on to his side. He felt the swoosh of the wooden blade as it grazed his cheek and stabbed the sand. Seizing the chance to counterattack, he cut up at Bato, aiming at the throat. The gladiator jerked his head at the last instant. The blade nicked his ear. He jumped back, half mad with anger as blood trickled down his neck. His glare turned to a grin as Duras disappeared into the shadows of the dormitory. Bato turned to follow him, and Macro was shaping to pursue them when a voice at his back stopped him short.

'Sir!' one of the guards shouted. 'Look! To the south.'

Macro swung his gaze towards the open gate. Five gladiators had broken away from the battle and were charging the guards at the post next to the gate. Seeing the imminent danger, the guards lowered the portcullis and drew their swords. Macro promptly felt his throat constrict.

'Oh shit. They'll raise the gate!'

He was temporarily torn between pursuing Bato and securing the gate. But with only four guards left standing, and Macer having deserted, he knew he lacked the manpower to regain control of the dormitory. There were sixty cells in the dormitory, with two gladiators to a cell. Attacking it with a trickle of poorly trained and out-of-shape guards would be doomed to failure. On the other hand, as long as the gladiators were trapped inside the ludus, the people of Capua were safe. He quickly decided that isolating the threat was his best strategy, at least until he possessed the means to force the issue with Bato.

Macro turned to the men. 'Who's second-in-command here?'

A young guard with blond curly hair raised his hand. 'Glabrio, sir.'

'You've just been promoted, lad.' The young man gave an anxious nod. 'Now, where the fuck are the other guards?'

192

The young soldier nodded to the dormitory. Hideous screams echoed from deep within it, and he and Macro shuddered at the appalling fate awaiting those guards unfortunate enough to find themselves trapped amid a throng of vengeful gladiators.

'It's too late for them,' Macro said, snapping Glabrio out of his trance. 'Listen carefully. There are only two exits from the ludus. I'll take care of the gate. I want you to fall back to the lanista's quarters and seal the door. We have to make sure there's nowhere for Bato and his men to run.'

'What about Macer, sir?'

The optio stared darkly at the junior officer. 'Macer has deserted. I'm in charge, lad. And I'm ordering you to bloody well seal off the other exit! If you prefer, I can write you up for dereliction of duty, and you can run the gauntlet at dawn. Am I clear, Glabrio?'

The young soldier nodded after a momentary pause. 'Yes, sir!'

'Good. Take one guard with you.'

Macro eyed the arms of a grizzled guard. Judging from his scars, the man had seen combat at one time or another. Unlike his commander, the optio thought glumly.

'You! Name!'

'Bassus, sir.'

'Ever fought in a proper battle?'

Bassus nodded quickly. 'I was in the Eighth Legion for twenty years, sir. Saw plenty of action down by the Danube.'

'Today's your lucky day, Bassus. You get to cut down a bunch of mutinous gladiators and save the imperial ludus from disaster.' Macro gestured to the struggle unfolding at the gate.

The orderlies unloading the wagon had been scythed down by the onrushing gladiators; amphoras lay shattered on the ground, their contents spilling across the sand. One of the guards lay on his back, clutching his guts and screaming for his mother. His comrade put up a brave resistance, but he'd been forced back to the outer door by one of the breakaway gladiators. The other four gladiators split into two pairs, grappling with the two sets of coiled cord ropes used to raise the portcullis.

'We've got to stop them from escaping,' Macro said to Bassus. 'If they break out, half the locals in Capua will find themselves at the wrong end of a blade. Same goes for us if the Emperor discovers our fuck-up. We've got to take them down.'

Bassus looked dumbfounded. 'Seal the doors, sir? Forgive me, but we'll be trapped too.'

'Can't be helped,' Macro answered firmly. 'We're all that stands between a mob of angry gladiators and the people of Capua.'

Macro hurried towards the main gate. Bassus staggered at his shoulder, his breathing laboured as he struggled to match the optio's pace. He was clearly exhausted from the skirmish. Years spent living in the relative comfort of the ludus, far from the rough and tumble of life on the frontiers of the Empire, had dulled his edge. Macro prayed that the guards' superior weapons would be enough to stop the gladiators from gaining complete control of the ludus.

There was a barbaric cheer from the main gate as the portcullis slowly rose off the ground. In front of the outer door, the guard managed to cut down his gladiator opponent and dropped to one knee, clutching a wide gash on his right ankle.

'Take the bastards on the left,' Macro shouted to Bassus. 'I'll cut down the two on the right.'

Bassus nodded enthusiastically. Belting out a hoarse roar, Macro charged at the gladiators to the right of the portcullis. His veins coursed with hot rage and one of the gladiators glanced up at the onrushing optio and hesitated. Filling his lungs, Macro let out an animal snarl and leapt forward. The gladiator quickly dropped the rope and moved to meet Macro head on, bracing himself for impact. At the last moment Macro thrust his shield out, smashing into the gladiator. The shield juddered in his grip, sending tremors up his forearm. He had no time to admire his handiwork. A piercing grating noise told him that the portcullis had finally been raised. The last gladiator on the right was frantically securing the rope.

The optio quickened his pace now, moving forward fearlessly towards the gladiator as he darted for the open mouth of the gate. Macro dived at him, nicking his calf muscle with the tip of his blade. A gout of red and pink oozed out of his leg. The gladiator spun round, hobbling with pain. Macro froze. The gladiator was clutching a sword taken from a dead guard. Incensed by his injury, he thrust his sword at the optio. Macro threw his head to one side at the last instant, the edge of the blade grazing his cheek. The gladiator sprang forward. There was an explosive grunt as the full weight of the man crashed on top of Macro's shield, slamming the optio to the ground. He placed the sole of his hobnailed sandal on the gladiator's chest and kicked out with all his might, launching the gladiator into the air. The man landed heavily a short distance away, the sword clattering out of his hand. As Macro scraped himself off the sand, he saw the gladiator roll on to his belly, crawling towards his sword. Macro had a moment to react. He glanced up and saw the portcullis directly over the floored gladiator. The spikes glistened like wolves' teeth.

'Leave the ludus!' Macro shouted to the guard standing in front of the outer door. 'Lock it behind you, and whatever you do, don't open it up!'

The guard nodded and hobbled out through the doors, slamming them shut behind him. In the same instant Macro spun to his left and hacked through the tautened portcullis rope with his sword with a single clean blow. The rope snapped apart, and the gate crashed heavily to earth. The gladiator on the ground screamed as the spikes punched through his arms, legs and torso, impaling him.

'I've always wanted to do that, sir.'

Macro looked over his shoulder at Bassus. He stood beaming over the bodies of the two gladiators who'd been operating the ropes on the left. They now lay sprawled on the sand.

'What's that, Bassus?'

'Carve up a couple of Thracians. Devious buggers, sir. Couldn't trust any of 'em further than you could piss.'

Macro chuckled drily. 'There's one or two men I could describe that way.'

He sucked in a breath through his teeth as his thoughts turned to Pallas and Murena. The imperial secretary and his aide would surely make him pay a heavy price for the gladiator rebellion. He quickly shook his head clear. There would be plenty of time to worry about the Greeks later. First he had to put a stop to Bato.

'Sir!' Bassus exclaimed. 'Look . . .'

The guard pointed to the dormitory. Two gladiators were dangling a guard from a window on the first floor, gripping him by his feet. The guard was still alive. The gladiators began hacking through his ankles with a pair of saws. The guard howled in agony, thrashing wildly as the saw teeth sliced through bone, before he fell to earth with a thud. Another guard had been set alight and pushed from a window. He landed not far from his stricken comrade and rolled desperately on the ground in a futile attempt to put out the flames.

'Good gods,' Bassus said with a shiver.

Macro turned away from the terrifying spectacle. 'Back to the lanista's quarters. Now!'

They raced across the training ground to the sounds of shrieks and moans as the freed gladiators exacted revenge on the remaining guards inside the dormitory. In the shadow of the porticoes at the northern end of the training ground Macro caught sight of Bato emerging from the dormitory block. Freed gladiators poured out after the Thracian. Bato made a lewd gesture at Macro with his hands and crotch, while around him rampant gladiators uprooted the paluses and overturned the stone sundial.

'Sir,' Bassus said. 'We have to go!'

Macro ground his teeth at the sight of the mutinous gladiators, then hurried on to the lanista's quarters in the gathering dusk, muttering under his breath.

'I swear to the gods, Bato will pay for this.'

CHAPTER TWENTY-FIVE

Macro raced down a wide corridor alongside Bassus, away from the ludus training ground. At the end of the corridor the two men scrambled up a set of marble steps and stopped in front of a solid double wooden door fitted with ornate bronze doorknobs. Macro clasped the knocker, a bronze ring running through the mouth of a wolf's head, and rapped three times on the door.

'Who's there?' a muffled voice asked from the other side.

'It's Macro! For fuck's sake, open up!'

There was a brief pause, followed by a series of metallic clanks and groans as someone fiddled with the heavy lock. Then the door creaked open to reveal Glabrio, breathing a sigh of immense relief.

'Thank Fortuna!' He smiled uncertainly. 'Thought you might have been done for, sir.'

Macro brushed past the young soldier. 'It'll take more than a few barbarians to cut me down, lad. I've been sending men like Bato over to the afterlife for thirteen years.'

'I've never seen anything like it.' Glabrio shivered as he slammed the door shut and secured the lock. 'I used to be with the urban watch here in Capua, sir. Putting out fires and breaking up fights outside the taverns, that sort of thing. Never thought I'd be fighting for my life against a mob of fanatical gladiators.'

A depressing sight greeted the optio in the lanista's quarters. The few surviving guards from the skirmish huddled in a group in the middle of the room. Among them was Macer. They were in a state of shock, drenched with sweat and blood. The orderlies and household slaves stood further back, their wretched faces stitched with anxiety at the sudden outbreak of violence, their eyes collectively focused on Macro for reassurance that their miserable lives were not in immediate danger.

Macro noticed a dishevelled figure pinned down under a guard, who pressed down on the man's back with his knees. The figure rocked his shoulders, trying to shake the guard off. His legs and arms were purpled with bruises and his curly hair was matted with blood.

'Got one of the bastards, sir!' the guard declared proudly. 'The slaves found him hiding in one of the side rooms and alerted us when we got here. He was clearly intending to ambush us, sir.'

'Urghhh,' the figure croaked.

Macro thought he recognised the groan. He approached the man, wrinkling his nose at the putrid smell coming off his filthy skin and hair. At the optio's instruction, the guard reluctantly slid off the man's back and Macro lifted the figure by his chin to get a better look at him.

'Pavo!' he exclaimed. 'What in Hades happened to you?'

'Sir . . .'

Macro ordered one of the household slaves to fetch a cup of wine. A few moments later the slave returned and passed the cup to the young gladiator. Pavo downed the wine in one gulp while an orderly who had experience of working in the infirmary examined his injuries. The sutured wound on Pavo's shoulder had been ripped open and resembled a pair of puckered lips. His jaw was swollen and his lips were distended. The orderly applied a new gauze dressing to his shoulder wound while Pavo sat gingerly upright.

'You're covered in shit,' Macro observed drily.

'I know, sir.'

'And you smell like Gallic cunny.'

'I seem to remember it was you who allowed Aculeo to put me on latrine duty.'

'Just saying.' Macro shrugged. 'Seems to happen to you a lot.'

The young gladiator groaned. 'This is no time for humour . . . sir. I am in rather a lot of pain.'

'That's your problem, Pavo. Always bloody complaining. Now, what happened?'

The young gladiator glared at Macro through his puffed-up eyes. 'They ambushed me, sir. In the baths. I overheard them plotting the rebellion. Then they left for me dead. I managed to escape when they went to begin the uprising. I came here to warn you. But it was too late.'

'Bato's thugs?'

Pavo nodded and swallowed hard. 'They're planning to escape the ludus, sir. Make their way to the hills and set up as a brigand outfit.'

'Shit.' Macro rubbed his jaw.

'Why didn't they all make a run for it back there when they had the chance, sir?' Bassus asked. 'Only a few tried to escape, rather than the entire mob. It doesn't make sense.'

The optio considered the guard's words for a moment before tightening his gaze at the sealed door. 'If Bato is planning a new career in brigandage, he needs men – and plenty of them. There'd be no point in escaping with only a handful of gladiators. That's why he ambushed us rather than flee the ludus immediately. He needed the keys to the dormitory block in order to release all his mates. Someone was kind enough to let him get his hands on them.'

Macro turned to look at Macer as he spoke and he saw the commander slipping away from the crowd in the middle of the room towards the door. Anger surged in Macro's heart and he leapt towards the man and clamped his hand round his wrist.

'What the hell do you think you're doing?' Macer yelped. He tried wrenching his wrist free of Macro's firm grip. 'Release me at once! I wish to leave. I have no desire to die because of your foolishness.'

'You're going nowhere,' Macro snapped. 'Everyone is to stay here until the rebels have been crushed.' Even in the dim glow of the candles, the expression on his face must have been visible to Macer, because he shifted awkwardly on his feet and swallowed hard.

'This is all your fault,' he said waspishly.

'That's rich, coming from the coward who dropped the keys to the cells.'

Macer narrowed his eyes at Macro until they were slits as thin as his lips. 'Your stubbornness has led us down a path of destruction, Optio. I warned you that Bato commands a loyal following. I implored you not to aggravate the man. Corvus at least heeded my advice. He knew it was best to keep Bato under control with the odd indulgence. If only you had listened to me, none of this would have happened.'

'I was doing my job. It's not my fault you let Bato have the run of the place.'

'I'm sick of being lectured by a common soldier,' Macer sneered. 'You may have been decorated by the Emperor, but I served in the Praetorian Guard. I don't have to listen to your tirade, Macro.'

'You're a failed Praetorian. Worse, you're a fucking disgrace.'

Macer stiffened. 'Several of my men are dead. The blame for that lies squarely with you. Thanks to your incompetence and your refusal to heed my repeated warnings, a dozen or more gladiators are also dead – each worth thousands of sestertii, I might add, and the personal property of his imperial majesty. I shall write this incident up and present my report to Pallas at the first opportunity.'

'By all means. Then I'll explain to Pallas how you ran away and left your men to fend for themselves. Even those sly Greeks take a pretty dim view of cowardice.'

Macer pressed his lips together.

'Glabrio!' Macro yelled.

'Sir?' the guard answered.

'Take this man down to the basement and chain him up.'

The guard approached Macer and seized his upper arm.

'You can't do this!' the officer protested.

'I already am.' Macro raised his sword and pointed the tip at Macer's soft chin, drawing a panicked look from the commander. 'Now don't make any noise down there. I don't want to have to come down and convince you to shut up.'

Glabrio bundled Macer towards the steps leading down to the cellar. 'You'll pay for this, Optio, I swear!'

Macro watched the commander depart. Beside him Bassus clicked his tongue.

'What's the plan now, sir?'

Macro pursed his lips as he considered his options. 'We're low on numbers. Apart from the guards, we've only got a bunch of orderlies and household slaves, and none of them has a hope in Hades of wielding a sword. We're no match for our enemy. The odds don't favour us.'

He felt a leaden weight descend on his shoulders. Taking a deep breath, he thought for a moment before continuing.

'We can only hope to crush the rebellion by regaining control of the ludus. The main entrance is reasonably secure. Even if Bato and his men manage to lever up the portcullis, that outer door won't budge. But sooner or later the gladiators will figure out that they can break through this door without any great difficulty. Then the lot of us are done for.'

'So what are we waiting for?' Bassus said. 'Let's take the fight to 'em, sir!'

Macro shook his head bitterly. 'As I said, we don't have the numbers to take the dormitory by force. There are about a hundred remaining gladiators versus only a few of us. As things stand, we have no way of retaking the ludus. The best we can hope to achieve is to contain the gladiators within these walls. But that's a temporary measure. It's only a matter of time before Bato forces the issue and attacks us with everything he's got. We'd be able to hold out for a short while, but sooner or later that Thracian pig and his men would overrun us.'

'What about asking the nearest ludus for help?' Bassus enquired.

Macro grimaced in frustration. 'I've thought about that already. But it's a non-starter. The closest one is half a day's travel. It's too far. By the time any reinforcements arrived, Bato would have barged his way through here and left us all for dead.'

'So that's it, sir? We're done for?' Pavo asked softly.

'Not necessarily,' Macro answered tersely. He turned to Pavo. There was a glint in his eye as he smiled at the badly bruised gladiator. 'You're forgetting that the Emperor is en route to Capua from Puteoli.'

Pavo nodded. 'Murena mentioned it at our meeting last week. Told me the old fool wants to cast his eye over the imperial gladiators ahead of next month's games.'

'The Emperor travels with a large retinue. Pallas will be with him, of course. And the other freedmen Claudius insists on surrounding himself with.' Macro flashed a wide grin at Pavo. 'But more importantly, he'll be accompanied by his German guards.'

Pavo slapped his hand against his thigh. 'By the gods, you're right! I've seen the Germans at the imperial palace. There's got to be at least two hundred of them in Claudius's personal body-guard. Even with half their number, we could soon put an end to Bato and his rebellion.'

'The Emperor was due to arrive in Capua today, if I remember correctly.'

'Yes, sir,' Pavo answered eagerly. 'At a villa on the hills above Capua. I've been there. It's not far by foot. If we send a messenger now, the Germans could reach us by nightfall, sir.' He paused, his brow furrowed. 'But what if Murena refuses to come to our rescue? Knowing that Greek snake, nothing would please him more than to see the pair of us get slaughtered by a mob of rabid Thracians.'

Macro shook his head. 'He's not in a position to refuse to help us, lad. This is the imperial ludus, the property of the Emperor. Once Murena gets word of the rebellion, he'll shit himself at the thought of the gladiators tearing the place down. That conniving Greek and his master Pallas will have no choice but to send out a full complement of Germans. Then we can take back the ludus.' Macro's expression suddenly soured. 'The only downside is it means having to grovel to Murena. He and Pallas will bloody love it. They'll have me by the balls. I'll be indebted to both of them. Worse, they might very well blame me for the rebellion in the first place.'

'There is no other way, sir,' Bassus said, throwing his arms into the air in exasperation. 'You said so yourself. The private ludi are all too far away. Murena is close by. He's the only chance we have to save this place . . . and ourselves. Besides, if you don't ask him for help and Bato's men overrun us, the Emperor will demand your head for losing his gladiators and his ludus.'

'Saved by a couple of Greeks.' Macro shook his head. The thought rankled.

'We don't have any choice.'

Macro bit his tongue as he wrestled with the dilemma. Begging for help from the aide to the imperial secretary offended his principles. He was a resourceful soldier, with a proud record of overcoming desperate odds on the field of battle. But even he could see no way out of their predicament without calling on outside support. Swallowing his pride, he thumped his fist on the desk.

'Bollocks!' He swung his gaze towards the door as Glabrio returned from the cellar. 'Glabrio!'

'Yes, sir?' the guard replied.

Macro gestured to the front door. 'I want you to leave immediately for the Emperor's villa. Pavo will provide you with the precise directions. Get there as soon as possible. When you reach the villa, tell Murena it's an emergency. Make sure he understands that the safety of not only the ludus but all of Capua is at stake. We need every German guard he can spare.'

Glabrio nodded dutifully. After being given directions by Pavo, the guard hurried out of the ludus. Macro watched him leave, a sense of excitement building in his chest at the thought of the impending reinforcements.

'Now all we have to do is hold our position until the Germans arrive.'

A thought clouded Pavo's mind. He bit his lip as the door closed behind the guard. Macro noticed the unease written into the young gladiator's features.

'What's bothering you, boy?'

Pavo pursed his lips. 'It's something that Bato's followers said in the baths, right before they set on me. About their plan, sir.'

Macro frowned. Pavo did not appear to like what he had heard. 'Well, what is it?'

Pavo closed his eyes as a wave of hot pain shrieked in his ribs. 'According to his thugs, Bato and his men only plan to escape once they've freed their comrades and ransacked the ludus.'

'The money raised from the gladiator sales,' Macro acknowledged gruffly. 'Bato got wind of it and demanded I hand it over. Go on.'

'A successful brigand outfit needs weapons, sir. That's what I overheard in the baths.' Pavo stared at the optio and gulped loudly. 'His men were discussing the possibility of acquiring some proper weaponry.'

Macro looked wide-eyed with horror at the gladiator.

'Oh shit. The armoury.'

CHAPTER TWENTY-SIX

Pavo regarded the optio with a look of deep concern. Faint screams emanated from the dormitory block on the other side of the ludus as the gladiators continued to riot and murder indiscriminately. Bassus and the other guards tightened their gazes on Macro. In the background the slaves stood still and silent, listening in to the conversation.

'Aren't the weapons locked up?' Pavo asked.

Macro laughed in his throat. 'That's a generous way of putting it. The gate protecting the weapons is rustier than my Greek. Your son could break it open, let alone Bato and his mob.'

'That's if they haven't already done so,' Bassus cut in. 'We may be too late.'

Pavo shook his head. The effort made him wince. Every muscle in his body ached horribly. He bit back on the pain, swallowed it into the pit of his stomach, remembering the stoic resilience of Titus and his forebears, drawing strength from their bravery in the face of adversity.

'Bato won't have got to the armoury yet.'

Macro rubbed his heavily furrowed brow. 'How can you be so sure?'

'I overheard him saying that he plans to execute the Celts in their cells first.'

'Makes sense, sir,' Bassus said with a curt nod. 'One of the Celts killed Bato's brother in a training-ground bout. The Celt was punished, but Bato has hungered for revenge ever since.'

'What about the other Thracians?' Macro asked. 'Do they hate the Celts too?'

Bassus nodded. 'The killing of the tribal chief's brother is a matter of honour among the men of Thrace, sir. Bato's men crave the shedding of Celtic blood as much as Bato himself.'

Macro thumped his fist into the palm of his hand. 'We have to do something about the armoury before Murena sends us reinforcements. The Germans would make simple work of a mob of unarmed Thracians. But fighting heavily armed gladiators is a different prospect. These men are highly trained killers. They'd certainly put up stiff resistance. We'd suffer heavy losses. Some of them might even escape to the hills.'

Silence greeted his words.

Then a thought struck Macro. His eyes glowed with grim determination. 'While Bato and his men are busy carving up Celts for supper, we'll burn the armoury down. Render the weapons useless.'

'Crude but effective, sir,' Pavo said. 'Although I doubt the Emperor will be pleased about the damage to his ludus.'

'He'll be less pleased by the damage to his empire if we don't,' Macro countered.

'You are forgetting one thing, sir,' Pavo cautioned.

Macro looked blankly at him. 'What's that?'

'We're trapped,' Pavo answered simply. 'As soon as you stick your head out of the door, a mob of angry gladiators will descend on you like dogs after scraps of meat. They'd rip us all limb from fucking limb. Pardon my Gallic, sir.'

Bassus wagged his finger at the gladiator. 'There is another way out. One that Bato and his followers won't know about.'

Macro turned to the guard. 'What do you mean?'

'We can use the drainage tunnel, sir. It runs under the perimeter of the ludus. One of the gladiators tried to escape through it once, so Corvus sealed it off at this end with a metal grille. But from this side, two or three of us ought to be able to follow the tunnel in the direction of the armoury.'

Pavo raised an eyebrow. 'The tunnel will take us all the way to the armoury?'

'I'm afraid not,' Bassus responded with a frown. 'There was no need for it to be accessible from the armoury. It does, however, link to the infirmary, which is next to the armoury. All we have to do is crawl into the tunnel through the reservoir in the cellar and follow it south, then climb up through the drain and make our way down the corridor.'

'Then it's settled,' Macro decided. 'We'll use the drain tunnel.'

He wheeled away from Pavo and carefully removed the bronze medals strapped across his chest. He handed them to an orderly. 'Take care of these, eh? They were given to me by Claudius. I'll need two good men to come with me. Bassus, you'll do. That leaves one more . . .'

The optio's eyes settled on Pavo.

'Me?' The young gladiator snorted and shook his head. 'Forget it. I'm in no fit state to fight.'

'We're in the middle of a crisis, Pavo.'

Pavo looked unconvinced. 'Even if I did help, what good would it do me? They're going to crucify me at the games anyway, sir.'

'Unless they can't afford to.'

Pavo scratched his elbow. 'I'm not sure I follow.'

'Think about it, lad. You have a chance to make yourself indispensable to those slippery Greeks. Once we've stopped the rebellion, Bato and his loyal followers will have to be executed. Set an example to the other men. The ludus is thin on gladiator numbers as it is. With Bato and the other Thracians out of the way, Pallas and Murena won't dare try to bump you off. There's no one to take your place at the games, and the mob in Rome won't accept a second-rate gladiator as the main event.'

Pavo clenched his teeth and bit back on the pain throbbing between his temples. The young gladiator hated the idea of being outwitted by the homespun soldier, but Macro had made a convincing argument.

'Listen,' Macro continued. 'Every one of Bato's followers that you cut down is one fewer gladiator to fight at the games. Help me put an end to the rebellion and you'll have a fighting chance of staying alive and getting to face Hermes. You won't just be a victorious gladiator. You'll be the Roman fighter who helped crush another Spartacus.' The optio shrugged. 'Or you can give up, sit here stinking of shit and wait for the Greeks to kill you. Or Bato. Whoever gets to you first, I suppose.'

Pavo felt the blood pound in his veins. He groaned in his throat as he stood fully upright, but the rage in his heart drowned out the chorus of pain. 'I'll join you, Optio.'

Macro studied Pavo for a moment. Although Pavo was a high-born aristocrat, the worst kind of Roman in Macro's eyes, there was something he warmed to in the lad. He was taciturn and occasionally naïve, but he was also surprisingly tough and bloody-minded, qualities that reminded Macro of himself as a young recruit to the Second Legion. He nodded his approval.

'That's more like it, lad. Glabrio!' Macro yelled, turning away from the gladiator.

'Yes, sir!'

'You're in charge here. Whatever happens, you don't let anyone through that door. If every slave in this room has to lay down his life defending this position, so be it. Once the Germans arrive, assemble the men at the main gate and post a lookout in the watchtower above. Wait for the first sign of smoke from the burning armoury. That'll be the signal for you to attack.'

'Yes, sir,' Glabrio said sternly. 'But what if the Germans don't get here in time?'

'I imagine Murena will be sweating out of his arse once he learns of Bato's actions. He'll send the men as soon as possible.' Macro turned away from the guard and smiled at Pavo. 'Now hurry up, lad. Bato and his mob might be leaving the dormitory at any moment. There's no time to lose.'

A short while later, Macro, Bassus and Pavo crept through the tunnel in near darkness. Pavo lit the way, carrying a lamp he had retrieved from the lanista's quarters. Macro followed, with Bassus bringing up the rear, the men clasping their swords above their heads to protect their weapons from the sewage. The lamp cast eerie shadows across the curved stone walls, and Pavo tried hard to focus on the mouth of darkness ahead of him rather than look down at the foulness swirling at his feet.

'How many times have I got to get covered in shit in one day?' he grumbled to no one in particular.

'Best get used to the feeling,' Macro said. In the darkness his voice seemed very close. 'If we somehow survive this rebellion, we'll be up to our necks in it with that slimy pair of freedmen. Besides, from the look of you, I'd say you have plenty of experience of wading through shit.'

'Such a refined sense of humour,' Pavo replied drily.

A wave of nausea tickled the back of the young gladiator's throat. He caught a strong whiff of fresh faecal matter and felt his back spasm. He involuntarily dropped his head and emptied his guts. The sound of his retching travelled down the tunnel.

'Better out than in, boy,' Macro said.

'Don't know what you two are complaining about,' Bassus added cheerily. 'This isn't so bad. You want to take a walk through the Subura at night. Shit all over the place, I tell you.'

'Gah! Rome,' Pavo uttered throatily, spitting out the bitter tang of vomit on his tongue. 'If I never set foot in that city again, I'll be a happy man. It's a dangerous place to be rich, or notable.'

He fell silent, staring ahead and trying to recall the distance between the lanista's quarters and the armoury to the south, on the eastern side of the ludus. He suddenly stiffened at the sound of a distinct squeal emanating from further down the tunnel. The bristles stiffened on the back of his neck and he peered at the dense blackness ahead with a cold sense of foreboding stirring in his stomach.

'What is it?' Macro hissed from behind. 'Why have we stopped?'

'Rats!' Pavo yelped. 'I hate rats!'

An instant later hundreds of the creatures burrowed out of the darkness and scurried through the sewage. Pavo quivered with disgust as the vermin scampered between his legs, scratching his knees. The young gladiator swept his hands in front of him, swiping them away. But they kept coming, scuttling up his hands and running along his back. In a blind panic he lowered the lamp and swept the flame back and forth across the rats, causing them to shriek and disperse.

'Got you!' he said as he sent another scorched rat darting away from the flame.

As he lifted the lamp he noticed a rat creeping up his right arm. It squealed at him. Pavo flinched. The lamp fell from his grasp and plopped into the sewage, extinguishing the flame and plunging the tunnel into utter darkness.

'What happened?' Macro asked.

'I dropped the lamp.'

'Really?' Macro gritted his teeth. 'Why can't you stop buggering things up, boy?'

The young gladiator was still for a moment as he strained his eyes. 'I can see something up ahead.'

A sliver of light shone in front of him. He squinted, but in the subterranean darkness it was impossible to discern how far away it was. He crept towards it, a tingling sensation working down his spine. The thought of gaining revenge over Hermes kept him going. Pavo no longer felt offended by the misery of life as a gladiator, cheered in the arena and bullied in the ludus. He had plenty of high-born friends in Rome whose lives were equally treacherous and squalid. Only their surroundings differed. But he had a higher purpose: to honour his father's name and restore it to its former glory. Only by killing Hermes could he achieve that. Yesterday, he reflected, his circumstances had seemed hopeless. Now his heart filled with steely determination. By defeating Bato and his thugs, he could save himself from crucifixion. He had a chance of staying alive long enough to win his fight against Hermes. He smiled in the pitted darkness at the thought that Bato's mutiny might work in his favour.

'Almost there,' he said.

The three men shuffled on in the pitch black, and the sliver of light swelled to reveal a drain set into the roof of the tunnel. Torchlight shimmered in the room above. Moving at a slow pace to keep his movements silent, Pavo finally stopped beneath the drain. He craned his neck up at the light and squinted.

'What can you see?' Macro whispered.

'Shelves stacked with gauze dressings, sir.'

'Yes! The infirmary!' The optio shook his head. 'Never thought I'd say that.'

'What now?' Bassus asked from the back.

Macro jolted Pavo. 'Go on, lad. Get up there. Quick, now. We don't have much time. If I have to wallow in this filth much longer, I'm in danger of smelling as terrible as you.'

Pavo gripped the sides of the drain and hauled himself up. It was a tight squeeze, and he had to strain to drag himself out on to the hay-strewn floor of the infirmary. Clasping his sword, he surveyed the infirmary as Macro and Bassus hauled themselves out of the drainage tunnel after him. The typical surgical instruments of hooks, bone drills, spatulas and saws had been looted by the earlier mob. A strong smell of garlic and sage hung in the air, mixing with the stench of human waste to form a putrid, sickly-sweet aroma.

Pavo stilled his breath as he moved north down the corridor leading to the armoury, softening his step and keeping the tip of his sword pressed ahead of him at hip height. In the distance the heightened screams of men carried across the training ground as several unfortunate Celts underwent prolonged torture and suffering at the hands of their former comrades. A little way down the corridor Pavo spied the armoury, its iron bars glittering in the glow of a nearby torch. His heart thumped furiously in his chest, blood twisting in his veins at the thought of wrecking the plan of Bato and his followers. As he neared the gate, the thumping increased in pace and fear spread through his heart.

Figures were pouring into the armoury. The lock had already been dismantled and the gates wrenched open. Pavo stopped dead in his tracks as Macro and Bassus drew alongside him. The three men looked on in dismay at the throng of gladiators, their broad shoulders and prominent chest muscles illuminated by the flicker of an oil lamp. The Thracians did not notice the small party further down the corridor.

'Shit,' Macro hissed under his breath. Pavo turned to him. Even in the intermittent glow of the lamps, the frustration was clear on the optio's face. Macro tensed his muscles and drew his sword. 'There's only a few of them. Come on. We can take them down.'

Pavo and Bassus gripped their own swords tightly. Once the last of the mob had entered the armoury, Macro raised his weapon.

'Now!'

With a terrifying roar he charged towards the armoury, with

Pavo and Bassus at his sides. The gladiators pillaging the armoury turned as one to see the three men storming out of the shadows in the corridor and closing in on them. They were too late to react. Grabbing a shield from the armoury floor, Macro parried the thrust of the first gladiator he came upon. Then he slammed his shield into the man and knocked him back against two of his comrades. He stabbed the man in his groin before he could get to his feet, wrenching the sword free. Pavo and Bassus grabbed shields of their own and attacked the other gladiators.

'Get stuck in!' Macro laughed. 'Don't show them any mercy!'

One of the Thracians hastily grabbed a spear from a rack on the wall and singled out Pavo, charging at him in a mad fury. The young gladiator tensed his strong muscles, his mind racing as the spear tip glanced off the shield braced in front of his chest. Pavo filled his lungs and charged the man, knocking aside the spear and then driving the tip of his sword into the rebel gladiator's groin before cutting up into his stomach. The man spasmed furiously as blood cascaded out of his wound. Pavo gave the sword a twist for good measure, then wrenched his weapon free and watched the gladiator collapse to his knees. Glancing around, he saw Macro smashing his fist into another gladiator's face. Grabbing the stunned gladiator by his throat, Macro hurled the man off his feet and sent him crashing into a rack of javelins arranged along the far wall. Behind the optio another gladiator seized a curved dagger and lunged at him, spitting with rage.

'Macro, watch out!'

Pavo raced towards the optio as he spun round to face the gladiator armed with the curved dagger. He slammed his right shoulder into the gladiator, knocking the blade away a moment before it slashed at Macro. The force of the blow dropped the gladiator to the ground. As he made to scrape himself off the ground, Pavo thrust his sword into the rebel's exposed neck. The man rasped, his fingers clawing at the point sticking out of his throat. With a final grunt Pavo wrenched his blade free. Blood spurted out of the wound.

'Learning a trick or two, I see.' Macro nodded admiringly at the Thracian.

Pavo shrugged casually. 'I had a good teacher.'

'That's the last of that sorry mob,' Macro said, gesturing at the sprawled gladiators. 'But there'll be plenty more of them on the way. The sooner we burn this place down, the better.'

Pavo surveyed the armoury while Bassus fetched an oil lamp. He noticed something and turned to Macro, pointing out several empty racks. 'It appears these gladiators were not the first to loot the armoury.'

'What are you talking about?' Macro asked.

'There are weapons missing, sir.'

Macro thumped his fist against the wall. 'Fuck! Bato must have removed some of them first.'

Pavo nodded. 'They probably took as much as they could carry, and intended to come back for the rest.'

'At least most of his men won't be armed. Good job too. There's enough weapons here to arm every one of the gladiators to the teeth.' Macro indicated the array of swords, spears and shields on display in the armoury. Some were unfamiliar to the optio's keen eye, and he supposed they had been modelled on the curved weapons preferred by armies in the east.

'Burn it,' he ordered.

Gripping a bronze oil lamp by its handle, Bassus held the flame to the nearest wooden rack. The air was quickly choked with fumes and a few moments later the rack erupted into flames. Bassus applied the flame to another rack and retreated with Pavo and Macro to the gate as the flames licked at the swords and spears, burning the shafts and handles. The guard threw the oil lamp into the swelling flames and joined the two men in the corridor. Macro grunted in satisfaction, his blood stirring at the sight of the weapons going up in flames.

'Sir!' Pavo exclaimed, clasping Macro's arm. 'Look!'

The optio followed the young gladiator's gaze beyond the porticoes and across the training ground. In the soft twilight he spied a horde of gladiators disgorging from the dormitory block and charging towards the burning armoury.

'The fire's alerted them,' Bassus observed. 'Now we're really in the shit.'

Several of the men were equipped with shields and swords. Others carried thrusting spears and daggers. Bato led the gladiators from the front of the pack. The Thracian rebel wielded a curved bronze shield and a curious four-pronged dagger. The steel prongs were bunched tight and straight in the shape of a cross, and were roughly a foot in length. Duras marched by his side wearing leather gloves with iron spikes sewn into the material. A three-pronged bronze fork was studded to the knuckles.

Bato grinned sadistically at Macro, his green eyes sparkling as they reflected the flames consuming the armoury. Smoke billowed out of the gates. The air was thick with the smell of charred wood. Beside the optio, Pavo clenched his fist round the handle of his sword in trepidation.

'There's got to be a hundred of them. They've got us trapped, sir.'

'Hold your ground, lad,' Macro said resolutely.

Bato slowed his pace as he neared the men. The flames roared behind them. The Thracian was momentarily distracted by the fire raging in the armoury. He pulled a sour face at the scorched weapons, then looked back at Macro and pointed at him with the prongs of his dagger.

'Ah, lanista! Trying to ruin my plan, I see. Sadly, you're too late. We already looted some weapons from the armoury. Along with the swords and shields taken from the guards we've killed, enough of my men are armed to easily overthrow you and the remaining guards.' He turned to Pavo. 'And I see you've brought your friend along. How convenient. Now I shall have the pleasure of watching you both suffer.'

'You might kill us, but your rebellion is doomed. You'll all be crucified.'

Bato laughed smugly. 'I think not. By the time the legions get word of our uprising, we will have disappeared into the hills. A lifetime of looting and pillaging awaits me, Roman. The only thing you have to look forward to is an excruciatingly painful death.'

'Go to Hades,' Macro bellowed huskily.

'You first,' Bato rasped.

As he made to charge at Macro, a sudden shout erupted from the south of the training ground, in the direction of the main entrance. The Romans and gladiators simultaneously turned towards the guttural cry. In the next instant the outer doors groaned open and a wave of shadows swarmed through the entrance and charged towards the gladiators gathered on the training ground. The look on Bato's face shrivelled to abject horror at the sight of the onrushing force. The men wore the breeches familiar to German tribes, and were armed with two-metre-long spears with shafts made of weathered ash with iron shanks mounted on top. Their swords were considerably longer than the standard legionary type. The gladiators stood rooted to the spot, stunned by the sight.

'Thank fuck for Murena!' Bassus cried. 'The Germans are here!'

CHAPTER TWENTY-SEVEN

Macro faced forward, his heart warming at the sight of ever more Germans pouring into the training ground.

'NOW!' he roared. 'Come on, lads! Let's stick it to 'em!'

The optio led with his sword towards the line of gladiators as Bato bellowed orders for his men to confront the advancing Germans. The spell broken, the Thracians slowly turned as one to face the Germans racing across the training ground. Several gladiators on the front line who were fortunate enough to be armed raised their pilfered shields to brace themselves against the impending attack. But the men were shaken by the bloodcurdling roars from the Germans and seemed hesitant to charge. Bato booted one gladiator in the small of his back, kicking him towards the oncoming shadows.

'Run at them, you dogs! Cut them down!'

His words were silenced as the Germans tore into the gladiators, thrusting their spears. The Thracian front line stood firm, planting their feet in the sand as the spear tips pierced their shields. Their unarmed comrades howled in agony as the tips punched through muscle and bone, impaling the gladiators and driving them back, pressing against their comrades to the rear. One of the men gave out a bloody gurgle as a German plunged his spear at him with such power that the tip exploded out of his muscular back. Undeterred, the gladiator began furiously hacking at the staff jutting out of his chest with his short sword. His German opponent snarled and thrust his spear in an upward motion, sweeping the gladiator off his feet and piking him in the air. Around him there was a blazing shimmer of steel as his comrades brought their long swords to bear and proceeded to cut down the enemy in a manic hail of stabs and thrusts.

Many of the gladiators were still armed with only clay shards or sticks, but the Germans showed no mercy, slashing at them with savage force. One gladiator charged at the Germans, swinging a wooden stake. He managed to jab one in the stomach and stunned a second with a sharp blow to his jaw. The gladiator let out a defiant roar as several more Germans descended on him, pounding him with their fists and thrusting ruthlessly at his prone figure. The man made a gurgling noise. A moment later one of the Germans hoisted the gladiator's decapitated head above the battle, the mouth slack and the eyes popped wide in a picture of mortal terror, a loose knot of veins and sinew dangling underneath it. Macro recognised the gladiator as one of Bato's loyal followers. With an animal roar the German struck another gladiator with the severed head, knocking him to the ground. Then he hurled the head through the air before continuing the attack against the remaining gladiators.

From the rear of the gladiator mob Bato watched the German advance unfold, his face a picture of mortal terror. Macro spied Duras tugging at his leader, imploring him to leave the fight as the Germans slashed their way through the defenceless gladiators. The Thracian pumped his fist at the optio. Then the two gladiators began picking their way out of the melee. Macro watched them flee and felt his pulse quicken. He gestured to Pavo and Bassus.

'Follow me!'

He raced ahead of the men, weaving through the gladiators engulfed in the relentless German onslaught. Ahead of him a burly Thracian swung round, blocking his path. Adjusting his stance at the last possible moment, Macro thrust his blade at the man, aiming for the lower chest. The blade juddered in his grip as the tip glanced off the gladiator's ribcage and pierced his vital organs. The gladiator mouthed a silent scream, his limbs trembling in agony as he stumbled backwards. Macro raced on. But the gladiators were being pushed back by the sheer ferocity of the enemy attack and he kept losing sight of his prey amid the crushing chaos.

At last he spotted two German guards who had cornered Duras

and Bato as they attempted to flee. One of the Germans thrust his spear at Duras. The bodyguard gripped the shaft before the tip could nick his flesh, and snapped the spear in two. He swung at the German and floored him with one blow to the chin, then pummelled the floored German into submission with his spiked gloves. At the same time Bato avoided the thrust from the second German's long sword, his lightning-quick reflexes allowing him to duck and attack in the same move, plunging the four-pronged dagger into the man's groin. The German gasped. Bato twisted his wrist, shredding the guard's manhood, grinning as he watched him fall to the ground. Then he pulled Duras away from the fight, leaving the savagely beaten German on the sand, his face caved in, his eyes, nose and teeth reduced to a glistening, bloodied pulp. They continued ducking and diving through the swarm of gladiators, heading towards the practice arena. Macro struggled to contain the rage building inside him.

'Bastards!' he snarled. 'Don't let them get away!'

Pavo caught up with Macro and surveyed the training ground. The sand had darkened. Puddles of blood glistened. Pockets of gladiators were fleeing the battle and heading for the sanctuary of the dormitory in a ragged retreat. The Germans hunted them down, bellowing their barbaric delight to a chorus of frenzied stabbing and thrusting.

Bassus pointed ahead. 'Look, sir!'

At the far end of the training ground a pair of silhouettes reached the western wall. Bato and Duras looked frantically around them. To the north, the Germans swarmed round the dormitory, cutting down even those gladiators who raised their hands in surrender, mutilating their corpses. One gladiator begged for mercy as the Germans booted him to the ground and plunged a spear into his guts. The man's eyes bulged in his sockets as the spear bored into his stomach. To the east, the battle raged. The two Thracians realised their only way of retreat was south.

Bassus squinted. 'They're heading to the practice arena.'

Macro growled in his throat. 'Good. Nowhere for them to run. Let's finish this.'

The three men broke across the training ground, stepping

between the slain gladiators and Germans. Darkness had now settled over the horizon and a full moon shimmered in the sky, washing the ludus in a pale light. The screams and clangs of the raging battle faded as they swept through the arched entrance leading to the arena and stopped in the centre, running their eyes across the wooden galleries.

'Where the fuck are they?' Macro whispered. 'Pavo, secure the gallery. Bassus, stay here. Guard the entrance.'

Macro and Pavo separated, cautiously searching the small arena for any sign of their prey. Then a scream pierced the air and Pavo swivelled his gaze away from the galleries and looked towards Macro. The optio stood unhurt. Pavo glanced towards the entrance just in time to see Bassus staggering under the arch, croaking with pain. Four prong tips jutted out of his throat. He shuddered, then fell limp. Bato stood past his shoulder, grinning feverishly. He yanked his dagger out of Bassus's throat and booted the dead guard to the ground, stepping through the arena entrance. At the same time Duras charged across the sand, his arms spread wide, his head lowered in a bull-charge posture, his features twisted into an almost inhuman look of hate. The bodyguard knocked the sword out of Macro's grip before he could thrust at him, clamped his hands on the stunned optio's shoulders and wrestled him to the ground.

Pavo spun back towards Bato. The Thracian toyed with his dagger.

'Your friend can't save you this time, Roman,' he seethed. 'Now I'll show you how a true First Sword fights.'

CHAPTER TWENTY-EIGHT

The Thracian leapt at Pavo in a blur of motion. The young gladiator had never seen a fighter move with such stunning speed and precision, his shoulders hunched, springing forward on the balls of his feet, so light and fast that he almost seemed to fly across the sand. He was upon Pavo in the blink of an eye, driving the dagger at his opponent's stomach. Pavo jumped back awkwardly. The prong tips scratched his flesh and a hot flush of blood trickled down the bronze First Sword belt wrapped round his loincloth. Spitting mad, Bato drove at Pavo again, giving the young gladiator no time to correct his stance. Grimacing through the waves of pain, Pavo batted away the dagger with his shield. The prongs gashed the shield, and the Thracian abruptly followed through with a stamp on Pavo's ankle, sending him reeling backwards, the shield wrenched from his left hand. Pavo dropped to the sand, a grim voice at the back of his head telling him that he could not defeat Bato, not with his injuries, not against such an agile and ruthless opponent. He glimpsed Macro a short distance away. Duras had the optio pinned to the ground, his spiked glove raised high, ready to strike a killer blow. But Macro thrust out a hand above his head, parrying the glove then headbutting Duras on the bridge of his nose. The young gladiator took heart from the optio's mettle.

'You're mine, Roman scum!' Bato jeered.

Pavo swung his eyes back to the Thracian. In a flash Bato plunged his dagger at the young gladiator, who turned cold at the sight of the prongs angling at his throat. Deprived of his shield, he thrust his sword above his chest, jamming his legionary blade between the steel prongs. There was an ear-piercing screech as metal scraped against metal, Bato driving the dagger down the length of the blade until the prongs struck the pommel of the sword. Then Pavo rolled to his left, wrenching his shoulder and releasing his grip on his weapon. The sword flew through the air, ripping the dagger from Bato's hand, and the two weapons clattered to the sand by the arena entrance. Pavo's heart was pounding and his breathing was hard. Seeing that his opponent had lost both his sword and his shield, the Thracian snarled with excitement and surged towards him. Ignoring the swelling pain in his ribs, Pavo launched himself to his feet with such speed that even the agile Thracian was caught unawares, and drove his fist into the rebel gladiator's stomach. A keening sound came from Bato's throat as he doubled over in pain. The shield dropped from his grip and hit the sand. Sucking in the pain, he straightened and parried another blow from the young gladiator. Then he balled his hands into fists and adopted a fighting stance.

'Come on, rich boy. Take your punishment,' he spat, a crafty smile tickling his upper lip.

Pavo shook his foggy head clear. Away to the side of the arena he spotted Duras, his hulking silhouette framed like a mountain against the moonlight. The bodyguard had locked his arms round Macro's neck, pulling tight. It was too dark for Pavo to see the expression on Macro's face, but the gargling sound of the optio struggling for air carried sharply across the arena.

Pavo turned his eyes on Bato, hatred for the Thracian raging inside his heart. He hefted his hands a few inches in front of his chin to protect his face. Bato pounced forward, but instead of swinging at Pavo's face he launched a devastating low punch that the younger man moved too late to parry. Fierce agony exploded in his guts as Bato hammered him in the side of his stomach, forcing him to stoop forward and lower his guard. Now Bato smacked Pavo on the jaw. The blow sent him reeling. A deafening crunch reverberated through the young gladiator's skull. White spots danced across his vision. His legs felt detached from his body. He could hardly stand.

'Get it over with,' he muttered grimly.

Bato chuckled cruelly. 'I'm not going to kill you, Roman. I'm going to take you and the lanista hostage.' He smacked his lips as a pleasing thought played out in his head. 'A decorated military hero and the imperial First Sword will do nicely when it comes to bartering for our lives.'

'Pallas will never negotiate with you,' Pavo said. A needling agony flared in his ribs. He gritted his teeth and fought down the pain. 'The Emperor would lose face by ceding to a mere Thracian. Your situation is hopeless. The battle is over. Surrender now and the rest of your men might be spared.'

'Fool,' Bato sneered. 'On your feet.'

Pavo glimpsed Macro in his peripheral vision. The stocky soldier was still trying to prise free of Duras's suffocating chokehold. Pavo boiled with rage at the thought of Bato triumphing. He had come too far, overcome too many obstacles. He had made a vow to Titus, and he wouldn't see it broken by this barbarian, or the two Greek freedmen, or anyone else who stood in his way.

With a burst of anger he stepped forward and launched a series of quick jabs aimed at Bato's midriff. His muscles, honed during the months of rigorous training under Macro's tutelage, found a hidden strength the young gladiator did not know he had. He had been transformed from a gaunt, angular young recruit into a well-developed fighter, and now his reserves of strength enabled him to take the fight to Bato. The Thracian lowered his hands to block the strikes, the speed and suddenness of the attack catching him off guard. With a swift push forward Pavo headbutted Bato. There was a dull crunch as the blow struck his jawbone, and Bato groaned in agony as his head snapped backwards. He stumbled away from Pavo but the young gladiator kept on coming, the blood pumping between his temples, his taut muscles shimmering with each blow he struck. Bato swung a desperate left hook, dazed by the onslaught. Now Pavo sidestepped the Thracian's sluggish fist and launched a powerful uppercut. His knuckles struck his groggy opponent clean on the chin, slamming the jawbone against the roof of his skull. Bato's eyes rolled into the back of his head as he fell away. In the same moment Pavo leapt at him, roaring at the top of his voice. The Thracian grunted as Pavo tackled him to the ground.

But Bato was not finished. Spitting out blood, he crawled

towards the sword and dagger, their tips glinting in the moonlight. Pavo rolled away and darted ahead of him, his lungs burning with exhaustion. He seized the four-pronged dagger before his opponent could snatch it and crunched the Thracian's fingers under his foot, grinding up knuckle joints. Bato looked up at him. He bared his bloodstained teeth at the young gladiator.

'You can't kill me. My followers will take revenge on you. They'll hunt you down.'

'Wrong,' Pavo replied. 'Most of your men have been routed by the Germans.'

There was a look of outright hatred on the face of the Thracian as Pavo thrust the dagger at him. Bato let out a throaty cry as the prongs pierced the nape of his neck. His neck muscles spasmed as the prongs tore through flesh and muscle and tissue, his legs and arms flailing in pangs of wild agony. He took one final glance at Pavo, cursing the young gladiator as he died.

A deep grunt snapped Pavo's attention towards Macro. The optio had sunk his teeth into Duras's forearm. Blood oozed. Jerking his head up, Macro spat out a chunk of flesh and wriggled free of the howling bodyguard. Duras clutched his bitten arm. Leaping to his feet, he dismissed the injury and swung wildly at the optio, swivelling at the hips, dropping his shoulders and launching punch after punch. Macro desperately tried to sidestep the blows.

'Macro!'

Pavo chucked the sword towards the optio, who caught it in both hands and spun back to Duras. In the same smooth arc of motion he plunged the sword into the bodyguard's abdomen. Duras's giant frame shuddered. His eyes bulged with fury as he clawed at his opponent. Macro snarled back, burying the weapon almost up to the handle. The bodyguard gave out a final anguished groan. Then he sank to his knees, blood pooling around him. Macro stepped back from the gutted bodyguard, breathing heavily.

Silence lingered over the practice arena for a drawn-out moment. Pavo heard the sound of his own blood rushing in his ears, loud as a thunderstorm. His pulse thumped furiously between his temples; his body was racked with tension. He stood rooted to the spot, blinking at Bato's sprawled figure, barely able to believe that the ringleader of the ludus rebellion was now dead. A sharp pang of pity hit him. In his previous life as a respected military tribune, he would have been quick to congratulate himself on slaying Bato. But in the past few months he had been subjected to the same living conditions and the same appalling treatment as Bato and his followers. The lot of a gladiator was, in his opinion, even worse than that of a common slave. At least slaves nurtured hope that their master might set them free. The most a gladiator could reasonably hope for was a quick and noble death in the arena, with the crowd screaming his name. It was a cruel and miserable existence, and Pavo could understand why men would seek to remove themselves from its yoke, even if he disagreed with the vicious acts of persecution and revenge adopted by Bato and his fellow Thracians.

A loud roar erupted to the north, shaking Pavo out of his stupor. He and Macro shared a glance.

'The Germans,' Macro reported.

Pavo raised an eyebrow at the optio.

'I've heard that battle cry a hundred times on the Rhine Frontier.'

Pavo fell quiet for a moment. 'I suppose it won't be long before they have the ludus back under control.'

Macro approached the young gladiator and gave him a pat on the back. 'Close call, that.'

'Quite. I've had enough of those to last a lifetime, sir.'

'All in a day's work in the Second, lad. Not for nothing are we the hardest bastards in all the legions.'

Pavo smiled weakly. 'If it hadn't been for me, you'd be dead.'

'Bollocks! I had Duras right where I wanted him.'

Pavo shrugged. 'Well, by my reckoning we're even now.'

Macro clasped the young gladiator's forearm. 'Thanks,' he said grudgingly.

At that moment a German officer stampeded through the arena entrance, his footsteps making a dull thud on the sand. His arms were covered with blood and his chest was heaving from exertion. He paused and looked at the two slain Thracians, then paced over to Macro and Pavo.

'You must be the lanista,' he said in heavily accented Latin to Macro.

The optio nodded stiffly at Bato and Duras. 'Spread the word to your men. The ringleader and his bodyguard are dead. His followers are loyal but not completely thick. Once they hear Bato has been chopped up, they'll lay down their arms.'

The German officer chuckled. 'There won't be any need for that, sir. The battle is almost over. Most of the gladiators have surrendered. A handful of Bato's fanatical supporters have retreated into the dormitory block. We're getting ready to move in and finish the job. Orders from the imperial secretary to kill them and stick their heads on spikes. Serve as a lesson for the rest of the gladiators, sir.'

The tone of his voice implied the German was not unhappy with this turn of events.

Macro said nothing. He felt no sympathy for the few gladiators trapped inside the dormitory. They had picked their side and lost, and now they would suffer the consequences. It was the same in the field of battle, and if the tables were turned and the Thracians had triumphed, he knew they would have spared no Roman lives.

The German officer cleared his throat. 'Murena wishes to speak with you, sir.'

The optio clenched his teeth, grunting in his chest. 'Murena is here?'

'He arrived with us, sir. He's waiting in the lanista's quarters. Wants you to report to him after you've cleaned up.'

'What does he want with us now?' Macro wondered tetchily.

The aftermath of the battle had left the ludus in tatters. Bodies were strewn everywhere, so much so that Macro imagined it might be possible to walk from one side of the training ground to the other without ever touching the ground. Grey pillars of smoke seethed out of the armoury as the roof covering that portion of the corridor threatened to collapse, groaning under the strain. The smoke smothered the sky, reducing the stars to faintly glowing orbs.

The optio and the young gladiator grabbed welcome cups of

225

water from an orderly attending to the wounded. Casting an eye across the training ground, Macro feared it would be a long time before the ludus returned to working order. The costs involved would be enormous. The rebellious gladiators had laid waste to every symbol of their imprisonment. The training posts had been uprooted and chopped to pieces. The sundial in the middle of the ground had been smashed apart. In a fit of rage, some of the Thracians had taken to operating on the ludus physician, Kallinos, with his own set of surgical instruments. A spatula protruded from his eye. His mouth was agape, his face locked in an expression of utter terror.

Passing under the porticoes, the German officer led Macro and Pavo up the blood-splashed marble steps to the lanista's quarters. Dread tied knots around Macro's bowels as he spotted the aide to the imperial secretary pacing up and down the main room. The damage to the ludus was the least of his worries. The loss of so many gladiators – more than half the strength of the school – would undoubtedly prohibit their participation at the forthcoming games. Not only would that be acutely embarrassing to the Emperor, it would threaten his ability to host imperial gladiator fights at all. Macro's impending sense of dread was heightened when he noticed Macer standing smugly next to Murena, soothing his reddened wrists. Both men looked at the imperial lanista and the young gladiator at his side.

'What in Hades is going on here?' Murena hissed sharply, throwing his arms in the air. 'Even a common soldier should be able to control a few gladiators. Letting the ludus fall into the hands of the Thracians is idiocy of the highest order! What will the mob say when they hear of this?' He fought to control the rage in his trembling voice. 'You have truly surpassed yourself, Optio. I am of a mind to have you banished to the mines for your stupidity.'

Macro shook his head angrily and glared at Macer. 'This isn't my fault, sir. This coward legged it at the first sign of rebellion and left his keys behind for the Thracians to grab. That allowed Bato and his mob to unlock every cell in the dormitory. If it hadn't been for this joke of a Praetorian, we would have contained the gladiators before Bato had a chance to increase his numbers.'

'Liar!' Macer's face exploded with fury. 'Sir, I gave the optio repeated warnings about the dire consequences of rough-handling the gladiators. But he insisted on bludgeoning the men rather than treating them with respect.'

'Respect?' Macro repeated incredulously. 'They're gladiators! Lowest of the low.'

'Thanks,' Pavo muttered under his breath.

'Enough!' Murena bawled, glaring at the commander and the optio in turn. Snapping upright, the freedman straightened his ruffled tunic and nodded at the German officer. 'This man tells me that by burning down the armoury you helped turn the tide in our favour.'

'It's true,' Pavo said.

Murena regarded the young gladiator coldly. 'That is not how the Emperor sees it. Nor is it how Pallas and myself view your conduct. You have damaged imperial property, both of you. That is a serious offence. Were it not for the fact that you have evidently helped fend off the rebellion by dispatching the ringleader, Pallas would be ordering you both to be nailed to a cross at dawn. You should consider yourselves highly fortunate.'

'You must be joking,' Macro said under his breath.

'What was that?' Murena snapped.

'Nothing,' Macro replied flatly.

The aide to the imperial secretary dismissed Macer with a curt wave of his slender hand. Once the commander was out of earshot, Murena sighed heavily and wrung his trembling hands as if trying to still his temper.

'It's true that Macer is an incompetent fool. We removed him from the Praetorian Guard after he almost got his men killed.'

'I knew it!' thundered Macro.

'Nevertheless, while he's not absolved of blame, it's clear that your hot-headedness has cost us dear, Optio. This rebellion leaves us critically short of gladiators for the upcoming games. With the remaining Thracians condemned inside the dormitory block, this ludus will be at half-strength. Unfortunately, that means we will have to come to some arrangement with another lanista. No doubt they will charge a high price for the use of their fighters. Not to mention the extensive repairs needed to the ludus, and the cost of replacing the dead gladiators. The Emperor is facing a bill of hundreds of thousands of sestertii.' The aide pivoted round. A contemptuous expression was etched on his face. 'Pallas and I agree that you must both pay for this damage.'

'What?' Macro blurted. 'You can't do that!'

'Oh, we can, Optio. We can do whatever we please. However, since it is abundantly clear that neither of you has the means to reimburse his imperial majesty, we must find some other way of settling your debts. I will have to discuss the matter with Pallas, but news of Bato's death has given me an idea.' The aide paused for breath. 'You will take the place of the Thracian at the games.'

Macro gaped at him disbelievingly.

Murena smiled coldly. 'You killed a man who was a central part of the entertainment at the games. I think it only appropriate that you take his place.' The aide flashed a scornful glance at Pavo. 'It was one of the most lucrative fights planned.'

Macro looked apoplectic with rage. 'Fight as a gladiator? Me?' He could think of no more shameful fate. He'd only ever heard of drunken former legionaries daring to debase themselves by fighting as gladiators. 'But . . . we saved your bloody ludus!'

'Calm down, Optio. Your identity will be disguised. Bato fought under a stage name. You shall adopt it, and wear the same helmet and clothing. That ought to do nicely in terms of convincing the mob. Bato was a big draw, and we don't want to disappoint the mob, now do we?'

'No, sir,' Macro barely muttered, still in a state of shock at his fate.

'Don't look so downhearted, Optio. You will only be required to appear in one fight, alongside dear Pavo.' He smiled wickedly at the gladiator. 'No need to conceal your identity, young man. You're already scum.' Pavo bristled with rage as Murena looked back to Macro. 'Should you survive, you can consider your debt to the Emperor wiped clean. You will then be free to return to the Second Legion. As an optio, I hasten to add.'

'What?' Macro growled. 'But . . . my promotion to centurion . . . we had a deal.'

'Consider yourself lucky to still hold the rank of optio. After your reckless approach to managing a ludus, I think it's fair to say you have demonstrated that you are wholly unworthy of leading men.'

'What about me?' Pavo asked.

'Pallas and I have decided not to crucify you, for the time being. But your fight with Hermes is off. We have arranged another opponent for the great man. The mob will be delighted that Hermes has at last recovered from his injuries and is back in training. Rest assured that for your part in this fiasco, Pavo, you will never see your son Appius again.'

Pavo's shoulders slumped. 'Well, who are we fighting?' he asked. 'A couple of lads from the imperial ludus in Rome, I suppose.'

Murena chuckled. 'No. You'll be pitted against rather more untamed creatures.'

'Gauls?' Macro asked.

'Animals, Optio. You're going to feature in the beast fights.'

CHAPTER TWENTY-NINE

Macro muttered a curse under his breath as the roar of the crowd echoed through the passageway of the Statilius Taurus amphitheatre. Almost a month had passed since the day of the mutiny in Capua and now the gladiators had arrived in Rome for the opening day of the games. From his position under the galleries Macro could see a vast column of gladiators, condemned criminals and comic performers stretched out in front of him in the passageway, trembling with anticipation as they waited for the signal from the arena attendant. In keeping with the tradition of the games, the procession would emerge on to the sand in full view of the spectators. Then Claudius would declare the games open. Macro remembered the order of the procession well. He'd witnessed several gladiator spectacles during his childhood. But he'd never imagined that he might one day enter the arena as a participant. He tasted something bitter on his mouth as the trumpeters blared and the attendants gave the signal and the head of the procession shuffled forward. The blood boiled in his veins as he neared the entrance.

'Condemned to fight wild beasts,' he growled. 'I'll never live down the shame.'

'Could be worse,' Pavo replied, nodding at a line of bedraggled prisoners of war directly ahead of them, their heads lowered and their shoulders emphatically slumped. 'One of the guards reckons that unfortunate lot are to be wrapped in animal skins, tied to wooden posts and ripped apart by panthers.'

'This is no time for splitting fucking hairs,' Macro snapped. 'I'm taking part in the games, lad. Me, a hero of Rome! I shouldn't be here.'

'Nor should I,' Pavo replied bitterly. 'At least you only have to get through this one bout. This is the third time I've had to fight. You should consider yourself lucky.'

Macro glared at the young gladiator. A thunderous cheer erupted from the packed galleries, cutting off his reply. Now the front of the procession slowly emerged on to the sands. Macro grudgingly faced forward, sweat trickling down his back in the fetid heat of the tunnel. As well as their suffocating helmets, the two men wore bronze cuirasses, leg greaves and protective arm padding. The armour weighed heavily on their muscular frames and merely shuffling along was enough to make them both break out in a sweat in spite of the cold. At the head of the procession the optio glimpsed the lictors, their bundles of wooden rods fixed with axes mounted above their shoulders. Behind the lictors was a colourful array of acrobats, dwarves and actors for the comic interludes, followed by a throng of arena attendants. The gladiators themselves were the last to emerge. The condemned men among them cut a depressing presence at the rear of the procession, staring ahead with deadened expressions. Other gladiators, champions of the provincial arenas, marched purposefully towards the entrance, eager to get the preliminaries over with so they could return to training ahead of their fights. All the men had chains clamped around their ankles and wrists. They were flanked by a large detachment of the Praetorian Guard.

'I can't see a bloody thing wearing this,' Macro fumed, fiddling with the visor on his helmet. 'How the fuck are we supposed to win our bout if we're half blind?'

'I suspect that is rather the point,' Pavo replied tersely. 'Beast fighters aren't the main attraction at the games, after all.'

'What's that supposed to mean?'

'If we can't see properly, it adds to the crowd's amusement.'

Macro glowered at the young man at his side, his rage evident even through the restrictive eyeholes in his visor. The indignity of taking part in the games burned in his chest, testing his patience.

'Shut up,' he muttered. 'It's your fault I'm in this mess in the first place.'

'What?' Pavo responded indignantly as the acrobats cartwheeled into the arena to a round of polite cheers. 'The imperial secretary to the Emperor was the one who condemned you to fight today. I had nothing to do with it.'

'Bollocks, lad! The only reason I'm here is because the secretary held me responsible for the gladiator mutiny at Capua.'

A sea of bobbing heads swarmed ahead of Macro as the two men drew near to the mouth of the tunnel. Pavo heard the faint din of musicians playing the flute and water organs out in the arena. Their delicate notes were abruptly drowned out by the shrieks and grunts of exotic animals transported on wagons being wheeled out to whet the spectators' appetite ahead of the beast fights and animal hunts. A few moments later there was a collective rumble as the spectators surged to their feet in eager anticipation.

'Claudius must have arrived,' said Macro.

'Gods, listen to that!' Pavo exclaimed as the mass of gladiators entered the arena to an earth-shuddering crescendo of noise. 'The galleries must be heaving with spectators.'

'Rather be up there than down here with this scum,' Macro retorted.

Privately he conceded that the mob had good reason to be out in force at the opening of the games. The Emperor had spared no expense to put on a stunning spectacle to win over the mob. Macro had spotted several posters advertising the event on the walls of taverns and merchant stores lining the path of the procession. Chariot races were being held at the Campus Martius, and earlier that morning an elephant-drawn chariot had conveyed Livia's image past a crowd lining the streets. As sponsor of the games, Claudius had brought together the pick of the gladiators and beast fighters from the imperial ludus in Rome and the smaller ludus in Capua. Macro shuddered at the vast cost of the event, which was rumoured to have run into several hundred thousand denarii.

Macro and Pavo were about to enter the arena when a voice shouted, 'You two! Stop there!'

The two men turned simultaneously as an arena official hurried towards them, his brow heavily furrowed.

'Who the fuck are you?' Macro demanded.

'Sextus Hostilius Nerva,' the official announced curtly. 'I'm in charge of the schedule. It's my job to make sure these games run smoothly and without any hiccups. You.' He pointed at Pavo. 'Name?'

'Marcus Valerius Pavo,' the gladiator responded.

'And your comrade?'

'Hilarus,' Macro said, bristling with shame. He took scant consolation from the fact that by fighting under the assumed name of Duras, he would at least conceal his true identity, preventing his superiors in the Second Legion from ever discovering his shameful secret. Assuming he survived, that is. He watched the beleaguered official consult a wax tablet, tracing a finger down the list of names. Clearing his throat, Nerva tapped his finger at a pair of names near the bottom.

'Wait here. Once you hear the command from the umpire, you're on. You're the second bout of the day, so make it look good, and whatever you do, don't die too quickly, eh?'

Fear instantly gripped Pavo.

'That can't be right. There are several pairings ahead of us.' The gladiator pointed at the list of names. 'Check the programme. We're the main draw. We're supposed to come last.'

The order of the bouts had been a source of hot debate in the ludus canteen in Capua, with gladiators torn between appearing in a later bout, with the guarantee of a bigger crowd and a larger reward for victory, and fighting in a minor preliminary bout and getting their appearance in the arena over with. In keeping with tradition, the beast fights were scheduled for each morning of the games, followed by the crucifixions of criminals at midday, with the gladiator bouts listed for each afternoon of the ten-day celebration.

'Change of plan,' Nerva replied aloofly. 'Sisinnes was scheduled to go first but he topped himself last night in his cell. The ungrateful sod bit off his own tongue and choked himself to death. Then we planned for Diodorus to make his debut, but he buggered off to the latrines and suffocated himself by thrusting a toilet brush down his throat. What a way to go.'

'Gods!' Pavo exclaimed.

Nerva shrugged. 'The beast fights always turn a few of 'em suicidal. The thought of getting torn to shreds, I suppose. Last year we had a dozen fighters strangle each other before the start of the games. Buggers up the programme, I can tell you. Then there are the ones nursing injuries.' He clicked his tongue, craning his neck at the arena. 'By Jupiter, I hope the weather doesn't turn foul. The schedule's tight enough as it is without rain messing it up further.'

Macro shook his head. 'A couple of beast fighters chickening out doesn't explain why we've been bumped up the list. There were plenty more bouts scheduled ahead of ours.'

'Orders of the imperial secretary,' Nerva replied, rolling his eyes. 'He's organising the games on behalf of the sponsor, Emperor Claudius. If you've got a problem with the schedule, I suggest you take it up with him.'

Macro and Pavo exchanged a look behind their visors.

Nerva continued. 'Once the procession is over, the Emperor will introduce the games and say a few words about the deification of his grandmother, Livia, then make some public pronouncements and give the obligatory thanks to the mob. We'll begin with a leopard versus a bull. Then it's your turn. Four of you will take to the sand.'

Macro slapped Pavo heartily on the back. 'Did you hear that, lad? Four of us against one beast! That shouldn't be too hard.'

Nerva chuckled. 'I wouldn't get your hopes up. You're fighting a lion.'

Macro and Pavo both froze.

'And not any old lion, but one specially trained for the arena,' Nerva went on. 'The handlers starve them for two days beforehand, then they're branded with hot irons to make them really vicious. I've seen one of these lions rip half a dozen veteran gladiators limb from limb. Four of you won't last long. Just try not to get too much blood over the place, eh? We're low on fresh sand as it is.'

'The men we're fighting with,' Pavo asked. 'Who are they?'

'What does it matter? You'll die all the same.'

'I want to know if they're skilled with a sword.'

Nerva consulted his tablet again and hummed. 'Late entrants, it says here. They're in the holding cell at the moment. Probably a couple of murderers who are for the chop. Doubt they'll increase your chances against the lion.'

He tucked his tablet under his arm and spun away down the passageway, whistling a tune to himself. Macro watched him depart.

'Bastard!' he growled, banging his fist against the wall in frustration.

'Ah, Optio!' a shrill voice cried from the shadows. 'Getting used to your new surroundings, I see.'

Macro looked up as Murena descended a set of stone steps leading up to the galleries and approached the two men. The imperial aide stopped in front of the gladiators, a slight grin snaking across his thin lips. His eyes glowed like polished metal.

'Cheer up, boy,' he said to Pavo. 'You're about to join your father in the afterlife.'

CHAPTER THIRTY

'What the hell do you want?' Macro thundered at the aide. 'Why, I've come to offer my wishes for your forthcoming bout, Optio,' Murena replied in his arrogant voice. He paused before adding, 'Or should I say . . . Hilarus.'

'You'll never get away with this!'

'But we already have. Speaking of which, how do you like your new name? Hilarus has a nice ring to it, don't you think?'

Macro seethed behind his visor. A chorus of angry snarls emanated from further down the passageway, where the wild beasts were kept in cages ahead of their scheduled appearances in the arena. Macro and Pavo had passed the chambers earlier, and the stench of fear and shit filled the air.

'Once the Emperor has finished addressing his loyal subjects,' Murena continued, 'the games will formally begin. Then you're on. Of course, you are featuring in the beast fight, not the animal hunts. Cavorting after antelopes and chasing donkeys hardly befits two such talented swordsmen.'

'This is a bloody insult!' Macro thundered.

Murena laughed. Footsteps trampled towards the exit located on the other side of the arena as the acrobats, dwarves and gladiators retreated from public view.

He turned to Pavo. 'As for you, gladiator – you will die. In this fight, or the next. Or the one after that. It makes no difference, I won't make the same mistake twice. Your luck has run its course.'

'You can't kill me. Not in front of the mob. I'm a hero in their eyes. If they see me die at the hands of a wild beast, they'll turn on Claudius.'

Murena chuckled harshly. 'I don't think so. You see, the mutiny in Capua has turned the mob against the gladiators. Nothing agitates them as much as fear of another Spartacus-style uprising.' The aide looked casually at his manicured fingernails. 'You were at Capua at the time of the mutiny, which marks you out for special treatment. Now every drunken fool in the Subura believes that you are a traitorous wretch. They'll cheer your death.'

'That's a lie!' Pavo bristled with rage. 'The mutiny had nothing to do with me. The Thracians were to blame.'

'Try explaining that to the mob. As far as they're concerned, gladiators are all the same. Scum.' There was a sinister gleam in the aide's eyes as he went on. 'Why else do you think we allowed you to fight under your own name? The mob has turned against you.'

Macro narrowed his eyes. 'You bastard! You'll pay for this.'

Murena laughed stolidly. 'It's a little late in the day for empty threats, Optio. Besides, should you ever dare to speak the truth about what happened in Capua, I'm afraid we will have to inform your superiors in the Second Legion that you participated in a beast fight. You don't need me to remind you of the consequences should they learn of your scandalous participation in the gladiator trade.'

A shrill note pierced the air, signalling the start of the beast fight. Macro looked round briefly as a leopard clawed viciously at a wild bull. The two creatures were tied together by means of a chain wrapped around their torsos, forcing them to enter into a violent confrontation. The leopard clawed again. Now the bull scrabbled back to the arena wall, sounding ghastly bellows of pain as blood fountained out of a glistening wound on its flank.

'Where's my son?' Pavo asked Murena.

'Appius? At the imperial palace. He won't live to see his third birthday.'

'You mean—'

Murena nodded. 'Your son is to be killed tomorrow.'

Pavo stepped back from the aide. His flesh crawled with abject terror. 'He's just a child . . . an innocent child.'

The aide waved a hand. 'I'm simply honouring the promise I made to you in Capua. You foolishly declined our offer and now Appius will be flung to the beasts. This time tomorrow, the entire Valerius family will be dead.'

Pavo was aghast. Tears welled in his eyes. Macro felt a stab of pity for the gladiator. The punishment might be excessive, he mused, but anyone who threatened the Empire had to suffer the consequences. Punishing a child, though? That was a step too far. He turned back to the aide. Pavo was speechless, overwhelmed with shock.

'What about our weapons?' Macro asked.

'Ah, yes, about that.' Murena shifted awkwardly. 'There has been a slight change to the details of your bout . . . You will be entering the arena unarmed.'

Macro's features darkened behind his visor. 'That's not a beast fight! That's how condemned criminals are sent to die. We're beast fighters. We should be equipped with spears and swords.'

The aide twitched with discomfort. 'And you shall have them, Optio. Just not at the start of your bout. I have seen to it that weapons will be distributed around the arena.'

'But that's not on!' Macro protested. 'The lion will cut us down before we have a chance to arm ourselves.'

Murena frowned. 'I don't appreciate your tone of voice. The mob is bored of ordinary gladiator fights. They want something new. As the sponsor, Claudius is under tremendous pressure to conjure up new methods of killing. Death being the only sure way of keeping the mob entertained. We must satisfy their barbarous urges if we are to hold a successful games and shore up support for Claudius. Otherwise all the hard work we have put into enhancing the Emperor's reputation will be wasted.'

'Tragic,' Macro replied sharply.

The aide appeared not to hear the optio. 'Besides, you're both wearing a full complement of armour rather than the standard tunic worn by the beast fighters. That should afford you plenty of protection.'

A roar sounded in the arena as the leopard finally overwhelmed the bull.

'This can't be happening,' Pavo murmured, his voice stricken with grief.

'Oh, but it is. Good luck,' Murena replied. A cynical grin creased his face. 'Or not.'

Pavo stared despondently at Murena as the aide turned his back on the two men and headed up the stone steps. A moment later two manacled beast fighters were herded towards Macro and Pavo by a handful of Praetorian Guards. Both fighters wore similar heavy armour and helmets. An excited murmur rippled through the crowd as the announcer dashed off the formalities ahead of the next bout. The guards grabbed Pavo and Macro by an arm each and shoved them towards the gate with the other pair of beast fighters.

An attendant gazed out across the arena, watching attentively for the signal from the umpire to usher the men on to the sand. The beast fighters huddled tightly together while one of the Praetorians unlocked their chains under the watchful eye of his comrades.

'That Greek snake,' Macro spat, soothing his reddened wrists once his chains were released. 'And this bloody armour doesn't help. I can hardly move.'

'I suspect there's a good reason for that,' Pavo responded sourly. 'Murena wants to get us both killed.'

'Bollocks!' Macro was incredulous. 'I'm a decorated soldier, lad, personally awarded my medal by Emperor Claudius himself. The pride of the Second Legion. They've got no reason to want to kill me.'

Pavo considered. 'You're the only other credible witness to what really happened at Capua. The only one who can prove we're both innocent. Murena said so himself. Could they trust you to hold your tongue?'

Macro snorted and snapped his gaze ahead as the attendants opened the gate. Nerva clapped impatiently at Macro and Pavo and the other beast fighters.

'We've got a big crowd today and every single one of 'em wants to see some blood. So give them what they want. And remember, the Emperor has paid good money to put on this show. Don't let him down by getting killed right away.'

'Perish the thought,' Pavo muttered drily.

Macro gripped Pavo by the arm. 'Do me a favour, lad.'

'What's that?'

'If by some fucking miracle we make it out of here alive, don't ever tell anyone I had to fight as a bloody gladiator. It'll be the ruin of me.'

Pavo nodded. Then the guards shoved the fighters in the back, thrusting them through the open gates and into the arena.

CHAPTER THIRTY-ONE

The beast fighters stepped out on to the sand. Grey clouds pressed low in the sky, carrying the threat of rain. Pavo glanced at the scene in front of him. Exotic trees and shrubs had been planted around the arena to recreate the look of a forest during an animal hunt. Several sword points and spear tips glinted amid the foliage close to the gate at the opposite end of the arena. Attendants frantically cleared up the mess from the animal fight, four of them dragging out the disembowelled bull while another pair hurriedly tended to the blood splatters, one sprinkling fresh sand over the blood and the second spraying rosewater on top. Two animal handlers had snared the leopard in a net and now dragged the beast back to the opened gate at the opposite side of the arena. Pavo glimpsed the lion in a steel cage in the mouth of the tunnel, its eyes glowing menacingly in the gloom. Once the leopard had been removed from the arena, the guards slammed the gate shut.

The four beast fighters were ushered towards the middle of the arena by the Praetorians, who accompanied them to make sure they didn't rush for the scattered weapons before the lion was released into the arena. Pavo winced with pain. The wound on his left shoulder had formed a pinkish scar and had failed to heal properly in the weeks after the mutiny in Capua. His shoulder felt stiff and heavy. A cool breeze fluttered over the arena. Macro stared at the galleries through the eyeholes on his helmet.

'Bloody hell,' he sputtered. 'I've never seen this place so full.'

Pavo raised his eyes. The optio was right, he conceded. The official capacity of the arena stood at twenty thousand, but many more spectators appeared to have crammed into the galleries for the opening of the games. Each of the four levels was packed, and even the walkways leading to the various exits were heaving with people eager for a glimpse of the fighters. The fifth tier of spectators was by far the most tightly packed, crammed shoulder to shoulder on the crumbling terraces above the more spacious galleries below. The mob swigged from jugs of wine which they passed to one another, their cheeks red from the close heat of so many bodies crammed together. The air was filled with the din of the crowd as they chanted about the sexual persuasions of the gladiators, to the mild irritation of the more privileged citizens seated on the lower tiers. The lowest was filled with magistrates and imperial high priests, with a parapet separating the spectators from the arena floor.

Above the gallery was the imperial box. Pavo spotted the Emperor seated in his ornately decorated chair, flanked by his German bodyguards, his distinctive purple toga draped across his frail shoulders. Pallas stood to the right of the Emperor and gazed down, grinning smugly. Murena stood at his side. He was frowning at the row of senators seated in the gallery above the imperial box. Pavo followed the direction of his gaze. One of the seats was unoccupied, he noticed. He spied the object of Murena's irritation at the entrance to the gallery. A grey-haired figure strode gracefully towards the empty seat, his piercing gaze fixed ahead, seemingly oblivious of his fellow spectators, the stripes on his fine tunic distinguishing him as a senator. His companions stood up obediently to make way for him, and as he took up his seat, he turned and stared down at Pavo. There was a glint in his eyes that stayed with the young gladiator.

Pavo quickly forgot about the man as a hail of boos and jeers rained down from the crowd.

'Die, you Thracian shit!' a spectator taunted Macro above the din.

'Fucking traitors!' another screamed.

'Shit,' Macro grumbled. 'Looks like Murena was right. The mob's turned against anyone associated with Capua.'

The attendants promptly exited the arena. In their hurry to keep the games on track, they had left some of the bull's innards on the sand, along with the lead chain that had bound the two beasts together. Pavo watched them depart. At the same time the umpire gave the signal to the animal handler positioned behind the opposite gate to release the lion from its cage. The gladiator felt his neck hairs stand on end as the Praetorians and the umpire scurried for the same exit as the arena attendants. Now Pavo was alone with Macro and the two other beast fighters. No sooner had the gate slammed shut than one of the fighters broke away from the group and ran towards the scattered weapons, stumbling along, burdened down by the heavy armour over his burly frame. Turning his head slightly, Pavo focused his gaze on the gate opposite. A cavernous roar echoed from the dark passageway beyond. Macro turned to follow the fighter, but Pavo slapped a hand around his thick wrist and held the optio back.

'Get off me, lad! The weapons are over there, we need to grab them!'

'Wait!' Pavo hissed. 'Look.'

The gladiator nodded at the lion encased in the steel cage. A moment later the animal handler slid the locking bar loose. The gate sprang open and the lion bolted out of the shadows into the arena. A roar went up in the crowd as the lion pounced on the beast fighter who had sprinted towards the weapons scattered across the opposite side of the arena from Pavo and Macro. The speed and ferocity of the attack drew a breathless cheer. Pavo stood his ground with Macro and the third fighter, his chest muscles tightening in fear as the lion pinned the fighter to the sand under its paws and started mauling his arm. The man let out a muffled howl as blood squirted out of a fresh wound and gushed over the sand. The lion yanked its head furiously from side to side, tearing at strips of flesh.

Screaming in pain, the trapped beast fighter tried prising apart the lion's jaws in a frantic effort to pull his arm free. The lion clawed at his hand, gashing his forearm. The man immediately clasped his other hand over the wound, lowering both hands from his face. In the blink of an eye the beast lunged forward and sank its teeth into his neck. Blood flowed freely out of the wound and spilled to the ground. The beast fighter's cries were mercifully choked off as the crowd screamed at the lion, imploring it to rip the face off its victim. Even Macro felt his iron resolve falter at the spectacle. Up in the imperial box, the Emperor jumped to his feet, clapping wildly as the lion disembowelled the fighter and began tearing at the entrails.

'If only we could somehow get past that monster and grab the weapons,' Macro said, staring forlornly at the swords and spears lying out of reach. 'Then we'd soon gut it like a bloody fish.'

Pavo turned to his former mentor. 'Macro . . . I mean, Hilarus,' he corrected himself quickly, remembering that they were not alone. 'I know how to defeat the lion. Just follow my orders.'

'You? Order me about? Piss off! Taking your advice was what landed me in this bloody mess in the first place.'

'My father had an estate in Antium,' the young gladiator began.

'This is no time for stories about your childhood, lad.'

'Listen to me! My father used to take me game hunting. He was an enthusiastic collector of wild animals. He brought many species back from his travels. Deer, ostriches, even the odd hyena. I know how to fight these beasts. How to trap and kill them.'

Macro nodded at the lion feasting on the beast fighter's guts. 'In case it escaped your attention, Pavo, we're not fighting hyenas. This is a fucking lion.'

'The same principles apply. The only way to survive is if we work together.'

'The Roman is right,' the third fighter cut in. He spoke in heavily accented Latin. 'That beast just cut Cygnus to pieces. It'll kill us too, unless we do something.'

Pavo glanced at the third fighter. The voice sounded oddly familiar to him but he couldn't quite place it.

'All right, lad,' Macro said grudgingly. 'You're in charge . . . for once. What's the plan?' He hated the idea of taking orders from a high-born brat. But he had no experience of killing wild beasts. He knew he had little choice but to place his faith in the young gladiator.

Pavo thought for a moment.

'The lion is faster and stronger than us. We'll never beat it in a straight fight. We need to lead it into a trap. I'll distract the beast. That should give you both a chance to grab the weapons.

Then I'll lure it towards you. As soon as it's in range, you spike it.'

Macro shook his head. 'Sounds like an idiotic plan to me.'

'If you've got a better one, feel free to share it.'

'He knows what he's talking about,' the third gladiator said. 'We should do as the Roman says.'

Pavo glanced at the third fighter. That voice again. Where had he heard it before? He dismissed the thought as the lion tossed aside what was left of the beast fighter and set its piercing gaze on the other men in the arena. Pavo crept towards the discarded metal chain, careful not to make any sudden movements that would attract the lion's attention.

'I don't know what you're doing, but for gods' sakes make it quick, lad!' Macro said, keeping his voice as low as possible. 'This bastard looks hungry.'

Pavo grabbed hold of the bull innards and smeared blood over his arms and legs. The strong smell choked him. Then he heaved the chain off the sand as the lion prowled towards the fighters, flicking its eyes from one to the next, as if deciding which would provide it with the heartiest meal. Filling his lungs, Pavo shouted at the lion and whipped the end of the chain towards it. There was a dull clank as the chain struck the lion on the side of its face. The blow temporarily stunned the beast. It half turned and snarled aggressively at Pavo, lifting its muzzle to sniff the air and licking its lips at the smell of blood clinging to the gladiator. Now it turned fully from Macro and the third beast fighter, narrowing its eyes at Pavo.

'Now!' he shouted to the two men.

In a swift motion Macro and the third fighter sprinted around the rear of the lion and raced towards the weapons scattered at the far side of the arena. Sensing movement behind it, the lion let out a full-throated roar and swung away from Pavo and back towards Macro and the third fighter. Pavo lashed out at the beast a second time. The lion roared as it spun back around. The dark slits of its eyes narrowed with animal rage as it hunched low, its tail beating on the sand in anger. Then it burst forward at Pavo, kicking up a cloud of sand as it pounded across the arena at a frightening speed. His throat constricting with fear, Pavo cast the chain aside, turned on the spot and ran as fast as he could away from the beast. He glimpsed Macro and the third fighter drawing near to the scattered weapons.

Even though Pavo was a natural athlete, and had practised sprint sessions under Macro's tutelage in Paestum, the body armour weighed down on him and hindered his pace, as if he was wading through mud. He could feel the ground trembling underfoot as the beast hurtled towards him. Its snorts and snarls reverberated inside his helmet. He spied Macro directly ahead of him picking up a spear and turning towards the lion. He glanced back and saw that the beast was leaping at him, its claws extended, its teeth bared.

'Do it!' he cried.

In the same breath he dived out of the way and Macro launched his spear at the lion. Pavo rolled on to his side as the lion gave out a deafening roar that sent fear trembling down his spine. Looking up, he saw the beast land with a dense thud directly in front of Macro. There was a hollow crack as the spear sticking out of its belly clattered against the sand and snapped in half under its collapsing weight.

'Yes!' Macro said, thumping a fist against his thigh.

His triumph was cut short as the lion spasmed briefly before lurching to its feet, roaring defiantly in spite of the splintered shaft protruding from its belly. Pavo looked on disbelievingly as the lion struck out at Macro, swatting the stocky optio aside with ease. He tumbled to the ground next to Pavo, a large gash visible across his thigh. The younger man glanced up as the lion drew close to the two fighters, groaning in pain.

'Shit,' Pavo muttered darkly. 'We've had it.'

A cold dread gripped him as the beast moved in for the kill. The thought of being ripped apart by the lion froze the blood in his veins. The arena trembled, the crowd rising as one to catch a glimpse of the gladiators on the verge of death.

'Come on, you bastard!' the third fighter yelled, jabbing a spear tip into the lion's back.

The lion jerked its head from side to side in an effort to shrug off the spear. The third fighter ripped the weapon out of the beast as it spun away from Macro and Pavo. Fresh blood dripped from the spear tip and a bright red gash streaked the lion's back. In the next instant the lion sprang forward at the fighter. The man grunted as the beast clawed at his chest, its massive weight pressing down on top of him. He fell back against the sand and the spear was wrenched from his grasp. Now the lion let out a deep roar as it angled its jaws at the prone fighter's neck. The fighter stretched his arm towards the spear, but the weapon lay tantalisingly out of reach.

'Kill it!' the third fighter begged his companions.

Pavo knew he had no more than a moment to act. He scraped himself off the ground and snatched up a spear lying on the sand close by. A short distance in front of him, the lion opened its jaws wide as it prepared to make its second kill. Planting his feet firmly, Pavo trained the spear point at the beast. His senses were heightened. He was keenly aware of the venomous pitch of the crowd, the shimmer of the sand under his feet. He flooded his lungs with air and launched the spear. The lion jolted upright in pain as the tip plunged into its back, blood splattering its golden mane. There were audible gasps of disbelief from the spectators as the animal rolled on to its back and pawed at the air, panting irregularly as it died.

Relief flushed through Pavo. The feeling quickly faded as discontented murmurs spread through the crowd. The spectators were furious that the fighters had survived, denying them the spectacle of the lion ripping the rest of the men apart. Conflicting emotions stirred inside Pavo, his elation at defeating the lion tempered by the grim certainty that he had succeeded only in delaying his own death. He glanced up at the imperial box, where Pallas and Murena shifted uncomfortably on their feet. Pavo couldn't help but notice that the stern-faced senator who'd arrived late seemed pleased with the result. Below the senator Pallas muttered discreetly to his aide. Nodding promptly, Murena shot up from his seat and disappeared down the nearest set of steps leading from the galleries.

'Get this fucking thing off me!'

Pavo snapped his eyes back to the third beast fighter. He was waving his arms and legs for help, pinned beneath the dead weight of the lion. Pavo hurried over to the man and rolled the lion off his chest. He offered his hand. The fighter brushed it away.

'Don't expect me to thank you for saving my life, Roman,' he growled scornfully. 'The only reason I agreed to help defeat that beast is because I didn't want it to kill you . . . I wanted to save that pleasure for myself.'

Pavo went white behind his visor as he noticed the familiar brand scarring the man's forearm: the mark of the house of Gurges. At last he placed the dull, heavily accented voice of the beast fighter.

'Amadocus . . .?' he said falteringly. 'Is that you?'

'Who the fuck else?'

The gate crashed open behind Pavo. Several guards poured out of the passageway. Nerva followed them, the official marching purposefully towards the beast fighters. He was stopped in his tracks by Murena calling out his name from the passageway. The aide pulled Nerva aside and began issuing orders to him.

Pavo looked back to Amadocus. 'What are you doing here?' he asked.

'Fighting in the games, what does it fucking look like? No thanks to you, Roman. Gurges went bankrupt after you beat Denter. I was sold to a lanista who owned a travelling troupe. Greedy bastard couldn't wait to get rich off my back. He threw me into the arena while I was still injured. I lost my bout, nearly paid with my life, too.'

Several attendants dragged the lion towards the opposite gate. Macro clamped a hand over the wound on his thigh, blood trickling between his fingers.

'My injuries ended my career as a champion of the arena.' The Thracian shook his head at his missing fingers. 'The lanista sold me off to participate in the beast fights. Told me it was that or the mines. You're the reason I ended up here, Roman. I swear as soon as I get the chance, I'm going to kill you.'

Murena waved Nerva away. The official hurried over to the beast fighters and nodded impatiently at Macro.

'Hilarus! Present yourself to the infirmary and get that wound cleaned up. The imperial aide will be along shortly. He wants a word with you.'

'Great,' Macro muttered under his breath. 'Just what I need.'

'What about me?' Pavo asked.

Nerva flashed a sinister grin at Pavo and Amadocus in turn. 'You two are to return to the antechamber with the other gladiators. You can watch the animal hunts while you're there. If I were you, I'd enjoy the show. Once those idiots are done prancing about, we've got a treat in store for the crowd. You've killed the lion – now let's see if you can do the same to an Atlas bear.'

CHAPTER THIRTY-TWO

A pair of guards escorted Macro down a series of corridors towards the infirmary. At this early hour the cots were empty. The medical orderlies diligently checked the equipment, preparing the stretchers and surgical instruments for the inevitable stream of patients that would follow. A strong scent of garlic lingered in the air as Macro entered the infirmary. He grimaced as he thought of the carnage that would soon overwhelm the orderlies. Memories rushed back to him of the field hospitals in battles along the Rhine, the stench of torn bowels, the rags soaked in fresh blood, the bodies piled high.

A wizened surgeon with grey eyes greeted Macro with a weary smile. 'It seems we have our first patient of the day. Step forward, gladiator.'

Macro remained at the door. He didn't like the tone of the surgeon's voice. 'It's just a flesh wound. I'll be fine.'

The surgeon craned his neck at Macro's gashed thigh and clicked his tongue. 'No such thing as flesh wounds when it comes to wild beasts, my boy. I've seen their cuts turn a gladiator half mad before he died. Allow me to have a closer look.'

Macro gritted his teeth as the surgeon prodded at his wound, inspecting it with his bony index finger. A wave of nausea washed over the optio. After what felt like a long time, the surgeon withdrew his finger and washed his hands in a bowl of water.

'You should live, provided we clean it out and suture it,' he announced, wiping his hands on a rag. 'Otherwise you might die in a day or two. Come with me.'

Macro reluctantly followed the surgeon into an adjoining room. He hesitated in the doorway as he caught sight of several needles, scalpels and saws arranged on a wooden table, their pointed tips shining in the wan candlelight. The surgeon turned to him.

'It won't hurt. A little pain when the needle pricks the skin, that's all.'

'That's what they tell you in the field hospitals.'

The surgeon smiled sagely as he drew up a wooden bench next to the operating table. Taking a deep breath, Macro sat down, his stomach churning as the surgeon prepared his instruments.

The surgeon cocked an eyebrow. 'I assume that you were once a soldier.'

Macro was about to remind him that he was a serving optio in the Second Legion when he remembered that he was still in the role of Hilarus. He bit his tongue and nodded.

'I've seen plenty of ex-soldiers grace my infirmary down the years. Some of them fallen into debt. Others discharged from the legions.'

'How long have you worked at the arena?'

The surgeon was lost in thought for a moment. 'Twenty years, give or take.'

Macro pulled a face. 'I wonder how men like you sleep.'

'Quite soundly, as a matter of fact. You get used to all the corpses and dismembered limbs after a while. The endless screams, too. The only problem is where to stock all the blood.'

Macro frowned at the surgeon as the latter cheerfully continued. 'Oh yes, gladiator blood is in big demand these days. Weddings, healing potions, ointments. Personally I think it's down to Pavo. After he defeated that barbaric Celt, Britomaris, children started playing at gladiators in the street. And the women.' The surgeon grinned at the soldier. 'They're practically fighting over which ones to shag.'

'Rome's changed a lot while I've been away,' Macro remarked with a rueful shake of the head. He reflected for a moment before continuing. 'You must be in for a busy day, what with all the beast fights.'

'I doubt it. In my experience, the beasts make quick work of the fighters. You should consider yourself fortunate to have survived. It's an extremely rare occurrence. Once the beast fighters are done, all that's left are the comedy interludes, followed by a few relatively minor bouts this afternoon. Tomorrow, however, we are expecting to be very busy.'

'Why? What's happening tomorrow?'

'Tomorrow is the day of the group fight.'

Macro looked up in puzzlement at the surgeon. He had heard of the relatively new notion of packs of doomed gladiators fighting one another until only one man was left standing. But he had never seen such a fight in the flesh.

'Oh yes,' the surgeon went on. 'The group fight is very popular now, especially with the rising cost of the games. The men who compete naturally come very cheap, as they're not professional gladiators but prisoners of war, murderers and thieves. Normally the sponsor would have to pay several thousand sestertii in compensation for a gladiator killed during the games. With the group fighters, it's a fraction of that. But, of course, such men are not properly trained and lack the appropriate skill with the sword. You should see the way those idiots blindly hack at each other. The wounds on their bodies are frankly appalling. Limbs hanging off, mutilated genitalia, all sorts.'

An orderly removed Macro's helmet, padding and leg greaves. He stared ahead as the surgeon tended to his wound, cleaning away the blood and sand with a damp rag before suturing the gash with a needle and twine. He was putting the finishing touches to the sutures when Murena appeared in the doorway.

'At bloody last!' Macro exclaimed. 'I've fulfilled my side of the deal. Now get me out of here and back where I belong.'

The aide ignored Macro and waved at the surgeon.

'Leave us,' he ordered.

After tying the end of the stitches into a knot, the surgeon rose from the bench and hurried out of the room, wiping his bloodstained hands on his tunic. Murena waited for him to leave, then spun back to face Macro. He looked flustered.

'How's the injury?' he asked.

Macro grunted. 'I've had worse. You get plenty of injuries serving on the Rhine. Speaking of which, when do I get to leave Rome?

I've had enough of this place. Too many crafty sorts for my liking.'

'I presume you're making a thinly veiled reference to me,' Murena responded. 'Subtlety is not one of your strong points, Macro. It requires a certain degree of wit to properly articulate.'

'Articulate this. You're a crooked shit, and the same goes for that snake Pallas. Now give me my travel authorisation. I'd best be on my way. If I stick around here much longer, I'll end up punching you in the face.'

Murena pressed his lips together. 'You can't leave. Your services are still required here in Rome.'

Something snapped inside Macro. He shot to his feet and marched up to the aide, temporarily forgetting the dull ache in his thigh, his features dark with fury. 'We had a deal. One fight, then I'd be free to go. You'd damn well better honour it, or else. I don't give a shit how close you are to the Emperor.'

'Calm down, Optio. Our deal stands, as soon as you have completed a final task – one of grave importance to the Empire.'

There was an anxious look on Murena's face, and Macro was momentarily intrigued, wondering why he and Pallas were so eager to keep him in service. Then he came to his senses, recalling his disgraceful participation in the beast fight, and shook his head.

'Forget it. I'm not interested. Rope some other poor bastard into your scheming.'

Murena moved to block his path as Macro headed for the doorway. The aide's eyes were laced with menace and his lips twisted at the corners. 'I'm afraid you can't return to the Rhine until you have completed this task. Then you are free to go. You have my word.'

'Your word is a load of crap. I trust you about as much as I trust a tart in the Subura.'

Murena stared back at Macro, his eyes twitching, nostrils flaring. He stepped aside from the door. 'Have it your way then, Optio. You may leave of your own accord and return to the legion, though why you find that freezing wilderness on the Rhine so alluring is quite beyond me.'

'Cold it may be, but at least it's clear who your enemies are.

You carry on butchering anyone who pisses off Claudius or whatever it is that scum like you do. I'm off.'

'A final word of warning,' Murena called out. 'If you do decide to turn your back on me, I'll see to it that word reaches your precious Second Legion about your activities in the arena.'

Macro slowly turned. A cold sensation travelled from his head to his toes. 'You wouldn't dare.'

'Really? Then you underestimate me, Optio. Needless to say, once Vespasian learns of your secret, your service in the military will come to a swift end. Rome frowns on men disgracing themselves in the arena. If you're lucky, some gang leader in the Subura might find you a place in his menagerie of thugs.'

Macro was torn. He desperately wanted to turn his back on Murena, but knowing that to do so would spell the end of his career in the Second Legion, and the loss of the hard-won respect of his comrades, appalled him.

'Fine,' he said finally through gritted teeth. 'But this is the last thing I ever do for you and Pallas. After this, we're finished. And if I never see another Greek for the rest of my life, it won't be too soon.'

Murena looked relieved. 'A wise choice, Optio. I knew you'd come round to our way of thinking eventually.'

He sat down at the wooden bench and planted his smooth hands on his knees, drumming his fingers as if deciding how best to proceed.

'What do you know about the Liberators?'

Macro shrugged. 'Sounds like the name of one of those fancy plays all the posh types go and watch.'

'I thought as much. A common soldier such as yourself is interested only in getting outlandishly drunk on cheap wine and engaging in acts of mindless violence with his fellow creatures. The politics of Rome probably mean nothing to you.'

Macro glared at Murena, impatient at being detained by the freedman. 'Get on with it.'

'There are men in Rome, some of them quite senior officials in positions of power, who are desperate to eliminate Claudius and return Rome to a republic. It seems these individuals remain committed to their cause despite the fate suffered by others who harboured republican ambitions. I am talking of men like Scribonianus and, of course, Titus, Pavo's father.'

Macro shrugged. 'So Claudius has a few enemies in the Senate. Even I know that's nothing new, and I couldn't give a shit about politics. Besides, when did Claudius start giving a toss about a bunch of old farts in togas?'

'Eloquently put, Macro. However, the Liberators are not to be taken lightly. They're highly organised, secretive and enjoy a significant level of support among the senators and dissenters opposed to the Emperor. We believe they are planning a fresh conspiracy.'

'Bloody Greeks,' the optio grumbled. 'Have to see a conspiracy in everything.'

Murena did not appear to hear him. He brushed a smudge of dirt off his tunic and said, 'Claudius is not short of enemies, both here and beyond the frontiers. It's the nature of the job. But information has come to the attention of the imperial secretary, and as loyal servants of the Emperor, we must act on it.'

'What sort of information?'

Murena pursed his lips. 'We fear that the Liberators plan to assassinate the Emperor at the games.'

At first Macro was too stunned to reply. Then he puffed out his cheeks, releasing all the pent-up tension in his muscles. 'There must be hundreds, if not thousands, of idiots talking about having a pop at Claudius. I'm no expert, but planning to give the Emperor the good news in front of the mob is about the stupidest plan I ever heard.'

'This plan is no idle threat, Macro.'

'Really? How do you know? Got some poor sod tied up and being tortured in the Mamertine, have you?'

Murena flashed a dark look at the optio. 'You're probably aware that we tried to enlist Pavo to help undermine the Liberators. We made him an offer in Capua. In exchange for bowing before Claudius in a public display of support for the new Emperor, we would spare his son. Pavo, of course, declined. He's quite the petulant brat, that one. Inherited his father's anti-authoritarian streak.'

'Get to your point,' Macro replied, injustice surging in his chest.

'After Pavo refused our offer, Pallas and myself had to resort to other means to move against the Liberators. Unfortunately, we can't detain every senator in Rome and torture the truth out of them, much as we would like to. It would not go down well with the mob. However, Fortuna has blessed us in the shape of a defector from the Liberators' ranks.'

'And why would such a man come over to you?'

Murena smiled thinly. 'We made him an offer he couldn't refuse. The defector, a trivial local magistrate, told us of the plan to assassinate Claudius at the games.'

'Sounds unlikely, if you ask me,' Macro responded tartly.

'The plan is certainly bold. But considering the success they have had so far in evading capture and undermining the Emperor's authority, we must presume that the threat is genuine.'

A distant cheer erupted above the infirmary. The ceiling shook, the walls groaning under the sheer mass of humanity bearing down on top of the arena. Murena frowned upwards.

'This place is falling apart,' he observed.

'Build a new one, then,' Macro responded gruffly.

'Oh, we shall. Perhaps not for a few years . . . but in time we'll build an arena like no other. We'll hold gladiator spectacles on an unimaginable scale, and our grip over the mob will be complete.' The aide stopped frowning and looked down at his feet. 'It's the most remarkable thing. Pallas and I were quite indifferent to the gladiator games at first. But now we see that they are truly a blessing from Jupiter. We'll have to host more of them in the future to keep the mob content and, more to the point, on our side.'

'Can't wait. Next time you arrange one of these fucking events, leave me out of it.'

The aide lifted his gaze to Macro. A hostile look flared in his eyes. 'According to the magistrate, the attempt on Claudius's life will take place tomorrow. And you are going to help us foil the plot.'

'How?'

'By stopping the assassin before he can kill the Emperor.'

'Correct me if I'm wrong, but doesn't Claudius have bodyguards for that sort of thing?'

Murena made a pained expression. 'The loyalty of his German knuckle-draggers is not in question. But they're likely to cut the would-be assassin to pieces, and it is essential that we take him alive. Capturing the traitor is our best chance of uncovering the names of the rest of the Liberators. If we get their names, we put an end to that nest of vipers at one stroke.'

Macro nodded in agreement. The German bodyguards were ferociously loyal to the Emperor and unlikely to show mercy to anyone who dared make an attempt on his life.

'At any rate, we could do with an extra pair of hands. The Germans sustained a significant number of casualties quashing the mutiny at the ludus in Capua, leaving the unit thinly stretched. There's also the fact that Claudius can't be seen to have too many bodyguards around him during the games. We're striving to portray the Emperor as a strong, fearless leader. It would not look good to have him seen in public hiding behind a mass of Germans.'

'Obviously,' Macro replied drily.

Murena cleared his throat. 'Your orders are to patrol the galleries and observe the spectators. Once the assassin reveals himself, apprehend him and take him to the imperial palace for questioning.' The aide's lips curled at the edges as he forced a smile. 'Then you will be free to go.'

Macro touched the stitches on his thigh. 'How do you know the attack is taking place tomorrow?'

Murena picked dirt off his shoulder. 'The magistrate told us.'

'He could be lying.'

'Unlikely. The imperial interrogators know what they're about. If he's lying, he'll be for the chop. But he had only limited involvement with the conspiracy. We don't know who else is involved, or for that matter who intends to strike the blow. And as I said earlier, it's politically impractical to round up every high-ranking public official and question them.'

'Why do you need me?' Macro asked, a deep frown weighing on his grizzled features. 'Why not use one of those lackeys in the Praetorian Guard?'

It was Murena's turn to frown now. 'We suspect that some of the Praetorians are part of the Liberators' conspiracy,' he said. He began pacing up and down the room. 'If you haven't already noticed, the guards have been relegated to arena duty. They are being kept as far away from the Emperor as possible without arousing suspicion in their ranks.'

'Hardly surprising,' Macro remarked in a low voice. 'Not that they'd be much use in any event. Bunch of overpaid amateurs playing at soldiers.'

Murena appeared not to hear him. 'This task requires someone with a good eye for danger and whose loyalty to Rome is unswerving. You have both qualities in abundance. The fact that you are a decorated soldier has persuaded Pallas that you are the ideal man for the task.'

Macro shook his head. 'It's an impossible job. There are more than twenty thousand spectators in the arena. How the hell am I going to keep an eye on all of them?'

'You won't have to,' Murena responded coolly. 'Pallas and I have given the matter some thought. We can rule out the assassin coming from the mob.'

'How can you be so sure?'

'He must come from the higher ranks because they are the ones seated closest to the imperial box. It's plausible that one of the senators might thrust a blade at the Emperor and strike a decisive blow before anyone could intervene. Any attempt on the Emperor's life from further away is laden with difficulties. One of the guards stationed at the exits would intervene before the killer had a chance to strike.'

'Why didn't you tell me about the conspiracy earlier?'

'The magistrate only spoke up this morning.'

Macro took a deep breath and fought a compulsive urge to snap the aide's neck.

'I'll do it,' he said after a pause. 'But after this, I'm pissing off back to the Second. No ifs or buts.'

'Agreed.' Murena nodded. 'This is your big chance to impress the Emperor. After the mutiny in Capua, he was inclined to have you crucified for carelessly destroying his personal property. You're highly fortunate that he has decided to place his faith in you.'

Macro was about to protest. But he reminded himself that the sooner he completed his task, the sooner he could return to the legion. He swallowed, pushing his rising anger into the pit of his stomach. 'When do I start?'

'Straight away.' The aide hesitated and stared intently at Macro. 'There is one more thing. It's vital that your presence around the Emperor is discreet. A Roman soldier by the Emperor's side might dissuade the assassin. Thankfully, I have the perfect cover for you.'

'A guard?' Macro asked.

Murena shook his head. 'As I mentioned, the guards are being kept at a safe distance from Claudius. No, you will pass yourself off as a freedman clerk working for me.'

'A bloody freedman!'

'It's the only convenient way of getting you close to the Emperor without arousing suspicion.' Murena narrowed his gaze. 'If you prefer, you can rejoin the beast fights.'

Macro clenched his jaw, bristling at the thought of having to endure further disgrace in the arena. His return to the Second Legion seemed more distant than ever.

Murena patted him on the shoulder. 'Good. Now if you'll excuse me, I have business to attend to. One of the other clerks will be along shortly to furnish you with the appropriate outfit. If you need me, I'll be in the imperial box.'

He turned to leave, but paused in the doorway and turned back to Macro, a cold look in his eyes.

'Don't let us down,' he warned. 'I'm relying on you to help me crush the Liberators once and for all. They may believe that by removing Claudius they'll usher in a brave new era of republicanism. They couldn't be more wrong. It is known that the legates of several of the legions are already positioning themselves to seize the throne should Claudius die. If the Liberators succeed, there won't be peace, but a bloodthirsty struggle for power.'

'Politicians stabbing each other in the back and seizing what they can?' Macro couldn't help sneering. 'If you ask me, that sounds exactly how things are now.'

Murena looked sternly at him. 'You may find the present situation in Rome disagreeable, but I assure you it would be far worse without the Emperor to maintain the status quo. If Claudius falls, Rome will descend into chaos.'

CHAPTER THIRTY-THREE

Pavo peered through the small barred window at the far end of the antechamber, gazing out across the sand. Fear made him tremble and feel sick as the moment of his bout against the Atlas bear drew closer. He was still exhausted from his efforts in defeating the lion, worsening his sense of dread at the impending confrontation. Even if he was fully fit, he stood little chance against a savage bear. But with tired limbs and sapped strength, he grimly acknowledged that his situation was hopeless.

At least a dozen beast fighters were crowded into the ante-chamber situated a short distance from the passageway where Macro and Pavo had first entered the Statilius Taurus amphi-theatre earlier that morning. A cloud of tension hung over them as they waited for their names to be called. Some passed the time by dictating their paltry wills to an official from the gladiator guild. Those with modest savings pressed coins into the hands of an opportunistic gravedigger in exchange for a burial plot beyond the city walls, rather than the usual grave pit that awaited most gladiators. The anxiety proved too much for one fighter, who retched on to the floor. The sour tang of vomit mingled with the fetid aroma from the makeshift latrine, simply a bucket in one corner of the pen filled to the brim with faeces and urine.

Fighting the urge to puke, Pavo focused on the animal hunt taking place on the arena floor. A fighter dressed in a tunic and armed with a short sword emerged from the tunnel, the attend-ants having already cleared away the lion and the dead beast fighter, along with the trees and vegetation. The man wasn't wearing a helmet. He turned to wave to the mob. Pavo caught a glimpse of his face and shook with disbelief.

The announcer read out the name of the animal hunter, but

Pavo already knew it well enough – Quintus Marcius Atellus. Pavo and Atellus had been childhood friends; they had studied Greek together and had played games in the streets. Atellus was the son of a wealthy landowner and, Pavo recalled, something of a spoilt brat, with his father keen to indulge his every whim.

Out in the arena there was a chorus of terrified squeals as a drove of hares and several ostriches were released on to the sand. Atellus laughed wildly, quickly cornering an ostrich. He plunged his sword into the panicked bird. Blood squirted out of its long neck and splattered his tunic. The ostrich flapped its wings erratically, shrieking in agony. Atellus then chopped up some hares with his sword as boos rang out across the arena.

'Why is Atellus competing in the games, I wonder?' Pavo mused.

'What did you say, Roman?' Amadocus barked at him.

Pavo half turned to the Thracian. 'Nothing.'

'Look at me when I'm talking to you!'

Pavo turned round. Amadocus stood in front of him with his armour removed, and Pavo now saw the full extent of his earlier injuries. A ragged gash ran diagonally down his chest and a wound to his left leg forced him to move with a slight limp.

'Not so high and mighty now, are you, rich boy?' Amadocus hissed, jabbing a finger at Pavo. 'This is what being a gladiator is all about. Rotting in a cell while you Romans walk around thinking your shit smells better than everyone else's. Now I'm going to make you suffer.'

An acute feeling of bitterness stung Pavo as he spoke. 'You have a short memory, Thracian. I saved you from the lion.'

Amadocus balled his callused hands into fists. 'And why the hell was I fighting against a wild beast in the first place? Because you came along and took my place in the arena against Britomaris. It should've been me matched against that barbarian. I would've won, too. I'd be the toast of Rome by now. Not sitting on my arse in this pit, waiting to die.'

'That had nothing to do with me. Blame those damned Greek freedmen of Claudius's.'

'I'm a true champion!' Amadocus thumped his fist against his chest. His facial muscles shook with rage, his thick accent mangling each word of Latin. 'I waited years for a chance to prove myself against the best in the arena and be numbered among the greats, slogging it out in the provinces, fighting the scum of the earth and patiently biding my time, just like the lanista instructed me to. Then you showed up and in a matter of weeks you're the people's champion. You bastard!'

Pavo pulled a sour face at his Thracian rival. 'The sword doesn't lie. You had your chances in the arena, you just didn't take them. The only difference between me and you is that I'm better with a sword and shield. Anyway, none of this matters. We're both about to be sent out to be slaughtered.'

The Thracian exploded with rage and lunged at Pavo. The gladiator backed away, trying to avoid being drawn into a fight, wanting to preserve his remaining strength for the beast fight. But Amadocus surged towards him. His outstretched hands grabbed Pavo by the neck and shoved him against the wall. A clamour erupted in the antechamber as some of the other beast fighters formed a semicircle around the men, fists pumping, cheering them on. The Thracian delivered a swift fist to the gladiator's groin. Pavo doubled up in agony and Amadocus launched a boot at his side and sent him crashing into the huddle of beast fighters. The fighters shuffled frantically away from the scrap as Amadocus hurled himself at the prone gladiator, pressing down on his opponent's arms with his knees, pinning Pavo to the ground.

'Roman scum! I'll make you pay!'

Pavo struggled to writhe free as Amadocus fastened his grip around his neck and squeezed his throat. His eyes bulged in their sockets. He couldn't breathe. The Thracian's fingers pressed hard against his throat cartilage. His brain felt as if it was swelling inside his skull.

'Die, Roman!' Amadocus bellowed.

Pavo fought off the aching tiredness in his limbs. He refused to die at the hands of the Thracian, even if meant exhausting his body ahead of the fight with the bear. He tensed his shoulder muscles and jerked to the side, pushing up on Amadocus with his palms as he turned. His strength caught the Thracian off guard. He let out a sharp cry as Pavo threw him off and sent him tumbling head first against the latrine bucket. The other fighters jumped back as its contents spilled on to the floor and drenched Amadocus in foul excrement. The Thracian spat waste out of his mouth and staggered to his feet. At that instant several guards thrust open the door and grabbed Amadocus before he could strike another blow at Pavo. Four of them clamped their hands around his arms. He tried in vain to wrestle free from the guards, snarling at Pavo the whole time, his hair dripping with filth.

At that moment Nerva burst in. The harassed arena official stepped around the stinking puddle as the guards restrained Amadocus.

'I'll kill you, Pavo!' the Thracian spat. 'This I swear!'

'I think the Atlas bear might have something to say about that,' Nerva declared as he glanced disapprovingly at Amadocus. 'It's time. Both of you. You're on.'

Pavo and Amadocus were manhandled towards the antechamber door by the guards. The other fighters stared silently at the men, painfully aware that they would soon be treading the same path.

'What about our weapons?' Amadocus asked.

'You won't have any,' Nerva replied flatly.

'Against a bear?' Amadocus spluttered, his eyes almost popping out of their sockets. 'Is this some kind of fucking joke?'

The official shot a severe look at him. 'Do I look like I'm joking?'

'On whose orders?' Pavo asked, shaking his groggy head clear.

'The sponsor, of course.' Nerva puffed out his cheeks and made a mark on his tablet with his stylus. 'Can't say I blame him. We're running behind schedule as it is. You were both supposed to die in your last fight.' He shrugged. 'First time for everything, I suppose. Now hurry up! I've got a tight schedule to keep to and the crowd is getting restless.'

Without further delay, Nerva led the small party of guards and beast fighters out of the holding pen and back down the passageway towards the gate. Ahead of them Atellus, the animal hunter, exited the arena and handed his sword to a nearby attendant. He noticed Pavo passing by and his jaw dropped in astonishment.

'By the gods, Pavo!' he announced gleefully. 'It's you!'

Pavo stopped in his tracks. He forced a smile at the land-owner's son. 'Atellus. What a pleasant surprise. You're competing in the games, I see.'

Atellus glanced down at his blood-splattered tunic and smiled. 'I've always wanted to fight in the arena. Thankfully my father is a favourite of the imperial court. He twisted a few arms and managed to get me added to the schedule. It's rather exciting, isn't it? The noise of the crowd, the feel of the sword in your grip. Nothing else like it . . .' He shook his head in amusement. 'I must say, you've started quite the fashion here in Rome. Thanks to you, the wealthy young men of Rome are in thrall to the games.'

His words sent a cold shiver through Pavo. 'You're participating of your own free will?'

'Of course. I was just taking part for a bit of fun. I wouldn't stoop to being a real gladiator.'

'You will never be that. Not while you shame yourself by massacring defenceless animals.'

Atellus laughed him off. 'Say what you like, but I can't wait to see the faces of my dinner companions tonight. They'll be green with envy!' His expression shifted and he cleared his throat. 'Anyway, I must go. Best of luck to you.'

Pavo watched his childhood friend saunter down the passageway, a leaden despair weighing heavily in his chest. He was struck by a sharp memory of his former life, the exotic food and heated political debates over a jug of good Falernian wine. The tragic injustice of it all struck him.

A clammy hand clasped his arm and one of the guards jerked him towards the open gate.

'Move it, scum!' the guard rasped.

Facing forward, Pavo took a deep breath and stepped out into the arena with Amadocus.

Jeers cascaded down on the two men from the now sparse crowd. There were several large gaps in the galleries, Pavo noted. Many of the spectators had grown bored of the morning programme of beast fights, in which dozens of men, some hunting in packs, others fighting individually, had been pitched against a bewildering variety of creatures, including giraffes, hippopotamuses and panthers. By now the novelty of the exotic beasts had clearly worn off and clutches of spectators were temporarily abandoning their seats, ducking out of the exits to refresh their wine cups at the merchant stalls lining the streets outside, ahead of the midday crucifixions. Pavo couldn't help noticing that several members of the remaining audience were stifling yawns as he took to the sand. The bitter realisation struck him that he would not even be granted the dignity of dying in front of a decent crowd.

With the arena almost a third empty, he could clearly hear the excitable mob in the upper terraces as they shouted abuse about him and his family in delirious voices. Several of the spectators made offensive hand gestures in his direction, their voices hoarse from hours of drunken singing.

The Atlas bear growled behind the opposite gate. A rank breeze fluttered across the arena as the gate creaked open, and a moment later the bear trudged out of the portal on all fours, followed by a small party of handlers. Some of the spectators seated at the lower galleries leant forward in their seats, commanding the beast to attack the fighters. As the bear neared, Pavo saw that a leash was fastened around its neck, with an animal handler standing to one side of it and pulling tight on the leash to the point of almost choking it. Behind the bear stood a pair of attendants, prodding it forward with wooden sticks. Four members of the Praetorian Guard kept watch at the gate, gripping the pommels of their swords in the event of trouble.

'How do we defeat this monster, then?' Amadocus asked.

'We don't,' Pavo replied coldly.

The Thracian rounded on him angrily. 'There must be something we can do,' he spluttered. 'You were full of bright ideas against that fucking lion! You're the expert here, do something!'

Pavo shook his head ruefully. 'I'm afraid without any weapons to defend ourselves with, we don't stand a chance. That bear is going to kill us.'

Amadocus was about to reply when he was interrupted by a guttural cry from across the arena. The bear had abruptly stopped in its tracks and was refusing to budge.

'What's going on?' Amadocus asked.

'I'm not sure,' Pavo replied. 'But it looks as if the bear's panicking.'

The handlers yanked on the chain and poked at the beast with their wooden sticks. The bear stubbornly refused to move and let out a deep wail. Infuriated by the animal's show of dissent, the handler tugged harder on the leash in an attempt to force it to continue towards Pavo and Amadocus. He only succeeded in enraging the creature. The bear thrashed violently at the leash, the chain tensing under the immense strain. Sensing the situation getting out of control, the handler shouted to the attendants for help. His companions bludgeoned the bear with their sticks. The beast brushed them away with a dismissive snort. As they retreated to a safe distance, the bear moaned and slumped to the ground.

Heated mutters broke out in the galleries. The handler turned to the imperial box in confusion. Pavo looked up to see Pallas glaring at Murena, and the aide to the imperial secretary shot up and gestured furiously to the Praetorian Guards keeping watch by the gate, urging them to assist the handler. Stirring into action, two of the guards hurried across the sand. One of them was brandishing a legionary sword. He stabbed the tip in the bear then jumped back. The crowd cheered. The bear howled. Droplets of blood glistened through its fur. In a blur of motion, the animal rounded on the handler and pawed at its leash.

Just then a spectator from one of the lower galleries threw his clay cup at the bear. The audience shouted its approval as the cup shattered against the side of the beast's head. The bear growled and spun around to face the direction of the spectator who'd thrown the cup. All eyes turned to the man. Pavo followed their gaze and saw an obese patrician seated in the gallery nearest to the arena floor, a perfectly round paunch visible under his toga. The handler pulled hard on the leash, snapping the bear away from the spectator. Spinning round, the bear lashed out at the handler, slashing at his guts with its long claws. The handler gasped. His bowels slopped out of the gash, emptying on to the sand, and as he collapsed, the leash fell from his slack grip.

Having broken free from its tight leash, the bear swung round to the arena wall and launched itself at the patrician with a

lightning-fast combination of power and speed. The colour immediately drained from the man's face as the bear pushed up on its
hind legs and stood upright. Stretched to its full height, it was
taller than the short drop between the gallery and the arena floor.
It thrust out a paw and tore into the dumbstruck patrician with
its claws. The patrician screamed as the claws grazed his chest.
He turned, trying to scramble to safety, but the bear, still standing
upright, immediately clamped its jaws around his arm and ripped
him from his seat. The patrician shrieked as the bear wrenched
its head to the side, pulling him away from the gallery, the slack
leash dangling uselessly from its neck. Then it relaxed its jaws and
sent the patrician tumbling to the sand below. It spun back around
and dropped to all fours as the patrician stumbled to his feet. He
turned to flee, but he was too slow. The beast slashed at him,
raking its claws violently across his face and chest. The man's
screams were abruptly cut off as the bear ripped his head off the
plump folds of his neck.

The exits were heaving with spectators desperate to escape the
wrath of the beast. At the imperial box on the other side of the
arena the Emperor looked dumbfounded. The German bodyguards
forced Claudius to his feet and escorted him towards the private
exit. Murena, clearly rattled, shouted an order at the guards
manning the gates. They frantically disappeared down the
passageway as the creature clawed the patrician's bloodied body.

'We have to do something,' Pavo urged. 'The bear isn't going
to stop until it's killed everyone in sight.'

'No need, Roman,' Amadocus replied. 'Look.'

He pointed to the Praetorians emerging from the gate and
cautiously approaching the bear. Each man brandished a hunting
spear seized from the arena armoury. The guards closed round
the bear in a rough circle, stabbing at it with their spears,
confounding the creature. One of the guards plunged his spear
deep into its side. Blood flowed out of the wound and gushed
over the sand. The bear howled horribly as the other Praetorians
encircled it, thrusting at the beast repeatedly. At last the bear let
out a faint whimper and dropped to the sand.

Nerva rushed out of the passageway, spitting with fury.

'The beast fights are off!' the official barked at Pavo and Amadocus.

'We're not going to fight?' the young gladiator asked.

'Are you mad?' Nerva gestured towards the patrician's mangled body. 'After that? Can't have fine upstanding Roman citizens getting mauled to death in the arena. Bad for business. If the spectators aren't safe during the fights, then the mob will stay away.' As if suddenly remembering something, he turned back to the passageway and snapped his fingers at a gathering of acrobats. 'You lot, get out here and for gods' sakes do something to distract the crowd!'

Pavo and Amadocus looked at the official.

'Does this mean our part in the games is over?' the Thracian asked hopefully.

Nerva laughed bitterly. 'No such luck. You're to be returned to your cells in the imperial ludus, along with the other fighters.' He shook his head. 'It's going to be a busy afternoon tomorrow, I tell you. There are sixty men listed to appear then.'

'Listed to appear in what?' Pavo asked nervously.

'The group fight,' replied the official.

CHAPTER THIRTY-FOUR

'Pssst! Wake up!'

Pavo stirred drowsily in his cell. He'd fallen asleep on the thin bedroll as soon as the guards had slammed the door shut, drained from the stress of the day's combat. Every bone in his body ached dully as he sat upright. He squinted at the gloom and saw a figure crouched outside the door, his piercing eyes reflecting the moonlight filtering in through a slit in the cell wall. The broad stripes of his tunic were faintly visible under his cloak. Pavo recognised the face as the elderly senator he'd seen arriving late to his seat in the galleries. The senator stared back at him, stroking his chin thoughtfully.

'Thank the gods. I thought you might be dead.'

'Who are you?' Pavo asked wearily.

The senator ignored the question as he ran his eyes over the gladiator and sounded a note of approval. 'You've shaped up nicely, I see. Titus always did say that the mark of a good Roman was one who understood the value of physical exercise. Not like those slobs you get these days, stuffing their bellies in the taverns. Here.'

The senator slipped a bundle through the bars, anxiously peering down the dimly lit corridor to make sure he wasn't being watched.

'Some food. To help you regain your strength.'

Pavo eagerly took the parcel. It was still warm. His belly rumbled noisily as he unwrapped the cloth and several chunks of stale bread and cooked meat tumbled into his lap. He hesitated to tuck into the food. He looked back at the senator, quickly sizing him up.

'I saw you fight this morning,' the senator continued. 'I must say, that was an impressive display. And I'm speaking as someone who was never very fond of gladiatorial sport.'

'That makes two of us.'

'You're probably wondering why I've taken the considerable trouble to pay you, the son of a disgraced legate, a visit. My name is Numerius Porcius Lanatus,' the senator declared in a stately voice. He had that annoying habit, Pavo noted, of answering a question other than the one being asked, a trait characteristic of all senators.

'Good for you, Porcius Lanatus,' Pavo responded.

'My name means nothing to you?' Lanatus asked. Seeing the blank look on the face of the young gladiator, he clasped his hands beneath his chin and considered Pavo at length. 'I was a friend of your late father, in the days when Titus was a mere military tribune and I was a provincial governor. Things were different then, but Titus and I were quite close. Perhaps he spoke of me.'

'Not that I can remember.'

Lanatus smiled softly. 'By the time you were born, I had already returned to Rome. I must admit, I was disappointed when your father decided to pursue a career in the military rather than join me in the Senate. Titus would have made an effective politician. But then he always did prefer swords to styluses. Much like his son, it seems.'

'The choice isn't exactly mine. Claudius sentenced me to die as a gladiator after they killed my father. Now they've condemned me to the group fight tomorrow. All I can do is make my peace with the gods and pray for a quick death.'

'Yes,' Lanatus said slowly. 'I've heard about the Emperor's plans for you. It seems terribly unfair, but then Claudius can't be trusted to keep his word. He'll do whatever it takes to secure the fawning adulation of the mob. Just like Caligula and Tiberius did before him. He's also beholden to those grubby Greek freedmen he insists on surrounding himself with. At any rate, I gather the mob is itching to see you fight.'

Pavo craned his neck to stare past the senator down the corridor. 'How did you manage to sneak past the guards? Only the imperial lanista and his staff are permitted to enter the ludus.'

'The duty guard is a fellow sympathiser.'

Pavo looked at the senator carefully. 'I'm not sure I follow.'

'He shares a certain attachment to republican values, as should all good, principled men. Especially fellows like you who have suffered greatly from the tyranny of the emperors.'

Pavo was silent for a moment. 'Some might call that treason.'

'True.' The senator nodded. 'Others might call it patriotism. That is, those of us who refer to ourselves as the Liberators.'

Pavo felt the hairs on the back of his neck stand on end. Placing the food to one side, he looked at the senator, his expression suddenly severe. 'Liberators, you say? Snakes would be a more apt description. You people are the reason my father is dead and I'm imprisoned in this cell waiting to be killed by a gang of barbarians. Get out of my sight.'

The senator shook his head sadly. 'That's no way to talk to a dear friend of your father's. Aren't you at least interested in what I have to say? After all, Titus shared our dream of returning Rome to the glorious days of the Republic.'

'What my father wanted was an end to the corruption.' Pavo was curt. 'He despised the regime for building lavish palaces while the soldiers under his command went without pay. He was concerned for the welfare of his men, not back-stabbing politics.'

'And we supported him fully in his endeavours,' Lanatus insisted.

Pavo snorted disdainfully. 'Where were you and the rest of the so-called Liberators when my father rose up against the Emperor?'

Lanatus's face darkened. 'We couldn't take the risk of publicly declaring our support for Titus. What do you think would have happened if we'd all come out of the woodwork and rallied around him? The Emperor would have executed us all.'

Pavo glowered at Lanatus. 'My father would still be here if it wasn't for you.'

'Titus sacrificed his life for Rome. I know his death pains you, but the Liberators are committed to realising his dream of a restored republic. That should be your dream too, if you truly honour him.'

'I've heard enough!' Pavo looked away, tasting a bitter tang in the back of his mouth. As someone who'd been born into great wealth, who'd lost everything and lived and fought among men regarded as the lowest form of human life, he felt he had a unique perspective on Rome and its political feuding. His sharp mind discerned how statesmen furthered their own ambitions by making hollow promises that the mob quickly forgot when a new gladiator spectacle was announced. In his mind, Lanatus and Murena were two sides of the same coin. Both were talented liars, destined to rise in Rome – as he himself never would now.

'I didn't come here to discuss politics with you,' Lanatus scolded. 'Actually, I came to make you an offer.'

'Then you're wasting your time. Whatever it is, I'm not interested.'

Lanatus stared back at Pavo. 'Rash as well as tetchy, aren't you? That'll be the Valerius blood in you. But I would caution against dismissing my offer out of hand. You'll want to hear what I have to say, trust me.'

'Trust you!' Pavo laughed. 'The man who hid behind his papyrus scroll while my father was thrown to his death in the arena?' He folded his arms and looked away. 'I'm done listening to you.'

'You underestimate me, young man.'

Pavo turned slowly back to face Lanatus. The senator looked at him with narrowed eyes as his lips flickered into a quick smile.

'I have something that will make you listen . . .'

He reached under his tunic and thrust his hand at Pavo, unclenching his fist to reveal a golden locket with a neck strap. There was an intricately detailed image of Icarus engraved on the front.

'This belongs to your son, I believe.'

Pavo nodded slowly at the locket. Every Roman boy was given one at birth to protect against evil spirits. His son's name had been engraved on the reverse, along with the date of his birth. He looked up at Lanatus. 'Where did you get this?'

The senator snatched the locket back. 'In due course. First, you must listen to me. I have a special task for you. The Liberators have been waiting for such an opportunity for months. Should you complete this task, then I may be able to help you.'

'Go on,' Pavo said warily.

Lanatus stroked the bridge of his nose. 'As you are no doubt aware, the last remaining survivor of the group fight is declared the winner and presented with a laurel crown by Emperor Claudius in person, along with a modest prize of one thousand sestertii. This gives us an opportunity.'

Pavo frowned. 'To do what?'

Lanatus glanced down the corridor before replying. 'Claudius lives in fear. Understandably so, given that his predecessor Caligula was assassinated by members of the Praetorian Guard. The Emperor will be surrounded by his German bodyguards while seated in the imperial box, making it impossible for anyone to get close to him. With one exception, namely the victorious gladiator.' He paused, allowing his words to sink in. 'Win the group fight, my boy, and you'll have a chance to avenge your father, and your family name . . . by killing Claudius.'

A cold shiver ran through Pavo. He looked at the senator with a mixture of suspicion and unease. And yet the thought of Claudius falling beneath his blade filled him with a strange thrill.

'Assassinate the Emperor . . . in front of the mob?' he whispered.

'Why not? A tyrant like Claudius deserves to die on the grand stage.'

'Perhaps. But even if I wanted to help, you're forgetting that there are sixty of us due to take part in the group fight. Nerva says only the last man standing survives. What if I get cut down? Then your plan is in tatters.'

'Ah, but that's the beauty of the group fights. You'll find your-self up against the dregs, the lowest of the low! Men with only basic training in how to hold a sword. And then there's you, with a reputation as one of the finest swordsmen ever to have appeared in the arena. To be honest, I was sceptical about your abilities. A boy born into a notable household, possessing an unnatural talent with the sword, seemed a rather far-fetched proposition. Until I saw you fight with my own eyes today. You showed admirable courage, skill and quick thinking to defeat that lion. I'm sure you can overcome the other gladiators tomorrow.'

'Perhaps. But what do I get out of this?'

'Revenge! It's well known that Claudius personally sanctioned your father's death. What greater prize could you wish for than the chance to kill the Emperor?'

'My fight isn't with Claudius. He's just some slobbering old fool. It's Hermes I'm after. He's the one who murdered my father. Hermes is the one I want to kill, not the Emperor.'

'Arranging a fight between you and Hermes is beyond my powers. He's reputed to be the greatest gladiator who ever lived. As such he enjoys unrivalled status and celebrity. I understand Caligula once tried to lure him out of retirement. Hermes refused outright. Caligula was outraged, but then he realised that any move against Hermes might be a step too far for the Roman mob.'

'But Hermes *has* come out of retirement. He's scheduled to fight at the games. Murena told me so.'

'Correct. He is, however, scheduled to fight another opponent to be personally selected by Claudius. I can do nothing about Hermes, I'm afraid. But I can assist you in another matter.'

Pavo cocked his head at Lanatus. His mouth felt very dry.

'I understand that your son is to be killed tomorrow. Thrown to the beasts. At least he would have been, were it not for that unpleasant incident with the bear today.'

'It doesn't change a thing. Murena and Pallas won't spare Appius. Those heartless Greek bastards will find some other way of killing him.'

'They already have. He's to be flung from the Tarpeian Rock tomorrow. It seems both the imperial secretary and his aide are keen to kill anyone who carries the Valerius name.'

Pavo considered. 'You said you would help me. How?'

Lanatus smiled slightly. 'Your son is at the imperial palace. How else do you think I discovered this locket?'

Hope and fear pounded inside Pavo's skull. He wanted to believe there was a chance to save Appius. He narrowed his gaze at the senator. The elderly man's eyes glinted as he went on.

'I've befriended one of the household slaves at the palace, an interesting young chap by the name of Quintus Licinius Cato. I'm a frequent visitor to the palace, and I had heard that young Cato was fond of poetry. I dabble in verse myself, so today I stopped by and offered to lend Cato a few scrolls from my collection. Some Catullus, and a few lines of Propertius.'

'What does this have to do with Appius?'

The elderly senator lowered his voice. 'Appius was there, Pavo. He's still under the care of the imperial slaves. I saw your son with my own eyes. He was wearing his locket around his neck. I took it from him so I could give you proof that I am a man of my word. Cato seemed quite attached to young Appius. The poor chap was clearly upset when he informed me that Appius will no longer be with us tomorrow.'

Pavo thumped his fist into his palm. 'Then there's still a chance to save my son.'

Lanatus glanced over his shoulder, and when he turned back to Pavo and spoke again, it was in a barely audible whisper. 'I have a plan. The imperial palace is almost empty while the games are being held. The Emperor, his imperial staff and freedmen are all in attendance and many of the slaves have been detailed for arena duty. All that's left are a few household slaves and a small detachment of the Praetorian Guard.'

'What's the plan?' Pavo asked rapidly, his pulse quickening, his mind racing.

'I'll make my way to the imperial palace during the fight tomorrow to lend Cato my poetry. I'm a familiar enough face at the palace. No one will refuse my entry. Once inside, I'll find Appius and pass him to one of my slaves at the entrance to the kitchen, which is unguarded during the games. From there he will be spirited away.'

A thought struck Pavo. 'Where will he go? He can't stay in Rome. Once Claudius is dead, there'll be reprisals against every gladiator in the land. Think of what Pallas and Murena will do if they catch Appius . . .' He found it too distressing to go on. He closed his eyes and tried to shut out the thought.

'I've already considered that problem,' said Lanatus after a pause. Pavo opened his eyes and watched the senator scratch his cheek as he continued. 'There's a friend of yours, I believe. A heavyset chap named Manius Salvius Bucco.'

Pavo blinked in amazement. 'Bucco was a fellow recruit during my time at the ludus in Paestum. But how did you find out about him?'

'The network of Liberators is far more extensive than you

might imagine, Pavo. A bodyguard of one of my friends used to be a gladiator at Paestum. He mentioned that you and Bucco were quite close. Apparently he had something of a gambling habit and owes you a debt.'

Pavo nodded. 'I got him out of a tight spot with a creditor.'

Lanatus smiled weakly. 'I sent one of my servants to Ostia to explain the situation to Bucco. He's on his way to Rome as we speak. He has agreed to take Appius in. My slave will meet him on the road and hand Appius over as soon as Claudius falls. He'll be in Ostia, safe and sound, before the authorities realise he's missing. His every need will be taken care of.'

Pavo was silent. He was apprehensive about placing his trust in Lanatus. But the alternative was to submit to a gruesome death in the arena. Murena had promised him that he would perish at the games one way or another, and Pavo knew he couldn't survive much longer.

'How am I supposed to kill Claudius? The attendants will take away my sword as soon as the fight is over. That's assuming I manage to survive the fight.'

'I've studied the programme in detail. The victor from the group fight will be taken to the infirmary immediately after the fight to be cleaned up and made presentable to the Emperor. When you arrive, I'll make my way down to the infirmary to offer my congratulations. Then I'll slip you a dagger, short enough to conceal in the folds of your loincloth. When you are escorted up the steps to the imperial box, you will simply reach for the dagger and end Claudius's evil reign.'

A cold fear worked its way through Pavo. He stared wide-eyed at Lanatus.

'How do I escape?'

'You don't,' Lanatus said simply. 'I thought you would realise that.'

'But the Germans will tear me to pieces!'

'Of course,' Lanatus responded gravely. 'But by then it will be too late. The Emperor will already be dead.'

The gladiator felt a cold tremor on his lips. 'I have to die to save my son?'

The senator's eyes burned brightly. 'Not just to save Appius, my boy. To save Rome. Think of the legacy you will leave. The Valerius name will be restored to its former glory, and you will be hailed as the Liberator who sacrificed his life in order to save Rome from ruin. Once Claudius is dead, I'll put forward an emergency vote to return Rome to a republic. This is your chance to be a hero, Pavo!'

The young gladiator fell quiet. He was aware of an enormous weight bearing down on his shoulders, and a wave of exhaustion washed over him. Turning away from Lanatus, he rose wearily to his feet and peered out of the narrow slit in his cell wall. The view overlooked the Campus Martius, stretching south towards the city walls. He glimpsed the outlines of grandiose baths and temples in the distance, their ornate marbled facades glowing under the pale moonlight, testament to the might of imperial Rome. The carcasses of several beasts lined the side of the Flaminian Way, the creatures dumped outside the arena after each fight. Now a small crowd of gaunt men in threadbare tunics gleaned what meat they could from the little that remained.

'Well?' Lanatus called from the other side of the cell. 'What's your answer?'

Pavo sighed. He was in an impossible position. If he accepted, his chance of gaining revenge over Hermes would be gone for ever. If he rejected the senator's offer, his son would die. At last he turned back to face Lanatus and said, 'I'm only doing this for my son.'

'A wise choice, my boy.' The senator straightened up, a relieved expression on his face, a fierce fire still burning in his eyes. Almost absently, he realised he was still clutching the locket. He chucked it to Pavo. 'Keep it. Perhaps it will bring you some luck. Now, it's late. I suggest you get some rest ahead of the group fight. Tomorrow you will take the life of the Emperor.'

CHAPTER THIRTY-FIVE

The sun glowed weakly behind the clouds the next morning as Macro took up his position close to the imperial box, trying to get comfortable in his freedman's tunic and failing. The belt fastened around his waist was too tight, and his stocky chest bulged inside his ill-fitting tunic. He cut a faintly ridiculous figure and he drew perplexed looks from the spectators seated in the nearby galleries.

'First a bloody gladiator, now a fucking clerk,' he muttered irritably. 'At this rate I'll be dressed up as a slave before the day is out.'

He shook off his anger and turned towards the arena floor. Half a dozen attendants were hurriedly raking the sand in preparation for the forthcoming bout. The galleries had gradually filled with spectators as the moment of the group fight drew closer. Now the arena heaved with the noise and bustle of a packed crowd, the smell of grilled meat wafting in from the street stalls. Macro gritted his teeth as spectators brushed past him in a mad dash for the few remaining seats.

The Praetorian at his shoulder noticed the sour look on Macro's face and grunted. 'Cheer up, mate. This is one of the perks of the job.'

Macro shook his head. 'I've had enough of gladiator spectacles . . .'

Turning away from the arena floor in disgust, he directed his gaze towards the imperial box. The puzzle of where the assassin might strike at the Emperor had stalked the optio all morning. He'd risen at dawn, making his way straight to the empty arena to explore its tangled warren of passageways. At the end of his inspection he had concluded that although there were plenty of exits the killer could use to escape into the streets, the Emperor and his retinue were well protected. The ornately decorated box was situated on a raised platform on the north side of the arena, affording a prime view of the gladiator bouts. The box featured its own private steps leading down to a guarded passageway that had a separate entrance also manned by a section of Praetorians. Getting near to the Emperor would be incredibly difficult. Macro had considered the possibility that one of the senators or foreign dignitaries immediately behind the box might be the assassin. But he doubted that any of them were physically capable of breaking through the party of German bodyguards, grabbing the Emperor and plunging a blade into his neck. There had to be some other approach where the assassin would be lying in wait. But for the life of him Macro couldn't figure out where.

'This isn't soldier's work,' he quietly seethed. 'I should be training men, not helping out those Greek tossers.'

'Oi! Get your hands off me!' a voice cried above the general murmur of the mob.

Swivelling his steely gaze to the right of the exit, Macro spotted two spectators quarrelling over a seat at the edge of the gallery. One of the men had grabbed a seated spectator by a fold of his weather-beaten toga. The seated man shrugged off the hand and shot to his feet. Macro rounded on them both in a flash ahead of the Praetorian Guard, pulling the spectators apart.

'What the hell is going on?' he demanded.

'This man stole my seat!' the first spectator protested.

'Piss off, I was here before you!' the second spectator snarled throatily. He smoothed out the fold in his toga, glaring at the first spectator through glazed eyes.

The first man glowered. 'This seating is reserved for the equites. If you're one of us then show me your ring.'

Macro raised an eyebrow at the second man. 'Well?'

The spectator looked away guiltily. 'I don't have it,' he slurred. 'I lost it in the tavern.'

'Another lie!' the first man fumed. He raised his finger and showed his ring to Macro. 'The man's an impostor. A pleb trying to pass himself off as one of his betters.'

Macro frowned at the second man. 'It appears you're in the wrong seating section, friend.'

The man flashed a withering look of contempt at him. 'Who the hell do you think you're talking to? Fucking freedmen,' he added bitterly. 'Bloody everywhere these days.'

Macro's temper snapped. He reached out and grabbed the man by the neck, forcing him to face forward and look towards the arena floor. A comedy troupe was entering from the east portal, acrobats juggling balls and midgets dressed up in costume. The spectator recoiled in shock as Macro whispered into his ear, 'Address me like that again and you'll have the best view in the arena. D'you hear?'

The man gulped loudly and raised his palms in mock surrender. 'Fair enough, mate. I'm sorry. You know how it is. Everyone's trying to get a seat for the games this morning. The group fight is the talk of the taverns. It's not every day you get two legends slogging it out in a free-for-all.'

'What are you talking about?' Macro hissed.

'Don't tell me you haven't heard! There was an announcement in the Forum first thing this morning. A message from the sponsor. All those gladiators who were supposed to get ripped to pieces by wild beasts have been drafted into the group fight . . . including that treacherous shit Marcus Valerius Pavo.'

'Stop spouting bollocks. I've heard about these group fights. They're just a cheap way of getting rid of the scum. Dozens of murderers and fugitive slaves carving each other up with about as much skill as a blind Gaul after a skinful of wine. The organisers would never risk a proper swordsman in that chaos.'

Macro released his grip on the man before he could reply. Down on the arena floor the comedy routine was trudging off and an umpire marched purposefully out of the eastern gate, followed by a procession of lightly armoured gladiators. Macro spied Pavo at the front of the column, staring rigidly ahead as the crowd hurled abuse at him.

'Gods, you're right!' he muttered. He experienced an acute stab of sympathy for his former pupil.

'Told you,' the spectator replied with a sneer. 'Tell you what, I don't fancy Pavo's chances in this fight.'

Macro rounded on the spectator. 'What do you mean?'

'There's quite a few who are handy with a sword who've been added to the programme. You've got your Egyptian swordsmen and your German barbarians. Amadocus is competing too.'

Macro felt his blood run cold. 'Bloody hell.'

The spectator nodded. 'Pavo being the champion gladiator, the other men will be desperate to give him the chop. I don't care how well he fared against the wild beasts; he's going to get slaughtered down there this morning.'

'Right, you bastards!' the umpire called out to the fighters as they wearily tramped out of the eastern and western gates and took up their positions either side of a chalk mark running across the sand. 'Nobody moves a bloody finger until I give the word. If I catch anyone trying to get stuck in too early, they'll be nailed to a cross before the day is out. Understood?'

'Yes, sir!' the gladiators chorused.

Pavo had awoken that morning Hades-bent on sparing his son from the same traitor's fate he'd suffered, and his father Titus before him. Entering the arena to a wall of noise, he recalled the gladiator tactics he'd learnt under Macro. The men slowly assembled on the sand, sixty in total. Some grimly resigned themselves to their fate. Others shook their fists at the crowd in postures of tragic defiance. A short, stocky gladiator stood to the right of Pavo, visibly trembling with fear.

'This is it,' he croaked. The man had no teeth, Pavo noticed, and a branding mark on his forehead marked him out as a fugitive slave. 'We're bloody done for.'

'First fight?' Pavo asked.

'And last,' the man replied bitterly. 'I shouldn't be here. I've never wielded a sword in my life.'

Pavo felt his muscles tense as attendants distributed the weapons to the men, steeling himself for the imminent fight. Accompanied by a line of Praetorian Guards, the umpire made his way around the fighters in turn, pausing in front of each man to personally inspect the sharpness of his weapon. In an attempt to bring some order to the group fight, which often descended into a chaotic brawl, the men had been arranged into two teams of thirty apiece, with the teams distinguished by their weaponry. Each fighter on Pavo's team was handed a curved sword two feet in length and a small round shield. The shield was smaller than the one he was used to in the legions and offered much less protection, and he was unfamiliar with the blade.

Their opponents on the other side of the powdered chalk line were equipped with two legionary swords but no shield. Both sets of fighters lacked body armour and protective helmets, wearing only their loincloths. He supposed the idea of the groups having contrasting weaponry was to force the gladiators with two swords, deprived of shields, to attack their opponents. Gripping his sword, Pavo noted a pair of German combatants on the opposite side of the chalk line conversing in their native tongue, their giant figures towering a full head over the other men, the swords looking ridiculously small in their hands.

The young fighter glanced in the direction of the imperial box. He saw Macro staring down at him from one of the exits, dressed in the manner of a simple freedman. The soldier nodded slightly at Pavo, who was struck by a sudden sadness that the veteran wasn't fighting at his side today. Across from the optio a line of foreign dignitaries and imperial staff filtered into the imperial box through the private entrance and made their way to their cushioned seats. A black rage ran through Pavo as he spotted Murena and Pallas taking their places beside the Emperor. The imperial secretary sipped wine from a silver goblet while he stared impassively down at the young gladiator, his skin pulled tight across his face, his lips thin as if they had been carved out with the tip of a knife. Pavo's heart burned with desire for revenge over the two freedmen.

He lowered his gaze to the fighters on the other side of the chalk line and felt his blood run cold. The gladiators armed with two legionary swords looked confident, gripping their weapons in the manner of seasoned fighters. The short, stocky man trembling beside Pavo was in keeping with the general demeanour of the rest of his companions. They were nervous and gripped their weapons clumsily. Gritting his teeth, Pavo realised that he'd need to call on all his experience and fighting skills in order to survive – and save his son.

'Prepare to die, Roman.'

Amadocus took a step towards Pavo, his neck muscles bulging as he drew the sword in his right hand level with his chin and pointed the tip at the young gladiator.

'We're on different teams, thank the gods.' The Thracian grinned cruelly. 'Now I'll get a chance to show everyone I'm the real champion of the arena. I've been waiting for this day for a long time.'

Pavo shook his head. 'You don't scare me. I've beaten better men than you.'

'Bullshit! I'm a champion of the arena. Not like those drunks and barbarians you've fought. As for this lot,' he ran his eyes across the gladiators around Pavo, 'I'll cut these useless shits down before the Emperor warms his arse on his cushion. Once they're out of the way, I'll hack you to pieces. Then I'll collect my reward.'

A shout from the eastern gate cut Pavo off before he could reply as Nerva ordered the attendants and guards towards the passageway. The gate clanged shut behind the last guard. Now every pair of eyes in the arena fixed on the umpire, and the same cold chill coursed through Pavo's veins that he always felt before a fight. Spectators heckled the umpire, urging him to give the signal so that the fight could begin. The umpire ignored the calls, waiting until all the weapons and equipment had been checked and the gates were secure. Satisfied that the preparations were complete, he at last removed himself to a safe distance from the fighters and raised his wooden stick high above his head. The crowd hushed. No one moved.

There was a dull thwack as the umpire beat his stick against the sand.

'Gladiators . . . FIGHT!'

At once the opposing group of gladiators charged towards the line, the Germans' full-throated war cries echoing above the roar of the crowd. Some of the fighters on Pavo's side froze with fear at the sight of dozens of sharp sword tips glinting at them. The stocky man to Pavo's right hurled his sword and shield at the onrushing opponents and turned on the spot, sprinting towards the eastern gate. Another fighter let his shield fall and, clasping both hands around the sword grip, turned the blade inward and jerked it up into the roof of his mouth, preferring to take his own life than suffer a grisly death at the hands of the veteran gladiators. The powdered chalk line quickly disappeared under the feet of the onrushing fighters.

A gaunt-looking man charged at Pavo. A grim determination swept through the young gladiator at the moment of battle. The life of his son was in his hands. He would not let Appius down. He tucked his shield tight to his chest and focused on the gladiator racing towards him. The man screamed manically at the top of his voice as he slashed at Pavo, bringing both swords above his head in a wide arc. The weapons trembled in his grip. Pavo side-stepped sharply to his left, avoiding the blow as momentum carried the ragged man forward, the two swords dragging his scrawny frame down and presenting his neck to Pavo. In a burst of motion the young gladiator thrust his sword at his opponent. The gaunt fighter had enough time to register a look of dumb surprise on his face before the curved blade plunged into his neck. He gasped in agony as it punched through his throat. Pavo wrestled his sword free of his opponent. Blood flowed freely from the wound. The man sank to his knees, gurgling curses at the young gladiator as he pawed at his gashed throat.

Pavo glimpsed a blur of movement in the corner of his eye. He spun round just in time to see two blade tips flashing in the air and slashing towards his throat as a burly, thickly bearded gladiator lunged at him. He jerked his head back with lightning reflexes, his muscles reaping the benefit of the hours of training under Macro in the ludus. His opponent jerked his shoulder, angling the blade up at the last moment. The blade tip nicked the young gladiator on the cheek. Pavo felt a hot pain flare on the side of his face and warm blood trickle down his neck. He shook his head clear as the bearded gladiator aimed his second sword at him. Now Pavo punched out with his small shield. There was a brittle clatter as the sword glanced off the metal boss, and a powerful shudder stung his forearm muscles. Then he pushed forward, crashing into his opponent with his shield clasped tight to his shoulder. The shield juddered as Pavo struck his opponent on the jaw, following up with a quick jab of his sword tip at the fighter's midriff. The man spasmed wildly as the curved blade sank into his bowels. Pavo flicked his wrist, angling the blade up into his opponent's chest and puncturing his vitals. The man clawed at Pavo, trying to gouge his eyes out. Pavo ripped his sword free and watched the man fall away, his heart pounding inside his chest like a beating drum. Each slain fighter brought him a step closer to securing the safe passage of his son out of Rome.

He glanced around him at the unfolding battle. The groans of the dying mingled with the relentless wet slap of metal slamming against flesh. The group fight had descended into a mass brawl and any pretence of organised combat between the rival groups was quickly abandoned as the mostly inexperienced fighters on Pavo's side were overwhelmed by the superior skills of their opponents. The crowd let out cries of delight as the two Germans tore into a handful of Pavo's terrified companions, some of whom hacked in an uncoordinated frenzy at their opponents while others tried to flee. One fighter threw his sword at one of the Germans in desperation. His opponent parried the makeshift missile and pounded towards his foe. Gripped by terror, the fighter ripped off his shield and chucked it at the German. The enormous gladiator brushed aside the shield and buried a sword in his enemy's groin. Pavo's companion howled in agony and keeled over, both hands clasped despairingly around the pommel of the sword protruding from his midriff. At least half of the fighters were now strewn across the sand, Pavo noticed. The survivors on his side were fighting for their lives in isolated pairs, hacking and slashing at their powerful opponents with increasingly desperate attacks.

'Roman! You're mine!'

Glancing across the corpse-strewn arena floor, Pavo glimpsed Amadocus limping towards him, his eyes burning with hatred, blood dripping from his mane of long hair. His jaws were clamped shut as he fought through the pain of several cuts. A heavily scarred man blocked his path towards Pavo. The man unwisely stood his ground, crouching behind his shield and blindly thrusting his blade at his Thracian opponent. Amadocus bared his teeth and stabbed at the man, who hefted up his shield at the last moment. The sword tip rang as it glanced off the boss. Losing patience, Amadocus cast aside one of his two swords, reached out and grasped the edge of his opponent's shield. The man tried to pull it back. But Amadocus was more than a match for him, even with an injured leg and missing fingers, and he proceeded to smash the shield against the man's face with brute strength. The man let out a nasal groan as the blow shattered his nose. He stumbled away from Amadocus, cupping his hands to his face. Amadocus thrust his sword at him with such force that the blade buried itself in his stomach up to the pommel. He wasted no time in kicking his stricken opponent aside, then he retrieved his discarded sword and hurried on towards his rival.

A full-blooded roar snapped Pavo's gaze back to the pair of Germans. They had finished picking off their hapless opponents, leaving Pavo as the last surviving fighter from his side.

'Don't stop fighting!' the umpire thundered. 'Only the last man standing wins!'

Now the two Germans turned on their comrades. Fewer than a dozen men were still standing. The Germans made short work of them, slashing through them with a series of coordinated attacks, severing spinal columns and punching through the napes of exposed necks. The bodies quickly piled up around their feet. The Germans looked around for another opponent and, spotting Pavo, simultaneously charged at the young gladiator to a rasping cheer from the mob, who were desperate to see their former hero cut down.

The man on the right lunged at Pavo first, the sharp points of his swords glinting in the light. Pavo bent at the knees and pushed out with his shield, meeting the attack head on. There was a jarring clang as the sword tips glanced off his shield boss and carried towards the sky. Now Pavo leaned forward and jerked his sword down at an angle, piking his opponent through his leading foot, slicing through tendon and bone. Blood spurted out of the wound and the German immediately tensed up with pain. He reached down to his impaled foot. Pavo retracted his arm and swept his shield in front of him in a wide horizontal arc, smashing into his opponent's jaw with the iron rim. The German's eyes rolled into the back of his head as he crashed to the sand.

'Scum, that's my brother!' the second German growled in broken Latin.

In the same draw of breath he launched at Pavo and slashed at him with the sword in his left hand. Pavo jumped back but the sword tip grazed across his front. A searing pain exploded in his chest as the tip pierced his flesh. His nerves screamed in agony and his fingers instinctively unclenched, releasing the sword from his grip. The German kicked his shield away as Pavo dropped to his knees, and shaped to plunge both swords at his felled opponent's neck.

'No! He's mine!' Amadocus bellowed savagely as he charged at the two gladiators.

The German spun towards the onrushing Thracian. Pavo glanced past his shoulder. He saw Amadocus stampeding towards the German, his eyes burning fiercely as he cut down his opponent with a stab to the abdomen. The German's eyes widened with shock as the blade sliced through his vitals. He gripped the blade, trying to prise it out of his torso, but Amadocus had a firm grip and quickly twisted it, churning up the German's bowels. In the same instant Pavo bolted upright and backed away from Amadocus. The German gasped in agony and fell away to the sand, landing in front of Pavo. His eyes went dim and a gurgling sound came from his chest.

The Thracian pulled his sword out of the fallen German and glanced across the corpse-strewn sand.

'Just you and me left, rich boy,' he chuckled as he looked back at Pavo. 'Guess what? This time tomorrow, it'll be me who'll be rich. Murena visited me last night in my cell. Promised me ten thousand sestertii, a farm in Brindisium, and all the cunny I could ever wish for in return for making sure you die.'

'And you believe a word that Greek rat says? You're even more stupid than you look.'

'You think you're so clever, Roman. You won't look so smart when my blade rips through your throat!'

Pavo stood frozen to the spot as the Thracian advanced on him, lips bared in a triumphant snarl.

CHAPTER THIRTY-SIX

Fighting through the burning pain in his chest, Pavo staggered backwards from Amadocus as his great rival lunged at him. The umpire waved his wooden stick at the Thracian, demanding that he give Pavo a chance to arm himself to make it a fair contest. Amadocus seized the umpire by his shoulder and stabbed the man in his stomach with a single clean blow. The crowd cheered, revelling in the sight of the official meeting a grisly end. Amadocus retrieved his blade and the umpire dropped to the sand, clutching his bowels to stop them spilling out.

Then the Thracian filled his lungs and resumed his charge at the young gladiator. Pavo quickly darted to his side and grabbed the two swords lying beside the gutted German. He looked up and glimpsed the gleam of a sword tip plunging down towards him. In a flashing blur he hefted the two swords as he twisted round, slamming them lengthways against the blade thrusting towards him. The rasping clash of steel against steel rang shrilly around the arena. Amadocus growled as Pavo pushed up on the balls of his feet and shoved the Thracian back a step. Amadocus came at him again but Pavo adjusted his stance and held both swords up in front of him, the blades close together, blocking the repeated thrusts. Amadocus breathed heavily, sweat running down his torso as the effort of his relentless attacks took its toll. But Pavo refused to get drawn into a slogging match. He knew that if he was to win against his old rival, he'd have to fight on his own terms, using his swordsmanship to overcome his more powerful opponent.

Amadocus attacked again, making a low keening sound in his throat. 'Fight, you Roman shit! Don't retreat like a woman.'

'Is that the best you can do?' Pavo taunted.

Amadocus snarled as he swung his blade. He stopped mid-swing, a cruel smile trembling on his lips as he spotted the flesh wound across Pavo's chest. 'You're bleeding, Roman. It's a sign. The gods must favour me.'

Pavo smiled. 'Fighting a wounded aristocrat and you're still struggling. You must be losing your touch, Thracian.'

Snarling madly, Amadocus stabbed at Pavo again, jerking his sword at the young gladiator in brutal thrusts. Pavo pushed out with his swords and deflected the attack. But he was beginning to tire. He could feel his muscles aching from the strain of keeping the swords raised. His breathing became increasingly ragged. Amadocus grinned as he sensed blood. He thrust his blade at Pavo, aiming for his torso. But at the last moment he jerked his wrist up and angled the blade at his rival's arm. Pavo twisted away from the thrust but the sword tip pricked his flesh and sent a stinging pain running down the length of his arm. He gasped for breath. His fingers spasmed and the sword tumbled helplessly from his grip.

'Got you now, Roman!' Amadocus sneered.

Pavo staggered backwards, his muscles palpitating with adrenalin and fear. Mocking taunts rained down on him from the galleries above the parapet. Now Amadocus reached down and grabbed the dropped sword before Pavo could reach for it. Armed with two weapons, his eyes full of savage intent, the Thracian jerked his arms back, tucking his elbows tight to his sides then thrusting both swords at Pavo's neck with immense force. For a brief moment the gladiator saw the life of his son hanging in the balance. Then, with one last burst of his failing strength, he dived to the right, evading the thrusts, and cut upwards with his remaining sword, stabbing Amadocus in his armpit.

The Thracian glanced down, stunned by the blade piercing his flesh, hot blood gushing down his torso and spattering the sand. Convulsing with anger, he lunged at Pavo. The gladiator winced in pain as Amadocus landed on top of him and the two men crashed to the ground. Pavo kicked out at Amadocus in a desperate attempt to throw him off. The Thracian punched him on the jaw. Pavo saw white. His vision cleared as Amadocus grabbed a curved dagger glinting on the sand. Now the audience shrieked with joy as the Thracian plunged the dagger towards Pavo's throat. Pavo threw his hands above his head to shield himself from the blow. His forearms were locked in a brace across the Thracian's forearm.

'It's over, Roman,' Amadocus rasped, pressing the dagger mercilessly towards his opponent. 'At last you die. Or beg for your life!'

Panic gripped Pavo as Amadocus growled and pushed the dagger tip towards his throat. He felt his muscles weaken from the weight of his rival pressing down on him. A great pressure built up in his chest and his ribcage throbbed with pain. Now the dagger tip pricked his flesh. Grief coursed through Pavo's veins at the fate of his son.

Swallowing hard, he summoned a final reserve of strength. The intense training under Macro flooded back to him. He pushed out his arms in an explosive thrust and shoved the dagger up and away from his neck. Amadocus briefly looked startled, unable to comprehend how the once slender recruit now possessed the raw strength and power to match him. Clenching his jaw tightly, Pavo locked his arm muscles and forced the dagger up inch by inch until the tip hovered a hair's breadth from Amadocus.

'You can't kill me! I'm the rightful champion, not you!'

'Say hello to Spartacus in the afterlife.'

The Thracian's eyes widened as Pavo pushed up with one last defiant effort and the dagger plunged into his throat, punching out of the nape of his neck, immediately reducing his grunt to a gurgle. A slight tinge of regret struck Pavo at the moment of his foe's death. Despite being sworn enemies, he retained a degree of respect for Amadocus. His rival had proved himself a fearless warrior, making up in sheer tenacity and fighting spirit what he lacked in skill. He watched as the rage in the Thracian's eyes dimmed and his mouth slackened, blood trickling from the corners of his lips. Then he rolled Amadocus aside.

A stunned silence gripped the arena, as if the spectators were unsure how to greet the result of the bout. Pavo prepared for another torrent of vitriol from the mob. Instead, loud cheers broke the silence.

'He's defeated Amadocus!' a spectator roared.

'Fuck the Thracian! Up with Pavo!' another shouted.

The applause spread through the galleries until every spectator was chanting his name. Pavo was filled with contempt at the fickle nature of the mob. He stared down at Amadocus, blinking blood out of his eyes, barely able to believe that he'd triumphed. He'd survived the beast fights and now the group fight – an achievement few other gladiators could lay claim to. At the end of his previous bouts he had felt uncomfortable about the fawning adulation of the mob, but now, having defeated Amadocus, he felt he richly deserved their praise. He reflected for a moment on his long journey from a scrawny recruit in Paestum to one of the titans of the arena in Rome.

Now there was only one thing left for him to do.

His sword felt heavy in his weary grip. He tossed it aside. He scanned the galleries, looking for Lanatus. There was no sign of him in the row of senators gazing down at the bloodied sand. By now Appius would have been removed from the imperial household and escorted towards Ostia and a new life with Bucco. Pavo experienced a pang of sadness at the thought that he would never see his son again. Strange, but now he was so close to completing his mission and killing Claudius, he was suddenly seized by doubt. He wondered whether he could trust Lanatus to fulfil his end of the deal.

He quickly dismissed the thought. He was too close to give up now. The life of his son depended upon him striking down the Emperor.

The sound of the gate creaking open broke his daze. Pavo lifted his gaze in the direction of the eastern gate and slowly scanned the scene in front of him. Utter carnage confronted the young gladiator. A tangle of limbs and torsos. Shafts of sunlight pierced the grey clouds, warming the cold sand, glimmering over the corpses and the bloodied sword points. The powdered chalk line was scarcely visible amid the debris of battle. The stench of blood choked the air, mingling with sweat and the piss and shit of evacuated bowels. Pavo stood still, numb with shock at how much blood had been spilled in the name of Emperor Claudius.

'Utter madness,' he muttered to himself.

He shook his head bitterly. Once more he found himself

disgusted with the mob. They had revelled in the group fight. Undoubtedly their cheers would lead to many similar events in forthcoming spectacles. He wondered where it would all end.

Nerva stepped out of the gate and trudged towards Pavo. He looked upset as he picked his way around the mass of dead gladiators. Attendants and guards followed him out of the passageway. The attendants began prising the swords and shields from deadened grips while the guards checked for any signs of life among the bodies, prodding at them with the tips of their swords. They moved swiftly from one slumped gladiator to the next. Behind them the two German fighters were piled on top of one another on a wooden cart.

'Look at this mess,' Nerva grumbled. He kicked away a severed hand in dismay. 'It'll take us bloody ages to clean this lot up.'

'What will happen to them?' Pavo asked softly.

'These worthless scum? Slung into a grave pit, most of 'em. The surgeon tries to save as much blood from these corpses as possible. To sell on, of course. What do you care?'

Pavo pointed to Amadocus. A large puddle of blood had formed under the Thracian. 'I want my winnings to pay for his funeral. At the very least he deserves a fitting memorial stone.'

Nerva arched an eyebrow at Pavo, sighing. 'Gladiators! You lot never cease to surprise me. Cutting each other to pieces one moment and buying each other gravestones the next. I'll never understand it.'

That's because you've never had to face raw steel in front of a baying mob, Pavo thought to himself, resisting the temptation to add the official to the sprawl of corpses in the arena. Nerva cast an eye over the gladiator and sucked his gums.

'You'll have to get that cleaned up.' He pointed to Pavo's chest wound.

Pavo lowered his gaze. The cut was not deep, but blood from the wound was streaming down his front. There was no pain. His mind was still racing with thoughts of victory, and the dangerous task that lay ahead of him.

Nerva nodded at the eastern gate. 'Make it quick. The Emperor is waiting.'

CHAPTER THIRTY-SEVEN

A strange calm settled over Pavo as he paced down the corridor. The infirmary was overflowing with casualties and Nerva ushered him into an adjacent room sparsely furnished with stretchers and cots where the wounded could recuperate. Through the crumbling walls Pavo heard the anguished cries of stricken gladiators going under the surgeon's scalpel. The flesh wounds on his arm and chest now throbbed painfully, but his mind was focused elsewhere. He closed his eyes and rehearsed his imminent attempt on the Emperor's life. When he opened his eyes again he saw a spindly figure standing in the doorway. The deep lines of his face were illuminated by the soft twinkle of the oil lamps in the passageway.

'Ah, gladiator! Congratulations on your victory!' Lanatus announced grandly as he approached. There was a spring in the senator's step and he was hardly able to contain his glee. 'How refreshing it is to see a noble Roman emerge victorious in a gladiator bout. Not like those aristocratic wastrels we saw yesterday, chopping up hares and ostriches to massage their egos.'

Pavo looked blankly at the senator. 'Where's Appius?'

Lanatus glanced nervously around the room at the faces of the other wounded gladiators. He leaned forward and whispered into Pavo's ear. 'For gods' sakes, man, keep your voice down! If anyone hears us, we're done for. We can't afford to slip up. Not now. The fate of Rome depends on us.'

'For you, perhaps.' Pavo wore a fierce expression. 'I only care about my son. We had a deal.'

'And it will be honoured,' whispered Lanatus, composing his features. 'You should be grateful for this opportunity, Pavo. You're about to go down in history as the man who ended the life of a dictator and restored Rome to its true greatness. I'm somewhat envious of you, if you must know.'

'Kill Claudius yourself, then.'

The senator looked coldly at Pavo, his lips clamped tightly shut.

'My son,' said Pavo.

'The boy is safe.'

'And on his way to Ostia?'

'Not yet,' Lanatus responded coolly, keeping his voice low. 'Only once you fulfil your side of the deal. Kill the Emperor, then I'll send Appius on his way with that friend of yours, Bucco.'

Pavo glared at the senator. 'I'm not doing anything until Appius is safe.'

'I will agree to no such thing,' Lanatus hissed. 'The important thing is your son is out of the Emperor's clutches. He's in a secure place. And I'll honour my word, Pavo, despite your insinuation to the contrary. Appius will be removed from Rome the moment you spill the Emperor's blood.'

A pair of orderlies entered the room bearing a stretcher. Pavo dimly recognised the wounded gladiator from the group fight. A deep gash was visible on the side of his stomach, glistening bright red like a pair of puckered lips. The wound looked fatal. The gladiator was delirious. Lanatus waited for the orderlies to lay down the stretcher in the corner of the room and roll the glad-iator into one of the empty cots. Once they had exited, he turned back to Pavo.

'You are in no position to argue with me. Either you kill the Emperor and Appius lives, or else you collect your reward and the boy dies.'

Pavo grimaced. Lanatus left him with no real choice. He gave a grudging nod. The senator sighed heavily through his nostrils.

'Good! Smile, Pavo. You're about to become the saviour of Rome.' The flicker of the oil lamps illuminated his grey eyes as he reached under his tunic and discreetly removed a small dagger, which he grasped tightly in his right hand, keeping it hidden from view. His caution was unnecessary. The other men in the room were writhing in agony from their wounds. No one paid him any attention as he slipped the weapon to Pavo. The gladiator glanced at the dagger, the enormity of what he was about to do hitting him like a fist. He hurriedly tucked the weapon into the folds of his loincloth, making sure no one saw him. At that instant two guards entered the room. Lanatus quickly took a step back from Pavo and cleared his throat.

'I've kept you far too long, my friend. You must be keen to collect your prize from the Emperor.' His eyes glowered as he added, 'Be sure to give his imperial majesty my best regards.'

With a quick smile of encouragement he turned on the spot and departed. The guards brushed past him, each grabbing Pavo by an arm and dragging him out of the room. They roughly shoved him down the passageway, passing several entrances to the galleries before arriving at a set of marble steps. The walls here were richly decorated with a stucco relief depicting the Emperor giving the sign of mercy to a vanquished gladiator. Four Praetorian Guards stood either side of the steps, and a familiar face was waiting to escort Pavo up to the imperial box.

'Macro!' Pavo sputtered.

'Lad,' Macro responded gruffly. 'Still in one piece, I see.'

'Barely.'

The optio grunted. 'Not a bad performance. A bit of work needed on your movement, and some of your thrusting attacks were frankly pathetic. But overall, you did well.' His expression softened as he spoke, and Pavo felt his chest swell with pride. A few words of modest praise from his former mentor counted for more than the acclaim of the mob. He cocked his head at Macro.

'What are you doing here?' he asked. 'And why are you dressed like that?'

'Blame that bloody Greek snake,' Macro snapped gruffly as he led Pavo up the marble steps. 'Murena has got me posing as one of his clerks. I've been suffocating inside this fucking tunic all morning.'

'But what for? I thought you were heading back to the Rhine?'

'Me too,' Macro growled. 'And I would've left Rome by now if it hadn't been for some bastards plotting against Claudius.'

'Plotting to do what, exactly?' Pavo said, feigning ignorance.

'To assassinate him,' Macro answered stonily. 'Pallas and Murena reckon some traitor is planning to cut down the Emperor today, right here at the games.' He squinted at the darkening clouds as they neared the imperial box. 'If they are planning on giving Claudius the chop, then they're leaving it late. There's only a handful of bouts to go.'

Pavo felt the burning pain in his arm, the searing graze across his chest.

'Tell you what,' Macro added in a stern voice. 'When the assassin reveals himself, he's in a world of shit. We've got orders to take him to the imperial palace for questioning. With luck he'll give up a few names before the torturers have finished with him.'

Pavo shuddered at the thought. The doubts swelling in his mind grew more insistent as he reached the top of the steps. Killing Claudius would not bring him peace, he realised. He would only achieve that with revenge over Hermes. But a voice in his head countered that he had no choice in the matter. Not if he wanted to save Appius.

'I've come too far now,' he muttered under his breath.

'What was that, lad?'

Pavo quickly lowered his head. 'Nothing.'

Shaking his own head, Macro ushered Pavo into the imperial box. Murena was waiting impatiently for them, his brow creased into a heavy frown.

'Ah, Pavo! Come to collect your reward, I see.' Murena lowered his voice. 'Now remember, his imperial majesty has a stutter and a tendency to slobber at the mouth when he's excited. Draw attention to neither.'

Pavo nodded. The smell of grilled meat tickled his nostrils and he noticed several imperial slaves gathered at the sides of the box bearing jugs of wine and trays of pork and honeyed figs, which members of the imperial household picked at. Across from the box he could see the arena floor below. Orderlies were still cleaning up the carnage from the group fight, raking the bloodied sand and scooping up discarded entrails. Pallas stood to the side of Claudius, who was seated in his ornate chair and flanked by a handful of clerks, with his German bodyguards standing guard at the sides of the box.

Twenty thousand spectators craned their necks to the imperial box to catch a glimpse of Claudius greeting the victorious gladiator. Pavo felt the sweat on his back freeze as the Emperor slowly rose from his chair and approached him. Pallas clicked his fingers at a nearby servant, who carried over a silver tray piled high with coins and a palm branch, the traditional gifts presented to the winner of a gladiatorial bout. Pavo took in a sharp draw of breath as he carefully slid his right hand down towards his loincloth. There was no going back now. He spotted Macro standing to one side, his eyes narrowed at the surrounding galleries, unaware that the assassin was standing a short distance from him.

Now Claudius stopped in front of Pavo. He wrinkled his nose at the stench of sweat and blood coming off the gladiator. Murena folded his hands behind his back. There was a gloating look in his eyes. Pavo could hear the blood rushing in his ears as he felt for the cold tip of the dagger.

Then Claudius opened his arms in joy and flashed a broad grin at Pavo. 'W-w-what a s-s-show!' he stammered. 'That was a remarkable p-p-performance out there, y-y-young man!'

Pavo was momentarily taken aback by the Emperor's good mood. He'd expected Claudius to be enraged by his victory. He noticed that the Emperor's response prompted a puzzled reaction from Murena, too. At the same moment the servant presented the silver tray to the Emperor, so that he could personally hand Pavo his prize money and palm branch. The young gladiator gritted his teeth as his fingers closed round the handle of the dagger.

The Emperor waved the servant away. 'Coins and p-p-palms are no fitting reward for a t-t-true champion!' he declared to Pavo. His eyes suddenly lit up and he clapped his hands. 'You d-deserve a proper reward. And I have just the thing. Your son shall be s-s-spared!'

Pavo froze with his fingers resting on the dagger.

'My son?' he asked numbly. His lips were cold. He was in a state of complete shock. 'You mean he's still . . . at the palace?'

Claudius frowned curiously. 'Why, of c-c-course he is. Under the watch of the Praetorian G-G-Guard.'

Lanatus . . . the bastard, Pavo thought, realising that the senator had lied to him. He had never intended to save Appius. Relaxing his grip on the dagger, he subtly removed his hand from the folds of his loincloth, his muscles shaking with rage. He had come so close to killing Claudius – and it would all have been for nothing.

Murena looked bewildered. 'Your majesty,' he began humbly, 'I must ask you to reconsider. Is it truly, ah, wise, to spare the life of this man's son? This is Marcus Valerius Pavo, son of the traitorous legate Titus . . . the man guilty of attempting to return Rome to a republic.'

'I k–k–know who he i–i–is!' Claudius snapped without looking at the aide. 'I am no f–fool.'

The aide smiled nervously. 'I meant nothing of the sort, your highness.'

'We must not m–m–make the same mistakes as our predecessors. We must l–listen to the mob.' Claudius gestured to the galleries with an unsteady sweep of his hand. Murena and Pavo both looked up at the spectators. They were still cheering the gladiator's name. 'Romans know a h–h–hero when they see one. This young m–man's father was a traitor, but the son has r–r–restored his reputation in the arena. He fought with great honour.'

'But your majesty—'

Murena drew a stinging rebuke from the Emperor. He simmered in silence as Claudius turned back to Pavo.

'Murena t–tells me you were condemned to d–d–die at these games.' Pavo nodded. 'Instead of money, I shall g–give you your f–f–freedom. No m–m–man who fights so hard should suffer an insulting death.' There was a harsh glow to his eyes as he added, 'Even the s–s–son of a traitor.'

The aide looked apoplectic. 'I must protest—'

'Enough!' Claudius barked. 'I have s–spoken, Murena. And you shall carry out my orders as my loyal s–s–servant.'

Murena looked sheepishly at his feet, unnerved by the abrupt show of authority from the Emperor. 'Yes, your majesty.'

'There is something else I desire . . . your majesty,' Pavo said, addressing the Emperor. Claudius looked at him and raised an eyebrow.

'Something other than f–freedom? S–s–speak of it.'

'I wish to fight Hermes.'

Murena looked ready to explode. The muscles in his face twitched with an indescribable hatred for Pavo.

'What a s–s–splendid idea!' Claudius exclaimed, slobbering at the mouth with excitement. 'The t–t–two greatest gladiators in Rome, pitched in a fight to the d–death! It sh–sh–shall be the perfect end to the games.' He turned to Murena. 'Don't you agree?'

'As you wish, your majesty,' Murena responded with ill grace.

Pavo felt as if an enormous weight had been lifted from his shoulders. Finally, his wish had been granted. He would have his fight against the gladiator who had killed his father in the arena and brought shame upon his family name. He choked back his emotion. It was hard to believe it was actually going to happen. Then he remembered something else as the Emperor turned away from him.

'There is one more thing, your majesty.'

Claudius stopped and glanced back.

'Y–y–yes?' he asked curtly. There was a flicker of irritation in his eyes, and Pavo wondered whether he had pushed his luck too far. Claudius had already promised to spare Appius and grant him his fight against Hermes. 'Well, w–w–what is it?'

Pavo stiffened his neck muscles. 'I want the right to choose my trainer for the fight.'

Claudius gave the matter some thought for a moment, then nodded impatiently. 'V–v–very well. My aide will sort out the d–details.' He stared coldly at Murena. 'Isn't that so, Murena?'

'Yes, your majesty.'

The Emperor grunted a response and returned to his seat as the attendants finished clearing up the arena and the announcer introduced the next fighters. Murena glared at Pavo, his eyes narrowed and his lips pressed tight, trembling with outrage.

'You will pay for this,' he muttered. 'I'll make sure of it.'

Pavo grinned. 'Aren't you forgetting something? The man I want to be my trainer.'

Murena shaded white with rage. A general cheer went up in the galleries as the next gladiators stepped out into the arena.

'Give me the name,' the aide seethed, his voice barely audible above the shouts of the crowd.

Pavo nodded at the optio at his side.

'I want Macro to train me,' he said.

CHAPTER THIRTY-EIGHT

The next morning Pavo gazed across the Circus Maximus and waited to catch a glimpse of the man who had killed his father. Tens of thousands of spectators had braved the morning cold to fill the chariot-racing stadium situated between the Aventine and Palatine Hills, filtering out of the entrances leading up from the arcade of shops at street level and making their way along the tiers to their seats. Instead of arriving to watch the usual programme of chariot races, the spectators had descended on the Circus Maximus to watch a rare gladiator bout. The sun glimmered faintly above the Palatine Hill. Palls of smoke drifted up from hundreds of forges amid the distant tenement blocks as Rome stirred slowly into life. From his seat at the lowest tier, Pavo braced himself against the chill breeze sweeping across the stadium and tried to quell the dread coursing through his veins.

'Where the hell is Hermes?' Macro cursed in the seat next to Pavo. 'I'm freezing my bollocks off out here.'

Pavo turned to his older companion. Macro had been in a foul mood since the two men had arrived at the Circus Maximus earlier that morning to watch Hermes take part in a sparring match against a less well-known opponent. Pavo had awoken at dawn in his cell at the imperial ludus, where Macro had presented himself with orders to escort the young gladiator to the Circus Maximus. While the excursion ought to have been a welcome break from the drudgery of the ludus, Pavo felt a growing sense of unease building in his chest. In two months he would take to the sand against Hermes, his nemesis, in a fight to the death.

'He must be appearing shortly,' the young gladiator replied. 'There's a full programme of chariot races due to take place after this contest. The organisers can't afford a lengthy delay.'

Macro folded his arms across his stocky chest and grunted. 'He'd better get a move on. It's colder than a Vestal Virgin's cunny this morning.'

Pavo glanced quickly past his shoulder at the upper tiers and frowned. 'What exactly are we doing here, Macro?'

'I told you. Pallas and Murena ordered me to bring you here to watch some journeyman gladiator from Macedonia put the great Hermes through his paces. Seems they wanted you to see Hermes fight before you face him in the arena.'

'Odd that they'd want me to observe my opponent,' Pavo mused. 'I'd have thought they would be doing everything in their power to sabotage my preparations for the fight.'

Macro shrugged. 'Who cares? This is a rare chance to see Hermes in action. If you ask me, it's the first good idea Pallas has ever had.'

Pavo frowned and rubbed the bristles on his jaw. He disliked his new beard, but shaving was a luxury that belonged to his former life. 'Still, why hold a mere sparring contest in public at the Circus? A practice bout in front of such a crowd is unheard of.'

Macro grunted. 'Hermes is more of a showman than a gladiator these days. No doubt the organisers are keen to make a profit on the back of it. This lot are dying to see him in action,' he added, jerking a thumb at the packed tiers.

Pavo glanced up at the crowd. At least a hundred thousand spectators had crammed into the stadium. He could only dream about attracting such a crowd, especially for a practice match with blunted weapons.

'Have you ever seen Hermes fight, Macro?'

The optio shook his head. 'Too busy carving up barbarians, lad. But I've heard plenty about him. Seems like every new recruit to the Second has seen him fight at one time or another. They can't stop bloody talking about him in the mess room.'

'I see,' Pavo replied tersely.

'Doubtless his wealth has something to do with it,' Macro grumbled. 'Your average gladiator being on a par with a runaway slave or a murderer, and all that. Most gladiators are lucky to last a year. Hermes has been fighting for twenty years – and he's richer than half the old bastards in the Senate.'

Pavo winced and shifted uncomfortably in his seat. 'We should be on the training ground, not watching Hermes go through the motions.'

'Try to enjoy it, lad.' Macro eased back and slapped his young charge on the shoulder. 'Anyway, I don't see what you've got to be so glum about. You've got what you wanted, haven't you? A fight against Hermes and the chance to avenge your old man.'

Pavo pursed his lips. He knew Macro was right. From the moment Hermes had beheaded his father, the young gladiator had burned with the compulsive desire for revenge. But he could not ignore the unease coiling in his guts.

'Pallas and Murena are up to something,' he reflected sourly. 'I'm sure of it.'

'That's life in Rome for you,' Macro muttered. 'Too many Greeks for my liking.'

With a firm grunt Macro turned away from Pavo and narrowed his steely gaze at the racetrack, which had been transformed into a gladiator arena for the purposes of the morning display. A chalk-line ellipse had been marked out, stretching from the twelve starting gates at the western end to the second turning post at the near end of the dividing barrier running down the middle of the track, adorned with various monuments and statues of the gods on top of an ornate shrine. Guards from the urban cohort had been drafted to manage the crowds at the stadium. In the distance a scattering of men and women peered down from the tenement blocks teeming along the slopes of the Aventine Hill overlooking the stadium. This was Macro's first visit to the Circus Maximus, and he found the experience a bittersweet one. As a boy he'd missed out on the excitement of the chariot races, since his father, Amatus, had taken a dim view of gambling. On race days Amatus used to keep his son busy cleaning cups and wiping down the tables in the dingy tavern he owned in the Aventine. Macro never imagined then that he would one day watch Hermes fight here.

Earlier that morning the optio had attended a special

announcement held in the Roman Forum. A huge crowd had gathered to hear official confirmation of the fight between Pavo and Hermes. Rumours had spread from the arena to the taverns in the immediate aftermath of the former's triumph in the group fight. The air in the Forum had been drenched in the fragrant aroma of exotic spices from nearby market stalls while the sun burned in a clear sky as the speaker's voice boomed off the surrounding porticoes. The two men would be competing as provocators – a type of heavily armoured combat that Pavo had never taken part in before. Only seasoned gladiators fought as provocators, Macro knew, due to the skill and muscle necessary to move about the arena.

At the same time the sponsors had announced that the date of the fight had been pushed back two months to give both fighters ample time to prepare for the contest. Few among the crowd complained about this development. The tavern owners and merchants hawking memorabilia now had more time to make a healthy profit from the many thousands of gladiator fans who had descended on Rome, and the bookmakers stood to make a killing from cashing in on fervent speculation over the contest. The decision had puzzled Macro, who had assumed the imperial secretary would want to rush Pavo back into the arena as quickly as possible, giving him little time in which to rest and prepare for his fight. Coupled with the offer to watch Hermes in action at the Circus Maximus, Macro shared his young charge's concerns. There was always some scheming motive behind everything that Pallas and Murena did, he knew.

At that moment the central starting gate opened and a deafening roar went up in the stadium. Macro swivelled his gaze back to the track as the umpire emerged from the shadows with a pair of attendants following close behind him bearing a pair of blunted short swords. A few moments later a gladiator stumbled out of the same gate. A bronze helmet covered his head and the large rectangular shield in his left hand quivered as he trudged towards the officials gathered in the centre of the ellipse.

'Who's the poor fellow facing Hermes?' Pavo wondered aloud.

'Criton,' a voice said to his right. 'He's going to get battered!'

Pavo turned towards a spectator wearing a stained tunic. There was a glazed look in his eyes and he gripped a wineskin in his right hand.

'Criton?' Macro repeated. 'Never heard of him.'

The spectator grinned. 'That's because he's a second-rate gladiator from Macedonia. Belongs to a travelling troupe. Hardly worthy of sharing the same arena as the colossus of Rhodes.'

Macro glanced back at the track as Criton received his weapon from the attendant. 'He is fortunate that this is just a sparring contest, then.'

'Why is Hermes matched with such a lowly sparring partner?' Pavo asked the spectator, ignoring Macro.

'Simple. Hermes has only just come out of retirement. No doubt he would've returned sooner, if those bastards hadn't ambushed him in the street and broken several of his bones. He's recovered faster than anyone expected, but he's still in need of a warm-up contest ahead of the big fight.' The spectator nudged Pavo conspiratorially. 'Between you and me, that rich upstart Pavo is in for a nasty surprise.'

'Oh? How so?' Pavo briefly considered revealing his name to the spectator but decided against it. He was curious to find out more about Hermes from one of his adoring fans.

The spectator paused and took a swig from his wineskin. Drops trickled down his chin and dripped on to his tunic as he continued.

'Don't get me wrong, I hear Pavo is handy with a sword. Especially for a rich boy. But Hermes is a completely different jug of garum to anything he will have faced so far. He is strong – and he's quick on his feet for a big man.'

Pavo shrugged. 'There's plenty of other gladiators that applies to equally.'

The spectator leaned in. Pavo wrinkled his nose at the powerful whiff of wine on the man's breath. 'But you won't find another gladiator who is also so good with a sword. The fifty bouts he's won is ample proof of that.'

Macro swung his gaze to the spectator with a sneer.

'Load of bollocks! Everyone knows the lanistas protect their best gladiators to negotiate a better price when it comes to renting them out. I bet half the fights Hermes won were against a bunch of cooks and fullers.'

'Obviously you're not a fan.' The spectator pulled a face at Macro. 'You'll change your mind when he gives Criton a proper thrashing.'

'Why is Hermes coming out of retirement anyway?' asked Pavo. 'After all, he's a freedman gladiator, not a condemned man. Whenever he's fought in the past few years he's been able to demand a fortune from the sponsors.'

The spectator shrugged. 'No one knows for certain. Plenty of sponsors have tried to coax him out since he announced his intention to retire for good. Emperor Caligula, among others.'

'So why change his mind now?'

'I've heard rumours that one of the Greeks working for Claudius had something to do with it,' the spectator replied.

Pavo was about to enquire further when a wild cheer erupted in the tiers. The stadium trembled. The sense of anticipation in the crowd was palpable as the spectators rose to their feet as one and directed their gaze towards the far end of the racetrack.

'Look!' the spectator exclaimed. 'Here he comes!'

Pavo and Macro followed his line of sight. A single gate stood at the eastern end of the track, beyond the bronze turning posts. A hushed silence swept over the stadium as the gate opened. Pavo felt the hairs bristle on the nape of his neck as a huge figure marched boldly out, his vast muscles glistening with sweat. The veins on his muscular arms bulged like tensed rope. The man was significantly bigger than his opponent. Pavo could not recall ever seeing a gladiator of such large proportions.

'Shit,' he whispered, his blood chilling. 'So *that's* Hermes.'

CHAPTER THIRTY-NINE

The champion of Rome entered the Circus Maximus to a burst of thunderous applause. Several spectators occupying one of the upper tiers unfurled a large banner proclaiming their support for Hermes. The spectator standing next to Pavo jumped to his feet and shouted himself hoarse as he joined in with the chants chorusing around the stadium.

'He wins every fight, makes his rivals look shite! Hermes! Hermes!' the fans sang.

'Fuck off, Criton!' a nearby spectator rasped above the general din.

Pavo glanced at Criton. The Macedonian stood next to the umpire, his hands trembling with fear. The champion acknowledged his fans with a vigorous pump of his fist, drawing another round of fervent applause as he strutted towards the temporary arena, bowing to the section of the crowd displaying their banner.

Macro snarled. 'Look at this idiot, grandstanding to the mob. He wouldn't last long in the Second. No place for showboats in the legions.'

Pavo studied Hermes as the champion passed his seat. The gladiator was in tremendous shape, he thought. As well as the standard helmet, manica, leg greave and chest protector worn by the provocator type of gladiator, he also wore a leather belt, studded with gold, wrapped round his torso above his loincloth. The belt glimmered faintly in the pallid morning light as one of the attendants handed him his blunted sword, which he took in his right hand. He gripped his large shield in his left. An image of Cerberus, the three-headed dog who guarded the gates of the Underworld, had been painted in bright colours on the front of the shield.

A short distance away Criton stood rooted to the spot, seemingly frozen in fear as the umpire went through the rules of engagement with the two gladiators, his voice almost drowned out by the crowd. When he had finished, he retreated to the chalk line and a cheer went up in the stadium as he gave the signal for the fight to begin. The spectator next to Pavo shouted deliriously as he urged Hermes to savage his opponent.

'Show him no fucking mercy!'

'Beat him senseless, Hermes!' a woman close by shrieked.

Criton immediately charged at Hermes, panicked into action by the heated fervour of the crowd and the scale of the occasion. With a lusty roar he planted his right foot on the ground and launched a quick thrust with his sword, aiming the smooth tip at his opponent's armoured chest. Hermes immediately shifted to his right, evading the thrust and striking his sword against Criton in one smooth motion. His sword clattered on the side of his opponent's helmet and the brittle clang of metal slamming against metal rang sharply around the stadium. Criton stumbled forward, his legs almost buckling as the impact momentarily disorientated him. Frantically shaking his head clear, he retreated from Hermes, repelling his foe by repeatedly thrusting his sword at him. But Hermes advanced steadily behind his shield, deftly deflecting each blow as he patiently let his opponent wear himself out.

'Criton is in trouble,' Macro remarked. 'Hermes is toying with the wretch. If he isn't careful, he's going to get badly roughed up.'

Pavo didn't reply. He was engrossed by the contest unfolding in the stadium. Still crouching behind his shield, Hermes closed in ominously on his opponent. Criton thrust his sword again. The colossus from Rhodes parried the attack. Frustrated by his inability to land a blow, Criton let out a full-blooded roar and lunged at Hermes. But the champion effortlessly parried his opponent's sword thrust, swiping his shield arm in a wide arc and deflecting the weapon away from his chest with swift and brutal speed.

In the next instant he dropped to a low crouch and shunted the bottom edge of his shield down at Criton's bare feet. A sharp crack like wood snapping was followed by a howl of agony from the Macedonian as the shield rim crushed his toes. Criton dropped his shield. Bright red spots of blood stained the sand as he hobbled frantically away from Hermes, his movements clumsy and ragged with the heavy armour weighing down on him. Now Hermes pounded towards his stricken enemy, moving with greater speed and intent on striking the decisive blow. Criton looked up and saw Hermes bearing down on him. Roaring manically, the Macedonian gripped the sword with both hands and plunged it in a downward thrust that Hermes neatly parried. Then Hermes shot forward in a blur of motion and kicked the bottom of his opponent's shield, tilting the top edge towards him. To gasps of disbelief from the audience, he slammed his sword down on top of the shield, wrenching it from Criton's grip and battering the Macedonian with it. The blade fell from Criton's hand as Hermes booted him backwards and sent him crashing to the sand. The gladiator towered over his soundly beaten foe. With a guttural roar he chucked his sword and shield aside in an arrogant gesture that Pavo found distasteful. Criton scrambled towards the chalk line, signalling to the umpire to end the fight. Nodding, the umpire raised his wooden stick.

The decision provoked a raft of angry shouts from the spectators. The man next to Pavo was spitting with fury at the prospect of the fight being cut short. The attendants looked to the umpire as he shifted uncertainly on his feet. Doubtless the organisers had chosen a weak opponent to fight Hermes because they didn't want to risk the champion suffering an injury a few days before the closing of the games. But clearly the short-lived contest had failed to satisfy the mob.

Hearing the cries of displeasure from his fans, Hermes paced over to Criton as he lay prone and defeated on the ground. The umpire attempted to block his path. Hermes shoved him out of the way and stooped down beside Criton, tearing off his opponent's helmet to howls of delight from the spectators. Before Criton could crawl out of danger, Hermes grabbed the floored gladiator and pummelled him repeatedly in the face. Then he lifted Criton to his knees. Clamping one hand over the Macedonian's mouth, he grabbed the back of his skull with his free hand and let out a savage grunt as he snapped his opponent's neck with a violent jerk of his arms. Criton spasmed as he uttered an agonising cry of despair. Then he went limp and Hermes released his grip. A frenzied cheer rose from the crowd as Criton slumped to the ground.

The spectator shook Pavo by the shoulder. 'I told you! Best gladiator ever, is Hermes.'

Pavo forced a smile. A dreadful feeling stirred inside him. He had never witnessed such a ruthless combination of brute strength and skill. He watched Hermes make a series of bows to his fans before strutting towards the gate at the eastern end of the stadium and leaving the startled attendants to drag away the lifeless corpse of his vanquished opponent. As soon as Hermes had disappeared, two more gladiators staggered blindly into the makeshift arena to continue the pre-chariot race entertainment. They were wearing full-face helmets without eyeholes in the visors, to the mild amusement of the audience. The spectator sitting next to Pavo and Macro abruptly rose from his seat and departed in search of more wine from one of the taverns located outside the stadium. Macro saw that the colour had drained from Pavo's face and slapped his thigh.

'Come on, lad. Let's get out of here. We'll head to the ludus and start training. In two months' time we'll have whipped you into decent fighting shape.'

They shuffled past the spectators and headed for the nearest exit leading from the tier to the arcade. Pavo moved slowly. He felt as if a great weight was pressing down on him. Based on what he had just seen, defeating Hermes seemed an impossible task, even allowing for time to recover from his injuries and properly train under the optio. As they descended the steps leading out of the Circus Maximus, he felt certain his journey as a gladiator would end in defeat. The champion was too powerful. Hermes would kill him in front of the Emperor. Just as he had killed his father a year ago, Pavo reflected gloomily.

The sun had brought some warmth to the street outside. Brothel touts and bookmakers loitered around the arcade, scavenging for business from the spectators disgorging from the numerous exits.

Pavo noticed a gaunt-faced woman curled up at the side of the arcade with her infant child. The baby wailed, its screams piercing the air as the mother begged Pavo to spare a few coins. Anguish swept through him and his mind wandered back to thoughts of his own child, followed by an immediate sense of relief.

'Soon Appius will be free,' he reminded himself, blood pounding between his temples. 'Even if I fail to beat Hermes, my victories haven't been in vain. I saved my son.'

'Maybe. Then again, maybe not.'

'The Emperor gave his word – Appius has been spared.'

'You'd do well not to trust anything he says,' Macro responded flatly. 'Especially with those Greeks persuading him to do as they say. Back-stabbers in the imperial household are like whores in the Subura. Bloody everywhere.'

Pavo glared tetchily at his mentor. Just then a blunt force thumped him in the small of his back and sent him crashing to the ground. He landed in the filth that covered every inch of the street.

'Out of the way, scum,' a gruff voice shouted. 'Make way for Hermes!'

Pavo glanced up and saw a burly man with mean eyes like the pointed tips of a sword elbowing his way past, kicking and punching a path through the crowd. The champion of Rome followed closely behind as the burly man ahead of him fended off the enthusiastic supporters eager to catch a glimpse of their hero. One of them pointed at Pavo.

'Look!' he exclaimed noisily. 'It's him . . . Pavo!'

'We saw him at the group fight!' the man next to the supporter shouted.

Pavo stood up, wiping the palms of his filthy hands on his loincloth as Hermes and his companion stopped in their tracks. Both men slowly turned to face him. The burly man scowled at Macro while Hermes, his helmet removed after his fight, glowered at Pavo. A prominent scar was visible on his upper lip which twisted his expression into a vicious snarl. His eyes burned brightly at Pavo, as if a fire was raging in their sockets. The cries and shrieks of the crowd around the champion of Rome abruptly faded and a tense silence settled over the street as hundreds of spectators simultaneously turned towards the confrontation. Hermes bared his teeth at his future opponent. Pavo noticed splashes of blood across his wide chest from his fight against Criton.

'Well, well,' he hissed in a grating voice. 'Look who it is. The traitor's son . . . and the next man to die by my sword.'

Pavo stood his ground but swallowed nervously as Hermes marched towards him. Every inch of the champion's body rippled with muscle. He was aware of Macro standing by his side. The expression on his face was hard and menacing.

'I'm told you asked to fight me instead of accepting your freedom,' Hermes demanded. 'Is it true?'

Pavo flushed angrily. He nodded. 'I've wanted to fight you for a long time. Since the day you killed my father, Titus.'

'Titus?' Hermes repeated, cocking an eyebrow. 'Yes, I remember the man well. You know what else I remember? How that old fool squealed like a baby as I went to cut his fucking head off.'

Rage coursed through Pavo's veins as Hermes burst into laughter. The burly man at his side laughed too. Some of the spectators joined in. Hermes cracked his knuckles.

'I had the privilege of honouring the Emperor's wishes and killing a traitorous general,' he added menacingly. The laughter quickly died out. 'Now I get to carve up his son in the same arena. Killing you will be a pleasure. Truly, the gods are generous.'

Pavo struggled to contain his rage. 'My father was a good man.'

Hermes laughed cruelly. 'Titus was a treacherous cunt. He deserved to die. As do you, for taking the foolish decision to fight me. A mistake that I will make you pay for in blood, rich boy.'

He took a step closer to Pavo. The two men stood face to face. Pavo could smell the rank breath and the foul sweat coming off his father's killer. Hermes stared at his opponent. Pavo held his gaze, ignoring the anxiety pulsing in his throat. The crowd pressed around the two gladiators.

Pavo balled his hands into fists. Macro darted towards him and

314

clamped a hand round his wrist. 'Save it, lad,' he growled. 'Take out your anger on the training ground.'

Hermes looked amused. 'Who is this?'

Macro stepped forward. 'Lucius Cornelius Macro, optio of the Second Legion.'

Hermes stifled a laugh in his throat. 'You're being trained by a soldier from the legions?' He slapped his thigh and shared a chuckle with his companion.

'Macro was personally decorated by Emperor Claudius,' Pavo replied through gritted teeth.

The champion turned to Macro. 'What did you do, bribe a few high-ranking officials?'

Macro hardened his gaze. 'I earned it in blood. Chopped up a load of angry Germans and led an expedition back across the River Rhine after our centurion was killed in a raid.'

Hermes paused for a moment, narrowing his eyes at Macro. Then he wiped his lips with the back of his hand. 'Fuck me, a proper Roman hero.' He turned to the burly man at his side and smiled wanly. 'Did you hear that, Cursor?'

His companion laughed and shook his head. Hermes returned his gaze to Pavo.

'This is why you're going to lose, traitor. You have some grizzled veteran of the legions to mentor you, whereas I have the best gladiator trainer in the empire.' He gestured to the burly man. 'Gaius Calpurnius Cursor.'

Pavo frowned. He recalled the name from a distant gladiator fight. 'The former champion who defeated Tetraites, the Butcher of Bithynia?'

Hermes nodded triumphantly. 'The same. With his knowledge and my skill, I'm going to crush you.' He glanced at Macro, a menacing gleam twinkling in his eye. 'Perhaps you would care to join Pavo and his father in the afterlife, soldier.'

Macro stepped towards Hermes, bristling with anger. 'I don't have to listen to scum like you.' He tipped his head in the direction of the crowd. 'Now piss off back to whatever hole you and that fat trainer of yours crawled out of.'

Cursor thrust himself forward and jabbed a finger at Macro.

'You can't talk to Hermes like that. He's the champion of Rome and a freedman. Show him the proper respect.'

'Champion my arse,' Macro hissed. Cursor glowered at him with brutal intent. 'Hermes is a six-foot-tall sack of shit who cuts down anyone the Emperor sticks in front of him for a few cheap laughs from the mob. Freedman or not, he's lower than a fucking slave. By the look of him, I'd say his trainer is even lower.'

Cursor drew a lungful of air and launched himself at Macro. At the same time, Hermes dropped his shoulder to unleash a punch at Pavo. Reading the move, the young gladiator leaped at the champion, half mad with rage, filled with a manic desire to kill the man here on the street in full view of his adoring fans. But Hermes thrust out his arms and grabbed hold of him, lifting him off his feet. The champion let out a deep explosive grunt and hurled Pavo into a nearby market stall. A jarring pain shuddered down his spine as he fell on top of a row of trinkets. Statuettes and cheap bracelets scattered across the flagstones. The crowd parted around the two gladiators with shrill cries of alarm. Pavo struggled to rise from the shattered ruins of the stall, but Hermes was on him in a flash, kicking him in the side of his torso. Hot pain flared across his ribs.

'Get away from him!' Macro thundered as he threw off Cursor and rushed towards Hermes, tackling him to the ground with a savage roar. Temporarily stunned by the attack, Hermes writhed underneath the weight of the stocky soldier. At the same time Pavo scrambled clear of the debris and put a hand to his head, feeling something hot and sticky matting his hair. He pulled away his hand and saw blood smearing his palm. He looked up just in time to see Cursor charging at Macro, his eyes wide with hatred.

'Macro, look out!'

As Macro glanced up, Cursor locked his arm round the soldier's neck, wrenching him off Hermes. Gasping for breath, Macro kicked out at the gladiator trainer, slamming his foot back into the man's groin. Cursor doubled up in agony, releasing Macro. The optio spun round and unleashed an uppercut that caught Cursor clean on the jaw. The gladiator trainer grunted. There was a dull crack as his jawbone shattered. His mouth went slack and his eyes rolled back. Without pausing for breath, Macro lowered his head and charged at his stricken opponent, burying him under a mad flurry of blows. In the meantime, Hermes had picked himself up. He spat out blood and set his piercing gaze on Pavo.

'Got you now, traitor,' he growled.

A sudden cry went up from somewhere in the crowd, distracting the two gladiators. Fighting back the burning pain on top of his skull, Pavo glanced past Hermes and saw a handful of men from the urban cohort barging through the crowd. They used their heavy wooden staves to clear a path and surrounded the gladiators and their trainers. A moment later the officer in charge of the cohort emerged from the heaving throng.

'That's enough!' he fumed as his men hauled Macro off a bewildered Cursor whilst two more seized Hermes and dragged him away from Pavo. When the officer saw Hermes, he was speechless for a moment, staring in obvious admiration at the gladiator.

'Why, I've seen you fight before . . . You're Hermes!' he exclaimed.

The gladiator nodded. 'That's me.'

'I was in the crowd when you defeated that Illyrian scum Demetrius. Best swordsmanship I ever saw, that.' Remembering his duties, the officer quickly composed his face and snapped his fingers at the two soldiers holding Hermes. 'Release this man at once. That's no way to treat a legend of the arena.'

His men did as ordered. Turning away from the gladiator, the officer searched for someone else to blame for the fracas and his eyes settled on Macro. 'You. Take your gladiator and clear off to the imperial ludus. We don't want your kind making trouble here.'

'Get your hands off me!' Macro boomed, pulling himself free of the men holding him. His nostrils flared with rage as he glowered at the officer. 'These bastards waded in with their fists.' He gestured at Hermes and Cursor. 'The lad and I gave them what they deserved.'

'Liar!' a voice cried from the crowd. 'The stout bastard started it.'

Other fans of Hermes shouted their agreement. The officer glanced at them before turning back to Macro and screwing up his face.

'From where I'm standing, it appears that you're the one who attacked first. As for the merchant, I'll see to it that a bill for damages is drawn up. It'll be docked from your pay.'

'Hermes started it!'

'I don't give a shit,' the officer retorted. 'Now get out of here or I'll have the pair of you thrown in the Mamertine and you can spend the night in that festering hole with the rats.'

Macro shuddered at the thought. Muttering curses to the gods under his breath, he brushed past Cursor and waved for his young charge to follow as the guards set about dispersing the crowd. Some spectators flocked to the nearby taverns built into the ground floor of the arcade to refill the jars of wine they had brought with them for the day. Others sought out bookmakers to place bets on rival teams ahead of the scheduled chariot races. Pavo tenderly placed a hand on his seeping head wound and winced with pain. As he made to follow Macro, Hermes stepped forward and blocked his path, contorting his snarl into a grotesque grin.

'Do you remember what happened to your old man after I butchered him?'

Pavo gritted his teeth and made no reply. A sharp memory flashed before him as Hermes leaned in and dropped his voice to a scratched whisper.

'Don't tell me you've forgotten, boy?' Hermes smirked. 'Allow me to remind you. His head was piked on a stake and put on display in the Senate House, to serve as a warning to others of the perils of conspiring against Rome.'

There was a flash of anger in Pavo's eyes. He clamped them shut and clenched his jaws. He had tried to forget the bitter memory of the day he had learned of the final indignity suffered by his father. Now a flood of rage ran through the young gladiator and every muscle in his body immediately tensed.

'They left his head on display for days,' Hermes went on. 'Birds picked at it. Eventually the smell got so bad they had to take it

318

away. I hear one of the imperial servants dumped it in the River Tiber.'

'I will kill you,' Pavo hissed, 'for what you've done to my family, I swear to the gods.'

Hermes sneered at him. 'I don't think so, traitor. The gods always favour me. In two months' time, the next head on a stake will be yours.'

CHAPTER FORTY

'Slow down, lad!' Macro bellowed at training the following morning in the grounds of the imperial ludus. 'You're supposed to attack the palus. Not chop the fucking thing in half.'

Pavo appeared not to hear his mentor. He thrust his training sword manically at the wooden post, gripped by an uncontrollable rage as he mentally imposed the face of Hermes on top of it. There was a dull thwack as the tip of his sword struck the palus at the point of an imaginary neck. Beads of sweat flowed freely down his back. He had been hacking and stabbing aggressively at the palus since Macro arrived at the ludus at dawn to commence the day's training. He'd worked up a fierce sweat despite the bleak winter chill. His muscles were still sore from participating in the group fight and the flesh wound on his chest had formed a lumpy scab. But the dull throb of his injuries was nothing compared to the leaden feeling in his guts. Pavo had not been able to sleep the previous evening, tossing and turning in his cell as he pictured his father's severed head on a stake, mocked by his enemies. His desire for revenge had twisted into something darker, an unspeakable urge to maim Hermes. He did not merely want to kill the champion of Rome. He wanted to make him suffer, as he himself had suffered these past months. Snarling through his gritted teeth, he slammed the blade of his sword against the heavily scored palus, as if hacking through Hermes's neck, his muscles tensed with rage. The sword splintered down the blade as it clattered into the training post. Macro immediately snatched it from Pavo's grasp.

'What the bloody hell do you think you're playing at, lad?' he bellowed impatiently.

Pavo glared back, chest heaving. 'Training, sir. As per your instructions,' he replied bitterly. 'You did order me to take out my anger on the training ground.'

Macro snorted and shook his head. 'I told you to use your rage as a motivation, lad. All you're doing is blindly hacking at the palus. Good gods, you're not even practising the moves I taught you. If you try hacking at Hermes like this in the arena, he'll cut you down before you've broken into a sweat.'

Grief and frustration overwhelmed Pavo. He lowered his head and his shoulders slumped heavily. 'I'm sorry, sir,' he panted. 'But Hermes is a step too far. He's unstoppable.'

Macro seized Pavo by the shoulders and looked him hard in the eye. 'Hermes isn't a god, he's a scum gladiator. He'll have a weakness. We've just got to work out what it is.'

'You saw the fight against Criton,' Pavo protested. 'He didn't seem to have any weaknesses that I saw.'

'Criton hardly launched an attack worthy of the name,' Macro countered sternly. 'We'll make a better fist of it. And look at it this way: if you lose, at least you'll go down fighting. Do your old man proud, eh?'

Pavo nodded without conviction. In moments like these he cursed his upbringing. For all his knowledge of the Greek trag-edies and the history of Rome and his fancy fencing lessons, he lacked the ruthlessness and determination to survive of a true warrior. One could not learn how to be tenacious and brave from lessons in school. Macro had both these qualities in abundance, a result of the many years he'd spent as a soldier fighting on the bloodied frontiers of empire. The optio possessed the kind of education one could only hope to acquire through hard graft, Pavo reflected.

'Perhaps I should have chosen freedom over revenge,' he said softly. 'When the Emperor gave me the chance.'

Macro was about to reply when a faint roar erupted from the arena east of the imperial ludus. He knew what the roar signified: the day's schedule of beast fights had begun. The optio shivered in his bones and looked sharply away from the direction of the arena.

'Pull yourself together, lad. You've come too far to piss it all away now. Besides, you don't want that showboating tosser stealing the glory, do you?'

'No,' Pavo said coolly. 'But how in the name of the gods am I supposed to beat him?'

Macro paused for a moment and mulled it over. He was interrupted by a voice shouting at them from the opposite end of the training ground.

'Macro! Pavo!'

Turning in the direction of the voice, Pavo squinted and saw a tall, lean man marching towards them from the administrative building to the left of the gates. 'Shit,' he muttered. 'Cornicen . . . the bastard.'

'The imperial lanista?' Macro raised an eyebrow. 'He's got it in for you, eh?'

Pavo nodded grimly. 'He's close to Hermes and Cursor. Too close for my liking.'

Since Pavo had been housed at the imperial ludus at the start of the games, Gnaeus Sentius Cornicen had done everything within his paltry powers to make the young gladiator's life a misery, giving him two rank meals a day and the coldest, dampest and filthiest cell to sleep in. It was a cheap tactic, thought Pavo, and characteristic of the officious lanista. Cornicen seemed especially eager to pander to the wishes of those who wielded real power and influence while he oversaw the Emperor's prized collection of gladiators.

Macro grunted. 'Probably trying to please those slimy freedmen of Claudius.'

Cornicen drew near to the optio and his charge.

'Put down your weapons and stop training, Pavo,' he snapped.

Macro glowered at the lanista with barely disguised contempt. 'You're interrupting our training session.'

Cornicen stared at him for a moment. 'I don't answer to you, Optio. And I'll interrupt you when I damn well please. Especially when a member of the imperial household requests your presence. The aide to the imperial secretary, no less.'

Murena, Pavo thought, shivering at the memory of the aide.

'And I'd like a Syrian tart and a jug of good Falernian, but we don't always get what we want, do we?' Macro responded smartly, dismissing Cornicen with a wave of his hand. 'Whatever Murena wants, it'll have to wait until we break for a rest.'

The lanista cleared his throat. 'Training is over for today, Optio. Report to the imperial palace immediately.'

'But we have to train!' Pavo protested.

'Not my problem,' Cornicen said with a sneer. 'Frankly, the sooner Hermes gives you the chop, the better. You've been nothing but trouble since you set foot in the ludus. This is a place for true champions, like Hermes. Not argumentative brats who can't keep their damn mouths shut.'

Pavo stared at him for a moment before Macro grabbed him by the arm and led him after the lanista, who was marching hastily towards the gates at the opposite end of the ludus. They swept past the other gladiators training at the two dozen paluses arranged further to the north. Hermes briefly stopped attacking his palus and glanced darkly in their direction. Cornicen had ordered Hermes and Pavo to train separately, clearly fearful of a repeat of the brawl outside the Circus Maximus. Keeping them apart was at least manageable, since Hermes was a freedman gladiator and he was not required to be billeted at the imperial ludus. Pavo had learned from one of the other fighters at the ludus that Hermes had been loaned the use of a lavish villa beyond the city walls. The villa belonged to a senior magistrate apparently seeking favour with the Emperor by tending to the needs of his prized gladiator.

Cornicen ordered the guards to open the gates of the ludus, and Macro and Pavo stepped out on to the Flaminian Way. The gates slammed shut behind them. The guard towers on either side cast long shadows over the flagstones as the sun fully rose. Shafts of sunlight cut through the thick cloud, casting golden bars of light over the ornate facades of the temples arranged on the slopes of the Capitoline Hill to the south.

'What does Murena want with us now?' Pavo seethed.

Macro shot Pavo a look. 'How the fuck should I know? Whatever it is, I can promise you one thing, lad. It won't be good news.'

Pavo bit back on his anxiety as they proceeded down the

Flaminian Way. The ludus had been constructed in the shadow of the arena. Presumably, thought Pavo, so that the organisers in charge of the games could conveniently usher gladiators and condemned men from their cells to the arena with less risk of them escaping. Flies buzzed around the two men as a handful of attendants slung the mutilated corpse of a wild boar on to the side of the street. Several animal carcasses lay in a heap next to the boar, their flanks stripped clean by starving Roman citizens desperate for a scrap of meat. As the two men headed towards the imperial palace, Pavo's mind kept returning to the scene of his presentation at the imperial box

You will pay for this, Murena had warned Pavo. *I'll make sure of it.*

His neck muscles stiffened as it occurred to him that the aide had summoned them to the palace in order to exact his revenge. He and Macro would not be the first Roman citizens to disappear in the reign of Emperor Claudius, and Pavo dimly understood that Murena would do anything to prevent his fight against Hermes from going ahead. For a moment he wished that he had the chance to fight Murena and Pallas in the arena instead. Their deaths would give him almost as much pleasure as revenge over Hermes.

He followed Macro down one of the many alleys leading from the main streets. Ahead of them stood the wrought-iron gates at the front of the palace, the impressive marble steps visible beyond. Guards stood on duty outside the entrance. Macro approached the gates ahead of Pavo and gave his name; the guards promptly nodded and waved both men through. A household servant escorted them up the marble steps. They climbed four more flights of stairs before heading down a wide corridor with an intricate mosaic on the floor. In one corner a clerk sat at a desk, writing with a stylus on a wax tablet. At the sound of their footsteps he glanced up from the tablet and nodded to a door at the far end of the corridor.

'He's waiting for you,' he said brusquely.

The servant opened the door and ushered Macro and Pavo inside. Then he turned and departed down the corridor, leaving the optio and the gladiator to consider the splendour of the office. A high window overlooked the Forum. Animal skins trapped the heat rising from the hypocaust floor, warming Pavo's numbed feet. In the middle of the room stood a large oak desk overflowing with scrolls and wax tablets. Murena stood up from the chair behind the desk and greeted his guests with a smile, his teeth gleaming like marble in the sunlight streaming through the window.

'Greetings, Macro,' he announced grandly. 'You haven't been in the office of the imperial secretary before, have you?'

'The gods have spared me that particular delight until now.' The optio cast his eyes over the furnishings and grunted. 'This is where you and Pallas scheme and plot against your enemies, is it?'

Murena laughed weakly and flicked his gaze towards Pavo, his thin lips curling at the corners. There was a gleam in his eyes as he studied the gladiator. 'You're looking well, young man.'

'What the hell do you want?' Macro spat, his chest swelling with fury.

'That's no way to greet a friend,' Murena replied with fake cordiality as he calmly folded his hands behind his back. 'Really, Macro, your manners are rather boorish, even for a man of the legions. No wonder that promotion to centurion has proved so elusive. You appear to lack the necessary political skills.'

Macro looked stonily at the aide. 'To Hades with your politics. I'm a soldier, not a fucking senator.'

'Eloquently put. As ever.' Murena paced round the desk and considered his feet, a deep frown creasing his face. 'Tell me, how did our esteemed champion, the pride of Rome, perform at the Circus Maximus yesterday morning?'

'You mean Hermes?' Macro clenched his jaw. He preferred the economical language of the legions to the flowery prose employed by the imperial aide. 'He beat Criton to a pulp and then snapped his neck. Not that Criton tested him. I reckon your average Praetorian would have put up a better fight.'

'I see,' Murena responded quietly. 'A pity. I had rather hoped Criton would provide a more thorough examination of Hermes's abilities.' The aide paused for a moment, his lips pressed tight as he continued to stare at his feet. Murena had changed, thought Pavo. Perhaps it was the stress of organising the games for the Emperor that had taken its toll. The aide seemed frail and visibly drained. His hair was unkempt and the arrogant glint in his eyes had dimmed.

'What the hell is this about?' Macro demanded. 'If you're hoping to rope us into another of your schemes, forget it.'

Murena feigned innocence. 'Calm down, Optio. I have come here with the blessing of the imperial secretary – to offer our assistance in your endeavour.'

Macro frowned. 'Eh? Get to the point. We've got a fight to train for.'

Murena stared at him for a moment. 'I'm glad you mentioned the fight. That is precisely the purpose of this meeting. It concerns our mutual foe.'

Macro's eyes narrowed suspiciously. 'What the fuck do you mean?'

Murena smiled wanly. 'I'm here as a friend . . . to help you beat Hermes.'

CHAPTER FORTY-ONE

For a moment both Macro and Pavo were too stunned to reply. A frigid silence hung over the men as Murena allowed his words to sink in. At length Macro spoke.

'You must be joking,' he growled. 'You'd rather lick a latrine clean than offer to help us.'

Murena stared at Macro but disguised his irritation. 'I am quite serious,' he replied evenly. 'Both Pallas and I have our reasons for wanting to ensure the death of Rome's most treasured gladiator.'

'You're wasting your breath,' Macro replied harshly. 'We've nothing to say to you.'

Murena made a considerable effort to suppress his hatred of the soldier. Clearing his throat, he said, 'I appreciate that we have had our differences in the past, Optio. I was hoping that we could set those differences aside and discuss our common cause.'

'Bollocks! A Gaul will become emperor before I have anything more to do with the likes of you. Now, if you're finished, we have to return to training.'

Macro turned to leave the office. Pavo clasped a hand round his wrist and leaned in to his ear while the imperial aide stood glowering at the two men.

'Is this wise?' Pavo asked, lowering his voice so that the aide could not hear them.

Macro pulled a face. 'You're not seriously suggesting we listen to what this bastard has to say – after everything he's done to you?'

Pavo shrugged. 'He might be able to help.'

Macro looked apoplectic. 'Good gods, lad!' he hissed through gritted teeth. 'Two days ago they tried to send you to the after-life in the group fight!'

'I know,' Pavo replied, biting back on his hatred towards the aide. 'But what choice do we have? We both saw Hermes beat Criton senseless yesterday. We need all the help we can get.' He tipped his head in the direction of the aide. 'Even if it's from a back-stabbing Greek.'

Macro clicked his tongue and thought for a moment.

'Shit. You're right.' Fuming through his nostrils, the soldier turned back to Murena. 'All right. We'll hear you out.'

Murena stared coldly at Macro. 'Everything Pallas and I have done was on the orders of Emperor Claudius. I hope you appreciate that there was nothing personal in our actions.'

'Just tell us how you plan to help,' Pavo intervened.

A smile flickered across the aide's lips. 'I know how badly you wish to see Hermes fall in the arena.'

Pavo clamped his eyes shut, remembering the vow he had made not to rest until he had avenged his father's death. Anger pounded in his veins as he considered his predicament. On the one hand, he hated Pallas and Murena. They were at least partly to blame for his fall from grace, and the thought briefly occurred to him that they might have been responsible for the sickening display of his father's severed head. But on the other hand, Pavo was utterly determined to kill the champion of Rome, even if it meant seeking a truce with the freedman who had conspired to dishonour the Valerian family. As much as the notion rankled, he privately conceded that he had no alternative if he wished to defeat Hermes.

He opened his eyes and nodded. 'More than anything else.'

Murena smiled mischievously at Pavo and inspected his fingernails. 'If those lowlife bookmakers scraping out a living around the Circus Maximus are to be believed, Hermes is the overwhelming favourite for the fight.'

'That's true enough,' Macro intervened. He nodded gruffly at his young charge. 'We'll do our best to prove those greedy bastards wrong, won't we?'

Pavo winced at the show of defiance from Macro. He admired the optio for his courage and steely resolve in the face of death. But a sick sensation gnawed in his guts as he faced the prospect of a grisly downfall in the arena. Even Macro's show of support could not mask the awful truth. Defeating Hermes was almost impossible.

Murena clasped his hands beneath his chin and gazed out of the window. After a long moment he said, 'Pallas and I have ways of, shall we say, levelling the odds.'

Pavo leaned forward. 'Why do you want to help? If Hermes wins our fight, I shall die. Isn't that what you've been trying to achieve these past months?'

Turning sharply from the window, Murena looked at the glad-iator for a moment. 'You may not be aware of it, young man, and I am sure the optio is entirely ignorant of such things, but within these walls a vicious struggle for power is unfolding as we speak. A struggle as desperate as any gladiator combat taking place in the arena.'

His words drew a humorous grunt from Macro, who rolled his eyes at the freedman.

Murena stared intently at the soldier. 'I know the politics of Rome hold no interest for you, Optio.' He snorted with derision. 'No doubt you would rather be debasing yourself with drink at one of the taverns, or perhaps satiating your Euripidean needs at a brothel.'

Macro looked puzzled. 'Eurip-what?'

Murena smiled and shook his head. 'Never mind. It is impor-tant for you both to understand something. The imperial secretary has advised Claudius from the day he was proclaimed Emperor. With my assistance, Pallas has guided his imperial majesty through the stormy waters of the early days of his reign. His political insight has helped to establish Claudius as the rightful heir to the purple toga.'

'Some might say the murder of his enemies helped as well,' Pavo noted drily.

The aide glowered at the gladiator, stung by the truth of that statement. Several months after Claudius had ascended the throne, Pavo knew, influential senators and prominent members of the imperial court were still disappearing from the streets of Rome.

'We have served Rome well,' Murena argued defensively. 'Pallas has proved to be a highly valuable confidant and earned the trust of the Emperor on important matters of state. But now we find our positions of influence threatened by another freedman. He has become rather close to Claudius of late. I speak in confidence, of course.'

'What's his name?' Pavo asked. 'Perhaps I have heard of him.'

'Narcissus.' Murena screwed up his face, as if the name left a vile taste in his mouth.

'So what?' Macro offered a casual shrug. 'One scheming freedman replaces another. What's the big fuss? You're all as bad as each other.'

'Believe it or not, some of us place the needs of Rome above our own interests. While the mob is drinking itself senseless, indulging in gambling and lewd shows, men such as myself and Pallas work tirelessly to administer the Empire. If it were not for us, Rome would have gone to the dogs long ago.'

Pavo looked curiously at the aide. 'And Narcissus is different?'

'Narcissus has his own agenda. He sees Pallas as a threat. If he succeeds in winning the confidence of the Emperor, he will no doubt turn Claudius against us. At the very least we will be banished into exile . . . or worse.'

'Perish the thought,' Macro muttered.

Murena appeared not to hear the soldier. 'Without us, there would be no new programme of public works, no sponsoring of the games. Narcissus is gravely mistaken if he believes we will surrender our position without a fight.'

'What does any of this have to do with Hermes?' Pavo asked.

The aide sighed deeply and lowered his head. 'As you are no doubt aware, Hermes had resisted all attempts to lure him out of retirement.' When he looked up at Pavo, his eyes betrayed a hint of fear. 'Until Narcissus stepped in and persuaded him to return.'

Pavo raised his eyebrows. 'How did he manage to tempt Hermes?'

'A great big fucking pile of money probably did the trick.' Macro sniffed.

'Hermes has no need of coin,' Murena countered pithily. 'He has more money than you can possibly imagine. Before he announced his retirement, he was earning up to a hundred thousand sestertii per appearance.'

Macro puffed out his cheeks. 'I'm clearly in the wrong business. I never knew killing scum paid so well.' The sum dwarfed the basic legionary pay of nine hundred sestertii. As an optio, Macro earned double pay, but as a centurion he could look forward to a much bigger salary. Even so, it fell well short of the fortune commanded by the gladiator.

Murena studied him with his pale eyes. 'Watch your tongue, Optio, or there may well be a future for you in the arena . . . a short future, that is.'

Macro flushed with anger. Murena smiled mockingly at him and paced up and down beside the window as he went on. 'Pallas suspects that Narcissus has persuaded Hermes to return by some other means.'

'But how?' Pavo asked blearily.

'We're not sure.' Murena stopped pacing the room and shrugged as he looked at the young gladiator. 'Narcissus is a slippery customer. He has turned scheming into an art form.'

Macro raised an eyebrow sardonically. 'Reminds me of someone, that. Can't think who.'

Murena ignored the jibe. 'Claudius is predictably thrilled with Narcissus. By securing the return of the Emperor's favourite gladiator, Narcissus is one step closer to winning his trust and estranging Pallas and myself. The games are our last opportunity to undermine him.'

Pavo saw it all then. The imperial secretary's grip on power was slipping from his tenuous grasp. Narcissus, for his part, would be unlikely to spare his rivals once he had won the Emperor's trust. Pallas and Murena could expect exile to an impoverished province at best. If Narcissus was truly vindictive, they might be thrown to the beasts. Pavo smiled inwardly at the prospect of the freedmen suffering – as he had done ever since they had cast him into the ludus in Paestum.

'That's why you want to help us beat Hermes?' Macro asked, rubbing his jaw. 'So you can undermine this other freedman?'

'Precisely, Optio. At the behest of Narcissus, Hermes is being publicly championed by Claudius. However, if Hermes loses, the Emperor will not be pleased. Narcissus will be held responsible – and will fall from favour.'

'Tragic,' Macro said. 'But I don't see why we should help dig you out of your hole.'

There was a calculating gleam in the aide's eyes, like a sword tip glinting in the sun. 'You still want your promotion to centurion, don't you, Optio? Pallas will be in no position to successfully petition the Emperor should Pavo lose.'

Macro clenched his jaw. He missed life on the Rhine. The drills, the discipline, even the watered–down swill that passed for wine in the camps. He shrugged off all thoughts of his return to the army and frowned. 'There's one problem. Hermes is an absolute beast. I'll push the lad as hard as I can, but there's no guarantee he'll win.'

Murena grinned. 'Ah, but I can give you a decisive advantage in your preparations.'

'What kind of advantage?' Pavo asked.

Murena ignored the question and addressed Macro. 'How is the boy faring, Optio?'

Macro sucked in a lungful of air and thought for a moment. 'Well enough. Once he's recovered from his last fight, I'll put him through a rigorous workout. We'll have him fitter than ever before. Whether that's enough to beat Hermes, only the gods know.'

The aide stroked his chin. 'As I thought. Well, I have good news for you both. Pallas and I have been giving the matter some thought, and we both agree that you could use a sparring partner.'

'I selected Macro as my trainer,' Pavo responded testily. 'I don't need anyone else.'

Murena smiled patiently. 'Macro may be able to teach you the tricks of the trade, but this sparring partner is one of the best in the business.'

'Who is he?' Macro asked.

'Publius Didius Ruga. He's a retired gladiator and bodyguard to the senatorial elite. He also happens to be the only man to have faced Hermes in the arena and lived to tell the tale.'

Pavo looked bemused. 'I wasn't aware that anyone had survived against Hermes.'

'Ruga competed as a gladiator during the reign of Emperor Tiberius. I understand his match against Hermes lasted so long that the Emperor gave him the thumb of mercy. His injuries were too severe to allow him to continue as a gladiator, so in an act of generosity one of the senators present appointed him as his bodyguard.'

'Why would Ruga agree to help us?' Macro cocked his head to the aide.

'Ruga never recovered from the shame of his defeat by Hermes. He claimed the contest was rigged in Hermes's favour. He burns with hatred towards Hermes almost as much as our young gladiator does.' The aide paused and smiled slyly. 'There is also the small matter of the fact that Ruga was recently relieved of his duties by the senator.'

'Relieved?' Macro repeated with a frown.

'Ruga is a drunk, Optio. I believe he started drinking heavily after his defeat by Hermes, to numb the almost constant pain he is in. I have spoken with him and promised to solicit the senator in question to help him get his old job back – on condition that he trains you.'

Macro nodded at the news. Although he was skilled with a sword and could impart general combat strategies to Pavo, as a soldier he knew better than anyone that the best way to prepare for battle was to gain inside knowledge of the enemy. A gladiator who had come close to defeating Hermes sounded like the ideal sparring partner.

Murena turned his gaze on Pavo and cleared his throat.

'In the meantime, you will continue your training somewhere else.'

'Why?' Pavo asked.

'I have no wish for a repeat of your fracas with Hermes outside the Circus Maximus. Besides, the lanista is a close acquaintance of Narcissus and it's possible he might try to sabotage your training schedule. I have rented a room for you, Macro, in a tenement block on the Aventine Hill, next to the Drunken Goat tavern.

There is a courtyard at the back. You and Ruga will train Pavo there.' A wicked smile crossed his lips as he flicked his gaze over to Macro. 'The streets are filled with drunks and degenerates. I'm sure you will feel at home.'

Macro bit back on his anger as Pavo responded to the aide. 'The Emperor has agreed to release me from the ludus?' he asked, his voice fragile with hope at the prospect of escaping the confines of his rat-infested cell.

'Under certain conditions. Pallas has convinced his imperial majesty that a death threat has been made against you by one of the other gladiators. Macro will escort you back to the ludus each evening. Try to escape and your son dies.'

Pavo grimly resigned himself to the prospect of having to remain in his cell at night. He went quiet as Macro scratched his chin and frowned. 'What about training equipment?'

The aide pursed his lips. 'I have sourced a few training swords and shields from the Praetorian Guard barracks, along with some weights. But by and large you will have to make do.'

'Great,' Macro grumbled. 'So while Hermes gets to hone his strength at the imperial ludus, we'll be slumming it in a courtyard, using whatever leftover equipment you can lay your bloody hands on.'

'You will have to improvise,' Murena responded haughtily. 'Isn't that what you soldiers are supposed to do best?'

Macro gritted his teeth, a dark expression clouding his grizzled features.

'There is, ah, one more problem.' Murena hesitated. 'I'm afraid the fight is going to be brought forward.'

Pavo and Macro swapped a look.

'How far forward exactly?' Macro asked.

'To next month, Optio. Starting today, you will have thirty days to prepare.'

Macro sucked the air between his teeth. At his side, Pavo's face turned pale, his shoulders sagging with despair.

'That's not enough time,' Macro said. 'In four weeks I'll have put some muscle on the lad, but that's your lot. We won't have had a chance to properly study Hermes and prepare against him.'

334

'There's nothing to be done,' Murena replied harshly. 'Claudius has decided to undertake a tour of the public works being built around the Empire the following month. The decision is out of my hands. You will have to cope as best you can.'

Macro managed to bite his tongue. In recent months he'd made a concerted effort to keep his temper in check, knowing that it had cost him promotion in the past. But being back in Rome and doing the bidding of the imperial freedmen was sorely testing his patience. More than ever, he desired to leave the city. He made a solemn promise to himself never to return.

'Even Britannia has got to be safer than this snakepit,' he growled under his breath.

Murena appeared not to hear him. 'Any questions? Good. Then I suggest you go and meet Ruga. He's waiting for you at the courtyard. I have already provided Cornicen with the necessary authorisation for your temporary removal from the ludus. He seems rather glad to see the back of you, Pavo.'

The optio straightened his back. Both he and Pavo turned to leave. Murena raised a hand, gesturing for them to halt. He stared at the soldier. 'I hope I do not need to warn you of the dire consequences of failure.'

Macro snorted. 'That old trick won't work. You just said that Pallas will be stripped of his authority if Hermes is the victor. Without your power, you're just a couple of spindly Greeks making empty threats.'

'But we still know your secret. After all, who could forget your appearance in the arena? And we will not hesitate to share it with Vespasian should you let us down.'

A hot rage swirled inside Macro. He clenched his hands into fists, the indignity of appearing in the beast fight burning like a hot coal in his chest. He stared at Murena. The aide nodded at the door.

'You may wait for Pavo at the main gates. I have something to discuss with him . . . in private.'

Macro turned to Pavo in surprise. The latter merely shrugged at his mentor, a blank look on his face. Shaking his head, Macro marched out of the office, taking one last glance at the aide before he closed the door. Murena sighed.

'Now that we are alone, I have something I would like to show you.'

'Appius?' Pavo asked hopefully. 'Do I get to see him at last?'

Murena answered with a note of pity. 'Not yet, young man. Claudius promised to spare your son a gruesome death. He said nothing of releasing him from custody. However, should you defeat Hermes, I can personally assure you that Appius will be freed.' There was a feverish glow to his eyes as he went on. 'What I am going to show you will give you, shall we say, a little extra motivation for your fight. Follow me.'

Pavo frowned suspiciously as Murena paced round the desk and led him out into the corridor. Macro had already departed for the main gates and the clerk was still busy making notes on his tablet as Pavo followed Murena down the corridor. At the end, they descended several flights of stairs until they reached a narrow passageway at the bottom. Two Praetorians guarded the entrance to the passageway, the light from oil lamps dimly illuminating their features. Murena nodded at them and the guard on the left promptly stood aside while his comrade ushered them down the passageway. It was cold and clammy and dark, and the young gladiator shivered, a sinister chill sweeping through him. They were entering the underground tunnels built beneath the foundations of the imperial palace complex, he realised. He'd heard of the existence of such tunnels, used by the Emperor and his entourage to move between the palace complex and his other estates without risk of being assassinated on the streets of Rome. Caligula had been murdered in one such tunnel by several conspirators. A sudden fear gripped Pavo. Perhaps Murena intended to kill him after all, he thought. His legs trembled as he followed the Praetorian and Murena down the tunnel. They passed several cell doors. At length the guard stopped in front of one and unlocked it.

'Leave us,' Murena ordered the guard.

'What's going on?' Pavo asked, panic creeping into his voice as he hesitated in the doorway.

Murena stared at him for a moment. His eyes smiled with intent. 'Enter, young man. There's a friend of yours in here.'

Something cold and sickening stirred inside Pavo. Reluctantly he stepped into the cell, anxiety tying knots in his stomach. Murena stood to one side. The cell was cramped – smaller than his own billeting at the imperial ludus, Pavo thought – and the instantly recognisable stench of blood and faecal matter lingered in the air. The flicker of oil lamps in the passageway cast a gloomy red hue. A series of torture instruments were laid out on the floor next to the door. Pavo felt his stomach churn as he spotted a patch of blood glistening on the stone next to his feet. Then he heard a timid groaning and his eyes were drawn to a crumpled figure slumped against the back wall. Manacles were clamped round his wrists and ankles. The man had been stripped down to his loincloth and on closer inspection Pavo realised that his fingernails and toenails had been ripped out. His torso was covered with burn marks and bruises. Murena clicked his fingers. The man wearily lifted his head and his dull eyes rested on Pavo. Blood dripped from his chin. His lips were purpled. The gladiator felt his entire body jolt.

'Dear gods . . .' he started.

'Senator Numerius Porcius Lanatus,' Murena cut in almost cheerfully, suppressing a smile. He glanced at Pavo. 'An old friend of your father's, I believe, in the days when Lanatus was the proconsular governor in Africa. Senator Lanatus also happens to be a Liberator. One of the leaders behind that shadowy network, no less.' He stooped down beside the elderly senator and grinned. 'Isn't that right, Lanatus?'

The senator stared back defiantly.

'Go to Hades, Murena,' he croaked. Pavo recoiled in horror as he saw that Lanatus's teeth had been ripped out of his mouth.

'I rather think that is what you will soon be doing, my dear friend,' Murena sneered. He ruffled the senator's thin grey hair and turned back to Pavo. 'One of the duty guards at the imperial ludus was exposed as a friend of the Liberators. We tortured him and he gave up the name of Lanatus easily enough.'

The senator winced, his chest heaving with pain. Standing upright, Murena turned to Pavo. 'Do you know why I have brought you here?' he asked evenly.

Pavo shook his head. The blood ran cold in his veins. Murena took a step closer to him and said softly, 'We solicited a confession from Lanatus. The palace interrogators tortured the old fool to within a hair's breadth of his life, but he eventually told us everything. They always do.'

The gladiator tried to feign ignorance. 'What does any of this have to do with me?'

'Don't play games with me, Pavo. Lanatus confessed to his role in the conspiracy to assassinate the Emperor. He told us about the plan to slip you a weapon in the aftermath of your victory in the group fight. How you were supposed to slit the Emperor's throat when you entered the imperial box to receive your award. I must admit, it was certainly an audacious plan.'

'I had no choice! Lanatus told me that unless I helped, Appius would die—'

Murena raised a hand. 'I'm not interested in your pathetic excuses,' he snapped. 'The only reason you're not being nailed to a cross at this moment is because Pallas and I need you to win. The very fact that you chose not to go through with the conspiracy suggests you at least had some doubts about the wisdom of committing such a heinous act.'

'What do you want?' Pavo asked warily.

'Victory, of course. I will not tolerate your defeat by Hermes.'

Pavo threw up his arms. 'Hermes is the greatest gladiator who ever lived. Even at my best, I might lose.'

'Then you will have to train harder. Win your fight, and no one else need ever learn of your part in the Liberators' conspiracy. Lose, and I will make sure that all of Rome is made aware of your treachery. The mob will ridicule you as a Liberator, Pavo. Your family name will be irreparably sullied. And poor little Appius will suffer a fate worse than death: he'll grow up as the disgraced son of a traitor.'

CHAPTER FORTY-TWO

'What was all that about?' Macro growled irritably. Pavo had left Murena at the entrance to the underground tunnel and rejoined Macro outside the main gates of the imperial palace where he was pacing impatiently up and down. A chill wind picked up and fluttered through the alley.

'Sir?' Pavo said absently. His mind was still shaken by the sight of Lanatus in the cell. He shuddered at the thought of the unimaginable horrors the senator must have suffered at the hands of the imperial interrogators. Only the political aspirations of the imperial secretary and his aide had spared Pavo the same fate. But if there was one thing worse than death for a high-born Roman, it was the loss of prestige, and he felt his blood boil at the prospect of being exposed as a traitor. Murena was right. Appius would grow up in disgrace, the Valerius family name stained by his actions. Now, more than ever, he needed to win.

Macro frowned. 'You look like you've just seen a cheap tart without her make-up on, lad. What's wrong?'

'Nothing,' Pavo replied. He looked carefully at his mentor, studying his face. He quickly decided that Macro was in the dark about his involvement in the conspiracy to assassinate Claudius. He breathed a sharp sigh of relief and forced a smile. 'Murena merely wanted to remind me of the importance of the fight.'

'Eh?' Macro sputtered. He went on, 'What's with the long face, then? You should be kissing Fortuna's arse, lad. Those bloody Greeks are on our side . . . for once.'

Pavo shrugged wearily. 'Perhaps we've made a mistake.'

Macro grunted. He was still in a foul mood from the encounter with Murena and the painful reminder of his appearance in the beast fights. 'You think too much. That's what reading all those books does to you.'

Pavo pushed aside the appalling mental image of Lanatus in his cell and cocked his head at his mentor. 'It doesn't strike you as odd that Murena and Pallas are offering to help, sir?'

'Gods know. They're Greeks, after all. Buggers are raised at birth to be slippery. Right now they see Narcissus as the greater threat. That means they're willing to work with you. My enemy's enemy, as the saying goes.'

Pavo tilted his head to the side, conceding the point. 'But they have spent the past several months trying to kill me. Surely they'd rather work with someone – anyone – else?'

'Bloody hell!' Macro threw up his arms in bewilderment. 'You know what those freedmen are like. Pallas will do anything to hold on to his title as the Emperor's chief arse-licker, even if it means cosying up to the disgraced aristocrat he's been trying to kill. No offence.'

'None taken,' Pavo replied flatly.

Macro shook his head. 'Anyway, you were the one who agreed to work with Murena.'

'Fair enough. But I don't believe his reason for wanting the defeat of Hermes. Pallas is a natural schemer. I'm sure he could think up a plan to undermine Narcissus that wouldn't involve aiding the likes of us.'

'None of our business, that. All we need to know is that Ruga has given Hermes a good run for his denarii in the past and he'll know a thing or two about how to stop him. With a bit of luck you might stand a chance of actually winning.'

'You're forgetting one thing.'

'What's that?'

'We only have a month in which to prepare for the fight, sir.'

Macro rubbed his hands. 'Then we'd best knuckle down to training. Put some bulk on you, lad.' He glanced down at Pavo's lower half. 'Especially those gangly legs of yours. I've seen more muscle on those bookish types who sit in the literary salons discussing poetry.'

The streets were bustling and loud with the hubbub of traders' voices as Macro and Pavo headed south from the imperial palace towards the Aventine Hill. Children's voices rang out above the metallic clank of shopkeepers releasing bolt locks as they opened their shop fronts for the day. Macro moved at a brisk pace, thoughts weighing heavily on his mind. Although he did not share his concern with his young charge, he worried about the lack of time in which to prepare. Normally three to four months was required to properly train even a veteran gladiator for a fight against a fearsome opponent. Pavo had a mere four fights under his belt and would be facing a supremely fit champion.

Macro surprised himself with how badly he wanted to see Pavo triumph. Respect for high-born Romans did not come naturally to the optio, who had grown up in humble surroundings. But Pavo had proved himself not only a talented swordsman but a hard-working student who possessed an indomitable spirit. Even with the might of the imperial household against him, he had never buckled under pressure and his fighting qualities would make him a worthy officer in any legion. And as his mentor, Macro felt a certain sense of pride.

A short while later Macro and Pavo threaded their way through the seething mass of humanity crammed on to the Aventine Hill. Decrepit tenement blocks stood several storeys high, cutting out what little natural light there was and casting a fetid gloom over the downtrodden inhabitants. The air was filled with the dull hammering of coppersmiths hard at work and the occasional cry of crazed drunks coming from within the dimly lit taverns scattered throughout the district.

'What in the name of the gods is this place?' Pavo spluttered. 'And what is that smell?'

Macro slapped a hand on the gladiator's shoulder and gave him a hearty shake. 'This is the Aventine Hill. The beating heart of Rome.'

There was a squelching sound as Pavo trod in something wet and slimy. Stopping in his tracks, he looked down in horror at a foul brown puddle. There were similar puddles all along the street. The young gladiator fought a strong urge to puke as he realised that a river of filth was literally running through the street. Macro chuckled at his companion.

'Open sewer,' he said matter-of-factly. 'The Aventine is riddled with 'em.'

Pavo looked for somewhere to wipe his fouled feet. 'This is not the heart of the city, sir. It is a repugnant slum. How anyone can live like this is quite beyond me.'

Macro widened his eyes. 'You're one to talk, lad. The gladiator who lives in a rank cell, eating maggot-infested gruel twice a day.'

Pavo furrowed his brow at Macro. 'My conditions are not out of choice, sir. They were imposed on me by Cornicen, as you well know. It's not my fault the imperial lanista singled me out for special treatment.'

'Always get on with the lanistas, don't you, lad?' Macro joked.

The younger man glared at the optio and waved a hand in front of him where men with dishevelled beards and wearing threadbare tunics shuffled solemnly through the streets. Babies wailed from within crumbling tenement blocks.

'My point is that these people have chosen to wallow in their own filth.'

Macro cocked an eyebrow at Pavo. 'Haven't been to the Aventine before, have you?'

'Never,' the young gladiator replied proudly. 'My family home was on the Appian Way. I rarely ventured within the city walls. Sometimes to attend processions in the Forum or listen to the debates going on in the Senate.'

Macro shook his head. 'Lucky for you. I once lived in this pit. And I can assure you, I had no choice in the matter, like the rest of these poor devils.'

They passed a bakery. A crowd of stick-thin Romans meekly gathered outside, waiting to exchange their grain rations for loaves of bread. Pavo knew that millions across the Empire depended on the grain ration. Perhaps Macro was right, he considered. Perhaps these individuals weren't scroungers on the grain dole, as he'd previously assumed. He fell quiet, lost in thought as they moved through the streets.

Macro stayed silent at his side. After his mother had run away from the family home when Macro was a child, he had moved with his father to the Aventine Hill to be closer to his uncle

Sextus. The sprawling streets and angry shouts of mid-morning drunks were instantly familiar to the soldier.

At the end of the street they spotted a rundown tavern built into the ground floor of a four-storey block. A brightly painted sign hung from a wall outside. A chorus of loud belches and roaring laughs emanated from inside. Pavo frowned at the sign and read it out loud.

'The Drunken Goat. Come thirsty, leave merry.' He shrugged. 'Has a certain ring to it.'

Macro nodded at an arch next to the tavern.

'Must be this way.'

The two men passed under the arch and entered a courtyard at the back of the tenement block. The courtyard reminded Macro of the place where Draba had trained him many years ago. Refuse was piled in the corners and the air was thick with the stench of decay and damp. Two pairs of wicker shields and wooden swords were stacked against the wall. They were the same as the training weapons issued to new recruits in the legions, deliberately designed to be heavier than real weapons so that novice swordsmen developed their muscles as well as honing their sword-fighting techniques. High tenement blocks surrounded the courtyard, and even with the clouds clearing in the sky, the shafts of sunlight found it difficult to penetrate the gloom.

Macro looked around the courtyard and frowned.

'Bastard is late,' he muttered, kicking one of the training shields in frustration. 'Typical gladiator. No discipline.'

At that moment a full-throated roar erupted from inside the tavern. The wooden door at the back crashed open and a huge figure staggered out. Pavo turned towards the man. His burly torso was heavily scarred, but the scars were nothing compared to the appalling injuries to his face. His muscles were slack with age and he had a large paunch. The man raised his small, dim eyes to Macro.

'Publius Didius Ruga?' Macro asked, taken aback by the sight in front of him.

'That's me.' His voice was slurred. He thumped a mangled fist on his lacerated chest. 'Finest fucking gladiator in the days of Emperor Tiberius, I'll have you know.' He burped.

At first Pavo could not believe that the maimed veteran in front of him had once proved himself the equal of Hermes. He studied Ruga as the man approached him, limping slightly. Ruga cocked his head at the young gladiator.

'You must be the thick bastard Murena was telling me about,' he said disdainfully.

'I beg your pardon?' Pavo replied with a start.

A cynical smile creased the veteran's face. 'Anyone who wishes to fight Hermes is a fool. As my scars should make clear. What's your excuse, boy?'

Pavo stared at Ruga. 'I'm no fool. Hermes took the life of my father,' he replied coldly. 'And I don't want to merely fight Hermes. I want to kill him.'

Ruga kept smiling. 'I'm sure you do. But fifty or so gladiators have stepped out to face Hermes and not one of them has triumphed. What makes you think you can do any better?'

Pavo glanced at the optio. 'I have the best trainer in Macro. He's one of the finest soldiers in the legions. He knows more than anyone about handling a sword.'

Ruga bowed his head in the direction of the soldier. 'With all due respect, Optio, your student's past achievements in the arena count for nothing. Fighting Hermes is like taking on five gladiators at the same time.'

'Bollocks to this. I don't have to justify myself to some washed-up swordsman,' Macro said impatiently. 'Look here. We've got a month until the big fight. Now can you help us or not?'

'That depends.'

'On what? From what we've been told, you already struck a deal with Murena. Unless you train the lad, you can forget about returning to your old line of work as a bodyguard.'

Ruga glared at the soldier. Without replying, he paraded over to the training equipment stacked against the wall and picked up one of the wooden swords. He pointed the tip at Pavo and said, 'Show me what you can do.'

'You're not serious,' Pavo spluttered.

'Defeating Hermes is about more than pure skill, boy. It's about having the desire to win. More than that, it's about not shitting your loincloth when Hermes is coming at your throat with a foot and a half of sharpened steel. Getting my old job back with Senator Macula is all well and good, but I'm not short of coin for the odd drink, and I'd rather walk away now unless you prove to me that you've got a hell's chance of cutting down that fucking savage.'

'You're drunk,' Pavo said in disgust.

'I've still got what it takes, boy.'

Pavo raised an eyebrow. The retired gladiator paused for a moment as he reached down with his free hand and unsheathed a wooden dagger fixed to a leather strap fastened round his tunic. Several lines of text were engraved along the length of the blade. He held the dagger closer so that Pavo could read it. The retired gladiator's name was engraved on a brass plate fixed to the blade. Next to it were the date and the name of the last opponent he faced in the arena.

'Hermes,' Pavo whispered as he read the name.

Ruga grunted. 'My rudis of freedom, presented to me by Tiberius after I came closer than any man to overcoming the colossus from Rhodes. I may be worn as old boots now, but I can still teach you a trick or two.'

Sheathing his rudis, Ruga chucked the training sword at Pavo, scooped up the second sword and kicked off his sandals in readiness for combat.

'Sir . . .?' Pavo asked, glancing at Macro.

The optio shrugged. 'You heard the man. Show him what you've got.'

'Yes, sir.' Pavo gulped.

He gripped the sword in his right hand. The lead weight in the pommel made the weapon heavier than a standard short sword, and he slowly adjusted to the increased weight as he turned to face Ruga. Macro clapped his hands to signal the start of the bout, but Pavo hesitated. Ruga bared his teeth at the young gladiator, seeing the uncertainty in his eyes.

'Come on, boy!' he growled. 'Attack me!'

Pushing his concerns about injuring the retired gladiator to one side, Pavo inched towards his opponent. Ruga studied him intently as Pavo lunged at him, thrusting the tip of his sword at his exposed neck. In a lightning flash of movement Ruga leaned to his left and deflected the attack with a sudden flick of his sword before pushing forward on his right foot and cracking Pavo on the bridge of his nose with a deft upward thrust. Pavo saw white for an instant. Ruga took two steps back, his lips parted in a drunken grin.

The younger man tasted something salty in his mouth and put a hand to his face. Hot blood trickled out of his nose. Ruga moved with a litheness that belied his hefty physique. Shaking his head clear, Pavo filled his lungs and launched a low thrust at Ruga, driving the tip of his sword at his groin. Ruga jinked to the right this time, circling Pavo as momentum carried him forward. A jarring pain shuddered through the young gladiator as the veteran slammed the weighted pommel of his sword against his back. Clamping his jaws shut and fighting the nausea rising in his throat, Pavo spun raggedly round and staggered away from his opponent. Ruga was bustling with vigour now, his aged muscles pumping, his eyes wide with fury.

'Come on!' he goaded. 'Surely you can do better than that?'

Enraged at having allowed himself to be caught out twice, Pavo charged at the retired gladiator with renewed determination. Ruga launched a stabbing move at his chest. Pavo quickly feinted and responded with a driving thrust that caught the veteran on the chin. Ruga hopped backwards. Pavo attacked him quickly a second time, his skill with a sword bewildering the retired gladiator. Ducking a solid thrust to the throat, Ruga jabbed his sword at Pavo's midriff. The younger man quickly parried with a flick of his wrist, arcing his wooden blade across his chest.

Now Pavo snatched a breath and brought his sword crashing down towards his opponent's temple. At the last moment Ruga jerked his sword up above his head and blocked the attack. Immediately the veteran cursed as he realised he'd left his torso exposed. Pavo punished him before he could backtrack, booting him in his paunch. Ruga staggered backwards. Pavo stormed forward and moved in for the decisive blow. He lunged at the veteran, aiming his training sword at his throat. But in a swift stroke Ruga dropped to a crouch and ducked the blow. Extending his right arm, he swiped his sword across the ground, knocking the younger man off balance. Pavo stumbled. Ruga followed up with a fist to the guts that sent his opponent tumbling to the ground with a desperate grunt. A sharp pain tremored down Pavo's spine as he slammed against the flagstones.

Ruga was on to him in a flash, kicking away the sword that had fallen uselessly from his floored opponent's grip. At the same time he pressed the tip of his own sword against the younger man's neck. Out of the corner of his eye Pavo spied Macro shaking his head in dismay.

'If you were fighting against Hermes, you'd be dead,' Ruga croaked between snatched breaths. 'Right now you couldn't beat the champion of Rome if he was fighting blind.'

Pavo climbed awkwardly to his feet, furious with himself for losing to a retired gladiator – and one who was clearly the worse for wear. He shook his groggy head clear and gestured for his sword.

'Again,' he demanded. 'I'll beat you this time.'

Ruga clenched his hand into a fist. His eyes twinkled. 'That's more bloody like it, boy! Never give up. That's the attitude you'll need if you want to defeat Hermes.' He scratched his straggly beard and considered Pavo. 'You have excellent reactions. I can see the optio has trained you well. But there's still plenty of work to be done with your movement and defence. With the right training, you may have a chance.'

'We have a month until the fight,' Macro cut in, quietly satisfied that Ruga could be of value during their training programme. 'Do you think it's possible to get him ready for Hermes by then?'

Ruga smiled. 'Perhaps. But it's going to be tough. From now until the day of the games we'll need to work him harder and longer than any gladiator who has ever trained for a fight.'

'I'll do it!' Pavo exclaimed defiantly. 'Whatever it takes. Hermes will fall by my sword, I swear.'

'Good. Then we begin immediately,' Ruga said as Macro nodded his approval. 'Just as soon as I've got my breath back and had another drink.'

CHAPTER FORTY-THREE

'A provocator fights with thirty pounds of equipment,' Ruga boomed, his hoarse voice echoing around the courtyard the following afternoon. He counted off the items on his scarred fingers. 'Helmet, armour, sword, shield. He has to carry a much heavier load than any other gladiator type. And if you're going to defeat Hermes, you need to rethink the way you fight. You must learn how to move, how to defend, how to attack without tiring. One thing's for sure. If you approach your fight the way you did yesterday, you'll knacker yourself in next to no time, and Hermes will stick you like a pig.'

A mild breeze whipped up, swirling dust around their feet. Macro stood at the edge of the courtyard, his cloak draped across his muscular shoulders, squinting in the gloom as Ruga put the young gladiator through his paces. The optio had been present at the Forum the previous day, where an announcement had been made to the excited crowd gathered to hear details of the forth-coming bout. Instead of hosting the fight at the Statilius Taurus arena, the sponsors had declared that Hermes and Pavo would fight in a temporary wooden arena constructed in the Roman Forum. Macro knew enough about the history of gladiator combat to see that the decision was a masterstroke from Pallas. His old trainer, Draba, had regaled him with stories of how, in the days before a dedicated arena had been constructed, gladiator events were frequently staged in the Forum. Hosting a one-off fight there would conjure memories of the great gladiator bouts of the past. Macro had departed the Forum after the announcer revealed the details of the prize on offer for the victor, a new title never before bestowed on a gladiator: Champion of the Arena.

He touched a hand to his temple. His head throbbed dully

from the effects of the jug of cheap wine he'd sunk the previous evening with Ruga at the Drunken Goat. The two men had worked into the night, drawing up a training schedule that would give Pavo a fighting chance against Hermes. With only four weeks to prepare, they had decided to divide the programme into morning and afternoon sessions, with the former focusing on strength and stamina and the latter dedicated to working on Pavo's combat technique and strategies.

Training began shortly after dawn each day. There was a short break at midday for a simple meal at the Drunken Goat – boiled pork and root vegetables accompanied by a piece of stale bread. Pavo considered it a relative feast compared to the barley gruel and vinegary wine he'd been served in the imperial ludus. Although he now trained and ate outside the ludus, Cornicen still went to great lengths to make his life a misery, even removing the straw bedding in his cell. At night Pavo lay shivering, swearing to the gods that he would not allow such petty tactics to get in the way of his desire to beat Hermes and avenge his father. In the afternoons Ruga stirred from his drunken slumber and sparred with the young gladiator, teaching him the sword-fighting techniques he'd need to counter the astonishing speed and power of his nemesis.

'The secret to beating Hermes is to ignore everything you've learned about fighting,' Ruga announced as he grabbed one of the training swords and pointed the tip at Pavo. 'Hermes is a master of the counterattack. He deliberately lures his opponents into a trap, then packs them off to the Underworld with a choice stab to the throat. Attacking him is fraught with danger.'

The optio shook his head. 'But the lad has to attack. Sitting back is asking for trouble. If he does that, Hermes will just pick him off.'

'Macro is right,' Pavo cut in. 'Hermes destroyed Criton in such a manner three days ago at the Circus Maximus. I can't defend against his brute force. No one can. He's too strong.'

'Ah, but Criton made a fatal mistake.'

'I'm not sure I follow,' Pavo replied doubtfully.

Ruga grinned. 'Here. I'll show you.'

349

The retired gladiator passed his training sword to Pavo, who gripped it round the weighted pommel. Then Ruga hefted up one of the two large rectangular wicker shields propped against the wall, clasping his left hand round the grip at the centre of the shield. He tapped the flat surface of the shield with his right hand and gestured to Pavo to attack.

'Well, boy?' he rasped. 'What are you waiting for?'

Pavo forced his tensed muscles to relax and held his ground for a moment. He studied Ruga carefully, determined not to get caught out this time. His opponent had no sword to attack with, so it ought to be relatively simple to rout him. Ruga held the shield in a sturdy grip, with his elbow tucked tight to his chest, the top edge level with his chin and the bottom edge reaching down to his knee. The shield thus covered the main part of his body.

Taking a deep breath, Pavo surged at Ruga and plunged the wooden tip of his sword down at his shins, hoping to draw the veteran into lowering his shield and exposing his chest to attack. In a blur of motion Ruga twisted at the waist and parried the blade with an outward sweep of his shield. Pain exploded in Pavo's forearm as the shield edge slammed into him. He fought to stop himself involuntarily releasing his grip on the sword. Now Ruga pushed forward on the balls of his feet and charged at him, tucking his shield close to his left shoulder.

Pavo gasped as the shield clattered into his chest, badly winding him. The force of the impact knocked him backwards. In the same instant Ruga hoisted the shield up above his head, angling his forearm so that it lay flat. Then he jerked his arm forward, thrusting the edge at Pavo. The younger man's head snapped back as the leather trim slammed into his chin and sent a burst of hot pain screaming through his skull. His legs buckled. He dropped to his knees, gasping for breath. He tasted vomit in his mouth. Ruga stood above him and dropped the shield to his side, patting the top edge, his glazed eyes as wide and bright as polished coins. He grinned at Pavo.

'A provocator's main offensive weapon is not his sword, but his shield. Hermes knows this better than anyone. The mistake Criton made was the same as nearly every other gladiator has made against Hermes.'

'They attack with their sword!' Pavo realised, thumping his fist against his thigh as he got to his feet. 'As soon as they thrust at Hermes, he retreats behind his shield and picks them off at range.'

Ruga nodded. 'Your sword is a foot and a half long. Using it brings you into thrusting range. Your shield is twice that length. Forget about trying to impale the bastard on the point of your sword like they teach you in the ludus.'

A thought struck Macro. 'Good advice for staying out of trouble, I suppose. Keeping range and all that. But it doesn't solve the problem of how Pavo is supposed to cut the bastard down.'

Ruga frowned at the optio. 'How do you mean?'

Macro picked up the shield, testing its weight and strength, his face furrowed in deep concentration. 'Normally a gladiator can get a good thrust between the ribs. Smoothly push the blade up until it nicks the heart and lungs.'

Ruga nodded again. 'Go on.'

'As far as I can see, a provocator is armoured from head to bloody toe. Leg greaves, arm manicas, full-face helmet, chest protector, the lot. They've got more protection than a decent fort.'

'It's true,' Pavo added, stemming the blood trickling out of his nose. 'We saw how Hermes hid behind his shield against Criton. He presented a solid wall of armour to his opponent.'

Macro scratched the back of his head and puffed out his cheeks. 'The trick is how to break through that armoured front. There's only one obvious striking point on the body . . . the throat.'

Pavo turned to Ruga. 'How am I supposed to get past his shield and armour?'

Ruga snorted. 'Many opponents have asked themselves the same question. That's why Hermes is regarded as the finest gladiator ever to grace the arena. Stopping him is hard enough. Defeating him is almost impossible.'

'Then how did you come so close?' Pavo asked.

There was a pause as Ruga glanced away. At length the retired gladiator limped over to a stone step at the side of the courtyard and sat down. He sighed wearily, a distant look in his eyes as he spoke.

'We were fighting in front of Emperor Tiberius. The closing

fight of the games at the Festival of Saturnalia. Thirty thousand spectators had flocked into the arena to see us fight. They certainly got their money's worth. Our match seemed to last for ever. Neither of us could find a way through the other's defences. By the end of it, we were both bloodied, bruised and exhausted. I thought I had done enough to just shade it and win on a decision. Sure enough, the umpire raised his stick to indicate the victor . . . me.'

Pavo and Macro shared a disbelieving look. 'You actually *beat* Hermes?'

Ruga laughed bitterly. 'I thought so. That's why I took off my helmet, to receive the adulation of the crowd. Then Hermes charged at me. Bastard hacked at my face and left me with this.' He pointed to the scars.

'But what about the umpire calling an end to the fight?'

'He reckoned I misunderstood his signal. Pah! Load of bollocks.'

Ruga fell silent. Pavo glanced up at the darkening skies, anger pounding in his veins, his hands balling into tight fists until his fingers almost drew blood from his clammy palms.

'I swear to Jupiter, I won't fall for the same trick. Hermes is mine.'

That provoked a cynical laugh from the retired gladiator, and as he lifted his head, there was a cold and sober look in his eyes. 'Don't you see, boy? The fight was fixed so that Hermes wouldn't lose. He's the Emperor's favourite gladiator. When you step out into that arena, you won't just be facing another gladiator. You'll be taking on the Emperor's chosen man.'

'Harder!' Macro yelled. 'Put your back into it, lad!'

Grinding his teeth and tensing his muscles, Pavo struggled to lift the weight of the four-wheeled wagon in the street outside the Drunken Goat. Macro stood under the arch leading to the courtyard and watched as he gripped the front edge of the platform and attempted to lift the wagon a second time. Ruga looked on from the courtyard. Pavo's arm muscles burned and he bent slightly at the knees as his legs strained with the enormous weight. The baskets filled with stones loaded on to the oak platform trembled as the wagon slowly tilted off the ground. Pavo held it there for a moment. Every fibre of his being screamed with pain and told him to drop it. But he clamped his eyes tightly shut and thought of Hermes, and the suffering he had endured to arrive at this point. He had come a long way to gain his revenge. He would not give up now.

'Release!' Macro barked.

With a pained roar Pavo snatched his hands away from the underside of the platform and jolted back a step. The wagon juddered as the front end crashed down. Macro stepped forward and counted the baskets.

'Fourteen. Not bad. We'll make a champion out of you yet, sunshine.'

Pavo winced in pain but felt pride burning inside him. 'Champion of the Arena,' he mused before glancing at Macro. 'Do you really think I can do it?'

'Not if you sit on your arse daydreaming I don't. Now give me another set . . . with more weight this time.'

Pavo's heart sank and Ruga laughed heartily. Macro waved at the tavern owner to add another basket to the load. The wheels groaned under the extra weight.

'But sir—'

Macro cut him off with a wave of his hand. 'Not a word, lad. You want to beat Hermes, you'll have to be strong enough to move around the arena with that armour bearing down on you. Got it?'

'Yes . . . sir,' Pavo mumbled, momentarily regretting his decision to appoint Macro as his trainer.

The optio had pushed him harder than ever before in the four weeks since he began training for the fight. The first week had been torturous, and Pavo barely had the strength to walk as he returned to the imperial ludus each evening after training and slumped on to the freezing floor of his cell. But by the end of the second week he had grown visibly stronger. At the start of training he'd struggled to wield the larger shield used by the provocator gladiators, his bicep stinging under the strain. Now his enlarged muscles allowed him to effortlessly grip the shield as he practised his attacking moves with Ruga each afternoon. With just one day left until he confronted his sworn enemy, Pavo dared to believe that victory might be within his grasp.

Macro slapped a hand against his thigh and nodded firmly.

'Now . . . lift!'

Although his expression remained stony, Macro felt his chest swell with pride as Pavo resumed his weightlifting exercise. The optio had feared the worst when his young charge won the right to face Hermes. But there was a steeliness in Pavo that surprised Macro. He had never seen the lad burn with such intensity as he had done in the past four weeks. Macro had put him through a series of punishing physical exercises designed to increase his lower body strength. The wagon lifts, as he termed them, were just one of a series of exercises that he had devised to compensate for their lack of training equipment. The owner of the Drunken Goat had taken an interest in the three men who ate lunch at his establishment each day, and after hearing the story of the brave young lad who was going to fight Hermes, he had offered to lend a hand; hence the wagon lifts.

But a cold dread gnawed at Macro. His own fate was tethered to that of the young gladiator. If Pavo fell in the arena, the imperial secretary would reveal the optio's participation in the beast fights to the officers in the Second Legion, bringing his military career to a swift and inglorious end. That grim thought forced Macro to redouble his efforts and leave no stone unturned in his bid to prepare Pavo for his fight. As well as the wagon lifts, Macro had his charge pushing a heavy cart up the Aventine Hill to bulk up his thigh muscles, and doing circuits of the courtyard with a training shield in each hand.

'By the gods, he has to win,' Macro muttered to himself, clenching his scarred knuckles into tight fists.

He was interrupted by a shrill crashing noise as Pavo released the wagon and one of the baskets fell and shattered an amphora leaning against the wall of the inn. Wine spilled across the flagstones. Pavo soothed his aching wrist and winced at the tavern owner.

'The imperial secretary will reimburse you,' Macro said.

The tavern owner waved a hand at the optio. 'Forget the wine. Just win the fight and teach that arrogant scum Hermes a lesson.'

'Probably watered down anyway,' Macro remarked glibly to Pavo as one of the tavern workers quickly set about scooping up the shattered clay shards from the street.

Ruga moistened his lips. 'I could do with a skinful myself.' He flashed a broad grin at Pavo. 'Tell you what, boy. Beat Hermes and the first jug of wine is on me.' '

Pavo forced a smile. Strange, but since being condemned to the ludus, he had never given any thought to a life beyond the arena. He supposed it was the same for nearly all gladiators. The high fatality rate made thoughts of freedom irrelevant and even dangerous. For his own part, the overpowering desire to avenge his father and restore honour to the Valerian family name had excluded all other considerations.

'Chin up.' Macro clapped his hands. 'We've still got work to do.'

Pavo raised his weary head and grimaced. 'Can't we rest now, sir?'

'Plenty of time for that in the afterlife! Now, give me one more set of lifts.'

'Yes . . . sir.'

As Pavo grasped the wagon, a voice from down the street interrupted him. 'Training hard, I see.'

A shiver ran down Pavo's spine. He stood bolt upright and spun away from the wagon, turning his gaze beyond the Drunken Goat. Macro and Ruga glanced in the same direction to see Murena striding towards them, sidestepping the clay shards and spilled wine. The guard accompanying him dismissed the tavern owner and his workers so that the aide could talk freely. Murena looked at Pavo and clicked his tongue approvingly.

'It seems Ruga and the optio have been fulfilling their side of our arrangement.' He continued to stare at Pavo. 'You've toned up nicely since we last met.'

Macro flashed a dark look at Murena and folded his arms defensively across his chest. 'What the fuck are you doing here?'

'Relax, Optio,' Murena replied, smiling with fake warmth. 'I have simply come to watch Pavo train. Pallas is understandably curious to learn how our young gladiator is getting on.' He reset his gaze on Pavo and nodded. 'Very well, by the looks of it.'

'Not bad,' Macro agreed guardedly. 'Given that we've only had a month to prepare.'

The aide stroked his smoothly shaven jaw with his bony fingers. 'And how do you rate his chances against Hermes?'

Suppressing his contempt for the freedman, the soldier took a deep breath and thought for a moment.

'The lad has done everything we've asked of him. Between myself and Ruga, we've pushed him hard. Hermes will never have faced a gladiator in such good condition.'

Murena's eyes narrowed as he continued to smile at Pavo. 'You didn't answer my question, Optio. Will he or will he not defeat Hermes tomorrow?'

The soldier shrugged. 'Hard to say. Even with the two of us training him morning and afternoon, he is up against the greatest champion in all of Rome. You know how the old saying goes. The only safe bet about fighting in the arena is that one man walks out and the other gets dragged out by a hook.'

Something shifted in the aide's demeanour as he switched his gleaming gaze to Macro. 'I am well aware of the vagaries of glad-iator combat. It's one of the reasons Pallas and myself were reluc-tant to promote such fights as a means of controlling the mob.'

'And now you're relying on Pavo to save your careers,' Macro remarked. 'Funny how things turn out, isn't it?'

The smile disappeared from Murena's face. 'Rome is full of treachery, Macro. A common soldier such as yourself will never grasp the difficulties of governing millions of feckless subjects. Pallas and I will do whatever is necessary to stay in power.'

Macro yawned. 'Save your lecturing for some other poor sod.' He nodded at Pavo and jerked his thumb towards the Drunken Goat. 'Come on, lad. Time for a quick rest and some food before you begin your final training session with Ruga.'

'Don't be late to the arena tomorrow, Optio.' Murena smirked. 'I would hate you to miss the pre-fight entertainment we have planned.'

'What the hell are you talking about?' Macro asked, narrowing his eyes.

Murena looked pleased with himself. He stared hard at Pavo. 'Let's just say there will be a special role for the Liberators guilty of conspiring against Emperor Claudius.'

Pavo shivered in his bones. Macro turned away, shaking his head, and went into the tavern. Pavo followed him inside. The aide watched them both leave. Ruga turned to head after them but Murena instantly swept forward and blocked his path.

'Out of my way,' the retired gladiator growled.

'Not yet. I have something I need you to do . . . if you want your job back.'

Ruga shook his head firmly. 'I'm training the boy, just as you demanded. That was our deal. One month with the lad and I'd be free to return to my old job as bodyguard to Senator Macula.'

Murena weighed up his response as he led Ruga into the courtyard, away from the bustle and noise of the street. 'Pallas and I must take into account the possibility that Pavo might lose tomorrow.'

'There's always a possibility of defeat,' Ruga conceded. 'But he has a better chance of victory against Hermes than most. What else could you possibly want?'

'A contingency plan.'

Ruga hesitated and glanced back to the street. 'I'm not sure I like the sound of that.'

'I'm not asking for your approval, gladiator,' Murena snapped. 'You will do as I say, whether you like it or not.' Composing himself, the aide lowered his voice. 'Tell me, are you friends with any other retired gladiators?'

Ruga pursed his lips. 'A few. Those who pay their dues to the gladiator guild mostly.'

'And they are looking for work?'

'Some of them. Why?'

Murena smiled thinly. 'Good. Now listen carefully . . .'

CHAPTER FORTY-FOUR

The crowd packed into the temporary arena rumbled and then burst into spontaneous cheers as another gladiator was cut down on the sands. A chill ran down Pavo's spine as he waited in the gloomy tunnel alongside Macro for his turn in the arena, the scaffolding directly above him shuddering as if with fear at the howls of pain coming from the butchery. Through the entrance to the arena he glimpsed the frantic glimmer of steel as a scrawny man armed with a short sword and a small round shield but no armour hacked madly at his elderly opponent.

This was the pre-match entertainment Murena had mentioned. It involved the guilty Liberators behind the conspiracy to assassinate the Emperor fighting to the death. The sight of a dozen public officials stabbing and slicing at each other in front of the baying mob made Pavo sick to the pit of his stomach. He frowned as the frail gladiator, Senator Lanatus, struggled to raise his shield to defend himself and stumbled frantically backwards from his opponent, begging for mercy.

'Looks like the magistrate is about to gut the senator,' Macro remarked as he narrowed his gaze towards the arena entrance. 'Not long now, lad. As soon as this scrap is over it'll be your turn to take to the sand.'

Pavo felt a cold tremor of dread tremble down his spine. 'What will become of the winner of this fight?' he wondered aloud.

Macro shrugged. 'Crucifixion, perhaps. If he's lucky the guards will execute him.'

'Gods.' Pavo shuddered and shook his head. He thought again of his agreement with Murena and Pallas. He secretly feared that the imperial secretary would reveal the truth of his involvement with the Liberators whether or not he won, but he knew he had no choice but to trust the two freedmen to keep their word.

In the next instant a shriek rang out as the magistrate plunged his sword into Lanatus's exposed chest. The senator convulsed on the spot. Blood spewed out of his mouth as he sank to his knees on the sand. The crowd cheered the death of another Liberator. Some spat at the dying senator. Others shouted obscenities at him as a pair of guards rushed out of the tunnel and seized the magistrate.

Macro clapped his hands. 'Right, lad. You're up next.'

Taking a deep breath to steady his nerves, Pavo forced his tensed muscles to relax and nervously counted down the moments until he stepped out into the arena. The air was dense and cold and felt icy in his lungs. This was it, he thought. The moment he'd been training for since he had been thrown into the ludus in Paestum, stricken with grief over the brutal murder of his parents, his son taken as a hostage and the ruin of his reputation and that of his family.

Revenge.

The tunnel he waited in was situated directly beneath the groaning wooden grandstands of the temporary arena, constructed in the centre of the Roman Forum on the same spot where the gladiator games were hosted in the time of Julius Caesar. The guards had arrived at the imperial ludus at dawn to escort him to the arena. A stab of fear had stirred in his veins at the sight of it. Although it was considerably smaller than the Statilius Taurus amphitheatre, the setting was infinitely more spectacular. The grandstands were flanked by a pair of marbled basilicas whose long porticoes and intricately decorated bas-reliefs glowed weakly in the pallid morning light. Beyond the arena Pavo had spotted the Arch of Augustus looming over the Forum, a symbol of imperial prestige. Macro had greeted him at the tunnel entrance. As Pavo made his final preparations, he had the strange sensation that even the gods were gazing down on Rome that day, eagerly awaiting the fight.

'Now remember what we discussed,' Macro said calmly, shaking Pavo out of his anxious stupor. The guards dragged the surviving magistrate out of the arena to a chorus of jeers and the optio had to raise his voice to make himself heard. 'Don't stay still for an instant. Keep moving. You don't want to give that bastard a chance to corner you. Make him work, lad. Move, parry, attack. Just like we said, eh?'

'Move, parry, attack,' Pavo recited tonelessly.

Macro nodded. He gripped Pavo by the shoulders and stared him dead in the eyes. 'I won't lie to you, lad. Fighting Hermes is going to be bloody hard work. Ignore the pain and focus on your task. The same as they teach you in the legions.'

'Easy for you to say,' Pavo replied. 'You're not the one fighting a legend.'

Macro shook his head. 'My neck is on the line, lad. Same as yours.'

A sudden despair overcame the young gladiator, his fists trembling with utter rage. 'Those Greek bastards! Roping us into their scheming. I hope they both rot in the Underworld.'

'No worries there,' Macro hissed through gritted teeth. 'Best thing for it is to make sure Hermes is waiting for them when they get there, eh?'

Pavo glanced up and down the tunnel. 'Why isn't Ruga here?'

Macro shrugged. 'Gods know. Probably getting pissed in some dubious watering hole.'

Pavo nodded distractedly. Behind the anxious thrill of his imminent appearance in the arena, a hot panic flared between his temples. Hermes was the favourite for the fight, and through the creaking grandstands he could hear the chants of the mob cheering his opponent's name. He felt as if all of Rome was against him then.

An attendant stooped at his feet to fasten the straps on the metal greave round his leg, pulling them tight so that the cloth padding was pressed against his shin. That was the last of the armour he had been issued. His bronze body armour was wrapped tight round his chest, causing him to sweat profusely in spite of the chill. The crowd quietened as the announcer ran through the formalities. Pavo listened. A sudden wave of nausea lodged in his throat.

A mild cheer rang out as Pavo's name was announced.

Macro said quietly, 'It's almost time.'

Pavo nodded. 'It's been an honour, sir.'

'Likewise, lad. Even if you were sometimes a prickly shit.'

A pattering of hurried footsteps echoed further down the tunnel. Pavo instantly spun round and squinted in the gloom at a figure hurrying towards him. He stood sharply upright as the figure neared and he recognised the short, portly man with the plump face. His cheeks were shaded red with exertion and beads of sweat glistened on the folds of his neck. Pavo blinked as he stood rooted to the spot, as if not believing the face staring back at him.

'Bucco . . .?' he spluttered at last. 'By the gods, what are you doing here?'

Pavo had not seen his comrade in many months – not since he'd transferred to the imperial ludus in Capua. Now the sight of a friendly face in Rome warmed his heart and steadied his nerves. The two men clasped arms. Attendants brushed past, bearing buckets filled with sand to sprinkle over the bloodstains.

Bucco caught his breath. 'I came as quick as I could,' he said. 'Some imperial aide called Murena told me I could find you here. It's good to see you, friend.'

'Murena?' Pavo looked at Bucco in surprise. 'He sent you?'

Bucco nodded. 'Woke me up this morning at my lodgings in the Subura.'

'You mean to say you've been in Rome all this time?'

'A month or so. A man came looking for me in Ostia claiming to be a servant of Senator Lanatus. He told me to come to Rome to take your son.'

'Another lie,' Pavo muttered icily.

'What's that?'

'Nothing,' he replied quickly. 'What happened when you arrived in Rome?'

'The senator refused to see me.' Bucco scratched his elbow. 'After I was turned away from his house, a couple of Praetorians grabbed me and hauled me off to the imperial palace. They asked me what my business was with Lanatus. I explained everything, and the next thing I knew, some greasy official handed me your son.'

Pavo froze. His stomach clenched anxiously. 'Appius . . .' He looked frantically up and down the tunnel. 'Where is he? Did you bring him with you? I must see my son before I face Hermes. I want to say goodbye to him, in case . . .' He clenched his jaw, overcome with a bitter grief.

Bucco smiled weakly at his comrade. 'I've been under strict orders not to bring him to you since I took him in from the palace. The aide, Murena, didn't want to interfere with your training sessions. I had no choice but to agree.'

Pavo frowned. 'Then where is he?'

'With my wife, Clodia, at our lodgings in the Subura. I sent for my family after I decided to stay on in Rome and try my hand at acting.' Bucco lowered his head. 'Your son can speak now,' he added quietly. 'He has been saying a few words.'

An almost unbearable grief seized Pavo just then. He clenched his fists, his heart beating furiously inside his chest. There and then he vowed to defeat Hermes. He would not lose to his nemesis. The welfare of his son hinged on his winning the fight and saving the reputation of the Valerian family name. He clamped his eyes shut and mouthed a silent prayer to the gods to protect his son. He opened them when Macro placed a hand gently on his shoulder.

'It's time, lad.'

Pavo glanced at the soldier and nodded. Then he quickly turned to Bucco.

'Can you promise me something?'

'Name it.'

Pavo paused for a moment. He glanced away from Bucco towards the entrance to the arena and choked back tears. Lips trembling, he took a deep breath and turned back to his comrade. 'If I die today, Appius is the last in the line of the Valerians. There is no other family to look after my son. Should I fall, raise Appius for me.'

Bucco forced a smile. 'I shall,' he promised.

Pavo nodded softly. 'Thank you, Bucco.'

'May the gods be with you, my friend.'

Pavo took a deep breath as the bucina players blared notes on their bass instruments and the feverish roar of the crowd filled the arena. Macro gave him a final pat on the back and a moment later a pair of officials thrust the young man down the short entrance tunnel. The ground shook underfoot with the rumbling anticipation of the crowd. Pavo felt a sick feeling in his guts. His armour weighed down heavily on him and his sweat flowed freely. He mopped his brow as he arrived at the entrance and took one last look over his shoulder. Macro nodded at him with a look of steely determination. Bucco stood by his shoulder and smiled faintly, his dim eyes filling with tears. Facing forward, Pavo grimly accepted his shield from one of the attendants. An image of Nemesis had been painted on the front. He smiled wryly. How appropriate, he thought. Then the second attendant slipped the full-face helmet over his head, dramatically reducing his field of vision.

Pavo swallowed hard. His neck muscles instinctively tensed. His breathing rasped inside the helmet as he sucked in cool air through the small airholes. The blood rushed in his head and he waited for the attendant to give the signal.

Then he marched into the arena to face his sworn enemy.

CHAPTER FORTY-FIVE

Grey clouds pressed heavily in the sky like grain sacks fit to burst at the seams as Pavo stepped out on to the sand. The visor on his helmet severely restricted his line of sight, cutting off his peripheral vision and forcing him to concentrate on the scene directly in front of him. As a consequence he could not see the ground at his feet and he shuffled tentatively at first as he approached the chalk line that marked the wide circle in the centre of the arena within which the gladiators were required to remain during their bout. This was a regular feature of fights to the death, forcing the competitors to remain in close proximity to each other instead of retreating to the sides of the square arena.

As he neared the circle Pavo lifted his gaze to the hastily constructed imperial box situated on the northern stand. The Emperor sat at the front, flanked by his German bodyguards and his entourage of imperial lackeys. The box was distinctly less impressive than the ornate structure at the Statilius Taurus arena, Pavo decided, and shorn of its elegance Claudius cut a rather sad and pathetic figure, smacking his lips as he sat in his chair, giddy with excitement at the prospect of the fight. A violent pressure pulsed behind Pavo's eyes as he spotted Pallas and Murena to the left of the Emperor. To his right stood a middle-aged man with crow's feet around his eyes, flashing a practised smile at Claudius. Pavo dimly recognised him.

'That must be Narcissus,' he muttered to himself.

He lowered his eyes to the mouth of the tunnel on the opposite side of the arena as two attendants filed out and approached the centre circle bearing the weapons to be used for the fight. As they reached it, the umpire pricked his thumb against the tips of the two swords in turn. Nodding to himself, he raised his thumb to the Emperor, confirming the weapons' sharpness and drawing a crescendo of cheers from the mob. Pavo drew close to the umpire. A sick feeling gnawed at his guts as he realised he was standing on the same spot where his father's severed head had been displayed to the mob. The thought filled him with anguish and anger.

A moment later Hermes stormed out of the same tunnel through which the attendants had emerged, into a deafening wall of noise. A section of the crowd rose to its feet, vocally clamouring for their hero to tear his opponent limb from limb.

'There's only one Hermes!' his fans shouted, roaring themselves hoarse. 'Only one Hermes!'

The very ground trembled as Hermes marched towards the circle. He was wearing the same body armour as Pavo, although his shield carried his signature image of Cerberus and his champion's belt was wrapped round his waist above his loincloth. Pavo felt the sweat on his back turn cold with fear as Hermes approached him. The colossus from Rhodes appeared even more muscular than he remembered. His biceps were solid and smoothly curved, as if fashioned from marble. The veins on his forearms were like cords of rope. He paraded to the crowd, bowing to all four grandstands in turn. Pavo felt his heart briefly soar as he heard a number of spectators jeer Hermes and cheer his own name.

'Pavo's going to cut your head off!' a voice bellowed clearly above the din.

Staring out of the grille that covered his face, Pavo glanced back past his shoulder and spied Macro looking on from the mouth of the tunnel. Bucco stood next to the soldier. Pavo drew strength from Macro's presence. His gruff honesty and stubborn dedication to the task at hand put many of Pavo's high-born friends to shame, and he had learned more from the soldier in a few months under his wing than the years spent studying the classics and observing the great debates in the Senate. He was sure that Macro would make a fine centurion one day.

The umpire gestured for both fighters to lean in as he explained the rules of the bout.

'Now listen,' he barked so that both gladiators could hear him above the noise of the crowd. 'The rules are simple. It's a fight to the death, which means there's no mercy from the Emperor today. If neither of you is able to kill your opponent outright, I'll call an end to the contest and the judges will declare a winner.'

He pointed to three magistrates wearing fine togas and seated on the bottom row along the northern stand, below the podium. Each gripped a wax tablet and a stylus, poised to make a mark whenever one of the participants landed a clear blow on his opponent. Pavo turned back to the umpire as he went on.

'The loser must accept the judges' decision with good grace. Whoever loses, I expect you to die like a true Roman. I want a fair fight, and that means no tugging at each other's armour, no chucking sand and no stepping outside the chalk line. If you step over the line, you forfeit the match – and your life. Understood?'

'Yes,' Pavo said.

'Let's get this over with,' Hermes rasped from behind his helmet. 'I can't wait to cut this brat to pieces, just like I did to that treacherous Roman shit Titus.'

'My father was an honourable man,' Pavo retorted. 'You're just scum, Hermes.'

The champion erupted into laughter, his massive shoulders heaving. 'Fool. Once I've carved you up, I'll take my place among the greats.'

Pavo frowned. 'What do you mean?'

'Narcissus has promised that a statue will be built in my honour, celebrating my victories. It will go on display in the Campus Martius. I'll be idolised by Romans across the Empire.' He snorted in amusement. 'Why else do you think I came out of retirement? I was already the greatest gladiator who ever lived. Now I'll be recognised as a true hero – more than old Titus ever was.'

Pavo lunged at Hermes, gripped by an indescribable hatred and unable to hold back his rage. The umpire thrust out his hands, separating the two gladiators and ordering them back two paces. With his tall, sinewy build and black eyes sunk deep into his skull beneath his bald head, the man carried the air of a strict school-teacher, and both gladiators immediately obeyed his command. When the umpire was satisfied that both fighters were under control, he nodded to the attendants. They handed a sword each to Pavo and Hermes, then quickly retreated towards the tunnel entrance. The crowd suddenly hushed. The moment of the fight was finally upon them. All eyes fixed on the umpire. Pavo stared ahead at Hermes, picturing his face behind the visor, imagining his scarred upper lip twisted with hatred. The younger man tightened his grip on the handle of his sword and took a deep breath.

At last the umpire filled his lungs and bellowed, 'FIGHT!'

Hermes took Pavo by surprise, pushing forward instead of retreating behind his shield, instantly slamming his sword arm out and angling the tip of his weapon at his opponent's exposed neck beneath his helmet. Pavo froze for an instant, the sword tip twinkling softly as it surged towards his throat. Then he hiked up his shield just in time and the sword rang dully as it glanced off the top edge and veered above and to the side of his head. In the next moment Hermes let out an animal growl and charged at Pavo with his shield tucked tight to his shoulder. Pavo crouched behind his own shield. The frame shuddered violently as Hermes clattered into him. Pavo dug his feet into the sand and held firm, the honed muscles in his legs tensing to stop him from falling backwards. The powerful impact trembled up his forearm and stung his shoulder muscles as panic flooded his mind. His strategy for the fight had been based upon the assumption that Hermes would rely on the counterattack. He had not prepared for his opponent to charge at him. Now Hermes sidestepped to his right and thrust his sword at Pavo's unguarded flank. Spinning round to face his opponent, Pavo quickly dropped to one knee and ducked behind his shield, blocking the pointed tip before it could puncture his midriff. The crowd screamed in delight as the sword rattled against the shield boss and glanced off.

Heart pounding, Pavo glimpsed Hermes above the rim of his shield. The champion was hacking his sword down like an axe chopping wood. Pavo instinctively hoisted his shield horizontally above his head in a smooth, swift motion, his arduous sparring sessions in the courtyard with Ruga firmly ingrained in his muscles. There was a thunderous crack as Hermes's sword hammered against the shield. Pavo felt a vicious pain shooting through his wrist as it absorbed the shock of the impact. Now he pushed up, every sinew and muscle in his legs straining as he threw off his opponent's sword and knocked Hermes off balance. He jerked his flat shield forward, just as Ruga had taught him. Hermes grunted as the iron-rimmed edge slammed against his bronze chest protector. A wild cheer erupted from a section of the crowd as Hermes was momentarily stunned. Others booed vehemently. Glancing over his shoulder, Pavo realised he had been pushed back from the centre of the combat circle. He now stood a few short paces from the edge, the chalk mark clearly visible in the sand.

He swung his gaze back to Hermes, perspiring hard inside his helmet. Droplets of sweat trickled down his forehead and into his eyes, temporarily blurring his sight. Ahead of him Hermes quickly recovered from the shield blow and brought the base of his sword crashing down on top of Pavo's shield, battering it to the ground before booting it aside. Pavo felt his heart skip a beat as the handle was savagely wrenched free of his aching grip. The shield landed a short distance to his right. Cursing the gods, he reached out to retrieve it, but Hermes reacted in a flash, slashing his sword at his opponent's outstretched arm. An intense searing pain stung Pavo's flesh as the sword tip grazed his bicep, nicking the muscle. Hissing sharply between gritted teeth, he snatched his trembling hand away from the shield, blood seeping from his glistening wound. Now Hermes swung his sword down at his opponent and Pavo immediately jerked his own weapon above his head. A rasping clang echoed around the arena as the two swords slammed into each other just above his helmet. Filling his lungs, Pavo roared and sprang to his full height, throwing off Hermes. The champion stumbled backwards, visibly shaken by the sheer strength of his opponent. He made a deep keening sound in his throat.

Pavo lunged at him, sensing a chance to draw blood. Hermes batted away Pavo's thrust with an outward sweep of his shield before raking his shield arm back across his chest and smashing the iron rim against his opponent's helmet. A clangorous sound rang through Pavo's skull. For a brief moment an unsteady blur clouded his vision. His sight cleared just as Hermes booted him in the guts. Pavo bent double and gasped at the cold air. Nausea burned in his throat. He staggered backwards, his muscles seized with anxiety. Hermes struck out at him with a brutal thrust of his sword. Pavo raggedly parried the move. Seething behind his visor, Hermes punched his shield into his opponent with unstoppable force. The younger man lost his footing, groaning in despair as he tumbled to the ground. His back crunched against the thin sprinkling of sand covering the travertine paving. He coughed and sputtered painfully inside his helmet. Every fibre of his being ached. The armour felt twice as heavy as it had done at the start of the fight. The spectators in Hermes's section of the arena rose to their feet, chanting and shaking their clenched fists in triumph.

'He's crossed the line!' one of the fans declared. 'Pavo has lost!'

Another section of fans who'd been chanting Pavo's name heckled their rivals, making offensive hand gestures and hurling insults in their direction. 'Dirty cheating bastards!' one of them shouted wildly. 'Pavo never crossed the line!'

Pavo gazed down at his feet. To his horror he saw that he had landed on top of the chalk mark enclosing the circle. His upper body lay fully outside the circle, with his trailing leg remaining inside by a hair's breadth. There was a collective rumble as the five thousand spectators crammed into the arena rose to their feet and craned their necks. Some shook their heads decisively. Others pointed to the floored gladiator and argued heatedly with their companions over whether or not he had crossed the line. Hermes raised his arms in victory as Pavo lay bewildered on the sand, gripped by despair, unable to believe that he had lost. Meanwhile the opposing factions shouted over each other, both sets of fans fired by the belief that their judgement was correct. Pavo swung his gaze back to Hermes as the champion swaggered towards him and stopped at his feet. His colossal frame cast a vast shadow over his opponent.

'On your knees, traitor,' Hermes grunted throatily. He was breathing deeply inside his helmet and his voice rasped through his airholes. 'Now you'll suffer a humiliating death in front of the Emperor . . . just like your old man.'

Pavo froze. Panic was beating like a drum in his chest. He swallowed his bitterness and struggled awkwardly to his feet, a feeling of dread tightening in his bowels as he prepared to face his gruesome fate. His heart sank like a lead weight at the thought that he had failed his father. He awaited his agonising death, awaited the moment when the champion of Rome would plunge his sword into the hollow between the base of his neck and his collarbone, piercing his heart. His only consolation was that he would join his parents and Sabina in the afterlife. To have come so close to revenge, only to fail at the last – it had all been for nothing, then. Dark droplets speckled the sand around Pavo as rain began to fall from the clouds hanging low above the arena.

'I'm sorry, Father,' he whispered inside his helmet.

'Halt!' a voice suddenly cried.

Both Pavo and Hermes looked towards the umpire. He was waving at Hermes, gesturing for the champion to step away from his opponent. Up in the imperial box, Pallas and Narcissus both stared intently at the umpire while Claudius consulted another member of his entourage.

'Pavo has not crossed the line!' the umpire exclaimed as loudly as possible, struggling to make himself heard over the competing yells of the crowd. 'The fight is not over!'

Hermes stood his ground and cocked his head at the official. 'Bollocks,' he spat as he jabbed the scuffed chalk line with the bloodied tip of his sword. 'This pathetic shit clearly crossed the line. Look at the chalk.'

The umpire shook his head stiffly. 'The rules state that the whole body must be outside the circle in order for the fighter to forfeit the contest. Pavo's leg was still inside. According to the rules, he is not out. He has not forfeited the bout.'

Hermes rounded on the umpire. 'But that can't be '

The umpire cut him off with a raised hand. 'I am the umpire, gladiator. My decision is final. Step back from your opponent and return to your position!'

Hermes towered over Pavo for a moment. After a pause he turned and paced sullenly back to the centre of the circle, fuming and shaking his head in disgust. The spectators closest to the action turned to their companions in the next row up and relayed the umpire's decision. Soon the news had spread throughout the stands. Hermes's fans, incensed by the verdict, loudly jeered the umpire and started pelting the arena with wine cups and cushions and anything else they could get their hands on. The guards around the exits set upon the offenders and hauled them out of their seats. Pavo's supporters remained standing, cheering deliriously and urging their hero on. The young gladiator noticed Pallas closing his eyes as he breathed a sigh of relief. Narcissus stood on the other side of the Emperor, his face locked into a tight-lipped scowl. A moment later a servant hurried over to Narcissus and whispered into his ear. Nodding severely, the adviser turned his back on the arena and headed for the exit. Murena and Pallas exchanged a smug look. Pavo glanced back at Hermes.

'An outrage!' Hermes snarled inside his helmet, loud enough for his supporters to hear.

At that moment the skies opened up. The gentle pitter-patter quickly swelled to a deafening hiss and there were cries in the stands as the spectators were soaked through by the sudden downpour. The rain fell over the Forum in freezing, slanting torrents, spattering the grandstands and turning the white sand a dark brown. At once several sections of the crowd shot to their feet and hurried towards the nearest exits, raising their hands above their heads as they tried in vain to protect themselves from the driving rain. Others loudly cursed the gods as their togas were drenched. In mere moments large swathes of the grandstands had emptied. Pavo watched as the rain washed away the chalk line, blurring the circle and making it impossible to judge where the gladiators were permitted to fight. The scuff mark where his leg had trailed across the line was quickly obliterated.

'Shit!' the umpire cursed. He cupped his hands to his mouth and shouted in the direction of the tunnel. 'The fight is suspended! Clear away the weapons!'

The attendants darted out of the tunnel entrance, eyes narrowed, jaws clamped tight and chins tucked to their chests as they braced themselves against the driving rain. Pavo could not hear a thing above the pinging sound of the heavy droplets striking his helmet.

The arena guards looked on helplessly as hordes of spectators scurried towards the exits. The German bodyguards hurriedly led Claudius out of a separate exit. Pallas and Murena and the rest of the imperial staff followed closely behind. One of the attendants ushered Pavo out of the arena, rain drumming loudly against his armour, the wet sand squelching underfoot. As he dragged his exhausted body towards the tunnel, Pavo could barely lift his head. By the time he reached cover, he was drenched through to his loincloth. Turning back to the arena, he saw Hermes trudging towards the opposite entrance. The champion, still raging over the umpire's decision, angrily shrugged off an attendant.

'What the hell were you doing out there?'

Pavo turned and lifted his eyes to Macro. The soldier nodded towards the arena floor, a cold expression on his weathered face.

'Sir?' Pavo panted, breathing unevenly through the airholes in his helmet.

Macro thrust a scarred finger at his chest. 'That performance was a joke! You almost handed victory to Hermes on a plate. If it hadn't been for the umpire, you'd already be cut to pieces. I bet Hermes could hardly believe his luck.'

Pavo shook his head. 'He's too strong and fast. You saw how he knocked me down. There's nothing I can do.'

Macro stepped into his charge's face and looked him sharply in the eye. 'Stop feeling sorry for yourself. I've been struck down a few times myself in skirmishes in the Second Legion. Do you know what I do when some German scum has me on the ground, eh?'

Pavo shrugged.

'I get up again, lad. Then I let the bastard have it. A good Roman soldier would rather shag a pig than surrender to his enemy. He's taught to fight to win or die trying. The same goes for you. So tell me, how badly do you want to beat Hermes?'

'Badly,' Pavo croaked.

'I can't hear you,' Macro growled.

'I want to beat Hermes, sir!' Pavo shouted hoarsely as he struggled to catch his breath. 'I want to kill the bastard!'

'That's better.' Macro thumped his young charge on the shoulder

372

while the rain continued to fall in shimmering rods of silver. He pointed to the sodden arena. 'When you go back out there, you show Hermes what a real champion is made of. If he hits you, you hit him back twice as bloody hard, d'you hear? Make that bastard regret the day he chopped up your old man.'

Pavo nodded vigorously. He hesitated for a moment. Then he glanced tentatively back out at the arena, filled with a sudden doubt. 'But how I am supposed to defeat him, sir? I'm doing exactly as you and Ruga taught me, but I still can't get past his defences.'

Macro grunted and scratched his jaw. 'Hermes is certainly a tough nut to crack. From watching the fight, I'd say the only way to beat him is by depriving the bastard of his most effective weapon.'

'What's that, sir?'

'His shield.'

Pavo snorted. 'And just how am I supposed to do that?'

Macro grinned. 'You know how Ruga reckons Hermes has no weaknesses?'

Pavo nodded uncertainly. Attendants brushed past him, bearing buckets of sand to scatter over the arena floor as the rain started petering out. He turned back to Macro.

'Well, I've been thinking about the way Hermes fought against Criton,' the soldier went on. 'And I think I've got an idea . . .'

CHAPTER FORTY-SIX

The rain stopped a short while later. Puddles shone across the wet sand as Pavo and Hermes re-entered the arena. The spectators hurriedly resumed their seats, having sought refuge under the tall porticoes lining the Forum, and the Emperor and his entourage returned to the imperial box. There was no sign of Narcissus, Pavo noted. He turned to the umpire and watched him pacing impatiently up and down the sand while a pair of officials sprinkled chalk over the faintly visible marking. Wielding his shield and short sword, Pavo stepped inside the freshly drawn circle and prepared to face his opponent again, repeating to himself the plan Macro had explained to him in the tunnel. He closed his eyes and prayed to Jupiter that the soldier's strategy would work.

Once the umpire had examined the chalk line, he paced back to the centre of the circle and gestured for the gladiators to approach and resume the bout. Hermes flexed his neck muscles and stared at Pavo as he warmed up.

'The gods won't save you a second time, traitor. It won't matter where you fall, once I've buried my sword in your fucking neck.'

'Go to Hades,' Pavo said coldly.

Hermes held up his sword. The blade glinted under the clearing sky. He grunted. 'Funny, that. Titus told me the same thing . . . right before I cut his head off.'

An almost inhuman anger took hold of Pavo. He saw red, his muscles twitching with hatred, his blood simmering as it ran hot through his veins. With steely resolve he took in a sharp draw of breath and firmed his core muscles as the umpire raised his stick and frenetic yells went up amid the crowd.

'Fight!' the umpire boomed.

There was a deafening roar from the crowd as Hermes sprang into a powerful attack, his sword point stabbing towards Pavo's groin. But this time Pavo neatly thrust his shield out and deflected the tip, his heart beating wildly as he drew a lungful of air and lunged forward. Raising his right arm above his head, he twisted his wrist inward so that the tip of his sword was pointing down at the ground. In the blink of an eye he extended his sword arm beyond Hermes's shield and stabbed at his opponent in a quick downward thrust, nicking him beneath the collarbone. Hermes howled in agony as the blade pierced his flesh. The champion responded by lifting up his shield to bat away Pavo's sword and thrusting at his throat. Pavo instantly jerked his head to the side. A grating shriek filled the air as Hermes's blade scraped along the surface of his helmet. The sound jarred shrilly between his ears and Pavo instantly jolted back from stabbing range and began manoeuvring round Hermes. The enraged champion pursued him round the circle, a bright red gash glistening on his neck.

Hermes went on the attack again, thrusting at Pavo as he drew within range. The young gladiator swung up his shield and deflected the blow, jabbing his sword at Hermes before the champion could recover to a defensive posture and nicking him on the shoulder. Pavo's pulse quickened. The plan was working. He focused solely on his opponent, shutting out the noise of the crowd and ignoring the nerves jangling in his throat. His senses were heightened. He was keenly aware of his breathing and the dull weight of the sword and shield in his grip as he lunged at Hermes, feinting high this time. The champion raised his shield, enraged and bleeding. Pavo smashed his own shield down towards his opponent's toes but Hermes nimbly backed off a pace and there was a muffled thump as the shield edge thwacked against the sand.

'Is that the best you've got, traitor?' Hermes sneered.

'Why don't you attack like a man?' Pavo mocked. 'Instead of hiding behind your shield like a coward.'

Hermes growled behind his visor. 'I'll cut you down now, scum! You're going to lose.'

He charged at Pavo, muscles shaking with fury as he clattered into his opponent with his shield and launched a mad flurry of blows with his sword tip. Pavo spun round at the last moment. There was a shrill metallic ringing as Hermes's sword repeatedly clashed against the shield boss. Adjusting his stance, Hermes instantly jabbed his sword low and slashed Pavo on the thigh. The younger gladiator dropped to his knee with a sharp cry of pain. Then Hermes thrust his shield out, smashing Pavo's sword out of his hand. The weapon landed with a dull thud on the wet sand. Pavo crouched behind his shield, blood disgorging agonisingly from his thigh wound. He gripped the shield, which thrummed as Hermes battered and thwacked his sword against it relentlessly. Guttural shouts rang out through the crowd as they sensed the fight reaching its climax. Every nerve in Pavo's body tensed with fear. With a fierce grunt Hermes kicked the bottom of Pavo's shield, tipping the top edge towards him. Then he brought his sword arm hammering down like a fist, wrenching the shield free of Pavo's weakening grip. It fell from his grasp. Hermes's fans went wild as he kicked the shield away and Pavo sank to his knees at the edge of the circle. Now Hermes stood in front of his opponent, breathing hard. He chucked aside his own shield in a fit of arrogance and saluted his fans as Pavo knelt defenceless beneath him.

'It's over,' Hermes gloated as he turned back to Pavo, a slight rasp to his voice. He tilted his head at the umpire. 'That cheating bastard can't save you now. You're mine.'

Pavo coughed up blood and slowly raised his gaze to Hermes.

'You're forgetting one thing,' he said weakly.

Hermes chuckled harshly. 'What's that, traitor?'

'You dropped your shield.'

Hermes immediately froze in horror as he realised his mistake. Macro had anticipated that the champion would cast aside his shield only when he believed the fight was already won – just as he had done in his sparring match with Criton. Pavo rolled to his left, scooping up his discarded sword and springing up on his toes as he pointed the tip at the champion's groin. Hermes's swift reflexes allowed him to swivel towards the tip and bring his own weapon down across his chest. A faint metallic ring sounded as he parried the thrust. Pavo dug deep and summoned one last ounce of strength, swiping aside his opponent's sword and shooting bolt upright before Hermes could recover, driving his sword tip at his opponent's neck. There was a brief glimmer as the tip caught the glare of the sun breaking through the clouds, followed by an explosive gasp of air as the sword punctured Hermes's throat and punched out of the nape of his neck. Hermes spasmed as Pavo drove the sword on until the pommel was almost touching his opponent's helmet.

The champion of Rome swayed on the spot for a long moment. The crowd gasped in disbelief as he pawed at the blade jutting out of his neck and made a strange gurgling noise. Then Pavo wrenched the blade free. Hot blood gushed out of the wound, splashing down Hermes's chest and staining the glittering belt wrapped round his waist. Hermes gave out a final wheezing grunt. Then he collapsed.

A stunned silence hung over the arena. Pavo looked on numbly for a moment, struggling to grasp that he had won. He blinked sweat out of his eyes and watched Hermes die, the wound in his neck disgorging a steady pump of blood that spilled on to the sand and formed a wide pool beneath his sprawled body. Then it hit him. The enormity of his achievement. He was overcome by waves of ecstasy and relief.

'By the gods, I've done it,' he whispered to himself, as if he could barely believe it was true. He closed his eyes and saw an image of his father flash in front of him. 'I have avenged you, Father . . .'

He let his sword fall from his grasp to the sand. There was no hot pounding in his veins as he'd experienced in the wake of previous fights. He felt only immense satisfaction that he had accomplished what he had set out to achieve many months ago. All the depredations he had been forced to endure, the deep humiliations he had suffered, the narrow escapes in the arena against some of the most feared fighters in Rome – he had met them all. He didn't know whether to laugh or weep. If someone had told him a year ago that he would be cast into a ludus, fight as a gladiator and return to Rome to defeat the great Hermes, he would have mocked them. Now, as he made a silent prayer to Fortuna and Mars, he was simply grateful that he was still alive.

Every muscle in his body throbbed with exhaustion and pain. He could hardly stand upright. The crowd erupted into a full-throated cheer. Even Hermes's fans joined in in recognition of the stunning display of power, skill and determination from the victor. Soon every spectator was roaring his name. Pavo was indifferent to the praise of the mob. Tomorrow, he knew, they would be in awe of another gladiator.

There was a tumult in the mouth of the tunnel. Pavo turned and saw Murena striding out of the shadows accompanied by a large detachment of Praetorian Guards. The imperial aide pointed to the victorious gladiator.

'Guards!' he shouted, his smooth voice cracking with anger. 'Arrest this man!'

Pavo was dumbfounded. Murena had betrayed him. A hot rage swept through his veins as the guards pushed forward, two of them grabbing him by the arms. Boos immediately chorused around the stands. Pavo was too weak to break free of the guards' grip. He cast a panicked glance across the arena, looking for Macro. He glimpsed him in the tunnel, where a handful of Praetorians were struggling to restrain the optio from entering the arena. One of the guards lifted the helmet from Pavo's head and the harsh light stung his eyes. He turned to face Murena. The aide to the imperial secretary approached him, an amused expression on his face. Pavo took a deep breath to compose himself.

'Release me at once!' he stuttered.

'Not likely,' Murena sneered, pulling a sour face at Hermes's sprawled body. 'Beating the colossus of Rhodes. I must say, that's quite the achievement. I had my doubts. But once again you have proved us wrong. Sadly for you, instead of the Emperor proclaiming you Champion of the Arena, you'll be hanging from a crucifix.'

Pavo felt the blood freeze in his veins. 'We had a deal.'

Murena smiled and took a step closer to the young gladiator. 'A deal?' he said in a low, mocking voice, barely audible above the chorus of disapproval showering down from the stands. 'Did you honestly think I would let you walk free, hailed as a champion, after you so nearly killed the Emperor? Of course not. You're a traitor, Pavo. Just like your father. The mob may love you now, but once they hear the truth, your disgrace will be complete. The Emperor may have spared Appius, but I will make sure he grows up as lowly scum.'

Pavo convulsed with anger. 'You bastard!'

Murena laughed. 'Rant all you want, my dear boy. Now we will make you pay.' He waved to the guards. 'Get this miserable traitor out of my sight.'

Pavo resisted, digging his feet into the sand despite his sapped strength. 'You can't do this!' he protested.

'Oh, but I can.' Murena laughed cruelly, his eyes narrow with cunning. 'I must say, this has all worked out rather nicely. Hermes is dead, Pallas and I retain our influence within the imperial palace and you are to be nailed to a cross. A fitting fate for the son of a treasonous general, no?'

Pavo clenched his jaws shut as black rage pounded viciously inside his skull. He was consumed by an urge to snap the neck of the imperial aide. Murena smiled gleefully at him.

'Send my regards to Titus in the afterlife,' he mocked as he turned to leave.

'That's the culprit!' a voice thundered from across the arena.

Murena halted and turned back round. Pavo looked towards the entrance at the opposite end of the arena and spotted Narcissus storming out of the tunnel, accompanied by Emperor Claudius and several of his German bodyguards. Narcissus appeared flushed with anger. He sidestepped Hermes's bloodied corpse and pointed an accusing finger at Murena.

Claudius frowned sharply.

'Are y-you quite s-s-sure of this, Narcissus?' he asked.

'Absolutely certain, your majesty,' the freedman replied brusquely.

Murena shifted uneasily on the spot, his face shading white with fear as he looked at Narcissus and the Emperor in turn. He smiled weakly. 'Is there a problem, your majesty?'

Claudius flashed a look of cold anger at the aide, his lips

quivering with outrage. 'N–Narcissus tells me that you hired s–s–several thugs – retired g–gladiators, no less! – to kill him.'

Murena was momentarily flustered. Murmurs erupted in the stands. The aide briefly lost his composure and something like panic flashed in his pale eyes. Pallas paced sheepishly behind Claudius. The imperial secretary did not even glance at his aide, Pavo noted. The two Praetorian Guards still held the gladiator by the arms and they glanced from Murena to Claudius, uncertain as to their orders.

'Is s–s–such a thing t–true?' Claudius asked after a pause, his temper rising.

'Of course not, your majesty!' Murena spluttered. 'I would never dream of conspiring against a fellow freedman. Narcissus is clearly mistaken.'

Narcissus glared at him. 'I don't think so, Murena.'

The aide shook his head. 'You have no proof to support this preposterous claim, Narcissus. Indeed, your very presence here exposes your lies. If I had paid some retired thugs to dispose of you, then why are you standing here before us?'

'Oh, but I have proof.' Narcissus folded his arms smugly across his chest and nodded to a figure standing amid the throng of German bodyguards. Ruga stepped forward and stood beside him. Pavo looked at Murena. There was a definite flicker of fear in the aide's eyes, he thought. Murena swallowed hard and glared at the retired gladiator.

'You . . .' he hissed.

'Publius Didius Ruga is not the one to blame here, your majesty,' Narcissus went on in a measured, calculating tone of voice. 'Ruga was bribed by Murena into taking part in a despicable plot with several of his retired gladiator comrades to kill me if Pavo lost his fight against Hermes.'

Murena countered frantically, 'These men are telling lies, your majesty!'

Claudius kept his gaze on Murena as Narcissus spoke. 'I am telling the truth. And Ruga here can confirm what I have to say. Murena ordered Ruga and his comrades to lie in wait in one of the alleys near the imperial palace. When he believed that Pavo was losing the fight, he gave the signal for one of the servants to lure me away from your side, your majesty, on the pretext that I was required at the palace on urgent business. Ruga and his comrades were then to ambush me in the alley.' Narcissus paused and smiled sardonically. 'A bold plan, I must say, if somewhat clumsy in its execution.'

'Outrageous lies!' Murena threw up his arms, his face burning with fury.

Narcissus ignored him and continued. 'Mercifully I already had my suspicions after Gnaeus Sentius Cornicen, the imperial lanista, reported to me that Murena had taken a special interest in training Pavo. I knew he was up to something. Thankfully Ruga refused to carry out the task; his first duty is to Rome, like any good Roman's, and he reported the ruse to his former employer, Senator Macula, late last night. The senator is a good friend of mine and he came straight to me with the news.'

Murena was speechless. Silence fluttered over the arena. Pavo looked on, scarcely able to believe what he was hearing. Now he understood why Narcissus had left the imperial box during the fight. He recalled what Murena had said when the aide had visited him in training the previous day. *Pallas and I will do whatever is necessary to stay in power.*

Claudius stared at the aide for a moment before turning his gaze on Ruga. 'W-w-well?'

Ruga bowed his head and nodded. 'It's true, your majesty.'

'These men are trying to deceive you, your majesty.' Murena looked pleadingly at the Emperor. 'I swear to all the gods, I had no hand in any such plot. Narcissus is attempting to turn you against me.'

Narcissus rolled his eyes at the aide. 'For gods' sakes, don't beg. It is rather unseemly, even for a freedman.'

'Your majesty, I would never—'

'Silence!' Claudius yelled, suddenly flushed with anger. Murena's lips quivered with fear as the Emperor turned to Pallas. 'Did y-y-you have anything to d-do with this t-treachery?'

Pallas feigned innocence while Murena visibly shook with fear a short distance away from him. 'I swear, your majesty, this is the first I have heard of these vile allegations. I assure you that my aide acted without my knowledge or permission in this affair.'

That appeared to satisfy Claudius. He scowled at Murena and waved to the guards. 'T-t-take this despicable t-traitor to the Mamertine! He can w-w-wait there until we c-crucify him tomorrow.'

Murena's eyes went wide with horror. Snivelling, he dropped to his knees in front of the Emperor. 'Please, most gracious majesty, I beg of you, let me live!'

The Emperor's expression hardened. 'Get to your f-f-feet, Murena. A man should e-e-embrace death with dignity.'

With that Claudius gave a stiff nod of his head and the guards dragged Murena towards the tunnel entrance, the aide screaming for mercy. Narcissus smiled as the crowd began to chant, 'Crucifixion for Murena! Crucifixion for Murena!' The spectators around the stadium were delighted that the day's entertainment had not ended with the gladiator fight. Turning away from Murena, the Emperor waved a frail hand at the men who were holding Pavo.

'R-r-release the gladiator. He has p-p-proved a noble swordsman.'

The guards obediently stepped away from Pavo. The young gladiator clutched the throbbing wound on his bicep and flashed a dark look at the Praetorians. He was beginning to understand why Optio Macro hated them. Claudius pursed his lips and considered Pavo for a moment.

'Perhaps I was w-w-wrong about you,' the Emperor mused. 'Rome needs m-more men such as yourself. There are f-few heroes these days. Too few to waste, while b-barbarians mass along our f-f-frontiers. You are free to g-go, young Pavo.'

Pavo looked astounded. Something like joy fluttered in his chest. He sank to his knees. Freedom. He had never thought he would taste it again. For a moment he was unable to speak. Drained from his fight, weary from the months of deprivation, he managed a half-hearted smile at Claudius.

'Thank you, your majesty.'

'Y-you have earned it, young m-man. In blood.' The Emperor

paused and considered something. 'A freedman needs money, especially a gladiator who has been f-f-fighting without any bounty. I sh-shall see to it that your family estate in A–Antium is returned to y-you.'

Pavo's smile widened slightly. He had spent many a holiday at the villa in Antium as a child. And the land surrounding the estate would provide a modest income.

Claudius abruptly dismissed Pallas and Narcissus from the arena and waved to a pair of attendants. One of them bore a silver urn filled with coins. The other carried a palm leaf. The Emperor looked at Pavo as the attendants swept across the arena.

'Now, to your f-f-feet, Pavo,' Claudius intoned. 'It is time for y-you to accept your title – Champion of the Arena . . .'

As the sun set over the imperial palace the next day, Pavo made his way down the marble entrance steps, clutching his wooden rudis of freedom. After the arena had emptied the previous afternoon, Claudius had ordered that the grandstands should remain in place for the following day's crucifixion. A sizeable crowd had turned up to watch Murena's execution. With both Lanatus and the aide to the imperial secretary dead, Pavo could rest easy. No one else was aware of his involvement in the conspiracy to kill Claudius, and Murena's desperate accusations against him had fallen on deaf ears. Pavo had been invited to the imperial palace following the public crucifixion to receive his rudis in person from Claudius in front of a large assembly of dignitaries. Although officially he could not reclaim his place among the senatorial class, the respect his father's peers showed him was obvious. Bravery was a rare commodity in Rome. Rarer than it ought to be, Pavo reflected.

Ruga and Bucco had been present to watch Pavo receive his freedom. In recognition of his help in training the gladiator to victory and exposing the conspiracy against Narcissus, Ruga had been given a new job as an imperial bodyguard, escorting functionaries as they went about their civic duties around Rome. Bucco had told Pavo that he intended to pursue his career as a comedy actor. At the end of the ceremony he had bid Pavo a warm farewell and the two men had sworn to remain friends. Pavo had a feeling they would be seeing each other again before too long.

Now Pavo grimaced as he made his way down from the entrance. The injuries sustained in his brutal clash with Hermes were still painful and he moved stiffly as he neared the wrought-iron gates at the bottom. The ornate colonnades cast long shadows over the steps. Squinting in the sunset, he noticed two silhouetted figures waiting for him. The new Champion of the Arena slowed his step as the Praetorian Guards stationed at their posts opened the gates. He limped towards the two figures outside. Then he caught sight of their faces and a surge of emotion swelled inside his chest.

Macro stepped towards him. His hand was clasped round the tiny fingers of a timid child by his side. The soldier grinned broadly at the stunned gladiator and cocked his head at the child.

'This little rascal belongs to you, I believe.'

For a moment Pavo couldn't speak. He dropped to his knees. Tears instantly welled in his eyes. 'Appius!'

Macro released the child's hand and gently nudged Appius towards his father. Pavo watched the child in amazement. Appius's gait was awkward as he approached his father, and Pavo felt a surge of pride as he watched his son walking on his own. He had been a baby the last time Pavo had seen him; now he was a small boy. Pavo felt a sudden pang of sadness.

'My son,' he stuttered. 'It's really you.'

Appius looked curiously at his father. Pavo imagined that he must appear unrecognisable to the young boy. A straggly beard covered the lower half of his face. His arms and legs were marked with bruises and scars from his battles in the arena. His once skinny frame was enlarged with taut muscle.

'I missed you so much, my boy.'

Pavo placed his hands on his son's small shoulders. So young. There was a flicker of recognition in his blue eyes, as the child tried to place the face in front of him. At last he reached out and touched the wooden rudis Pavo was holding.

'Sword,' Appius said.

'Yes, sword,' Pavo replied.

The child raised his hand and lightly touched a scar on Pavo's face. 'Father.'

Pavo smiled. Overcome with joy, he hugged Appius tightly and clamped his eyes shut. It had all been worth it. The training, facing down the slippery freedmen in the imperial palace, surviving every vicious foe in the arena. For this one moment, holding his son tight as a free man, Pavo told himself he would have endured any hardship.

At length he stood painfully upright and smiled at Macro.

'You're in a bright mood . . . for a change.'

'Course I bloody am, lad.' Macro waved the scroll in his right hand bearing the wax seal of the Emperor's office. 'I'm a centurion now. Best of all, I'm finally heading back to the Rhine Frontier, and this time there's not a meddling Greek in sight who can stop me.'

'When did you receive your promotion?'

'Earlier, while you lot were watching that shit Murena get nailed to a cross. Bucco asked me to stop by his lodgings in the Subura and bring Appius to you. I was more than happy to do so.'

'Things worked out rather well for us both in the end, Macro. Or should I say, Centurion.'

'Not too bad, I suppose.' The newly promoted centurion patted his chest. 'The Emperor gave me a thousand sestertii to go with the promotion. Very generous of him, that. It's a long trek back to the Rhine and I'll need the company of a few cheap tarts along the way.'

'You'll be leaving soon, then?'

Macro nodded as he tucked the scroll into his sidebag. 'At dawn.' He looked up and considered Pavo for a moment. 'What're you going to do now? Seeing as you're a freedman and all.'

'I'm a freed *gladiator*, Macro. There's a difference. Rome's social mores forbid me from returning to my former elevated standing.'

'Bollocks to social mores, lad! You're the most popular gladiator Rome has ever seen. They'll be talking of the way you fought back from the brink to defeat Hermes for years to come.'

Pavo smiled weakly. The centurion was right. Other gladiators had been popular with the mob, but as a high-born man Pavo carried a unique appeal. His feats had gone some way to restoring pride to the Valerius family name. Along with the return of his estate in Antium, Pavo received an urn filled with coins from the Emperor for his victory over Hermes, which he put to good use. He set aside a small sum for a proper grave and monument to be built on the Appian Way in honour of his father, with the balance going to the gladiators' guild, so that others who fell on the sand could be spared the indignity of being slung into a grave pit. In the wake of his victory Cursor had approached Pavo, offering to act as his trainer and manager, arranging show bouts across the Empire in return for a share of the profits. Pavo had politely turned down the offer.

'Is that the end of your career as a gladiator, then?' Macro asked.

Pavo nodded. 'I've no wish to step back inside the arena.' He looked down at his son and smiled. 'Besides, I'm about to begin a new career.'

Macro's expression darkened. 'Don't tell me you're going to follow Bucco and become a bloody actor!'

'No chance.' Pavo laughed. 'Actually, it's not so much a new start as a return to an old job.' He paused for a moment and looked at Macro with a determined expression. 'The Emperor has appointed me as a tribune to the Fifteenth Legion. I'm to leave for the camp at Carnuntum, near the Danube, as soon as I've put my affairs in order.'

'Tribune, eh?' Macro raised an eyebrow. 'Not bad . . . even if it is with those slackers in the Fifteenth. And the Danube is supposed to be the armpit of the Empire. The Rhine is almost civilised by comparison.'

'So I hear,' Pavo replied sourly. He glanced back at the imperial palace. 'I'm sure one of those slippery Greeks is behind all this. The imperial household seems rather keen on hastening my departure from Rome.'

'Give you your moment in the sun, then post you to some filthy backwater where you won't pose a threat to the Emperor, eh?' Macro shook his head, glad that he no longer had to deal with the politics and scheming of Rome. He nodded at Appius. 'What about your son?'

Pavo turned back to the boy and ruffled his hair. 'Appius will join me. As I travelled with my father across the Empire before him.'

Macro scratched his jaw. 'Fair enough. I suppose there are worse postings than the Danube. Judaea, perhaps. At least you'll have a chance to cut down more scum like Hermes. You seem to have a knack for chopping up barbarians.'

Pavo smiled. The two men clasped hands. Of one thing the new Champion of the Arena was certain. He would not forget Macro in a hurry.

'Look after yourself, lad,' the soldier said as he made to leave.

'And you too . . . Centurion.'

Macro turned his back. Pavo watched him trudge off. After a couple of steps he stopped and turned back to the former gladiator. 'One more thing, Pavo.'

'Yes, sir?'

The centurion cleared his throat as a pained expression crossed his weathered face. 'That business about me having to appear in the beast fights last month. We'll keep that to ourselves, eh? Not a word to anyone.'

Pavo smiled softly. 'Don't worry. Your secret's safe with me.'

'Where have you been all these fucking months?' Centurion Lucius Batiacus Bestia barked as he rolled up Macro's travel warrant.

A chilly wind carried through the Second Legion fortress on the banks of the River Rhine, stirring Macro's cloak as he stood stiffly in front of the gate at the southern end of the camp. The sentries had not been expecting any arrivals, and having been away from the camp, Macro did not know the password. After a sharp exchange of words, a message was sent to Bestia, the veteran centurion in the Second and Macro's superior. It was only when Bestia laid eyes on his comrade that the gate was opened. The sky was grey and the ground was a sea of churned mud as winter slowly gave way to spring.

'Well?' Bestia asked, tapping his foot. 'I'm still waiting on an answer.'

Macro weighed up his words carefully. It had been a little under two months since he had departed Rome and tramped north. The march back to the legionary fortress had been good exercise, and despite the snow in the mountain passes and the mud of the forest tracks, he had marched twenty miles a day, stopping only to eat and put his head down at night. The newly promoted centurion had had plenty of time to think about his excuse for his prolonged absence from his comrades. But now with Bestia giving him a long, hard look, his mind was suddenly blank.

'I, er . . . I mean . . .'

Bestia crossed his arms and frowned. 'I think I know what happened here . . . Centurion.'

'You do, sir?' Macro blinked and tried to compose his face, suddenly afraid that Murena or one of his imperial colleagues had somehow sent word back to the Second Legion after all. He stiffened his muscles and prepared for Bestia to give him the bad news that his career as a soldier was over.

Bestia grinned. 'You've been pissing away your reward money on tarts and wine. Then you panicked and realised you'd been away from your real mates for too long, so you used your new friends in high places to get you out of trouble with some half-baked excuse about being retained on imperial business. Bollocks! You don't fool me, Macro. You were up to your neck in cunny and Falernian this whole time.'

Macro kept a straight face but breathed a deep sigh of relief. Bestia would jibe him relentlessly about his extended period of leave for several months, but that would be the worst of it. A smile escaped and the veteran centurion grunted at him.

'There's a ragged bunch of new recruits due here any day now. They'll need to be whipped into shape. Doubtless some of them will head your way and will need training.' He paused and looked hard at Macro. 'That is, unless you're too busy making friends in the palace.'

Macro straightened his back and sucked in a lungful of cold Rhine air. 'It's good to be back, sir.'

Bestia laughed. 'Ha! Be careful what you wish for, Centurion.' He tapped his nose. 'Summer will soon be upon us. Those barbarians across the Rhine will be stirring. Mark my words, Centurion Macro. The excitement's just about to begin . . .'

GLOSSARY

Centurion: officer in the Roman army, commanding a century of eighty men.

Denarius: silver coin worth four sestertii.

Doctore: gladiator trainer in the ludus. Often an ex-gladiator himself.

Editor: sponsor of a games.

Hoplite: a Greek soldier armed with a round shield, spear and a sword. The inspiration for the hoplomachus type of gladiator.

Lanista: owner of a troupe of gladiators; imperial lanistas managed the Emperor's personal retinue of gladiators.

Lictor: civil servants, often ex-centurions, who accompanied the Emperor and senior magistrates in Rome. The lictors carried bundles of rods with an axe on the outside to symbolise the power over life and death.

Ludus: gladiator school, where the veterans and recruits trained, ate and slept.

Murmillo: type of gladiator nicknamed the 'fish man'. Typically only heavily built men would be selected to train as murmillos. They fought with short swords and large wooden shields and wore fin-like helmets.

Optio: second-in-command of a century of men in a legion, reporting to the centurion.

Palus: wooden training post used by trainees to practise their sword skills on.

Provocator: heavily armoured type of gladiator armed with a short sword and a legionary-style shield.

Retiarius: specialist type of gladiator armed with a trident and a net.

Rudis: wooden sword given to gladiators who earned their freedom in the arena.

Secutor: type of gladiator specifically paired with a retiarius.

Sestertius: large brass coin, the standard unit of price in ancient Rome. The average legionary pay was 900 sestertii per annum, and a loaf of bread cost half a sestertius.

Thraex: gladiator armed in the Tracian style with a small shield and a short sword.

AUTHOR'S NOTE

Rome had an uneasy relationship with its gladiators. Admired and loathed in equal measure, they often played a crucial role in keeping the mob content – and creating a wellspring of support for the Emperor. Julius Caesar set the trend by establishing his own school of gladiators and laying on great spectacles, free of charge, to the delight of the mob, who idolised him in return. Later on, emperors, high priests and dignitaries competed to stage ever more elaborate spectacles in order to win popular support. But these same aristocrats also held a scathing view of the gladiators themselves, believing them to be degenerates on a par with slaves. Becoming a gladiator placed a man in a permanent state of infamy, and stories of the sons of senators and equestrians signing on to gladiator schools – to pay off debts, or to seek out new thrills – scandalised the establishment. How commonly highborn men signed on at schools isn't known. Although most of the surviving inscriptions on gladiator gravestones belong to freedmen, they were more likely to be able to afford an inscription thanks to the generosity of friends and family. The slaves, prisoners of war and criminals who populated these schools would not have been so fortunate. But the fact that aristocrats who became gladiators were written about suggests that this was a fairly rare occurrence. Certainly the disgrace of a military tribune such as Pavo being thrown into a ludus would have given rise to heated gossip in bathhouses and inns throughout Rome.

Most gladiators died within a year or two of signing up, with the less talented fighters pitted against each other in brutal group fights. For many, the only hope of escaping death was to win their freedom by earning enough prize money to buy out their contract with their lanista. A select few fighters so impressed the watching Emperor during their bouts that they were awarded the wooden rudis of freedom on the spot, in recognition of their heroics in the arena – very much like the young high-born gladiator in his decisive grudge match.